P9-DNM-932

Robin Pilcher has spent too long behind the scenes. The son of the bestselling novelist Rosamunde Pilcher, he has worked as a farmer, assistant cameraman and PR consultant. Married with four children, he lives near Dundee, his birthplace. *Starting Over* is his second novel: his first, *An Ocean Apart*, is also published by Time Warner Paperbacks.

For more information about Robin Pilcher, please visit his website at: www.robinpilcher.co.uk

Also by Robin Pilcher

An Ocean Apart

STARTING OVER

Robin Pilcher

timewarner
paperbacks

A *Time Warner* Paperback

First published in Great Britain in 2002 by Little, Brown
This edition published by Time Warner Paperbacks in 2003

Copyright © Robin Pilcher 2002

The moral right of the author has been asserted.

A CIP catalogue record for this book
is available from the British Library.

ISBN 0 7515 3091 3

Typeset by
by Palimpsest Book Production Limited,
Polmont, Stirlingshire
Printed and bound in Great Britain by
Clays Ltd, St Ives plc

Time Warner Paperbacks
An imprint of
Time Warner Books UK
Brettenham House
Lancaster Place
London WC2E 7EN

www.TimeWarnerBooks.co.uk

I wrote this book remembering two of my good friends,
Iain Mallet and Roddy I'Anson

ACKNOWLEDGMENTS

Thanks to Peter Erskine for supplying me with information about his wonderful new golf course at Kingsbarns; Sam and Jeannie Cheston for help with all things Spanish; David Greer for his guidance on the oil industry; Winnie Jurk, who rapped my knuckles over my schoolboy German; Aurora Jauncey, who did likewise with my Spanish; Alice Gruzman, who helped refresh my dimming memory of Sydney by running around Vaucluse with a camera; and last but not least, my family, who once more put up with me talking away to myself for the best part of a year.

CHAPTER 1

A taste of spring. That's exactly how it should be described. Nature pervading the senses with the tangy texture of newly tilled soil, laced with the lightest sprinkling of salt that blew in on the cool breeze from the North Sea. Liz Dewhurst leaned against the rotting strainer-post at the head of the field and closed her eyes, pulling in a deep breath and moving her tongue across her palate to identify more. There *was* something else, but it seemed alien, ill at sorts with this carefully prepared recipe. She opened her eyes and watched the large John Deere tractor sweep past fifty metres below her, the masculinity of its six-cylindered roar giving way to the more genteel sound of the drill-spouts, clicking away like a thousand synchronized knitting needles as each placed its designated quantity of barley seed into the rich dark earth.

Liz smiled to herself and pushed away from the strainer. Diesel fumes. That's what it was. Her moment of sweet communion ended by a technological breakthrough.

'Come on, Leckie!' she called out, shrugging the strap of

the basket higher onto her shoulder and scanning the hedgerow for the Jack Russell terrier. He appeared from the undergrowth a hundred yards uphill, like a cork fired from a champagne bottle, and stood looking at her, a small power pack of energy weighing up the odds as to whether obedience should give way to further moments of pure joy.

'Come *on*!'

The tone of voice was enough. Obedience would seem a better option today. Hitting full speed at only two strides into its run, the dog tore down the hill towards its mistress, then veered off and dodged away down the field in front of her.

Liz made for the centre of the field, hoping to coincide her arrival there with the next pass of the John Deere, but as it turned on the end rig, the engine was cut, emptying the air of its noise, leaving only the weaker, yet more melodious sounds of the cab radio to take its place.

Bert was well settled into his lunch by the time she reached the tractor, alternately biting into a white-loaf sandwich and supping away at a plastic cupful of tea. Acknowledging her arrival with a chuck of his head, the old tractorman slid forward in his seat and gave the door a hefty boot open, allowing the fug of sweet pipe tobacco to escape from the cab's airless confines and waft down towards Liz.

'Hullo, Bert.'

'Weel?' Bert replied with his customary question to the greeting.

Liz turned and looked down the rail-track straightness of his drilling. 'How's it going?'

Bert took a noisy slurp of tea before answering. 'Tractor's pullin' braw, but yon machine ahent's a real scunner. Spoots aye seem to be gettin' fell chochit.'

Liz smiled up at the old man. Having lived all her thirty-seven years right here on the east coast of Fife, she was proud both of her Scottish roots and lilting voice, but sometimes she found it almost incomprehensible that both she and Bert should come from the same country, so broad was his accent. A native of Aberdeen, he spoke as if every word had been given a good chewing before being sputtered out in a whirring stream. And that lack of comprehension had not all been one-sided. At the *ceilidh* that her father had held to mark Bert's twenty-five years' service on the farm, the tractorman had risen unsteadily to his feet, clutching in his hand a glass of whisky that was as dark as the peat with which it was made, and remarked that 'the reason that me and the fermer hev got on sae weel ower the years is that neither of us hev understood a bloody word we've said tae itch ither!'

Liz bent down and picked up a handful of earth, rubbing it gently between fingers and thumb and allowing the crumbled soil to fall back to the ground. 'At least the conditions are perfect. I don't think they've been this good in years.'

Bert sat back in his tractor seat. 'Aye, weel, there's somethin' tae be said fer that at ony rate.'

Liz glanced to where the old cab-less Fordson sat idle at the bottom of the field. 'You wouldn't happen to know where my father's got to?'

'Aaay. He went off doon the gulley just afore ye

arrived.' He let out a throaty chuckle. 'He'll be sunbathin' on the rocks, nae doot.'

Liz laughed at the vision of her father lying prostrate on a rock, his coveralls zipped right up to the neck to keep himself warm. 'Aye, nae doot.' She gave her head a quick shake of admonishment, realizing that she too was slipping into the vernacular. 'Well, I'll away down and see him. I've got his lunch.'

She patted the basket with her hand and looked back at the tractorman. But he had already closed the door of the tractor to resume his own.

Liz set off at a brisk pace towards the gulley, hoping to catch her father before he made his way back to the field. As she went, a blinding pinpoint of light from the adjacent field, sun hitting polished metal, caught her eye, and she stopped to see what had caused it. Two distant figures, their fluorescent green coats clearly outlining them against the dark backdrop of the sea, stood on open ground two hundred metres apart. One held a long white pole at the vertical and moved this way and that in response to the hand-waving of the other, who, when not giving directions, was stooped over a surveying theodolite, the source of the reflected light. The sight of this hitherto innocuous task had an immediate effect on Liz, displacing her feeling of complete contentment for the day with a griping sense of foreboding. She watched them for a moment longer, then, with her hand held hard against the basket, she turned and began to run in tottering, uneven steps across the unworked land, as if physical distance might help separate her from the undesirable

4

infringements of the surveyors' actions. Only when she was sure that the undulating contours of the field hid all view of the neighbouring farm from sight did she slow to a walk.

The gulley that led down to the shore was dank and gloomy, the sun's rays being denied access to the dreariness of its inner sanctum by a canopied arch of unkempt hawthorn bushes, their roots exposed like gnarled arthritic limbs after years of undermining by an out-of-control rabbit population. Consequently, the full length of its rutted centre still brimmed with a succession of stagnant brown puddles despite the fact that it had not rained for the best part of a month. Liz kept to the driest part at the edge of the track, her upper body tilted to the side to avoid having her head caught by the tentacled branches of spiky hawthorn, and at the same time keeping an eye on the darting Jack Russell, just in case he decided to up-tail and vanish down one of the all-too-inviting rabbit holes.

With warming relief, she stepped back out into bright sunlight at the bottom of the gulley and climbed up high onto the overhang of craggy volcanic rock to afford her a better view of the shoreline. The wind, now sparkled with moisture from the crashing waves, had become more chilled, and she zipped up her quilted jacket to the neck and pushed away the strand of short blonde hair that blew about her face. The dog, who had been vainly sniffing out something of interest in these new maritime surroundings, suddenly let out a short yelp, heralding the discovery of her father's whereabouts, and headed off, his claws scrambling for purchase on the slippery rocks, in the direction of the lone figure that sat looking out to sea fifty yards upwind from where she stood. Liz turned to follow the animal at a more careful pace, her Wellingtons being too loose-fitting to be classed as ideal footwear for the purpose in hand.

Even though he would have certainly been forewarned of his daughter's proximity by the dog's appearance, the farmer continued to look mesmerically out to sea as she approached, the collar of his coveralls turned up as token protection against the wind, his white-browed eyes shielded by the peak of a battered tweed cap. He sat with the wriggling dog in his arms, his hand clamped tight over Leckie's mouth to avoid his over-amorous greeting.

'Hi, Dad,' Liz breathed out in a sigh of exhaustion.

At the sound of her voice, the farmer broke from his train of thought and turned to flash her a crooked smile. 'Well, lass. How're you doing?' He let go of the dog, allowing it to spill from his arms and run off to explore the peripheries of a nearby rock-pool.

'I thought I'd bring your lunch out to you.'

'Aye, well, there was no real need. I'm not that hungry.' He gave his head a quick, appreciative nod. 'But it's good of you, nonetheless.'

Liz sat down beside him on the rock, tucking the bottom of her jacket under the seat of her jeans to avoid its chilling smoothness. She wedged the basket into a crevice, damp with seaweed, behind her, then delved in and took out a Thermos and a plastic container filled with sandwiches. She poured out a cupful of soup for her father and handed it to him.

6

'Just as well I brought this down. You didn't look as if you were going to bother coming in for lunch.'

He took a loud swallow of his soup, but did not follow it up with any verbal response, instead just wrapped his large, calloused hands around the steaming warmth of the cup and cast his eyes far beyond the frothing breakers on the rocks.

Liz reached across and put a hand on his knee. 'Are you all right, Dad? You seem to be a bit away with the fairies.'

Her father let out a long sigh and turned to her, a wistful smile on his face. 'Och, I don't know, lass. Just having a few thoughts.'

'What kind of thoughts?'

He took another sip from his cup, then gave a short laugh. 'If you really want to know, I'll show you.' Handing her the cup, he leaned forward to pick up a pebble before pushing himself to his feet. He stood for a moment, as if readying his tall, angular frame for action, then, with a certain and, to Liz, quite alarming unsteadiness that was probably only to be expected of a man nearing his seventieth year, he jumped his way across the rocks to stand just out of the spattering reaches of the breaking waves.

'See that out there?' he called back to her, his voice barely audible above the noise of the sea. He pointed his finger towards a jagged needle of rock that protruded from the sea seventy metres offshore. Liz nodded in response. He moved back a couple of paces, executed a number of practice throwing actions to loosen off the muscles in his stringy arm, and then, with one ungainly skip forward, he launched the pebble, and almost himself, out into the

7

water. The small stone hit the surface with a feeble plop, not even a quarter of the way to its appointed target. For a moment, he stared at the point of impact, then, letting out a loud exclamation of derision, he made his way back to where Liz was sitting.

She shook her head as he approached. 'What was that all about?'

Her father sat down, letting out a heavy blow from the effort, then leaned over and took a sandwich from the box. 'I'll tell you.' He took a bite and, almost simultaneously, began his explanation. 'When I was a wee lad, about ten or eleven years old, my father brought me down here and showed me that rock. He said that the day that I could hit it three times in a row from that point where I just threw that stone would be the time when he'd let me take over the farm. Well, I thought there and then that I'd make him eat his words.' He shot a knowing wink at Liz. 'Aye but, lass, he was a wise old devil. No matter how much I tried, I fell short of that rock all the way through my teens. Then, once I'd the strength to get the range, it took me another two years to get the control. And when I eventually did hit it three times, he didn't believe me! So I had to do it all over again, with him standing as witness – and that took another six months!' He laughed. 'I was twenty-three by that time!'

Liz smiled at her father. 'You'd wonder how he knew that it would take that long. Do you think that *his* father put him through the same test?'

'Oh, aye, he did. And as far as I know, *his* father before that, too!'

Liz was silent for a moment before making the decision to ask the question. 'And did you ever do it with Andrew?'

The farmer took another bite of his sandwich and this time said nothing until he had swallowed his mouthful. 'Aye, I did – and the lad hit it three times when he was only nineteen.' He gave a long sigh and held out his cup to be replenished. 'But your brother was never that interested in the farm. And why should he be? I never minded that much. He was always a clever boy. Too bright to spend his days driving tractors about the place. He'd only have got bored. No, he made the right decision, going away to Australia like that. Managing director of a company and all.' He drained his cup, and flicking its residue out to be dispersed by the wind, he once more scrutinized the distant rock. 'Aye, it's like the family's own stone of destiny, that out there. I suppose it's sort of become like the physical pinnacle of my life, with those pebbles getting closer and closer to it as I grew up, and now, as I get older, getting further and further away. I suppose it won't be long now before I canna even heft them further than the shoreline itself.'

Liz took the cup from him and put it back in the basket. 'Come on, Dad, you're being a bit pessimistic, aren't you?'

He wiped his hands on the legs of his coveralls. 'Aye, well, I've had the mind to be a bit pessimistic over these past few months, as I'm sure you'll understand.'

'Yes. I can,' Liz replied softly. She screwed the top back on the Thermos and kept hold of it at its tightest position. 'You'll be missing Mum a good deal, Dad?'

He pushed back the peak of his tweed cap and scratched

at the top of his snow-white tangle of hair before settling it once more on his head. 'Of course.' He got to his feet and held out a hand to his daughter. 'You don't easily forget the scent of a flower just because it's died.'

Taking hold of the outstretched hand, Liz felt the power in his grip as he brought her effortlessly to her feet, then, picking up the basket, he set off across the rocks towards the gulley ahead of his daughter.

'Dad?'

'Aye?' He turned back to look at her.

'I haven't ever asked you this before, but – well – you don't blame me, do you? In any way – for Mum, I mean?'

Her father beamed a broad smile at her and shook his head. 'No, Lizzie, I don't. And never think it. It was just one of those sad coincidences, her getting ill when you and Gregor parted company. Of course, there was no doubt that we were all affected by it, with our families and the farms being linked so close, but no, lass, I'm pretty sure that it never hastened her end.'

Liz leaped the two rocks to where her father stood and put her arms around his chest, pushing her cheek against the exposed front of his woollen jersey and feeling the warmth radiate through from his lean frame.

'I sometimes wonder what it would be like if it had never happened.'

'What? You jumping in the back of the Land Rover with young Gregor?'

Liz pushed herself away from him, and looked up at a face that twinkled with amusement. 'Dad!'

His grin spilled out into a laugh. 'Och, you mean the

10

marriage? Well, I suppose one wouldn't have happened without the other, would it?'

Liz smiled and shook her head. 'No, you're right. It wouldn't.'

Her father pushed his hands deep into the pockets of his coveralls and gave a brief nod in the direction of the rock, its tip now becoming more pronounced with the ebbing of the tide. 'You can't change destiny, lass. You can't get your pebble back once you've thrown it. It's all been. It's in the past. Anyway, you wouldn't have that fine lad of yours if it was different, would you?'

Liz took in a long deep breath and let it out. 'I know that.' She paused for a moment. 'But sometimes I wonder if the future holds anything better.' She cast a wary glance at her father. 'They've been out on Gregor's farm again – doing more surveying for the golf course.'

He nodded. 'I know. Gregor phoned me this morning. They want to start here tomorrow.'

'What did you say?'

'I told him to hold off until we see what the outcome of the meeting is tonight.'

He watched the change of expression on his daughter's face, the usual open, smiling features being drawn down into a hardened glare of determination. 'We can't let it happen, Dad. We mustn't let them steamroller us into making a decision.'

Putting an arm around his daughter's shoulders, he drew her into his side, and lifting his other hand to her face, he pushed gently at the corners of her mouth with his thumb and forefinger to reinstate the smile. 'Listen,

Lizzie, we'll see what they have to say, and we'll do what's best.' He bent down and planted a kiss on the top of her head. 'But I don't want you getting all huffed up and bitter about it all, lass, because that's not you – that's not you at all.' He leaned his head forward to make eye contact with his daughter. 'D'you hear me?'

Liz looked up into his kind, weather-beaten face and could not help but break into a genuine smile. 'I'll try – but it's hard sometimes.'

'I know.' He grabbed her hand and pulled her up bodily onto the next rock, then turned and gave a shrill whistle for the dog. 'Come on, we'd better get going, otherwise Bert will have no worked ground in front of him.'

Together they picked their way slowly across the rocks back towards the gulley. Just as they reached the plateau on which Liz had stood to search him out, both caught the distant but constant rumble of thunder crescendoing as it approached them. Instinctively putting their fingers to their ears, they watched as the menacing cross-section of the Phantom jet sleeked towards them, hugging the coastline like a hunting fox, conspiring to keep hidden until the last from its unsuspecting prey. With an ear-shattering roar, it passed overhead, no more than two hundred feet above them, then banked hard to the right and streaked out seaward for the final run-in to its destination at RAF Leuchars.

No more than a minute later, Alex Dewhurst stepped away from the ball, just as he prepared to play his approach to the tenth hole on the New Course at St Andrews. He took two more practice shots, swinging his number eight iron in slow, rhythmic arcs, desperate to keep his concentration until the Phantom jet, which had set down on the runway at the other side of the estuary, had closed down the reverse thrust on its engines. When the noise had subsided, he re-addressed the ball, flexing his knees to settle his tall frame into the shot, then played through the ball with a swing as smooth as those that he had executed in practice. The ball soared high into the air, starting its flight left of the fluttering flag before catching the stiff sea breeze that blew in across the course. It pitched fifteen metres short of its target, but with no back-spin applied, it ran fast across the hardened fairway onto the razored surface of the green. It caught the borrow and swung in towards the flag, and eventually came to rest no more than three feet from the hole.

Alex kept the final position on his swing until he had seen the ball come to a halt, then let the club rest down on his shoulder. He turned to his opponent, and grinned. 'Of course it was meant!'

Tom Harrison's eyes had not left the ball. The captain of the university golf team stood no more than two clubs' distance from Alex, supporting his right elbow with his left hand and biting thoughtfully at a fingernail. He took a deep breath and glanced across at his younger opponent, shaking his head in disbelief.

'That is bloody *ridiculous!* That's about the fourth time today you've laid it dead from that distance!'

Alex stepped forward and scooped up the divot of turf

with the blade of his club. 'It doesn't always work that way.' He replaced the divot and stamped it back into the ground. 'But I suppose it does help being brought up on links courses. You just get to know how they work.' He speared the club back into his golf bag and swung it up onto his shoulder, then stood watching as Tom walked over to where his ball lay in the short, wispy rough at the edge of the fairway.

No, he thought to himself, it certainly didn't always work that way. Far from it. Despite having a handicap of five, quite often by this stage in a game he would have blown a couple of holes, simply through some niggling apprehension that momentarily bled his concentration. But then it always seemed to be a different matter when he was in a match situation. This was his forte, playing head to head against an opponent, playing to win. And he knew that, in this case, his reward for winning would probably be a place on the team.

Tom played his shot, but badly miscalculated the resistance of the rough, the consequence being that the ball stopped ten yards short of the green. 'Damn!' He picked up his bag and walked rapidly forward to catch up with Alex. 'So, go on. You were saying that you were at school around here.'

'Yes. Madras College. I wouldn't say that I exactly excelled myself there, but that was my fault, not the school's. I spent more time on the golf course than I did in the classroom during my final year, which did play havoc with my grades. But I was the captain of the school golf team, and I took it all quite seriously.'

Tom pulled a face at Alex's obvious self-deprecation. 'Well, you couldn't have done that badly if you got into the university.'

'Only there by the skin of my teeth.'

'Aren't we all? So, what are you reading?'

'Languages – German and French.'

'Ah, a *leenguist*, huh? And what about digs? I suppose you're in halls, being a fresher.'

'No. I still live at home.'

'Oh, right! I didn't realize that you lived that close to Saint Andrews.'

Arriving at his ball, Tom shrugged the golf bag off his shoulder and pulled out a pitching wedge in one practised move, then, with near nonchalance, stood over the ball and stroked it to within two feet of the hole. He turned to Alex, a hopeful grin on his face. 'A gimme?'

Alex nodded. 'Okay. A gimme.'

Tom crossed over to the ball and pushed it into the hole with the back of his club. 'So where exactly are you from?'

Alex took a putter from his bag and walked over to his ball. 'Balmuir. You've probably never heard of it. It's just a wee flea-bite of a place seven miles along the coast. My parents both farm out there.'

'Oh, I know Balmuir! That's where they're planning to build the new course, isn't it? I read about it in the local paper. "The best new links course in Britain," that's how they're describing it already.'

From the moment that Alex put the blade of the putter to the ball, he knew that he was not ready for the shot. Thoughts unconnected with the game flashed through his mind, and he suddenly felt apart from the ball, his brain totally out of tune with the movements of his hands. He tried to play for time by taking a couple of practice shots, but was only too aware of a tenseness that grated at the fluidity that been there beforehand. His eyes began to focus on other things – the logo on his ball, lying askew with the angle at which he was preparing to play his shot, a minute blade of grass that seemed to be lying against the grain in the carpet of green. All things that, up until that moment, had remained completely unimportant and unnoticed in the momentum of his game. He took back the club and hesitated. The sin. The cardinal sin. He pushed the ball towards the hole, and knew from the moment that he had hit it that it was to the left and well past.

He watched the ball as it took its designated path, bending his knees forward in the hope that the movement would in some way alter its course to the hole. But psychology gave way to physics, and the ball glided past its target exactly at the point that he had imagined. He stood watching it for a moment, then glanced across at his opponent, cocking his head to the side in an expression of resignation to his own fallibility.

Tom scratched at the side of his face with a finger. 'What happened there?'

Alex didn't reply, but walked forward to his ball, hiding his disappointment by scrutinizing the line once more, as if trying to lay blame on something other than his own ineptness at getting it into the hole.

'Is that all right?' he asked quietly. He bent down, his hand hovering above the ball.

'Yes, sure,' Tom replied. He exhaled in relief. 'Hell, you let me off the hook there, mate. Thought that was definitely me going one down.'

Alex scooped up the ball and went to pick up his golf bag, passing Tom without a remark.

Together they walked to the next tee in silence.

Even though it was still his opponent's honour to drive off, Alex watched as Tom dumped his bag on the ground and continued on to the bench that was situated at the side of the tee, nestled under the protection of a rampant gorse-bush. He sat down and folded his arms. 'I'm sorry, Alex. I psyched you out just then, didn't I?'

Alex smiled at him and shook his head. 'No, it was nothing. Just my concentration went.'

'I know. I saw it happen. What was the cause?' He paused for an explanation, but none was forthcoming. He asked again. 'Was it something I said?'

Alex shook his head. 'It doesn't matter.'

'Like hell it doesn't! Listen, forgive me if I come over as being a bit of a know-all, but it's perfectly true that seventy-five per cent of this game is played in your head, and to put it bluntly, Alex, if you're going to have any chance of playing for the team, I have to make sure that you don't spook quite as easily as that.'

Alex looked back to the tenth hole and watched as a ball came to rest on the edge of the green. 'Come on, Tom, we'd better get a move on, or we'll hold up play.'

Tom paid no heed to the remark. 'Oh, bugger them, let

them play through. Come on, tell me. It was something about the new golf course, wasn't it?'

Alex walked slowly over to the bench and thumped himself down beside Tom. 'Yes, you're right.' He paused. 'The plan is to build the golf course on our farms.'

Tom nodded slowly. 'And you don't want it.'

'Do I not! I think it would be a great idea. Can you imagine having a championship course right on your doorstep?'

'So . . . what's the problem?'

Alex shot his opponent a faint smile. 'It's a long story – but, in a nutshell, "family" is the problem.'

'Go on.'

Alex took off his baseball cap and ran his fingers through his thick brown hair. 'Well, if you really want to know – it's a bloody mess, really! My parents split up about six months ago, after eighteen years of marriage, the reason being that my mother found out that my father had been having an affair with this local woman for about two years.'

Tom bit at his lip. 'Ah, right!' he mumbled quietly.

'And that's only half the complication. Mum and Dad came from neighbouring farms, you see, so their parents thought, well, if the families are to be united in marriage, why not unite the farms as well? So that's exactly what they did. Farming was going really well at that time, and there were these massive grants coming from the European Community, so they lured into buying tractors and grain-driers and all the latest technology – all against the collateral of the farm, which, as it turned out,

18

was pretty bloody stupid. Anyway, times changed, prices went down, and the business began to suffer. And then, to cap it all, my mother found out about the affair.'

Alex stopped talking as the two golfers who had been playing behind them came onto the tee. They exchanged pleasantries about the weather and the condition of the course, and watched as both hit shots that made light of the awesome expanse of gorse-infested rough that separated the tee from the fairway. With a final wave of thanks, the two golfers went on their way.

'So?' Tom asked. 'What was the outcome?'

Alex took in a deep breath. 'The outcome was that both my parents and the farms split. My father shacked up with his girl-friend at his place, where in fact we'd been living up until that time, and my mother and I moved back to my grandparents' farm. And then, two months ago, just to rub salt into the wound, my grandmother turned up her toes.'

Tom blew out a noiseless whistle and leaned forward, resting his elbows on his knees and rubbing his face with his hands. 'Bloody hell!' he exclaimed, almost to himself. He looked at Alex. 'As you say, what a mess.'

Alex smiled at him. 'Exactly. And what's been left is this almighty financial wrangle about who owns what, or, to be more exact, who *doesn't* own what. The bank really has it all. Anyway, going back to the new golf course, my father thought that he had found an answer to all our problems. He'd been approached by this financial consortium that wanted to reinstate an old nine-hole course which had existed on the farm sometime around the First

World War. Their plan was to make it into an eighteen-hole championship course – as you say, "the best new links course in Britain" – which would mean constructing it across the two farms.'

Tom nodded his head slowly, beginning to understand the implications. 'And your mother's dead against it.'

Alex fired his fingers pistol-fashion at his opponent. 'Got it in one. And if you think about it, can you blame her? Her husband leaves, and then comes back, all sweetness and light, to ask her if she would mind giving up her family farm so that he can pay off his overdraft and live happily ever after with his girl-friend.'

'*Bloody* hell!' Tom exclaimed again, this time more forcefully.

Both were silent for a moment as each contemplated what had been said.

'Why don't you leave home?' Tom asked eventually.

Alex let out a long breath and shook his head. 'I can't. I don't think that would be fair on Mum. Her two men upping sticks and leaving in the space of six months. No, I've got to stay around. It's just that the atmosphere gets so . . . depressingly heavy, and everything is so insular. It's like being caught up in some appalling soap opera. Nothing new – or . . . well – of any consequence is ever talked about in the house. It's all about the wretched farms, and who's saying what behind whose back, and' – he pulled down the corners of his mouth – '"*Whose side are you on, anyway?*" There is just absolutely *no* outside interest taken at all.'

Tom got to his feet and stood up on the bench to see

20

how far the two golfers were in front. He jumped off, took a driver out of his bag and teed up his ball. 'Well, introduce something.' He swung his club back and forth.

Alex looked at him quizzically. 'What do you mean?'

Tom turned and leaned on the top of his club. 'Well . . . you can't just sit and wait for something to happen, for things to get better, because, you have to admit, it's a pretty hopeless situation. So why don't you try to take the lead? Introduce something new to talk about – I don't know – get a student lodger, or take a girl-friend home or something.'

'I don't have one at the minute.'

'Well . . .' Tom held out his hands in exasperation. 'I really can't tell you, Alex. It's your business, not mine.' He stepped forward to his ball and, without any preparation, hit it with enormous power straight down the centre of the fairway. He bent forward to pick up his tee. 'But what is my business is the fact that I can't risk having you blow a game when you're on the team.'

Alex was silent for a moment as he took in what Tom had just said. 'What exactly d'you mean by that?'

The captain of the university golf team smiled at him. 'I'm short of a guy on Saturday. Can you play?'

CHAPTER 2

When Liz and her father arrived for the meeting that evening, the mock-Tudor-beamed lounge bar of the Doocot Arms in Balmuir was already nearing capacity, even though proceedings were not scheduled to begin for another quarter of an hour. Liz took off her coat by the door and cast a concerned eye over the assembled company as they jostled about and craned over each other to study the various plans of the golf course project that were pinned to the display boards beside the bar.

She let out a nervous breath. 'I thought that this was to be a closed meeting tonight,' she said quietly to her father.

He caught the eye of Andy Brown, the owner of the village store, and nodded him a greeting. 'Aye, I was under that impression, too. Looks like they're going all out to drum up local support.'

'And I can guess whose idea that was,' Liz answered, her voice edged by the thought. She scanned the room for Gregor, but there was as yet no sign of him.

'Mr Craig! Mrs Dewhurst!' The voice came from the direction of a disembodied hand held high in the centre of those who perused the plans. For a moment, the volume in the room died as every face turned to look at them. A path was cleared to allow the speaker to make his way forward to where they stood, and as he approached, Liz watched as the company turned to murmur with one another, the subject of their gossiping made all too apparent by smirking smiles and the almost imperceptible jerk of heads in her direction.

That's right, Liz thought to herself. Have a good laugh. Don't worry, I know exactly what you're saying. Look, there goes Liz Dewhurst, the woman who couldn't keep her man. Satisfied him once after a Young Farmers' Dance when they sorely tested out the springs of his father's Land Rover, and then, having paid the consequences, couldn't keep up the momentum. He, on the other hand, with the purring care of that wee blonde-haired bombshell of a divorcée, Mary McLean, couldn't keep it down!

Jonathan Davies approached them, his hand outstretched to her father. 'Mr Craig, how nice to see you.' The two men shook hands, and then, to Liz's dismay, he planted a kiss on each of her cheeks. 'Well, what a turn-out!' he exclaimed, surveying the crowded room. 'I discussed it with Gregor, and we both thought that it was time to let the local residents in on the action.'

As I suspected, Liz thought, fixing the man with a false smile of greeting.

Davies put his hands together and gave them a quick, frictioned rub. 'So, what can I get you both to drink?'

Liz's father held up his hand. 'Thank you, Mr Davies, I'm not much of a drinking man. If there's a cup of tea going?'

'Right! I'm sure I can arrange that. And Mrs Dewhurst?'

'Liz – please. I'm not a great one for formalities.' Not the true reason, she thought to herself. It's just the name Dewhurst that grates on you.

Davies's face lit up at this welcome overture of friendship. 'Of course. Liz. So what can I get you?'

'Just an orange juice, please.'

'Right. Well, let's go over to the bar and I'll introduce you to some of the American contingent.'

He set off across the room with a springy, purposeful bounce, and Liz and her father fell into step behind him. He was a short man, no taller than her at five feet five, but he was as honed and as well-cut as the tweed suit he was wearing. An ex-naval officer with a bearing that met well with his past occupation, he had made his money with a firm of City stockbrokers before 'down-shifting' to Scotland, where he had sought out a collection of other monied parties to start up what had now become an extremely successful venture-capital group. At first, he had concentrated his expertise on identifying small, ailing businesses which he had bought, built up and sold on. Now, with a string of successful transactions to the group's name, he was going for the big one, having gone into partnership with an American-based finance company which specialized in the development of sports complexes.

After putting in his order at the bar, Davies moved over to the group of men that stood in a huddle in the centre of the room, and placed his hand on the bright-yellow-sweatered arm of a large, athletic-looking man to attract his attention. 'Michael?'

The man turned, and before Davies had the chance to continue with his introduction, he looked straight at Liz and flashed her a smile that seemed to accentuate both the brilliance of his perfectly set teeth and the nut-brown texture of his sun-tanned face. He was almost too ridiculously good-looking, as if he had just stepped off one of those billboard advertisements for toothpaste that showed a jagged white starburst exploding from the model's teeth and the word PING! in thick black-painted letters inscribed within.

'Michael, can I introduce you to Liz Dewhurst?'

The man reached out and grabbed Liz's hand before she had made any move to offer it and gave it a finger-crunching shake. 'Hi, Liz. Michael Dooney. A great pleasure to meet you.'

'And,' Davies continued, taking a step back to allow clear ground between Dooney and Liz's father, 'this is Mr Craig.'

Dooney launched himself forward to Liz's father and repeated his near-crippling action. 'Hi, Mr Craig. Michael Dooney. A real pleasure, sir.'

Davies held out his hands in a gesture to signify that all three were included in his address. 'We are particularly lucky to have Michael on board for this venture. He has been responsible for designing some of the top golf courses

25

in the United States over the past' – he turned to Dooney for verification – 'twenty years, is it, Michael?'

Dooney raised his eyebrows and let out a long puff as he made his own mental calculation. 'Nearer twenty-five now, I think, Jonathan.'

Davies smiled. 'Well, there you are. A veritable wealth of experience.' The beckoning of the barman caught his eye. 'Right now, I'll go and get your drinks, and maybe, Michael, you could introduce Liz and her father to the rest of your crew.'

Dooney flashed Liz his Colgate smile once more. 'It'd be my pleasure.'

His compatriots were all of a similar size and build to Dooney, although all but one were dressed in more formal attire. Dooney went round the group of four men, introducing them all in turn and giving a short résumé on the involvement of each in the project. Jack Dennis, the accountant; Bill Hennessey, the banker; Shane Reader, the property developer; and Hatton Devlin, the other casual dresser, Dooney's young assistant.

After formalities were completed, Dennis immediately engaged Liz's father in conversation, leaving Liz to the mercy of Dooney's flashing gaze. He moved forward from the other men, in doing so making it obvious to Liz that theirs was to be a one-to-one exchange.

'So, this is all pretty exciting, huh?'

Liz shrugged her shoulders. 'Well, it's early days yet, isn't it? I mean, there could be some objections to it.' She paused briefly, realizing that her comment might have given away too much of her own feelings towards the project. She smiled up at the course architect and added brightly, 'Couldn't there be?'

Dooney chucked his head to the side in appraisal of her question. 'Well, from what Jonathan has told me, it looks good at the moment. He's been liaising with the planners, and they seem to be quite pro the idea. It would certainly take the heat out of the golf courses at Saint Andrews, especially seeing that it's going to be a golf *links*, rather than an inland course.'

Liz smiled weakly at him. 'And that will make the difference?'

'Sure as hell it will! That's why the guys come over here to Scotland – to play the natural courses.'

Liz nodded her head. Go on, say it, you stupid woman. Say that you don't want the bloody golf course. Say that you don't want to give up the farm that has been in your family for five generations. Say that your husband has gone off with another woman, and that the last thing you want to do is give the farm over to him, so that he can be happy and—

'I hear your son's quite a golfer.'

Liz started at the question, her mind away on another plane. 'I'm sorry?'

'Your son. I hear he's a pretty good golfer.'

Liz let out a sigh that was entirely unrelated to Dooney's words of praise. 'Yes. You're right. He's actually having a trial today for his university team.'

Dooney gave her a wink. 'Good for him. So I reckon that he'll be over the moon at the thought of a golf course on his doorstep.'

Liz opened her mouth to reply, but was cut short by Jonathan Davies's voice rising above the noise in the room.

'I think we should maybe make a start to proceedings, even though Gregor isn't here. He did warn me before-hand that he might be a little late, due to a prior engage-ment.'

To Liz's horror, she was aware of a ripple of amusement running around the room as people took their seats, all due to Davies's unintentional *double entendre*. Her facial expression must have given a concise indication of how she felt, because suddenly her father was at her side, giving her arm a reassuring squeeze.

'Come on, lass,' he said quietly. 'Let's go and sit down.'

He made to move forward, but felt the resistance to his guidance as Liz stayed where she was. He turned to look at her.

'Dad, I don't want to stay here. I think I'll just go home.'

The farmer smiled at her and shook his head. 'Listen, lassie, don't take any notice of this lot. They're nothing but a bunch of ignoramuses. If you go off now, you'll just be adding fuel to their fire. So what do you say to just sitting down and seeing what these lads have to say?'

Liz bit hard on her bottom lip and nodded slowly, and her father took hold of her arm once more and pushed her quite forcefully up the narrow aisle to the front row.

As they were about to take their seats, the door of the lounge bar crashed open. Both Liz and her father, along with every other person in the room, turned to watch as

Gregor blustered into the room, shrugging off his waxed jacket, while at the same time keeping his foot against the sprung door so that Mary McLean could enter unhindered. Again, the slight hum of levity ran around those that were seated.

Liz sat down quickly, keeping her head rigidly to the front. She leaned stiffly over to her father, trying to make it as unobvious as possible to those behind that she was speaking to him.

'What is *she* doing here? This has nothing to do with her.'

Her father did not reply, but reached for her hand.

Gregor and Mary made their way quickly to the front. 'Sorry we're late, Jonathan,' he said, leaning across the top table and shaking hands with those who sat behind it. 'Hope we haven't held up the proceedings too much.'

Davies held up his hands. 'Not at all, Gregor. We've just taken our seats, so you've missed nothing so far.'

Liz watched out of the side of her eye as Gregor threw his jacket onto a seat on the opposite side of the aisle, then turned to nod her father a silent greeting.

'Right!' Davies called out, giving everyone the benefit of his most welcoming grin. 'Firstly, I know that I would go to the ends of the earth for a free drink, but nevertheless may I thank you all for making time in your busy schedules to attend tonight.' He paused while the audience gave due appreciation to his humorous entrée. 'Now, I know that there has been much discussion in the area about the pros and cons of our project, so I thought that it would be best if everyone had the chance to air his

29

views, and hopefully those present at the top table with me will be able to answer all your questions. It would be my aim tonight to have you all leaving here seeing this not only as an extremely exciting project, but also one which will be of great benefit to the local economy. So, without further ado, and just to whet your appetites, I think it would be best to hand over first to Michael Dooney, who will take you through the exact geographical layout of the course.'

From the moment that Dooney stood up, Liz listened only half-heartedly to the whole proceedings, her mind suddenly preoccupied with thoughts of now-distant times when she, Gregor and Alex were a complete and inseparable unit – living together, laughing together, working the farm together. She could picture so clearly those picnics at harvest-time, leaning against bales of sweet-smelling straw and watching proudly as their young son took his first precarious steps, staggering his way from mother to father and back again through the crackling stubble. She remembered watching Gregor at the controls of the giant combine harvester, his shirt-sleeves rolled high to reveal thick brown arms and bulging biceps, and her heart would skip a beat as she considered how the task seemed to accentuate his rugged good looks; and then there were the occasions when he would allow Alex up into the cab and, clamping the young boy between his knees, would let him steer the machine, open-mouthed with delight, across the field. She thought about the hilarious evenings spent right here in the bar after the day's work had been done, then returning home, their minds tingling with the effects of the drink, where their bodies would cast aside the fatigue of their labours, and they would . . .

No. She didn't want to remember that. It was no use remembering that. Those days were all over, finished with, never to happen again. God, had it really been so much her fault? Why had it gone so wrong? Had she really not been a good companion to him, a good lover? She glanced across the aisle to where Mary McLean sat, her head leaned to the side, a look of concentrated interest on her face. Could no one else see how utterly unconvincing that expression was, with her dolly-bird looks and lacquered curls? Liz looked down into her lap and picked at a piece of cotton thread that had come loose at the side of her denim skirt. God, am I that dowdy, that *unsatisfying* that he sees something better, something more pleasing in *that* woman?

It was a question being asked from the back of the room that brought Liz's attention back to the meeting. She looked up at the top table and realized that all the speakers had finished their presentations, and that she had missed everything that had been said. She turned to see who was asking the question, hoping that her action would make it look as if she were genuinely interested in the proceedings. The tweed-enveloped figure of Delia, the wife of Sir Hector Stanfield, owner of Balmuir Estate, stood six rows back, her hands clutched to the metal arch of the chair in front, onto which she leaned her whole formidable frame. This was all much to the agitation of Miss Mouncey, the occupier of the chair, a sparrow-like spinster whose attendance at the meeting heralded the fact that she had, for once, taken a break from her purgatorial pastime of polishing the brasses in the local church.

'You state quite convincingly, Mr Davies,' Delia bellowed out, 'that this is going to be good for the area. I would hope very much that this is true, but, to be quite honest, I do have my doubts. In my experience of these new developments, what will take place is that a whole load of people will be shipped out here to work, and we won't benefit at all. What we'll be left to put up with is a huge increase in the amount of traffic on our roads and hundreds of foreign people making a nuisance of themselves in our village.'

Liz could not help but join in with the cacophony of laughter that spread about the room. She watched as Delia took her seat and noticed that, to the woman's credit, a wide smile was spread across her lipsticked mouth. Good for you, Delia, Liz thought to herself, please keep it up. Please keep objecting.

Davies was on his feet and had started his reply before the drone of amusement had died. 'Lady Stanfield.' Liz studied his face as he waited for silence to be restored, his eyes sparkling with humour as a result of Delia's statement. Goodness, he was good. He had always proved himself to know all that he should about everybody. 'Lady Stanfield, the steering committee, to a man, is giving full support to the idea that this project should work for the good of the community, and as such we would hope to offer as many jobs as is thought practicable to those who live in the area. As far as the roads are concerned, we don't envisage that much of an increase in traffic, and for those who do come to use the complex we would hope that, no matter how far they have travelled to reach these shores, they would be more than willing to burgeon local businesses with their custom.' He picked up the glass of water from the table and took a drink, giving time for the general undertone of approval to percolate across the room. 'Nevertheless, I think that, at this stage,' he continued, 'we should just take stock of our present position by recapping on what has been said tonight. Outline planning consent has been granted, and as such we have continued apace with the surveying on Winterton Farm.' He glanced down to where Liz and her father sat, raising his eyebrows in anticipation of approval. 'And we are hoping that, if all goes well, we will be able to move on to Brunthill Farm tomorrow.'

Liz turned to her father and gave him an uncertain smile.

'Mr Davies. Can I ask a question?'

Liz recognized the voice of Danny McKay, another of Balmuir's local farmers, a man renowned as much for his imperiously outspoken views at National Farmers Union meetings as he was for his Bacchanalian visits to the local cattle market.

Davies gave his head a quick nod. 'Certainly, Mr McKay.'

'This project is going to be built across Winterton and Brunthill farms, is it not?'

Davies furrowed his brow, wondering if the slight slur in Danny McKay's voice might be the reason for his stating the obvious. 'That is correct.'

McKay let out a deep, scornful laugh. 'Well, taking everything into consideration, it would be in my mind that you would have more chance of flying to the moon than getting the owners of those two farms ever coming to an agreement!'

There was a sudden intake of breath from everyone in the room, followed by total silence only broken by the whispered tones of Danny McKay's wife telling him to sit down.

'Wheest, woman, it has to be said. Mr Davies, trying to make ends meet in farming is pretty damned hard at the minute, and quite honestly, if I was given the chance of an offer like yours, I'd grab it with both hands. But that's not the case, is it? So, my point is that if one particular party, or parties, has been lucky enough to be given the chance to get out, then they shouldn't be too selfish in making up their minds, so that we can all be in the position to reap some of those benefits that you've spoken about. So, I think I'd be speaking for everyone here in asking for assurance that neither Gregor nor Liz Dewhurst will allow their petty differences to mar the future potential of your scheme.'

Liz sat rigid, staring straight ahead at Jonathan Davies, seeing, for once, a flustered expression come over his face. She felt her cheeks flush uncontrollably, and a sudden pounding filled her head. She heard the chair beside her creak and watched as her father rose slowly to his feet. He turned and fixed Danny McKay with a steely glare.

'Mr McKay, I can tell you that this family has known some suffering over these past few months, yet not for a

34

minute have we allowed this to stand in the way of Mr Davies and his colleagues in their endeavours to draw up their plans. But nothing is certain just yet, and I can tell you that if a decision is made to end the project at any stage, it will be because of financial considerations made by both Gregor's and my family, and not because of what you term as "petty differences."' He looked round to Jonathan Davies. 'With apologies to the chair' – he turned back to scowl at the now red-faced farmer – 'I take your question, Mr McKay, as not only being out of order, but also damned offensive.'

An embarrassed silence descended upon the room as both men took their seats again. Liz found herself glancing unwittingly over to where Gregor and Mary McLean sat, and saw her huddling forward in her seat, trying to make herself as invisible as possible.

Davies cleared his throat and rubbed nervously at his forehead. 'Well, I think that we have probably discussed enough for this evening. If anybody has any further questions, my colleagues and I are going to be holding back here for a bit, so please feel free to come forward and ask them. So it just leaves me to thank you all for attending.'

The meeting broke up with a general movement of chairs and a buzz of hushed conversation. Davies picked up his papers from the desk and pushed them together in his hands, then made his way around the table to the front row where Liz and her father still remained seated.

He leaned forward to Liz. 'I'm so terribly sorry about that, Liz,' he said quietly. 'If I had realized at all that someone would come out with such a crass statement, I would never even have considered an open meeting at this stage.'

Liz shook her head. 'Don't worry. Something like that would have been said regardless of when you held it. It's the fodder on which our little community thrives at the minute, I'm afraid.'

Davies nodded and gladly escaped back to the bonhomie of his American colleagues. Liz let out a long sigh and turned to her father. 'Come on then, Dad,' she said, taking his arm. 'Let's go home. I'll go get the car and meet you at the front door.'

The small car-park at the rear of the pub had emptied as fast as the lounge bar after the meeting. Pulling her coat around her to protect her from the chill wind, Liz walked over to the Land Rover and put the key in the door.

'Liz?'

A car door slammed shut behind her, and she turned to watch Gregor walk across the car-park towards her. Breathing out a heavy sigh, she leaned back against the door, casting her eyes anywhere but at her husband.

Gregor stopped a short distance from her and pushed his hands into his pockets. He looked down at the ground and began scraping his shoe at a loose stone in the Tarmac. 'I'm sorry about that in there. Your father was right. McKay had no cause to say such a thing. He's just got it in for us – always has.'

Liz made no reaction to his remark.

'Have you seen Alex today?'

Liz shook her head.

'Just wondered how he got on at the trial.'

Liz shrugged and turned to open the door of the car. 'No doubt I'll find out when I get home.'

'Liz?' Gregor stepped forward and put his hand on her arm, but immediately withdrew it as he felt her pull away from his contact. 'Listen, Liz, we must talk sometime. We have to discuss this whole thing through properly. I had a meeting with the bank today, and they're getting pretty edgy about the overdraft. I don't think it'll be that long before they try to pull the rug out from underneath me – so I would guess that they'd do the same with you. What I mean is that I don't think that we can go on just burying our heads in the sand.'

Liz kept her hand on the car door, but turned to look at him, waiting to see if he had anything further to add.

'Liz, come on. Just listen for a minute.' He paused and let out a long sigh. 'The reason we have to talk is that I'm not so confident that this golf project *is* going to get off the ground. Jonathan said to me today that one of their investors has pulled out, and if his group don't find another investor in the next couple of months, then the Americans are going to cut their losses and move their money over to another project in the States. So, you see, we have to talk. We can't jeopardize this one chance of solving all our money problems. We have to think of our futures, of Alex's future. If we show ourselves to be right behind the scheme, then maybe they will delay making a decision for a little bit longer.'

Liz felt a sudden warmth from the realization of hope that built up inside her. Okay, so there had always been uncertainty about whether the project would get off the ground during the earliest of its stages, but over the last month she had been beginning to admit to herself that it was heading towards an inevitability. So to lose a valued investor at this stage would be crucial. This might be the way out. If they couldn't find the money, then her father, Alex and she would be left in peace, and Gregor would be left to sort out his own dirty washing. She folded her arms and stared straight at Gregor.

'Why did you bring her along tonight?'

Gregor bit at his lip. 'What?'

'You heard me. Why did you bring her along? It's got nothing to do with her.'

'Well, she just wanted to show interest.'

Liz let out a short laugh. 'I'm sure she did.' She turned and opened the car door and got in.

Gregor walked forward and grabbed the door, preventing her from shutting it. 'Come on, Liz, you've got to be a wee bit more reasonable than this.'

Liz pulled the door shut with unaccountable power. She grabbed hold of the steering wheel with both hands and stared mesmerically at its centre, fighting hard to control her emotions. After a moment she rolled down the window and looked at her husband. 'Reasonable?' she said quietly, a laugh of incredulity in her voice. 'Why the hell should I be reasonable? When were you ever *reasonable*?'

Starting up the engine, she crunched the Land Rover into reverse gear and lurched back, spinning the steering wheel so that Gregor had to jump aside to avoid coming into contact with the vehicle's already battered wing. As she pulled away, she glanced across at Gregor's pick-up, briefly catching the look of wild astonishment on Mary McLean's face.

She laughed to herself and said out loud, 'Oh, dear, oh dear, Barbie gets a fright!'

CHAPTER 3

The charcoal smell of burnt pastry wafting through the closed door of the kitchen greeted Alex as he entered the house that night, quickly followed by a painful expletive and the clattering bash of hot pie dish being discarded rapidly onto the sideboard.

'Look at that!' He heard edged anger in his mother's voice. 'What a damned waste! Where on earth is he?'

Alex stood motionless in the back lobby, physically sensing the air of tension that had become so commonplace in the house over the past six months. He caught hold of Leckie on his fourth attempt to jump up into his arms and stroked the Jack Russell's smooth coat in an effort to keep his welcome silent, at the same time straining to hear his grandfather's quiet but calming response.

'That's as may be,' his mother cut in, 'but he could have at least called.'

Alex took a deep breath to ready himself for the inevitable frosty reception and entered the kitchen, immediately wishing that he hadn't coincided it with giving a visible wince at the acrid fumes that filled the room. His mother stood at the paint-flaked central worktop, its surface cluttered by the opened contents of the day's mail, a large bag of Ewe Milk Replacer and his grandfather's tweed cap, upon which sat a large ginger cat whose tail swished as regularly as a pendulum as it stared fixedly at the pie. His mother looked up, catching his frown of distaste, then continued to busy herself in picking out the least-burnt bits of the steak pie before giving the side of the dish a hard tap with the edge of her spoon. 'You may well look like that. It's because you're so late that it's burnt – and don't add to the smell by bringing that dog in here. He's out in the lobby because he's rolled in something.'

Alex immediately thrust the small dog out to arm's length, and with an expression on his face that would have well befitted someone who had been asked to dispose of the decomposing body of a rat, he hurriedly projected the dog back out through the door, wiping his hands, on relieved impulse, on the seat of his trousers.

'Alex!'

Letting out a short, manic cry of frustration, he walked over to the kitchen sink and turned on the tap to rinse his hands. The water was scalding. '*Shit!*' He pulled his hands back fast from the steaming torrent, giving them a frantic shake to cool them down. He turned to see his grandfather, who was seated at the table, throw a glance of disapproval in his direction over his half-moon reading spectacles. 'Sorry.' Alex smiled apologetically. 'The water's hot.'

'So what happened to you?' his mother asked. 'Where have you been?'

'Well, I went to have a drink with Tom in the nine-teenth hole and sort of lost track of time.'

'You could have called.'

He took a dish-towel from the rail in front of the Rayburn and dried his hands. 'I know. I would have done. I'm sorry. But I really did lose track of time.'

His mother handed him a plate brimming with steak pie, boiled potatoes and broccoli. He stared at it for a moment, considering asking whether she would mind if he put one of the sticks of broccoli back in the bowl, it being his least-favourite vegetable, but thought better of it, thinking that it might not be too diplomatic a move under the circumstances. He walked across to the small table at the window and sat down opposite his grand-father, who was engrossed in the newspaper that was spread out on the yellow oilcloth in front of him.

'And did you drive back?'

'Yes.'

'What? After drinking?'

'Yes.'

Alex took a mouthful of food and glanced up to his grandfather, who looked at him over his spectacles and gave him a wink. Alex grinned back at him.

'I saw that, you two.' She walked across to her father and gave him a slap across his upper arm with her oven glove. 'There's no need to encourage him, Dad. He could lose his licence, and then he would be expecting us to drive him in and out of Saint Andrews.'

'Coke, Mum. I was only drinking Coke.'

'Ah. Right.' She stood for a moment realizing her misjudgement of the situation, then covered for her unease by stretching across to remove her father's empty plate, pushed to the farthest side of the table to make way for the newspaper. 'Well, that's all right then.' She walked back to the kitchen sink and rinsed off the plate before putting it in the dishwasher.

'So,' his grandfather started slowly, taking off his spectacles and laying them down on top of his newspaper. He folded his arms on the table and looked across at his grandson. 'How did it go, then?'

Alex smiled at him. 'I never thought anyone would ask,' he said, a tone of amusement in his voice.

'Well, I'm asking.'

'I got in.'

His grandfather brought his hands together in one resonant and triumphant clap. 'That's my lad! Well done, you! You played well, then?'

'Well enough. I thought I was going to blow it half-way round, but at that point, Tom Harrison, the team captain, announced that he wanted me to play on Saturday, and after that, I just seemed to pull it all together.'

Alex had just taken another mouthful of food when a blue rubber-gloved hand flashed past his eyes and a pair of arms, quite unexpectedly, encircled his shoulders and he felt himself drawn in against the busty softness of his mother's chest. She held him so tightly that there was too much resistance for his jaw to continue chewing, and one of the buttons on her woollen cardigan bit painfully into his ear. But he made no attempt to move away. 'I'm sorry, Alex.' She kissed him on the forehead. 'I had completely forgotten that this was your big day. Well done, darling, I'm really proud of you.'

She let go and moved back to the kitchen sink to continue scrubbing at the blackened innards of the pie dish. Alex looked across to where she stood, the harsh glare of the fluorescent light accentuating the paleness of her tired face. Damn this whole situation, he thought to himself. Damn Dad for doing this to her, for behaving like some young stud at *his* age. Because that's all it was with Mary McLean. Just a sexual attraction. He could see that himself. They didn't have anything in common with each other. She never went out on the farm or to the market with him, not as Mum used to do. And when they did speak, there was always an air of falseness in their conversation, as if they were simply a couple who had been thrown together on a blind date. But then he'd made his bed and he was going to have to lie in it.

He pushed the broccoli to the side of his plate and scraped what was left of the steak pie onto his fork. 'I also got a job caddying again for the holidays,' he said brightly, trying to inject a shot of levity into the gloomy atmosphere.

His mother looked round, pushing back a strand of hair with her forearm to avoid its coming into contact with the greasy froth on her glove. 'Have you? Well done.' Alex could hear her making every effort to express enthusiasm.

'Well, I just thought that I'd take the opportunity on the way back from playing, so I looked in at the caddymaster's office. He said there'd be no problem. Just turn up when the semester is over.'

The muffled trill of the telephone sounded over the last few words of his sentence. Liz turned from the sink and walked over to the dresser, pulling off her rubber gloves as she went. She stood for a moment looking at the empty base of the portable. 'Dad, where's the phone?'

'Ah, yes. Sorry. I used it earlier. I think it's in the hall.'

'Well, see if you can remember to put it back in future.' She opened the door into the hall and closed it with force behind her.

Taking the opportunity of her absence, Alex got up from the table and took his plate over to the plastic rubbish bin at the side of the Rayburn. He flipped open the lid and slid the watery stalks of broccoli off his plate.

'What's eating Mum?' he asked, reaching back into the bin to cover the evidence with a discarded *Farmer's Weekly*.

'Nothing at all, Alex, is *eating* your mother,' his grandfather retorted, a sternness to his voice, 'in the same way that nothing is *eating* at that broccoli that *was* on your plate.'

Alex pulled a short, embarrassed smirk. 'Right. I'm sorry. I didn't mean it to sound like that. It's just that . . .'

Mr Craig leaned back in his chair. 'Aye, I know what you're going to say. But your mother does have reason to be feeling a little upset.' He paused and closed his newspaper, and carefully folded it up. 'We had the golf course meeting tonight.'

Alex poured himself a glass of water and went back to

45

sit opposite his grandfather. 'What happened?'

'Just some of the locals behaved a bit unthinkingly towards her. Made her feel a wee bit uneasy. And then she had a few words with your father in the car-park afterwards about the project.'

'What was he saying?'

'Och, just that he thought that it was still the only way we could appease the bank and suchlike. He did say that these consortium laddies were having to stall a bit, being in need of another investor.' He let out a long sigh and leaned forward to pick up his spectacles, holding them by one leg and twisting them back and forth between thumb and forefinger. 'But . . . well, we'll just have to wait and see.'

'Do you think it will happen, Granddad? I mean, it's been so on-off over the past year.'

'Aye, well, from what I gathered at the meeting tonight, it looks now as if they've got everything in place to get started. I suppose it just depends on whether they get this other investor.'

Alex eyed his grandfather. 'And what about you, Granddad? Do you want it to go ahead?'

Mr Craig smiled across at his grandson. 'I can't help but admit that I've got awful mixed feelings about it, Alex. The farm's been in the family for five generations, and you know, old habits die hard. But there's no getting away from the fact that we're in a bit of a pickle financial-like.' He chuckled. 'Maybe in hindsight, we shouldn't have invested so much when we joined up with your father's family after your parents got married, but it seemed the right thing to do at the time.' He paused and Alex could hear the glass-paper friction as he rubbed his calloused hand across the grey stubble on his chin. 'But then all those "high heid yins" in Brussels changed their tune and told us to start taking land out of production, and that's really when farming changed for me. There was no great pleasure in seeing a good field left to grow weeds, and know that we were taking taxpayers' money for the pleasure of just letting it happen. To me, it sort of undermined the whole integrity and honesty of the business. And now we're being told to diversify *away* from farming, so I suppose we're just heeding their advice.' He shook his head. 'But I just never thought that it would mean we'd be giving up farming completely. I always had the notion that I'd end my days being a farmer.'

Alex stared out the window into the blackness of the night. 'Mum really doesn't want the project to go ahead, does she?'

'Not at the minute, no. But I think we can all understand her point of view. She's been hurt quite bad by what's happened – not only with your father, but also losing her mother. And really, since then, she's been running the business side of the farm, so I think she'd be loath to give that up, it taking her mind off everything and all.'

Getting up from the table, Alex walked over to the sink and discarded the remaining contents of his glass. He turned and folded his arms. 'I just feel that we've all got to keep going, Granddad. Not especially with the farm, but with, well, everything. I mean, I *know* that Dad has behaved like a stupid fool, and I realize that Grandma dying has been hard on both you *and* Mum, but we've got to keep going. To be quite honest, I don't know how much more of this eternal gloom I can put up with.'

His grandfather let out a quiet snort and shook his head. 'That bad, is it?'

'Yes, actually, it is. You know, Tom asked me today if I'd ever considered moving into digs in Saint Andrews, and for a moment I was really taken by the idea. But I wouldn't do it. At any rate, I couldn't afford it. But what we need to do is inject a bit of *life* into this household. We can't moulder around in sorrow forever.' Alex bit hard on his lip, understanding that he might have gone too far with this last remark. He walked over to his grandfather and put a hand on his shoulder, then pulled out the chair next to him and sat down. 'Sorry, Granddad, that didn't come out right. What I was meaning to say was that I just don't like seeing you both so . . . well . . . down all the time.'

His grandfather smiled at him. 'Listen, lad, I'm not "down," as you put it. At my age, you accept the fact that you're getting nearer the time when death plays its part some way or other. Aye, I miss your grandmother, but I'm not "down." I've got a great many good memories, you know, and that's what keeps me going.'

The door opened and they both turned and watched Liz walk back in. She replaced the portable on its base. 'That was your father, Alex. He said well done about getting into the team, and wondered if you would give

48

him a call about shooting pigeon on Saturday. He says they're hitting the oil-seed rape quite badly.'

'Did you tell him that I'm playing golf on Saturday?'

'Yes, but he was thinking of doing an evening flight. You'd be through by then, wouldn't you?'

'Probably,' Alex replied with little keenness. 'I'll give him a call in a minute.'

Mr Craig looked across at his daughter. 'Was that all he had to say?'

Liz took the kettle off the side of the Rayburn and filled it with water. 'No, he said that Jonathan Davies was concerned that what happened tonight in the pub might colour my judgement on the project, and he asked me to call him.'

'And did you?'

'Yes.'

'And what did you say?'

Liz spooned coffee into a mug. 'That we were still undecided.'

He chortled quietly. 'Probably not what Gregor had hoped you would say.'

'No.'

Alex took a deep breath and got up from his chair. 'Listen, I don't know what you both feel about this, but, well, I was speaking with Tom about everything on the golf course, and he suggested that we might get someone in – you know, as a paying guest in the house. We've got the spare room empty, and Granddad, you said yourself we were pretty strapped for cash. I just thought that maybe it wasn't such a bad idea. I mean, every little bit helps.'

49

Liz let out a scoffing laugh. 'I don't think things are *that* bad, Alex!'

'Maybe not, but at least it would be a bit of money coming in for housekeeping and the like.'

Liz took the steaming kettle off the Rayburn and poured water into her coffee. 'I think that that would be more trouble than it was worth, would it not?'

'I don't think so, Mum. I mean, a student or someone. They'd probably only sleep here, and I'm going into town every day. I could drive him and get him to pay for some of the petrol, so it would help me.' Alex looked from one to the other. 'Well, would you consider it?'

His grandfather flicked his head to the side. 'Not a bad idea. It may be peanuts, but Alex could be right. Every little bit helps.'

Alex looked at his mother. 'Well?'

She took a sip of coffee and slowly shook her head. 'I don't think we need anyone else in the household at the minute.'

Alex lifted his hands in exasperation and slapped them hard on the top of his head. 'Oh, for God's sake, Mum, come on! It's exactly what this household needs at the minute! If not for financial reasons, then certainly for emotional ones!' For a moment he stood looking at them both, their faces expressing dismay at his outburst, then, shaking his head at the futility of it all, he turned and picked up the portable. 'I'll see you both in the morning.' He left the room, closing the door behind him without a backward glance.

Liz made for the door, intending to call him back, but

was cut short in her actions by her father.

'Leave him be, Lizzie.'

'What did he mean by that?' she asked quietly.

'You've got to understand that he's finding it hard to work out how best to cope with the situation at present. He doesn't like seeing you suffering the way you are at the minute, lass. He's just trying to think of a way to help you out.'

Liz moved over to the table and sat down heavily on the chair next to her father. She rested her elbows on the table and rubbed at the tiredness in her eyes. 'I know.' She paused. 'Oh, Dad, I don't know what's wrong with me. My head is so full of *hate* at the minute. It seems to affect everything.'

Her father stretched across and gently patted her arm. 'Aye, I can tell that. But what Alex was saying to me when you were out of the room is right, you know. We have to keep going. We have to bring life back into this house, otherwise we'll all just sink into a huge bucket of gloom.'

Liz looked up and smiled at her father. 'It's that bad, is it?'

Her father gave her a wink. 'That's exactly what I asked Alex.'

Liz raised her eyebrows and blew out a long breath. 'So it *is* that bad.'

'Aye, I think it must be – for him, at any rate.'

Liz nodded. 'So we should maybe consider doing what he suggests.'

'I don't see why not. As he said, the spare room is free,

and he's certainly right in saying that we could do with a bit of extra cash coming in.'

Liz put both hands on the table and pushed herself to her feet. 'I'll go and have a word with him.'

Her father laid his hand on top of hers. 'Aye, you do that thing. And remember, lass, you mean more to that boy than anyone else in the world at the minute.' He got up from his chair and took his daughter in his arms. 'And that goes for me as well, d'ye hear?'

CHAPTER 4

The pigeon, nothing more than a shadowed outline against the darkening sky, weaved its way across the field towards him before setting its wings to plane down into the small copse at the edge of which Alex had been standing for the past two hours. He kept his head low, shielding his eyes with the peak of his baseball cap, just in case the fast-diminishing light caught in them the merest glint of reflection, enough for the pigeon, through the intricacy of its built-in radar vision, to sense that something was out of sorts with its intended night-time roost. Alex raised the shotgun and took a bead on its head, allowing for its forward motion, putting pressure on the trigger only when the bird had reached the outermost branches of the tree that stood behind him. The gun kicked hard against his shoulder, the air exploding with sound, and as the hollow echo faded away across the open fields, it was replaced by the frantic thrash of wings against branches, as those pigeons which had slipped into the centre of the wood, from directions unguarded by his father or himself, broke cover from the depths of the trees and made their escape.

The Jack Russell, who had been watching the progress of the pigeon as intently as Alex, took off into the wood, yelping excitedly at the prospect of finding another bird, fully intending to give it a good mauling before it could be finally wrested from his vice-like jaws.

'Leckie!' Alex yelled after the dog, his voice breaking into a laugh. 'Come here, you stupid idiot! I missed it!'

Leckie, however, never deviated from the mission-in-hand, his warcry diminishing until it was lost to the sound of the freshening wind that had begun to flush out any vestige of warmth that had been hitherto afforded to Alex by the protection of the trees. He pulled up the collar of his jacket and dug his hands deep into the pockets. Leaning back against the tree, he began stamping his feet on the hardened ground in an attempt to rid the tingling ache of cold from his toes.

'I think we're done for the night.'

The voice made Alex start, and he turned to watch his father approach through the trees. His shotgun was shouldered with one hand, and in the other he carried a plastic fertilizer bag, the weight of which caused it to knock clumsily against his Wellington as he walked.

Breaking open his gun, Alex took out the unfired cartridges and slipped them back into his belt. 'How did you get on?'

'Not too bad. About twenty-three. How about you?'

Alex looked down at the dismal extent of his bag. 'I haven't counted yet, but I think only about ten. I'm afraid I was a bit off-target tonight.'

His father glanced over to the pile of spent cartridges that lay scattered at the base of the tree. He let out a short laugh. 'Aye, I can see that. Well, you start picking those up, and I'll deal with these.' He laid down his gun and started to count the pigeon into the bag. 'Nine, ten, eleven. One more than you thought.' He gave the neck of the bag a twist and slung it over his shoulder, then, putting his thumb and forefinger into the sides of his mouth, he gave out one long, ear-splitting whistle to call back the dog. He bent down to retrieve his gun. 'Och well, it's just a drop in the ocean anyway. They'll still be back in force tomorrow, even though they've lost a few comrades tonight.' He waited until Alex had finished stuffing the empty cartridges into his pocket, then moved off into the field. 'Come on, we'll head for home.'

Alex tucked his gun under his arm and stood for a moment watching his father stride away in front of him, his short, muscular frame barely stooping under the weight of the heavy bag he carried over his shoulder. That's a good one, he thought to himself. And whose home would you be talking about?

They made their way in an uneasy silence across the open field, the only sounds being the wind and the brittle crunching of their feet on the frost-spangled leaves of the oil-seed rape. The near-full moon in the cloudless sky lit their way, their shadows cast in front of them in ghostly, yet perfectly focused forms. It wasn't until they had reached the brow of the hill, where the warming rectangles of light spilt out from the windows in the farmhouse to greet them, that his father spoke.

'So the match today was successful, was it?'

'Yes, it was. But only just. We won all the singles, but only managed to scrape a draw on one of the foursomes.'

'Who was it you were playing?'

'Aberdeen University.'

'Right.' His father paused, and Alex sensed that he was uncertain as to how he should continue the conversation. 'And then, what about your studies? How are they going?'

'Good enough. I've had a change of tutor for German which I thought might be a bit disruptive, but he's turned out to be a pretty sound guy, *and* he makes himself available for tutorials, which is more than can be said for the last one.'

'New, is he?'

'Yes, a Canadian. He's actually a professor, but he doesn't head the department or anything like that. From what I can gather, he's just coming up for retirement and was given a secondment to Saint Andrews from the University of Toronto.'

'One of those eccentric old duffers, is he?'

Alex let out a short chuckle. 'In ways. He's always pacing around the room as he talks, and he has this pipe in his mouth which he never succeeds in keeping lit. But, funnily enough, I wouldn't say that he really looks *that* old. He sort of reminds me of one of those old Hollywood film actors, but I can't for the life of me think which one.'

His father stopped, a querying smile on his face. 'Give me a clue, then.'

Alex shrugged. 'I can't. I just know that I've seen him in one of those old colour films. Maybe one of those 1960s thrillers.'

'Alfred Hitchcock?'

'No, that's not him.'

His father laughed. 'No, you nit, that's the guy who *made* those kind of films about that time.'

'Ah. Well, maybe.'

'I bet it's Cary Grant.'

Alex stopped in his tracks, his mouth open in thought, then he gave a loud click with his fingers. 'That's exactly who it is!' he exclaimed. 'You've got it! It's Cary Grant.'

His father chucked his head to the side and gave his son a companionable bump with his arm. 'There you are, then. One thing I know about is my films.'

They walked on into the shelter of the red pan-tiled farm buildings and passed round the side of the lambing shed, where his father's small flock of pedigree Suffolks was housed.

Letting the fertilizer bag fall from his shoulder, Gregor flicked on the switch by the door, the action immediately causing a flutter of alarm amongst his ewes as they noisily began to seek out their offspring in the close-stocked quarters. He made his way slowly down the central feed aisle, casting an experienced eye from one side to the other to make sure that nothing was amiss. Alex watched him, leaning his shoulder against the side of the door.

'Dad?'

Gregor reached the other end of the shed and turned. 'Aye?'

'Can I ask what you're planning to do?'

His father walked slowly towards him, giving the flock a second appraisal. 'I don't really know, Alex. I suppose it has to depend on whether the consortium can get this other investor.'

'I didn't actually mean that. What about you and Mum?'

Gregor had reached the half-way support stanchion of the shed. He stopped and looked at his son, but did not answer.

'Are you going to get a divorce?'

His father finished the inspection and came to lean his back against the opposite doorpost. He let out a long sigh. 'I don't know, lad. I'm not sure what I should do. I don't know what would be least hurtful to your mother.'

Alex shook his head and stared out into the night to avoid looking at his father. 'It's not just Mum, you know.'

He heard the crumpled rustle of his father's waxed jacket as he moved across the doorway towards him. A strong hand squeezed his shoulder, but he shrugged it off and walked out into the darkness, giving a quick whistle for Leckie, who had been busying himself on a ratting sortie, darting from one building to another.

'Alex!' He could hear anxiety in his father's voice as he walked away from him. 'Listen, lad, why don't we go into the house for a cup of coffee and we can have a talk about it?'

'Not tonight, Dad,' he shouted back over the sound of the wind. 'I've got an early start tomorrow, and anyway' – he stopped and looked back to where his father stood, silhouetted in the doorway by the light that shone out from the lambing shed – 'I want to go home.'

He turned and made his way towards his car. That

should give him a jolt, he thought to himself, that should hurt him. But as he walked he realized from the burning sting of tears in his eyes that the remark had had exactly that effect on himself.

CHAPTER 5

Agnes Winterbotham placed her Nilfisk vacuum cleaner into the cupboard under the stairs, then began her daily struggle of trying to get its unruly tube sufficiently curled so that she could close the door behind it. Giving its escaping spout a final kick with an elastic-slippered foot, she slammed the door and locked it, the action giving her as much satisfaction as if she had just managed to subdue an irascible boa constrictor. Delving into the pocket of her floral housecoat, she pulled out a yellow duster and walked along the swirl-patterned carpet in the narrow hallway, wiping the cloth along the radiator shelf as she went, being careful to avoid knocking off either the cactus plant or the delicate pink figurine of the 'Shepherdess with Lamb in Arms.' She opened the front door, snibbing it so that it didn't shut behind her, and descended the three steps to the pavement, where she began rubbing hard at the brass plaque which was bolted to the black-glossed iron railings that ran the full length of the little street. When she felt that its gleam was sufficient, she looked to each side of her to make sure that she would not hinder the path of one of the many students who were making their way, in different states of urgency after the weekend, along the street to their lectures. Then, taking two paces back, she first made sure that the name BALLINLUIG GUEST HOUSE stood out well for the benefit of any prospective client, before leaning her head to the side to confirm to herself that the VACANCIES sign in the window of the residents' drawing-room was set in exactly the right place for maximum appeal. Satisfied that all was as it should be, she ascended the steps.

As she reached out to give the brass knob on the front door a quick once-over, it flew open and a young man, dressed in brown terylene trousers and beige wind-cheater, appeared and immediately tripped over the threshold, precipitating both himself and the pile of books that he carried at her feet. She moved to the side and watched as he scrambled together the papers that had flown out of his 'Arcadia A-4' file, then, gathering up his books, he got to his feet and gave her a wide, teeth-plated smile, using the corner of the file to push his black bottle-lensed spectacles back onto the bridge of his nose.

He let out a long, embarrassed moan. 'Sorry about that, Mrs Winterbotham,' he lisped, his words accompanied by a fine spray of spittle.

Agnes looked kindly at the acne-infested face of the young boy, thinking to herself how unkind nature could be to bestow one person with so many disturbing afflictions. 'That's all right, Alasdair. Now, did you remember to call your mother this morning?'

Alasdair let out another indecipherable sound that gave her no real clue as to what the answer might be to her question, then turned and ran off down the street, his scarf flying out behind him like that of a First World War pilot. Agnes watched fondly as he went. What a nice boy, she thought to herself, so little trouble. Just the kind of guest that she liked. She let out a short sigh and glanced up to one of the upstairs windows, the lower half of which was closed down upon two pairs of grey socks that flapped in the morning breeze. Not like others she'd care to mention.

She walked back into the house, dropped the snib, and opened the door into the residents' drawing-room. Adjusting the two lace antimacassars as she made her way around the sofa, she gave each of the three cushions a generous plumping before laying them back in place. Then, running her cloth over the mantelpiece, she lightly dusted the ornaments before taking down the focal point of the display, a fading black-and-white photograph of her deceased husband. She gave the glass that protected the stern, shrouded-eyed face a gentle blow, then wiped the frame and replaced it, adjusting it so that it was exactly positioned where it had been beforehand. Standing back, she smiled at the bleak countenance and said quietly under her breath, 'Good morning, Hubert. It's another lovely day. Fresh, but lovely.'

A door slammed shut upstairs, so loud that she saw the photograph tremble in the shock wave. With a click of her teeth, she walked over to the mantelpiece, made the minutest adjustment to her husband's image, then hurried over to the door and opened it. She looked up the narrow staircase at the tall man who thumped his way down towards her, struggling to pull on a huge belted mackintosh over his leather arm-patched tweed jacket, while passing a battered leather brief-case from one hand to the other.

'Professor Kempler? Might I have a word?' Agnes held her hands together, squeezing her fingers so tightly that the area around the knuckles went white. She hated confrontation. In the past, she had always left this kind of thing up to Hubert.

'As long as it's quick, Mrs Winterbotham. I have to give a tutorial in ten minutes.'

He always pronounced her name incorrectly. It was pronounced 'bottom,' not 'botham.' Hubert would have put him right, probably quietly accentuating his rebuff with some comment about the ignorance of 'colonials.'

'Professor Kempler, I wondered if you might *try* to make a little less noise. It disturbs the other guests.'

The man clamped the brief-case between his legs while he did up the buttons on his raincoat. He glanced up the stairs. 'Forgive me for saying this, Mrs Winterbotham, but as far as I know, you only have myself and that spotty-faced youth as your guests at the minute, and I saw him head off in the most appallingly dishevelled state about five minutes ago.'

Agnes felt her face colouring fast. 'That is a cruel thing to say, Professor, and neither is it the point. The fact is that I am of a nervous disposition and I don't like noise.'

Arthur Kempler did up the buckle of his belt and took the brief-case from between his legs. He stuck his hand in

63

his pocket and pulled out a pipe and a lighter. 'I'm sorry, Mrs Winterbotham. I shall try to make less noise in future.' Then, before Agnes could utter another word of reproach, he flicked the lighter and held it to the bowl, emitting from his mouth a puff of smoke that even a myopic Red Indian would have found hard not to see.

Agnes was incensed by his action. 'Professor, please do *not* smoke your pipe in my house! I've asked you this before!'

Arthur cast his eyes heavenward, then made an accentuated play of pressing his forefinger into the bowl to extinguish the pipe before returning it to his pocket. 'Anything else, Mrs Winterbotham? I have to go, you know.'

Agnes crossed her arms to stop herself from shaking both with anger and nerves. 'Yes, as a matter of fact, there is.' She bravely took one pace towards him. 'I have also specifically asked you not to hang your shirts or your socks on the radiator to dry.'

Arthur Kempler held up both hands in desperation. 'And I've stopped, Mrs Winterbotham!'

Agnes continued slowly, trying to control her tone. 'Yes, but now you are placing your socks on the window-sill to dry, and, Professor Kempler, it does not look good for prospective—'

Arthur turned full circle this time, his flailing briefcase nearly decapitating the 'Shepherdess with Lamb in Arms.' '*Christ*, Mrs Winterbotham, how the *hell else* am I meant to get them dry?'

That was enough for Agnes. She had felt up until now that she could put up with his appalling house manners, simply because in early March room rentals throughout St Andrews were at a low ebb. But for anyone to take the Lord's name blatantly in vain in front of her! That was unforgivable! What would Hubert have thought at this kind of behaviour going on under *their* roof? There was obviously only one course of action to take.

'Professor Kempler, I am sorry, but you leave me no alternative other than to ask you to leave.' There. She had said it, and she was proud that there had not even been the slightest tremor in the tone of her voice.

Arthur stood looking at her for a moment, then swept his hand over his grey-flecked hair, a grimace on his face as he tried to force some kind of reconciliatory meekness into his manner. 'Listen, Mrs Winterbotham—'

Agnes realized immediately that she had the upper hand. 'It's "bottom," by the way, not "botham."'

Arthur nodded. 'I'm sorry, Mrs Winter-*bottom*.' Damn it, he didn't mean to smile. Get that smile off your face *now*. 'But could we not just try again? I really do promise that I'll make an effort, as I'm sure that you must understand that I don't have much time to look for other accommodation right now, it being in the middle of the semester.'

Agnes had caught the smile and gave him one last glare of contempt before turning on her heel and walking along the passage to the kitchen. 'I shall give you three days to find other lodgings, Professor Kempler, and I shall *not* be returning your deposit.' She opened the door into the kitchen and closed it behind her.

For a moment, Arthur stared at the lilac-blue barrier

that lay between them, then blew out one large, loud raspberry. 'Damned woman,' he said quietly and turned and let himself out of his former residence.

At the first chime of the bell, Alex looked up from his notes and glanced through the dusty panes of the study window at the church clock on the other side of the street. It was midday. He caught the eyes of his three fellow students and raised his eyebrows. From their looks, he could tell that they had gathered as little from the tutorial as he had done, and he was fairly sure that they were all of the same mind in wishing that the professor would come to a halt, so that they could go off to have a well-earned pint in the pub. But he continued to drone on unintelligibly through the twelve chimes, as he had done throughout the whole two-hour tutorial, pacing the floor in front of the huge marble fireplace, every third round holding his lighter to his pipe and letting out one huge cloud of smoke, before taking it from his mouth and allowing it to burn out over the next three rounds.

The professor was definitely having an off-day. Usually his tutorials were fired with debate and humour, and on many occasions he was sympathetic enough to break into English if he felt that the point of discussion was too important to be jeopardized through the students' lack of knowledge of the German language; or, what was more common, if he felt that the punch line of one of his many off-beat jokes might not receive the loudest groans of inappreciation that it deserved. But today had been completely different. Alex sat back in the armchair and picked at the piping on the faded loose cover, allowing his thoughts to meander away from the tutorial, as they had done throughout the session. He thought back to the golf match on Saturday and went over in his mind how much better he could have played the two approach shots to the sixteenth and seventeenth greens, and how they would have secured for him and his partner an outright win, rather than a draw, in their four-somes match. He thought back to his trial match with Tom Harrison, and his golf captain's words of advice. Maybe Tom was right that he should try to get another girl-friend. He hadn't really had a steady one since he had left Madras the year before. Okay, there was that girl he'd met in Freshers' Week, but that had only lasted a couple of weeks. He looked across at the only girl in the room, opposite him on the sofa. She sat, quite obviously doodling on her textbook, her legs curled up under her bottom, her elbow resting on the leather arm as she absently raked her fingers through her straight blonde hair. What about Madeleine, for instance? Yes, what *about* Madeleine? He'd not even considered it before, but why not? She was a really good friend of his, they'd studied a good deal together, and as far as he knew she didn't have a boy-friend. He looked hard at her in appraisal. *And*, what's more, she's pretty. His eyes moved down from her face and took in the curve of her breasts and the protrusion of her nipples against the tightness of her cotton T-shirt, all this being accentuated by the framing folds of her open-zippered waistcoat.

Alex suddenly realized what was happening, and gave

his body a shuddering jolt to get himself away from that train of thought. What the hell was he doing? He crossed his legs to relieve the sensual ache that had begun tugging at his lower abdomen. Come on, Professor, finish off this damned tutorial now, before the distractions get worse!

Arthur stopped and looked at his watch. '*Also, was machen wir? Es ist schon viertel nach zwölf! Gut! Machen wir Schluß. Am Freitag sehen wir uns alle wieder hier.*' There was a general creaking of old furniture as the students moved in their seats to gather up their belongings. Madeleine was first to her feet. She threw her books back onto the sofa and pushed her arms high above her head in an effort to stretch out some of the weariness that had assailed her body during the dreary session. '*Und Madeleine,*' the professor continued, '*ich finde es sehr beunruhigend, daß Sie in meiner Arbeitsgruppe keinen BH tragen. Ich bitte Sie, in Zukunft einen anzuhaben.*'

The aftermath of his remark, following the initial shocked moment of silence, could have been much worse, had Madeleine not immediately read the situation as being yet another example of the professor's zany sense of humour, taking it as his preconceived plan to end the otherwise mind-numbing tutorial in a breath-clutching climax. She broke the embarrassed hush in the fusty room with a loud burst of laughter, deciding to give the old boy as good as she had received. 'I beg your pardon, Professor!' she exclaimed, a look of surprised horror on her face, her three male colleagues noting, with relief, that there was little change to the colour of her cheeks. 'If I choose not to wear a bra, then I won't! Anyway, you're far too old to make a remark like that!' She put together the two ends of her waistcoat zipper, and shut away from sight the subjects of debate.

For a moment, Arthur Kempler stood with one hand holding his elbow, the other covering his mouth. He then closed his eyes and thumped the palm of his hand against his forehead. 'Madeleine,' he started slowly, 'that was an unforgivable remark, and I am totally ashamed of myself for ever having uttered it. You are absolutely right, of course. Not only am I too old, I have no business to make any observation at all on how my students dress. Please accept my most abject apologies. If I can offer any excuse for my unacceptable and unprofessional behaviour, it would be only that I happen to have a few rather distracting thoughts going through my mind at the moment.'

Madeleine glanced at her fellow students, then took the opportunity of rubbing salt into her tutor's wounds. 'That, Professor, is an understatement.'

Arthur held up his hands, as if defending himself from any further verbal onslaught. 'I know, I know! It's just that . . . well . . . I have this morning been unceremoniously ejected from my lodgings by a woman who would make Boadicea look like a nurserymaid.' He turned to shuffle together the papers on the desk and stuff them into the brief-case. 'Consequently, I have been forced to find somewhere else to live in the next . . . three . . . days.' Clicking his brief-case shut, he turned and leaned against the desk, glancing around his four students. 'So if any of you have a bright idea, I would be most grateful for your assistance.'

Madeleine waved her hand in the air. 'I don't suppose you'd be interested in a room in our all-girl flat, would you, Professor?' she fluttered in wicked innocence.

Arthur let out a guffaw of a laugh and pushed himself off the desk, walking between his students to the coat-stand by the door. 'Madeleine, my dear, with the self-confidence and sense of humour that are obviously in your possession, you will go far in life.' He took down his rain-coat and began shrugging it on, bowing to Madeleine as he did so. 'I thank you for your kind offer, but I must feel obliged to refuse.' He did up his buttons. 'But if, at any time, you see me emerging from a large cardboard box in a shop doorway on a cold, frosty morning, I would be most grateful if you might ask again.' He opened the door of the study and held out his brief-cased hand to usher the group out of the room.

While Arthur locked the door, the students made their way down the stairs, laughing quietly amongst themselves about the tedium of the session and the professor's extraordinary remark, their hushed tones echoing around the chambered confines of the stone stairwell.

When they had reached the next landing, Madeleine glanced up through the iron banister. 'Poor old boy!' she said to Alex when she had seen that the professor wasn't following. 'It'll be pretty difficult for him to get anywhere at this time of year. He'll probably end up in a doss-house.' She laughed. 'At least, he's got the coat to go with the image!'

Alex smiled at her observation, then almost immediately stopped dead in his tracks, a frown of contemplation coming over his face. Madeleine had carried on a couple of paces before she realized that her companion was no longer at her side. She turned and gave him an inquiring look. 'Alex? What's the matter?'

Alex shook his head. 'Oh, nothing much. Probably nothing at all. But listen, you go on to the pub with the others, and I'll meet you there in about ten minutes.'

Madeleine seemed still none the wiser for his explanation. 'What are you going to do?'

'Nothing. I just want to see Professor Kempler for a minute.'

Madeleine shrugged her shoulders and smiled at him. 'Okay.' She turned and started quickly down the stairs to catch up with the others. 'I'll see you in the pub, then.'

Leaning his back against the wall, Alex settled down to wait for the professor to appear, and began to work through his mind the practicality of his new train of thought. Was it worth considering? I mean, giving it a bit of lateral thought, would it be such a daft idea? Maybe it wasn't another student that was needed at home. Maybe it would be much better to have someone older, someone with experience in life, who could inject some light-hearted diversity – and even wisdom – into the household. Perhaps it was all too easy, latching on to the first person who just happened to be looking for somewhere to live, but then it might work. In fact, the more he thought about it, the more *workable* the idea became! The professor was an easygoing guy, he had a good sense of humour – well, a bit odd-ball would be more precise – but he didn't seem to be grumpy or obtrusive or anything like that – and what was more, he *had* to be getting on to be about the same age as Granddad, so they'd probably have quite a bit in common. And it would be much easier for Mum having someone that age, better than having a student whom she might feel she'd have to 'mother.' Alex pushed himself away from the wall. Well, no harm in putting the idea to him, anyway.

There was still no sign of the professor. Alex turned and made his way back up the stairs again, finding the door of the study open and the professor's keys hanging in the lock. The room appeared to be empty, but the top drawer of the filing cabinet, which was against the wall behind the desk, was open, and files stuck out from it like badly shuffled cards.

'Professor?'

Arthur's tall figure suddenly materialized from below the level of the desk, the look of surprise on his face crumpling into a grimace of pain as his head came into contact with the underside of the cabinet drawer. A sound rang around the room as loud and as lingering as the ringing of a gong. 'Ow! Dammit!' He closed his eyes tight and rubbed hard at the top of his head. 'Alex! What the hell are you doing? Ow, that hurt!'

'Sorry. I didn't know where you were.' Alex walked around the side of the desk and looked down at the disordered pile of files and papers scattered over the surface of the floor. Arthur bent down to push them together.

'That bloody woman! Said she wouldn't pay back my deposit. Now I can't find the damned piece of paper I signed.'

Picking up the files, he stuck them back, with little

regard to indexing, into the cabinet and slammed the door shut. 'So! What can I do for you?'

'Well, I wonder if I could have a quick word?'

Arthur's mouth twisted in trepidation at what he thought might well be the reason for his student's returning. 'Alex, I hope you're not going to take me to task over what I said to Madeleine. It was a stupid remark, and I really could kick myself for saying it. I hope that you don't think that you need to take it any further.'

Alex shook his head. 'No, I wasn't going to mention it.'

The professor smiled at him. 'Good! I'm glad.' He sat down on the edge of the desk, crossing his arms. 'In that case, please don't think me rude if I say that I hope this won't be too long a discussion, Alex. I really *do* have to find somewhere else to live.'

Alex cleared his throat. 'Well . . . actually, it was about that.'

'Really?' The expression on Arthur's face turned from one of resigned detachment to quizzical interest. 'Do you know of somewhere?'

'Well, it depends on whether you want to live in Saint Andrews or not.'

Arthur cocked his head to the side. 'I teach here, Alex. I can't very well go live on the other side of Scotland.'

'I didn't mean that. Would it matter to you if you lived *outside* Saint Andrews?'

Arthur shrugged his shoulders. 'At the minute, I'd consider anything. I don't have a car, but as long as there's some kind of regular public transport . . . What do you have in mind, Alex?'

'Well, it's just that we have a spare room in the house that we were thinking of renting out. I live on a farm with my mother and grandfather about seven miles out of Saint Andrews, and because things aren't going too well with the business, we discussed the idea of letting out a room to help with – you know – housekeeping and that sort of thing.'

Arthur nodded slowly, taking in what Alex had been saying. 'Can one get into Saint Andrews quite easily from out there? I mean, is there a regular bus service?'

'Yes, from the top of the farm road. But what I was going to suggest is that I drive in to university every day, so I could bring you in. That is, if you could maybe give me a hand with the cost of petrol.'

Arthur contemplated this for a moment, then held out his hands as if laying himself open to Alex's tentative offer. 'So, where do we take it from here?'

'Well, if you want, you could come out to meet my mother and grandfather, and have a look at the place. I'm afraid I have no idea what the charge would be for the room. You'd have to talk to my mother about that, but I'm sure that it won't be any more than you're paying at the minute in the middle of Saint Andrews.'

'Okay then. When would be a good time?'

Alex glanced at his watch. 'It couldn't be until a bit later, I'm afraid. I've got two essays to finish off for tomorrow, so I'm going to be spending most of the afternoon in the library. But I reckon I'd be through by, say, half past four. I could take you out after that, if it would be suitable.'

74

Arthur rose to his feet and walked over to the door. 'I think – or should I say I hope – that that sounds like a godsend, and because, unlike you, I have little to do this afternoon, I shall rendezvous with *you* at the library at, say, twenty to five.'

'Right.'

Arthur walked over to the door. 'You *will* call your mother about this, won't you, Alex?'

'I could try, but I don't think she'd be in. She spends most of the day out on the farm. But I'm sure it will be all right.'

'Okay. Well, I'll see you at twenty to five at the library.' They walked out onto the stone landing, and the professor closed the door of the study behind him. 'And thank you, Alex. You may have just saved me from a life on the streets of Saint Andrews.'

Brian Davidson, Balmuir's master butcher and the man renowned throughout Fife for being the purchaser of the Supreme Champion at the 1989 Smithfield Show, stripped the disposable gloves from his hands and threw them into a waste-bin, then came around the end of the counter to open the door of the shop. 'Now, see and enjoy your meal tonight, Liz. You couldn't get better than a roll of Aberdeen Angus beef, no matter what the French may say!'

Liz smiled at the man, the ruddiness of his beaming face quite accentuated by the white coat and mesh trilby he wore on his head. 'Thank you, Brian. Let's hope they appreciate the treat.'

She left the shop and walked across the narrow main street of the village to where the Land Rover was parked. It had been her intention to leave the package in the vehicle, but seeing Leckie jump across from the back seat and stand with his front feet on the steering wheel, a cockeared look of eager anticipation as he eyed the bag, she thought better of it and veered past towards the small Spar supermarket.

The bell on the door tinged as she entered, and she scooped up a wire basket from the stack that was pushed in beside the refrigerator unit. She took a pint of milk from the unit as she passed and made her way quickly around the single display section in the centre of the shop to pick up a packet of peas from the deep freeze, her only other requirement for the day. As she turned the corner, her eye was caught by the line of glossy magazines on the shelf. Consequently she did not happen to notice the enormous tweedy posterior that bent forward in front of her, the possessor of which was doing her best to get low enough to retrieve something from the hindmost reaches of the bottom shelf. Liz hit her target at speed, making Delia Stanfield straighten up faster than she might have done in many a year.

Liz clapped her hand over her mouth. 'Lady Stanfield! I am sorry! I wasn't looking where I was going!'

Delia took time to turn her formidable bulk around in the confined area, her eyes lighting up when she saw who her asailant was. 'Liz, my dear, it's you!' She rolled her eyes and let out a long sigh of regret. 'I was so hoping it was going to be some gorgeous young man!'

'Oh dear! What a real disappointment for you!' They both laughed, any potential embarrassment that the incident might have caused tempered by their humour.

Delia linked her arms through the handle of her basket and gave Liz's dress a quick assessment from head to foot. 'Well, you certainly are the working girl today, aren't you?'

Liz glanced down at her attire. The legs of her jeans, tucked into her Wellingtons, were smeared with milk from the leaking teat of a feeding bottle, and there was a yellow streak of something much less savoury down the front of her torn jacket where she had had to cradle one of the more sickly lambs. She looked up at Delia, an embarrassed look on her face. 'Oh, Lady Stanfield, would you just look at me! I was really hoping that I could make it in and out of Balmuir without anyone seeing me. We're over our heads with work at the minute, what with the sowing *and* the lambing, and I suddenly realized that we didn't have anything for supper. Problem is that Dad and I have all the orphan lambs over with us at Brunthill this year. It just seemed easier with the situation being . . . well . . . what it is.'

Delia moved forward and gently put her hand on Liz's arm. 'I do understand, my dear.' She paused, her glossy lips suddenly pulled tight into a thin line of contempt. 'That really was an appalling show at the meeting the other night,' she said in a hushed tone. 'What a dreadful oaf that man McKay is! I did *so* feel for you. Now, you might well consider it being none of my business, but may I ask how things are at present?'

Liz smiled at the kindness of the woman. 'Well, they're not really . . .'

Delia sighed and shook her head. 'Aren't men such fools? Only thinking of one thing all the time.' She rocked forward in a confiding manner. 'Hector had a dalliance once with one of our girl grooms. Didn't last, though. Soon put a stop to it.'

Liz found herself having to bite hard on her lip to stop herself from laughing, the image of the upright figure of Sir Hector and a hot-blooded girl groom being too incongruous to imagine. 'How did you manage that?' she asked.

Delia shrugged her shoulders. 'Found them in a clinch in the discothèque at a hunt Ball, so got hold of a jug of ice-cold water, walked up to him and poured it over his head. Ha, *that* soon cooled his ardour. Never went astray after *that!*' She put her hand once more on Liz's arm. 'Now listen, my dear, I know that the community council are really pushing for this golf thing to go ahead, but *you* must take your time in deciding. If you want any advice, please come to see me. Even though I was lucky enough to curb Hector's rambling instincts, I do understand exactly what you're going through.'

Liz smiled a thank-you at the woman. At that moment, the bell on the door sounded, and Delia, having the advantage of height over Liz, craned over the central display to see who had entered. She looked back at Liz, a furtive expression on her face. 'Oh, my word, speak of the devil! It's the *other* woman, my dear.' She pressed her bulk as far back against the display section as she could to allow

Liz to pass. 'You go on and I shall waylay her while you get out of the shop.'

'That's very kind of you, Lady Stanfield,' Liz whispered conspiratorially.

Delia gave her a wink. 'Not at all. As I said, I understand the situation.' And, as if settling herself to form the last line of defence at the Siege of Mafeking, she turned to block the aisle. Liz quickly retrieved a bag of peas from the deep freeze and made her way to the counter, hearing behind her the sound of Delia's voice reaching decibels never before attained in the shop as she greeted Mary McLean.

CHAPTER 6

Once he had become used to the agricultural state of the interior of Alex's Peugeot van and the heady cocktail of tractor oil and sheep, Arthur had found himself rather enjoying his trip out into the countryside. At the outset of their journey he had thought to break the formality of the student/teacher relationship by engaging Alex in general conversation about his family and his roots in Fife, but noticed that the boy's hesitancy as he drove through St Andrews and the lack of response to his questioning indicated that he was probably quite new to the art of driving. He decided therefore that it would be less of a distraction to Alex if he just kept quiet, and consequently settled himself back in the torn plastic seat and contented himself in looking out the window.

The little van swept up the hill out of St Andrews and rounded the corner at the Brownhills junction, leaving the late-afternoon sun to bathe the grey stone houses of the town and the ancient ruins of the cathedral in a strong, shimmering light. The road ran on adjacent to the sea, lying some distance away across undulating fields of newly tilled soil, its burnt-steel surface broken in ribbons of white by the cresting waves as it stretched off to the horizon without hindrance of land or vessel. Single-wired fences atop drystone dikes dipped and rose as they drove by, revealing, at their lowest ebb, fields in which double-tyred tractors toiled with frenetic power to prepare the seed-beds for the summer's harvest. In others, sheep fussed like protective nannies about their unruly young as they bounced on spring-loaded legs around straw-baled shelters tucked well into corners away from the cold cut of the prevailing wind. Occasionally the open view was narrowed as they passed through hamlets of whitewashed cottages, each of different size and shape but granted uniformity by the pan-tiles on their roofs, their terra-cotta surfaces shining to an almost translucent pink in the fiery rays of the dipping sun.

Arthur's relaxed contentment in perusing the scenery was such that, when the incident took place, the most immediate thought that flashed through his mind was that his Maker had predestined the fifteen-minute journey to be a restful and fitting climax to his otherwise disruptive life. They had just driven, at nothing more than a gentle pace, over the crest of a hill on the twisting road when they were suddenly confronted by a speeding car heading straight towards them, its driver having become frustrated at being caught behind a queue of traffic that was fronted by a large, slow-moving tractor. Both Alex and Arthur simultaneously slammed their feet hard down to the floor, and with a degree of luck, rather than of better judgement, the van responded to Alex's guidance by swerving in towards the side of the road and juddering to a stalled halt with one wheel up on the grassy bank. The white-faced driver of the approaching car managed to swerve his way through the narrowest of gaps between the Peugeot and the tractor before being sent scurrying on his way by an ear-splitting blast on the airhorn of the gigantic blue machine.

For a moment, Alex stared straight ahead at the lopsided view of the wall three feet in front of them, then blew out a long puff of relief. 'Sorry about that,' he said quietly, breaking his seven-mile silence.

'Wasn't your fault,' Arthur replied, turning back from viewing the disappearing car through the rear window. 'Damned fool's not long from his coffin if he goes on driving like that.' He studied Alex's ashen face. 'Are you all right?'

Alex nodded. 'That's the first near miss I've ever had.' His voice shook as he spoke. 'Do you think the van's all right?'

'Well, all we can do is reverse and see if a wheel falls off or the engine drops out. But don't worry. You did well to avoid him.'

Alex started the engine again and reversed carefully away from the bank. Arthur rolled down the window and craned out to see if he could detect any damage. He brought his head back into the van. 'Seems to be all right. Just a few clumps of grass stuck in your fender.' He looked across at Alex. 'Are you sure you're all right to continue?'

'Yes, I think so. We've only got about another half a

mile to go.' He engaged first gear and moved away slowly. 'That's not the first time that's happened here. Not with me, I mean, but with other drivers. Problem is that the road has Z-bends all the way from Balmuir to here, so it's about the first place you can even try to overtake for about a mile.' He gave Arthur a nervous smile. 'That's why this stretch is known locally as Smash Alley.'

Arthur gave him a reassuring wink. 'Well, we live to see another day, thanks to some pretty classy driving.'

Alex stuck to a cautiously sedate speed for the remainder of the journey, and Arthur noted the look of quiet relief come over the boy's face when he eventually brought the van down through the gears and indicated left off the main road. They turned in beside a lopsided wooden sign so lacking in paint that it was impossible for Arthur to ascertain the name of the establishment that they were approaching, and headed down a road pitted with pot-holes, the sides of which were spattered with loose Tarmac chips from past attempts at reparation. Alex began threading the van through these obstacles, the now-confident burst of speed at which he was accomplishing the task making it quite obvious to Arthur that he had probably been doing it for a good many years longer than he had been on the open road.

After two hundred yards of fairground driving they pulled into the farm steading, an assortment of buildings which Arthur quickly assessed to have seen better days. The rusted guttering that bounded the loose-slated roofs hung away in places from its mountings under the weight of green tufted weed that grew in its length, and where the unchannelled rain-water had run down the sides of the walls, white mould had clutched hard into gaps left by crumbling mortar. The tongue-and-groove timbers on the weather-bleached doors had swelled outwards, bursting their hold on each other, so that they were now of little use in closing off the darkened interiors of the buildings. And around the extremities of the property, half-hidden amongst tall yellowing clumps of grass, lay a graveyard of disused farm implements.

They continued round to the house, lying on the seaward side of the steading, and the initial sight of it made Arthur's urban-yearning heart drop the final few inches to the level of the metal oilcan that he had been holding upright with his feet for the duration of the journey. The door into the drab, grey-harled extension that jutted out at the back of the otherwise whitish house was an insipid shade of yellow, the lower half of it being almost indiscernible in colour due to the muddied streaks that had been splattered against it both by the elements and passing vehicles. At one side of the well-worn stone steps that led up to the door an old fertilizer bag had toppled over, spewing out its tangled contents of orange baler twine, while at the other side a discarded refrigerator rested hard on its open door, its stained interior filled with a plethora of dark brown medicine bottles.

Alex pulled the car to a halt and turned off the engine. 'Here we are, then.'

Arthur forced a smile onto his face. Good God, it was worse than Cold Comfort Farm! 'It's very nice, Alex.'

Alex laughed, noting the distinct lack of enthusiasm in

the professor's voice. 'No, it's not. It's ropy as hell, if you want the honest truth. Maybe I should explain that this is my grandparents' farm, and I don't think they ever had much inclination to do anything with the place. They just became quite happily used to it being like this.'

'But you live here now?'

'Yes.' He aimed a finger to a distant group of buildings that was just visible between the end of the house and an open-sided hay barn. 'We used to be there until about six months ago, but then . . . well . . . my parents split up, and my mother and I moved back here. Then my grand-mother died a couple of months back, so now it's just myself, my mother and my grandfather.' Undoing his seat-belt, he made to open the door, then turned back to Arthur, thinking that maybe further reassurance was necessary. 'I think my mother has great plans to get the place back in shape again, but time and money are both pretty hard to come by at the minute.' He pushed the door open on its creaking hinges and got out, and watched over the roof of the van as Arthur slowly appeared from the passenger's side. 'But I think you'll be pleasantly surprised when you get inside. It's very comfortable – and warm!'

Arthur flicked his head to the side. 'Well, that's pretty important. My landlady in Saint Andrews had a tight-fisted habit of turning off the heating at six o'clock every night, regardless of how low the outside temperature had dropped.'

Alex laughed. 'Well, I can promise you that it's like a hothouse in there. Anyway, come on and I'll show you around.'

As they made their way across the small courtyard towards the back door, there was a rasping screech as one of the steading doors was slid back on rusting rollers. A tall, thin man with a shock of wild white hair appeared in the doorway, a struggling lamb tucked under each arm.

'Och, it's yourself, Alex,' the man said, turning to push the door closed with his elbow. 'Wasn't expecting you to be home already. You're not practising your golf tonight?'

'No, not tonight,' Alex replied, walking towards him.

Mr Craig eyed the clumps of grass wedged hard into the bumper of the Peugeot van. 'Looks like you've been ploughing a bit, lad.'

'I know. I've just had a near-miss up on Smash Alley. Someone came at me on the wrong side of the road.' He bent down to pull the grass from the bumper. 'I don't think there's any damage done, though.' He looked up at his grandfather. 'Is Mum home, Granddad?'

The farmer gave the steading a quick scan for the Land Rover. 'No, I doubt she's back yet. She went into Balmuir for some purchases.'

'Right. Well, have you got a moment? I'd like you to meet someone.'

He looked over Alex's shoulder to where the tall rain-coated figure stood by the back door. 'Aye, well, I was just away to feed these wee devils, but I reckon they can hold off for a couple of minutes.' Sliding open the door with a shove of his boot, he pushed the lambs back through the gap. 'I doubt they'll go far,' he said, closing the door on them. Taking an old rag from his pocket, he gave his hands a brisk rub as he walked with Alex across the court-yard.

'Granddad, I'd like you to meet my German tutor, Professor Kempler.'

Craig nodded a greeting. 'Professor Kempler.' He stuck out his hand and Arthur took hold of it, feeling the soft-ness of his own hand grate in the man's calloused grip.

'Very pleased to meet you, Mr . . . ?'

A flustered look came over Alex's face. 'Sorry, I should have said. Mr Craig.'

'Well, it's a pleasure, Mr Craig.'

There was a moment of uneasy silence as the two men smiled pleasantly at each other, both waiting for Alex to begin explaining the reason for the professor's visit. He eventually took the hint. 'Granddad, I was having a tuto-rial with Professor Kempler this morning, and he just happened to mention that he was having to leave his lodgings, so he doesn't have anywhere to stay. I just thought that maybe he could have the spare room – you know, like we discussed.'

A look of clarity came over the old man's face. 'Ah, I see. Right, well, there's a thing then.'

Arthur looked from one to the other, detecting a lack of keenness in the farmer's answer. 'Maybe I'm jumping the gun a bit in coming out here today, Mr Craig. It was just that Alex said that there might be a chance that you had a room to let, and if that is the case, then I could very well be interested in renting it from you.'

The farmer scratched at the side of his face with his fingers. 'Aye, well, that's what we decided to do.' He looked at Alex. 'We did have a thought that it might be a student, Professor. I don't know if the room would be quite suitable for someone of your standing.'

Arthur laughed. 'Mr Craig, I am sure that what you have to offer would be a veritable palace compared to some of the places that I've ended up in over the years.'

The farmer smiled at the man. 'In that case, let's away and take a look then, shall we?' Walking over to the door, he levered off his Wellingtons on the doorstep and led the way into the house.

From the moment he entered, Arthur realized that Alex was true to his word. The house was indeed warm, though it was obvious that little had been done in the way of decoration for many a year. Moving in single file through the cluttered kitchen and along the narrow passageway to the front hall, Arthur found himself murmuring words of feigned appreciation as he cast an eye over the collection of dull little prints, hung too high on walls lined with a yellowing paper on which it was just possible to make out the dying colours of its flowered pattern. Mr Craig opened the dark-stained panel doors at either side of the hall, giving Arthur fleeting glances into a stark, formal dining-room and a neatly arranged sitting-room. Both, he determined from their slightly musty smell, had seen little use over the years.

Moving across to the staircase, the farmer bent down to slip home a dislodged stair-rod that held the threadbare beige runner in place. 'I'm afraid it all may seem to you a wee bit run down, Professor.' He took hold of the carved oak banister rail as if requiring its support, but then began to make his way with surprising agility up the stairs. 'My wife and I never had much expertise in this interior-designing lark.'

Arthur followed on with Alex hard at his heels. 'Well, in that case, you're a man after my own heart, Mr Craig. All I need of a place is a warm bed and a comfy chair.'

'Aye, well, I hope we may be able to accommodate you there.'

The stairs led up to a half-way stage, from which a passage ran off to rooms at the back the house, before turning back on themselves to continue up to the spacious front landing. Once there, Mr Craig walked across the skylighted area and opened a door, standing back to allow Arthur to enter first.

The room was of similar size to the drawing-room below, again with a slightly unused smell and with the same all-enveloping wallpaper, but Arthur judged it to be both clean and comfortable. A double bed, covered with a yellow Candlewick bedspread, was pushed against the wall opposite the window, its oak headboard sporting two frilled reading lamps, while in the highest part of the room a large wardrobe fitted snugly into the wide angle of the ceiling. In one corner to the side of the window an old leather-inlaid desk, probably the most valuable piece of furniture that Arthur had seen so far in the house, doubled as a dressing-table, while in the other a sagging armchair sat at an angle.

Having taken in the contents of the room, Arthur walked into the small recess created by the dormer window and looked out. The sun had by now sunk away, but even in the gloaming of the day he could well see why the house had been situated in such an opportune place. Save for a short foreground of rolling fields darkened by cultivation and a ragged line of windswept hawthorn bushes at the land's farthest extreme, the view was dominated by the North Sea, a colourless canvas that merged with no sign of demarcation into the dulling sky. He pressed his face close to the window. The view remained unchanged either way, except for the cluster of farm buildings that Alex had pointed out to him earlier, lying three fields distant to the north-east.

He turned back from the window to find Alex and his grandfather standing behind him with earnest looks of expectation on their faces.

'Well?' Alex asked. 'Do you think it'll do you?'

Arthur nodded. 'Looks fine. Perfect, in fact.' He looked across to the farmer. 'So, have you any idea how much you would be requiring for the room, Mr Craig?'

The old man scratched at the back of his head. 'Ah, well, that's a question now, isn't it? I couldn't rightly say, Professor. I think, on that account, it would probably be best if we waited until my daughter came home, and then you and she can—'

He was cut short by the sound of a door slamming in the hallway. 'Dad?' Liz's voice rang up the staircase.

Mr Craig gave Arthur a wink. 'Saved by the bell. There she is now.' He walked out of the room. 'Aye, we're up here, lass. We're on our way down.'

'Dad, is Alex all right? The front of the van looks as if he's hit something.'

He raised an eyebrow at his grandson before leading the way down the stairs. 'Aye, he's fine. Just had a wee incident on Smash Alley. Not his fault, though.'

Liz stood at the bottom of the stairs, still in her Wellingtons, watching as her father and Alex appeared at the half-way stage. 'What do you mean, a wee incident? And what *are* you two doing up there, anyway? Has something happ—' She stopped when she saw the stranger appear behind them. 'Ah, I'm sorry,' she continued quietly, watching as Arthur descended the stairs. 'I didn't realize you had somebody with you.'

Alex came to stand beside his mother. 'Mum, I'd like you to meet Professor Kempler, my German tutor.'

'Oh!' Liz uttered in horror. She put her hand to her head and brushed back her hair, an instinctive gesture to try to bring some semblance of decency to her appearance. She watched as the professor approached her, his hand outstretched, a broad smile on his face that creased the lines at the sides of his sparkling brown eyes. 'How do you do, Mrs Dewhurst. It's very good to meet you.'

'And you too, Professor.' She shook his hand, then held out her palms as she looked down at her filthy attire. 'I'm sorry about my clothes. If I'd known you were coming—'

'Oh, please, no!' Arthur interjected. 'It is I who should apologize. I have come completely unannounced and certainly should have known better.'

Liz smiled at the man. So this was the new German tutor from Canada Alex had told her about. My goodness, he certainly had preserved himself well if he was truly

91

coming up for retirement. And he certainly wasn't her vision of a professor. He was really . . . well . . . almost too . . . dashing! 'Well then.' She glanced at Alex and her father. 'So . . . to what do we owe this pleasure?' The smile suddenly slid from her face, to be replaced by a look of concern. 'There's nothing wrong, is there?'

'Of course not!' Alex exclaimed. 'What? Did you think I was being chucked out of university or something?'

'Well, I just thought . . .'

'No, it's nothing like that. Professor Kempler has come out here today because he's just had to leave his lodgings in Saint Andrews, and I thought that the spare room would be perfect for him. Anyway, we've just had a look at it, and he thinks it would suit him well.'

Liz somehow managed to keep the smile on her face, even though she felt like gasping out in dismay. 'Ah!' She nodded slowly, giving herself time to make sure that the smile was well and truly fixed. 'Ah! Right!'

Alex studied the inane grin on his mother's face. 'Mum?'

'Yes?' The smile still stuck.

'We did agree.'

'Yes, we did, didn't we?'

Arthur shifted uneasily from one foot to the other. 'Listen, I'm sorry, Mrs Dewhurst. I can see that I've put you in a difficult situation here. If it is at all inconvenient, I can certainly look elsewhere. I am sure that—'

'No!' Alex interjected sharply. 'Come on, Mum! This is what we agreed.'

'I know we did, but . . .'

'But what?'

Liz shook her head. 'I'm sorry, Professor, it's just that we're so busy at the minute. I don't know if we can . . . well, what I mean is that I didn't realize that Alex would get someone *quite* so soon, and . . . well, to be quite honest, I don't think that we're ready to rent out the room just yet.'

Alex threw up his hands in frustration. 'Oh, Mum!'

Arthur stepped in to calm the situation. 'No, Alex, I can quite see your mother's point of view. But if I might just take a moment to try selling myself to you, I really am very self-contained and I would not make demands on you at all. And I am quite adept at looking after my own room and doing my own washing, and I am also quite prepared to cook my own meals.'

'Oh, no, you wouldn't have to do that!' Liz exclaimed. 'I mean,' she said, softening her tone, 'if you were to stay, you wouldn't have to do that.'

Alex looked at his mother, realizing the glimmer of hope in her reply. 'So?'

'I don't know, Alex. We only discussed this a few days ago, and I didn't think you'd be getting anybody until April or May at the earliest. It's just not a very good time, what with all the farm work, and those men starting to survey the wretched golf course.'

'Mum, you heard the professor. He doesn't want anything other than the room – and he's pretty desperate for somewhere to live.'

Liz looked across at her father, who had been quietly leaning against the banister, pulling absently at an ear-lobe.

He gave her an almost indiscernible nod. She turned back to the professor, a resigned smile on her face. 'All right. You can certainly have the room, Professor, but I don't really know what I would charge you.'

Arthur pushed his hand into his pocket, taking up a resilient stance. 'Well, if you would like to name a price, Mrs Dewhurst, I'm sure we could come to a satisfactory agreement straightaway.'

Liz took a moment to think. Damn it, if he was going to be there, she would have to make it worth her while. 'Forty pounds a week, including your food.' She watched his face drop, and realized that she had overstepped the mark.

'Forty pounds a week!'

Liz felt her face colouring. 'I'm sorry. As I said, I really have no idea about the going rate. What about thirty—'

'Fifty.'

Liz looked at him aghast. 'What?'

'You're selling yourself short, Mrs Dewhurst. I am willing to pay fifty pounds a week, including my evening meal. Come on, the view itself is worth thirty pounds a week.' He paused. 'Wait, on consideration . . .'

Liz looked at him with open eyes, thinking that the deal was now going to fall flat. 'What?'

'Fifty-five on the condition that you let me smoke my pipe in my room.'

Liz was completely taken aback. 'Well.'

'Go on, Mum,' Alex said, a broad grin on his face. 'He never manages to keep the thing lit anyway, so it would be a bargain.'

Liz nodded. 'All right, Professor.' She put forward her hand to conclude the deal, but as Arthur went to take it, she unexpectedly withdrew it. 'I would like to make a condition of my own, if I could.'

Arthur eyed her. 'And what might that be?'

'That you stay and have something to eat with us tonight.'

Arthur laughed. 'Mrs Dewhurst—'

'Liz . . . please.'

He nodded. 'All right . . . Liz, that is not a condition. That is a pleasure!'

'Good. In that case, Professor Kempler, you have yourself a deal.'

CHAPTER 7

Roberta Bayliss pulled the old Holden out of the car-park of the Royal Sydney Golf Club and drove the short distance down Kent Road to the traffic lights at the junction with New South Head Road. At five o'clock on a Friday afternoon, the traffic streamed nose-to-tail out from downtown Sydney, the heat from the cars making the surrounding air shimmer in the still-fierce swelter of the day. She wiped away a bead of perspiration from her forehead and cranked up the air conditioning to its rasping limit, then sat back to wait for the lights to change, focusing her eyes on the refreshing coolness of the waters of Rose Bay just visible beyond the tennis courts in Lyne Park.

She really did not relish the idea of going to this birth-day party. Not that she would ever dream of letting her feelings show in front of her sister Eleanor, for whose sixty-fifth birthday the party had been organized. But it was just that, for her, birthdays were no longer occasions to be cele-brated. They only seemed now to serve as unwelcome reminders of years fleeting past, of the ever-shortening climb up the ladder to decrepitude and senility.

But maybe that was a really selfish thought – and even a stupid one, taking into account that here she was, as fit as a fiddle at the age of sixty, playing golf nearly every day. And, what's more, if hereditary factors were to be taken into account, there could be no worry about longevity nor of mental collapse setting in when she had both her parents still alive and kicking.

A short blast on a car-horn sounded behind her, and she glanced up to see that the lights had turned green. Pushing her foot down on the accelerator, she crossed over the thoroughfare and joined the line of traffic heading east along New South Head Road, the speed at which she accomplished the manoeuvre being the fastest that she would drive for the next ten minutes. Finally, having crawled the kilometre's distance, she turned left off the main road by the imposing edifice of Kincoppal School and made her way down Vaucluse Road, its narrow avenue bounded by large rambling houses whose extensive grounds were hidden from view by high stone walls.

At the road's farthest extreme, where it looped round on itself in front of the wooded area of Nielsen Park, Roberta slowly manoeuvred the car through a set of high wrought-iron security gates into a short, brick-paved driveway. Cutting the engine, she took her shoulder-bag from the passenger seat and got out of the car. She stood for a moment making adjustments to her cotton dress, not so much as a preening measure, but more because she felt so unused to wearing one. She found dresses to be such impractical garments, always creasing up or twisting round on her, and anyway, she was always aware that they clung to her body in all the wrong places, revealing herself in her true light as being small and lumpy. Even her friends at the golf club had registered bewildered surprise on witnessing her appearance from the ladies' locker room. How *different* you look, Roberta, they had said. Certainly not how *wonderful* you look! But maybe that was because they had only seen her dressed in trousers or shorts, those being not only her normal uniform for playing golf, but also her everyday wear.

She took a deep breath and began climbing the stone steps that wound their way up through the well-groomed garden in front of the house. She had gone no more than half-way when she heard the front door open and Dana, her niece's help, appeared at the top of the steps. Roberta stopped in her tracks and looked up at the large, smiling woman. 'Where's the party then, Dana?'

'Hasn't started yet, Miss Bayliss. The kids all wanted to go to the beach before tea, so they headed down to Nielsen. Becky said you could either stay here and wait, or go down and join them.'

'How long have they been down there?'

'No more than half an hour.'

'Well, I'll go on down.'

'You sure? It's pretty hot out. You're quite welcome to stay.'

Roberta smiled. 'The walk will do me good. Anyway, I might have a paddle myself.' With a wave of her hand, she turned and descended the steps, stopping at the car to take her Titleist sun visor from the golf bag in the boot. With perfunctory care, she pulled it on hard over her cropped grey hair, then walked down the drive and crossed the road into the park.

The tall gum-trees that stood in Nielsen Park gave such cooling shade against the heat of the day that she decided not to make her way to the beach immediately, but instead veered off in a westerly direction towards Shark Point, along one of the many concrete paths that criss-crossed the grassed area of the park. She walked at a fast pace, acknowledging the greetings of those whom she passed, until the trees eventually gave way to the unhindered view of Port Jackson. She stood for a moment watching the yachts out on the wide expanse of sparkling blue water, their multi-coloured sails stretched full in the offshore breeze as they tacked back and forth against the jagged backdrop of the city's skyscrapers. Then, rejoining the path, she headed across the top of the park and walked down onto the beach, where she found its short length lined with a multitude of elderly sun worshippers who appeared to be casting aside any cares about skin cancer in their attempts to soak up the last of the summer's sun. She kicked off her sandals and walked barefoot along the edge of the water, scanning the area for her sister's party.

'Bobby! Over here!'

She turned round to see her sister sitting on the stepped concrete wall at the top of the beach. She gave her a wave and skipped across the hot sand towards her.

Eleanor rose to her feet as she approached. 'You got the

message then?' she asked, peering at Roberta from under the brim of an enormous straw sun-hat.

'I did.' Roberta reached up and gave her sister a kiss on either cheek, their difference in height allowing her to do so without their respective headgear becoming a hindrance. 'Happy birthday, darling.'

Eleanor laughed as she sat down again on the wall. 'I don't know if "happy" is the word that would best describe it, but at least my well-earned pension matures today!'

Roberta sat down next to her. 'Well, I think you look wonderful.' She closed an eye to accentuate the scrutiny that she gave to her sister's face. 'In fact, I would go so far as to say that you could almost pass yourself off as my younger sister.'

Eleanor nodded slowly, her mouth twisting to one side. 'I don't know how I'm meant to take that. Do I give you a hug or just tear your hair out?'

Roberta laughed. 'Please, not the second! You did *that* often enough when we were kids!'

Eleanor dug her bare toes into the sand and raised her legs so that the two small mounds ran off the sides of her feet. 'Only when you deserved it.' She paused in a moment of reflection. 'Goodness, we fought some, didn't we?'

Roberta nodded. 'We sure did.' She put her arm around her sister's waist and gave her a squeeze. 'It really is great to see you, Ellie. We haven't seen each other for so long. How's life up on the peninsula?'

'Good.'

'And Gordon's well?'

'Longing for his retirement in July. He's had just about enough of the journey down to Manly every day. The poor man wanted to come down here today, but he had some meeting which he couldn't put off, so we're going out for a slap-up meal tonight, just the two of us.'

'Quite right, too.' Roberta cast her eyes along the beach. 'So, where's the rest of the party?'

'Becky's on bay-watch duty over there.' Eleanor pointed a finger to the far end of the beach where the tall, willowy figure of her daughter, dressed in a white T-shirt and short denim skirt, stood at the edge of the water with her arms folded. 'And the racket you hear out in the water sounding like a load of seals being fed at Taronga Zoo is in fact coming from my two grandchildren and their countless friends, who later will be joining me to celebrate my "coming of age."' She looked across at Roberta and gave her a wink. 'Thanks for coming, Bobby. I was needing a bit of "mature" support, seeing that big sis Mary found something more important to do with her time. I did have a niggling suspicion that you might have been tempted to have a few extra holes of golf and pretend that you'd forgotten about it.'

Roberta smiled and watched as Becky started to move slowly along the beach towards them. 'Wouldn't have missed it for the world.' The young woman caught sight of her aunt and waved. Roberta raised her hand in reply.

'That's a lie, for a start.' Roberta turned to catch a knowing smile on her sister's face.

'Not your cup of tea really, is it? A whole load of screaming kids tearing around at your ankles.'

'I don't mind it – once in a while.'

Eleanor stood up and looked out across the small bay to where the children were swimming. She called out to her daughter. 'Becky, Clem's getting pretty close to the shark-net, isn't he?'

'He's all right, Mum,' Becky called back, shielding her eyes against the glare of the sun. 'I'm watching him.'

Eleanor sat down again. 'I hope so,' she said quietly. 'I don't want my birthday celebrations dampened by one of my grandchildren getting snagged by a shark.'

'That's what shark-nets are for, aren't they? Keeping the sharks *out*.'

'All right, clever one. I just don't think you can be too careful. Those grandchildren are my pride and joy, you know, but maybe . . .' She stopped.

Roberta looked at her. 'Maybe what?'

'Nothing.'

'Were you by any chance going to say that maybe I wouldn't understand that, not having grandchildren of my own?'

Eleanor bit at her lip. 'Sorry, Bobby. That was a pretty thoughtless thing to say – or *begin* to say.'

Roberta shrugged. 'Doesn't bother me. I don't really notice it. Those kind of feelings just . . . well . . . have never been awakened in me, so I wouldn't know otherwise.' She looked at her sister. 'But that doesn't mean I'm not very fond of all Mary's and your countless offspring.'

Eleanor nodded. 'I know you are, but . . . don't you sometimes think to yourself secretly, deep down inside you, that you've missed out?'

Roberta laughed. 'No! Not at all.' She paused. 'Well, I don't think so. I've never wanted for more than what I have already. I've really been quite content with my life.'

'But you could have married, Bobby, couldn't you? I remember there being one or two quite meaningful relationships in your life. What about that Royal Navy guy from England, for instance? He was really keen on you.'

Roberta raised her eyebrows. 'He was a wimp, Eleanor, and you know it.' She eyed her sister. 'Anyway, why the sudden interest? You've never asked these kind of questions before.'

Eleanor shrugged her shoulders. 'I don't know. Maybe today is the first day that I have felt old age creeping up on me. Maybe I just want to settle differences and get to understand everything before . . . well . . . anything happens.'

'What an extraordinary thing to say, Ellie. We've no differences to settle.' She gave her sister a nudge with her arm. 'Come on, nothing's going to happen to you. You're as fit as a racehorse. And as far as getting to understand everything, what *is* there to understand? I never got married. That's it. I'm not the first woman in the world never to have got married.'

'I know, Bobby, but I just feel that you've not really done much with your life, other than sticking around at home with Mum and Pop. Here you are, sixty years old, and you're still there, still the tomboy – still the *baby* of the family. Mary and I both made the break when we were just out of our teens. Why did you feel that you couldn't – or even *shouldn't*?'

Roberta frowned in puzzlement at her sister. 'I don't know where you're coming from, Eleanor. What are you trying to say? Are you *jealous* or something?'

Eleanor laughed dismissively at the suggestion. 'Of course not!' She then glanced across at her sister, realizing that her flat denial to the question had not registered true with either of them. 'Oh, I don't know, Bobby. Isn't that just the best? I really don't know.' She sighed. 'Would you believe it? Sibling rivalry rearing its ugly head at *our* age! I suppose we'd never be talking like this if Mum and Pop were pushing up the daisies. But here we are, two sexagenarians, still enjoying the pleasure of being the "younger" generation.' She was silent for a moment, then reached over and patted Roberta's knee before rising to her feet. 'Come on, I think your crabby elder sister has said quite enough on the subject. It must be too much of the sun. Let's walk back to the house together.' As Roberta stood up, Eleanor caught her daughter's attention and waved her hands in semaphore style to indicate that they were both leaving the beach.

Kicking the sand off their feet on the concrete stepway that led up from the beach, they slipped on their shoes and began to amble their way slowly along the central path through the park, their arms linked together.

'Tell me about Mum and Pop,' Eleanor said. 'How are they? I don't think that I've seen them for about two months.'

'They're both well enough, I guess.' Roberta paused. 'No, actually, I have to say that Pop is not his usual sprightly self at the minute. We've only managed to get in three half-rounds of golf over the past week, and those have really knocked him out.'

Eleanor chuckled. 'Well, he *is* coming up to ninety, Bobby. You've got to realize that twenty-seven holes of golf in a week is something of a marathon for anyone of his age.'

Roberta shook her head. 'Oh, no, that's not the reason. He's just maybe got a bug or something. He'll soon be right as rain. Anyway, he's got to be, because we're heading off to Augusta for the Masters at the end of the month.'

Eleanor stopped walking and looked at her sister. 'Bobby, you're asking a lot of him, you know. He *is* old, you've got to understand that . . .'

'No, he's fine. As I said, it's just a bug. It'll soon—'

Eleanor took hold of her arm and held it tight. 'Bobby! He's *my* father, too, you know. I happen to be quite concerned about his well-being, because I want to make damned sure that he survives as long as he can.'

Roberta pulled away from her sister's grasp and glanced down at her feet, the look on her face immediately stirring an extraordinary realization in Eleanor. Here, standing in front of her, was the little girl she had known so many years before, the same pouting expression on her clear, boyish face, always put on whenever she had been rebuked for some misdemeanour or other. Eleanor understood now that she had not been that far off the mark back there on the beach. Bobby was still the kid of the family. She had never really moved on from her childhood.

She put her arm around her little sister's shoulders and

drew her in beside her as they continued walking. 'Listen, Bobby, I know you've done more for Mum and Pop over the years than either Mary or I ever could. And we have never doubted the fact that you were Pop's favourite. I think, in a way, that you filled the shoes of the son that he never had, playing golf with him and travelling the world to all those tournaments. But you're going to have to accept the fact that the time has come for him to start to slow down and take things a little easier. I know it's hard to take this in, but he is an old man now, and the reason why he has probably kept on playing golf is because he doesn't want to let *you* down.'

'But if he stops,' Roberta replied quietly, 'that'll be the end of him. I know it. He's got to keep going, Eleanor.'

They walked in silence for a moment before Roberta stopped and let out a heaving breath. 'You know what you were saying earlier on about me not getting married?'

Eleanor nodded. 'Yes?'

'Well, if you want the honest truth, there was never a time when I felt that I ever wanted to. You see, my perfect role model for a man has always been Pop, and I never really found a man who could quite match up to him. Not that he ever discouraged them or anything like that. In fact, sometimes he was quite blatant in his endeavours to get me married off. The decision was mine, Eleanor. He was, and still is, my greatest friend, and there's been no one in my life like him.' She let out a short, unconvincing laugh. 'So there you are. After all these years, there's your question answered.'

Eleanor smiled at her. 'You didn't need to answer it. I

knew already.' She paused. 'Bobby, the reason why I brought this whole thing up is because I'm not just worried about Pop. I worry about you as well, about what will happen to you when he eventually does go. You have to give it thought, my darling, you have to start trying to work out what you're going to do with the rest of your life, because you're too great a person just to curl up into a lonely little ball of sadness and self-pity.' She studied the changing expression on her sister's face as emotion began to break through her blind resistance to the reality of the situation. She had made her point. There was no reason to say more. 'Look, Bobby,' she said, moving across to her sister's side and putting her arm once more around her shoulders, 'I think the best idea would be for you and me to strike a deal to keep him with us as long as we can, don't you? My suggestion would be to cut out any idea of travelling to Augusta – or anywhere else, for that matter – and just get him fit for playing his golf. How about that? That should keep you both happy, should it not?'

Roberta nodded in silent agreement.

As they resumed their walk, a profusion of whooping yells grew in volume from behind them on the path, and they were quickly overtaken by a whirlwind of young party guests heading back to the house. Clem slowed down as he passed by. 'Hi, Granny! Hi, Great-Aunt Bobby! Come on, get a move on! Dana's got the barbie going *and* I think Mum's been to Doyle's for some oysters for you lot.' He turned and sprinted off after his friends.

Eleanor looked at Roberta, a sparkle in her eye. 'Do you fancy a race?'

Roberta's crestfallen features slowly broke into a smile. 'You've never beaten me before.'

Eleanor hitched up her skirt in her hand. 'Maybe not, but there's always a first time. Are you ready? One . . . twooo . . . threeee . . . GO!'

Roberta sprang quickly from her mark, and although she ran at no more than a jog, it was a speed far greater than that mustered by her elder sister, who felt the twinge of arthritis in her left knee as soon as she took her first step. Eleanor continued to walk along the path and watched as her sister ran the whole length of the park, only stopping when she had reached the pavement on Vaucluse Road. Roberta turned to look back at her, and seeing the margin of her win she let out a cheer of victory before crossing the road and making her way up the driveway of the house.

Eleanor let out a quiet laugh. Poor Mum, she thought to herself; how on earth had she ever been able to compete with *that* all her life? Then, as she walked on, the smile at the thought slid from her face and she slowly shook her head. Oh, Bobby, what *is* going to happen to you?

Chapter 8

The old ewe licked hard at the remnants of thin membrane that still covered the body of her first-born lamb as it lay spluttering its way into life beside her head, then let out a long, effort-filled groan as she pushed hard once again to try ridding herself of its more reluctant twin. Gregor Dewhurst disengaged his hand from her backquarters and got to his feet, flexing his fingers in an attempt to ease the numbing pain caused by the contracting of her cervix. He poured a fresh dollop of lubricating fluid into his palm, then knelt down to try again, closing his eyes to concentrate on his sightless task. He carefully pushed in around the lamb's head and felt for its knee joint, hoping to hook in a finger and release a front leg, so that he could align it into a more normal birth position. He sensed the next contraction coming on and grimaced as the ewe's powerful muscle once more clenched his hand in a vice-like grip. The lamb moved only the merest inch forward in the birth canal, but it was enough for him to detect the small triangular opening for which he had been searching.

He eased the leg forward until it was free from her cervix, then applied enough downward pressure to bring its shoulder clear. He blew out with effort as he waited for the next contraction, then, feeling her strain once more, he clamped the leg in his little finger and slid the cleft of his fore and middle fingers over the lamb's head and gently prised it free from her womb. Kicking in a clean layer of straw with his foot, he allowed the lamb to flop down onto the ground, and as its small diaphragm began to heave in air, he quickly cleared away the mucus from its mouth with his little finger.

'My word, wee one, that was a tussle and a half, wasn't it?' he said quietly, pulling away the remains of the placenta from its body. He picked it up by its front legs and swung it gently forward to lie at the head of the ewe beside its twin. 'There you are, lass, there's another one for you to deal with.'

He stood up and watched as the attentive mother began to work on her new lamb, feeling almost as contented as she at the eventual success of the delivery. He took the towel that was hanging over the top rail of the gate and gave his hands a hard rub, then settled back against the gate to make certain that the bonding process had begun.

In all the years that he had worked on lambing, he could not remember one that he hadn't enjoyed. He had never sickened of the job. Even during the one appalling downtime when he had found his flock to be riddled with contagious abortion, the pure surge of joy at finding one alive was indescribable. The creation of life had the ability of touching one's emotions to the core, the power to turn utter adversity and desperation into hope, in the way that a news report might show total jubilation amongst the rescuers of a small child who had been plucked alive from the concrete graveyard of its shattered home, days after the whole area had been devastated by an earthquake. He had never really been a religious man, but there was something so powerful, so tangibly spiritual about the process of birth that, after that particular lambing, he had felt compelled to go to church to give thanks.

And, of course, the feeling wasn't only associated with his lambs. He remembered the day Alex had been born, the whole procedure seeming so uncannily similar that he had felt the strongest compunction to roll up his sleeves and help the midwife with her task. He smiled to himself. Poor old Liz. She could tell what he was thinking by the look on his face. 'Don't you *dare* come near me,' she had screamed at him. 'Don't you think you've damaged me *enough?*'

He raised his arms above his head to stretch out the stiffness in his limbs and the tiredness in his body, which brought on a long and totally unpremeditated yawn. He glanced at his watch. It was six o'clock in the evening. Making a quick mental calculation, he worked out that he had been on the go for eighteen hours without a break. My God, what a difference it was, having to do the job by himself. Before, it had been a time of the year when the whole family had been involved, but now, with his parents living in happy retirement in their little cottage in

Balmuir, neither had felt the urge or inclination to come out to give him a hand. But, then again, one of the reasons for that had been Liz. Both his parents had been so thunderstruck by the split-up of his marriage and the barrier it had caused between their two families that hardly a word had passed between them since.

Then of course, there *was* Liz. She had been the master at lambing, having both a patience and stamina that could outlast him at any time, as well as being the possessor of small hands that could extricate the most difficult lambs at birth. Unfortunately, he couldn't say the same thing for Mary. The only time she had ever been into the lambing shed she had almost fainted at the sight of a birth, then had come up with the impractical suggestion that he should give epidurals to all his ewes.

He stared blankly at the new mother and her lambs, his pensive inactivity allowing a comforting surge of fatigue to sweep though his body. He had to admit to himself that he did miss Liz, and not just for the practical reasons. He never meant it to turn out the way it had, but it was just that circumstances had prevailed. He would have dearly loved to have more children, to have experienced once more the exhilaration at the birth of a baby, but it wasn't to be. Three times Liz had miscarried, and thereafter her frustration and disappointment had manifested themselves in complete disinterest and apathy towards sexual relations. It was only a temporary state of affairs as it turned out, no more than three months, but how the hell was he to know that? For a young man in his prime, it was too much to cope with. And then Mary had been there, flirtatious and willing, and she had provided the physical solace for which he so yearned. Yet he had never thought for a moment that it would end in such a calamitous way.

But that showed, on his part, naïveté in its extreme, and he knew now that he had demonstrated a complete lack of understanding towards Liz. She had been deeply hurt by her inability to have more children, and he had only helped to consolidate that pain by having an affair with another woman. It had to have been the final insult, the final kick in the teeth. The outcome was inevitable and the repercussions far-reaching, so much so that the whole situation was now both an emotional and financial mess. He could not bear the bitterness that Liz now felt towards him, nor the resentment Alex showed in his unwillingness to come round to the house. If he could only make Liz understand that the golf project would be a step forward, not only to financial betterment but toward finding some middle ground for an understanding between them. But she wouldn't speak to him. It was well and truly finished.

Nevertheless, he still had Mary, and he had always been both touched and proud at the stalwart resilience she had displayed when faced with the narrow-minded attitudes and behind-the-back remarks of the local people. Yet, as far as being a friend, she had her short-comings, there being little common ground between them. She was completely ignorant about the ways of farming, and sometimes the artlessness that she displayed in her efforts to appear interested in the golf project annoyed him. That was what he missed most about Liz.

Having been married in their teens, they had literally grown up together and had understood everything about each other. But it was totally pointless to make such comparisons now. Liz was gone, Liz was in the past, and it was Mary who was willing to stick by him and share his bed whilst others wouldn't even have him in their house.

The two lambs had struggled to their feet and now stood on splayed legs, pushing their noses into their mother's soft belly in an attempt to find some source of nourishment. Gregor took an aerosol can of antiseptic spray from his pocket and, picking each up in turn, gave their umbilical cords a good covering before latching them on to the ewe's teats. He waited for a further five minutes to make sure that each had enjoyed a healthy intake of colostrum, then, letting himself out of the pen, he walked down the feeding aisle, glancing from side to side to see if any other births were imminent. All seemed quiet, so he left the lambing shed and made his way across the yard to the house.

The airless heat in the kitchen hit him as soon as he entered, making the drowsiness he had felt in the cool of the lambing shed immediately become more like a drug-induced stupor. Pulling out a chair from the kitchen table, he slumped down and leaned his elbows hard on the table's scrubbed surface and began rubbing at his tired eyes. The door opened behind him, but he could hardly find the energy to turn around.

'Gregor!'

He pivoted his face round on his hand to look at Mary. 'What's the matter?'

'Look at your boots! They're covered in dung!' She waved her hand in front of her face to waft away the smell to which his own senses seemed to be completely immune, and walked over to the cooker to stir gingerly at the simmering contents of a pan, keeping herself at a safe distance so that she didn't accidentally splash either her pink tight-fitting blouse or her black pencil skirt. As he watched her, Gregor could not help but feel a pang of lust shudder through his body, even in his near-comatose state. It was extraordinary that even in the execution of a task as innocent as stirring a cooking pot, Mary was unable to disguise her natural provocation; the position that she adopted to carry out the task pushing her bottom upwards and outwards so that the fabric of her skirt stretched tight against the curve of her hips, making it ride high up the back of her legs. My word, Mary McLean, he thought to himself, you certainly have quite a body! She looked round at him, catching the look in his eye, and gave him a wink, followed by a remonstrative smile. 'I think you should try getting used to taking off your boots by the back door before coming into my kitchen.'

Gregor let out a long sigh and bent forward to unlace his boots. *Your* kitchen. Is it really *your* kitchen? Beforehand, he had never really thought of it as being anybody's kitchen.

'Oh, and I nearly forgot,' Mary said, pulling off a section of paper towel from its roll and giving her manicured hands a gentle wipe. 'Jonathan Davies called you from his car about five minutes ago. He's going to drop in on his way home.'

Gregor flicked back his head, a smile of disappointment on his face. 'That's a pity.' He toed off his boots and carried them over to the door of the back kitchen. He opened it and threw them in. 'Did he say what he wanted to talk about?'

Mary shook her head. 'Just said that he wanted a word.'

'Have I got time for a bath?'

Mary was about to respond when car lights swept across the kitchen window. 'There's your answer.'

Gregor let out a resigned sigh and returned to the back kitchen to greet Jonathan Davies. Mary watched him as he left, then opened up one of the cupboard doors to use the mirror that hung inside to give herself a quick once-over.

She heard Gregor welcome the man. 'Nice to see you, Jonathan, come on in.'

Mary scampered back to the cooker and nonchalantly began to stir at the cooking pot. She turned with a beaming smile on her face as the two men entered the room. Jonathan walked up to her, his hand outstretched. 'Mary, how nice to see you. Hmm, what a delicious smell! What *are* you cooking?'

Gregor watched with interest as Mary's face coloured as she took his hand, then listened as she began to explain to Davies the contents of her pot, and the many ingredients she had added to embellish their flavour. He had noticed this before, but had never quite been able to pin it down, and it was something he found to be almost unkind or even untrustworthy about Mary's character. She relied on him, she supported him and she was attracted to him, but as soon as another man showed any interest in her or what she was doing, no matter who he was or what age he was, she became singular in her attention to that one. And that was exactly what she was doing right now. It wasn't a mild flirtation, but an all-out offensive to attract the man. As far as Mary was concerned, there were only two people in the room at present – she and Davies. But maybe that was her greatest attraction. Although you never knew quite where you stood with her, while you were the man in her life, you were king.

Davies turned from the cooker, a broad smile on his face. 'Sorry to butt in on your supper like this, Gregor.'

Gregor shrugged. 'No bother. Do you want some? I'm sure there's enough, isn't there, Mary?'

She smiled but did not voice a reply.

'No!' Davies exclaimed, holding up his hands to accentuate his refusal. 'I wouldn't dream of it.' Walking over to the kitchen table, he sat down on its edge and crossed his arms. 'No, the only reason that I wanted to drop by was to tell you that I had a meeting today with an investment company in Edinburgh, and I'm pretty sure that they want to come in on the project.'

Gregor gave a double thumbs-up. 'Oh, that's great news, Jonathan! So we're still on line, then.'

Davies gave a tentative nod. 'Of course – from our end, that is.' He gave a quick glance towards Mary. 'I just wondered if you had had any further feedback from . . . well . . .'

Gregor eyed Mary as she busied herself around the kitchen, quite obviously fully aware of the subject around

117

which they were skirting 'No, nothing.' He paused for a moment. 'I'm afraid that I'm in a bit of a stalemate on that front at the minute. I was just wondering whether it might be a good idea if you made an approach.'

Davies slapped his hands down on his thighs. 'Did try, old boy. I went round there tonight to spread the good news, but it was only your father-in-' – he checked himself – 'her father and your son who were in.'

'So where was Liz?' He shot a look in Mary's direction, knowing immediately that he had said it with too much interest. Mary had caught his look, so he made a vain attempt to mollify his inquiry. 'I mean, was she out feeding the lambs or something?'

'No. Seemingly she had gone to the theatre in Saint Andrews.'

Gregor let out an abrupt laugh. 'The theatre! I doubt it. That's not her scene at all.'

Davies raised his eyebrows. 'Well, that's what I was told by Alex. They have one of his tutors from university staying in the farmhouse at present, and she'd apparently gone with him.'

For some reason, Gregor felt an unpremeditated rise of envy in his gut. He nodded his head slowly, longing to ask who this man was, but realized that Mary's agitation was becoming all too obvious in the way that she had begun to clatter dishes and cutlery onto the table.

Davies broke the uneasy atmosphere by rising from the table and clapping his hands together. 'Well, I must be off.' He walked over to Mary and this time bade his farewell by planting a kiss on both her cheeks. 'Goodbye,

Mary, and thanks for your impromptu cooking lesson. I must get my wife to try that recipe some time.'

Gregor followed him through the back kitchen and out into the yard. Davies opened the door of his car, then turned to look at him. 'You must see if you can have a word with Liz, Gregor. If this investment company comes good, then we should be ready to start almost immediately, but we really need to have the go-ahead from all parties, otherwise it can never be anything other than a complete non-starter.'

Gregor nodded. 'Aye, I understand that.'

'Okay. Good. Well, give me a call any time.'

'Will do, Jonathan. And thanks for dropping in.'

Gregor waited until Davies's car had driven around the corner of the steading before walking back into the house. Mary did not look at him when he entered the kitchen, but stood by the cooker ladling out her spicy stew onto two plates. He walked around the table and encircled her waist with his arms. She tried to shrug him away but he held fast. He bent forward and kissed the back of her neck. 'Are you hungry?'

'Why?' she asked, a tetchy edge to her voice. 'Aren't you?'

He gave her ear a gentle bite. 'Not for food, anyway.'

CHAPTER 9

A gentle breeze blew in through the window of Liz's bedroom, parting the curtains wide enough to allow a splash of sunlight to flicker momentarily onto her face. She opened her eyes and pushed her toes downwards under the bedclothes in one long, luxurious stretch before turning her head slowly on the pillow to glance at the alarm clock on her bedside table. Her brow furrowed. She quickly raised herself onto an elbow and picked up the clock, giving it closer scrutiny. Oh, for heaven's sake, it was twenty past eight! She picked up the clock and checked the alarm button. It was in the 'off' position. Throwing back the bedclothes, she jumped to her feet, discarding the alarm clock onto the bed with little regard to its future functioning. She pulled her nightdress over her head and scrambled around with the clothes on the chair, trying to separate those that she had worn the previous night from her work attire. She pulled on her knickers and hopped around on one foot as she got into her jeans, then walked blindly towards the door, struggling to find the misaligned armholes of her T-shirt and woollen polo-neck. Opening the door, she ran downstairs in her bare feet and raced into the kitchen.

Alex and the professor had just stood up from the breakfast table, their mugs and plates in hand. 'Ah, the sleeping beauty doth appear!' Arthur exclaimed, giving a dramatic bow in her direction which made the crockery rattle precariously in his outstretched hand. Fully aware of his past record with breakable objects in the house, Liz moved swiftly forward and relieved him of his load before it too was added to his tally.

'Why didn't you wake me?' she asked, shifting her gaze towards Alex in case it was construed that she was addressing the professor.

Alex opened the door of the dishwasher and slotted in his plate and mug. 'I thought that if you were sleeping on, then you were probably needing it.'

'But the lambs need to be fed. You know that.'

Alex shook his head slowly, as if making out that she was giving him little credit for his own common sense. 'Yes, I know that, Mum. That's why I've done them.'

'Ah,' Liz said quietly. 'Right. Well, thanks for that.'

Arthur gave her a wink. 'Thoughtful boy, eh?'

Liz did not respond to the remark. 'And what about Granddad? Have you seen him this morning?'

'He went off at about eight o'clock with the spraying contractor. Said that he was going to do a field walk with the guy, and that he wouldn't be in until about mid-morning. He asked me if I would feed the lambs, because he thought, like me, that you deserved a lie-in.'

'There you are, then!' Arthur declared, opening up the cupboard above the sink and taking out a mug. 'Everything is organized for you, so if you'd allow me now to do my bit, I'll make you a cup of coffee before your son and I hit the road.'

'No, please don't bother. I can do it myself.' She moved forward to take the mug from him, but he hugged it to his chest to avoid her outstretched hand.

'No, it would be my pleasure! The kettle's just boiled. White, no sugar, isn't it?'

'Yes. Thank you.' She turned to catch Alex beaming a wide smile at her. 'What are you looking like that for?'

Alex shrugged his shoulders. 'No reason.'

'There you are.' Arthur handed her the mug of steaming coffee, then turned and headed towards the hall. 'Alex, I won't be a moment. I've just got to get my coat.'

As the professor's footsteps sounded up the staircase, Alex folded his arms and leaned back against the draining-board. 'So, how was it last night?'

Liz took her coffee over to the table and sat down. 'Good. It was very funny, actually.'

'Not so highbrow as the first play, then?'

Liz laughed. 'No, I understood this one.' She took a sip of coffee and her face lengthened into an expression of disgust. 'Oh, my goodness, that's horrible!' Getting up from her chair, she hastily discarded the contents of her mug down the drain and set about making herself another one before Arthur re-entered the kitchen.

'And he hasn't tried to molest you yet?'

'No, Alex, he has not.'

'There you are. I told you that he'd be all right.'

Liz smiled at her son. 'Alex, I'm sure that molestation is the last thing that a man of his age would be thinking about.' She paused. 'Anyway, maybe age has nothing to do with it. Maybe I'm now just unmolestable.'

Alex flicked his head to the side. 'I don't know. I thought you scrubbed up pretty well last night.'

'Thanks, Alex.'

'Well, come on, it's pretty rare you being seen without a streak of lamb shit somewhere on your clothing.'

Letting out a cry of affront, Liz gave her son a sound punch on the arm before making her way back to the table with the new cup of coffee.

'Anyway, I'm not the only one who thought you looked pretty good last night.'

Liz raised her eyebrows. 'Your grandfather, I suppose. He just says that kind of thing as a matter of course. Trying to boost my flagging morale.'

Alex screwed a forefinger into the side of his head. 'No, actually, dummy, it was the professor!'

She shrugged her shoulders. 'Same thing, isn't it? The kindly compliment of an older man?'

'Oh, come on, Mum! Do yourself a little justice! He may be a bit older than you, but I wouldn't underestimate his judgement. I think he's seen quite a bit of life, you know.'

Liz pushed her spoon around in the coffee. 'Well, if you say so,' she said quietly, taking a sip from her mug. She cleared her throat. 'What . . . er . . . exactly did he say?'

'Only that he thought you looked . . .' Alex stopped speaking as he heard the professor's footsteps thump down

123

the stairs. He blustered into the kitchen, his raincoat flapping open behind him.

'Sorry about that, Alex. Suddenly remembered I needed some papers for today. Couldn't find them.' He opened his brief-case on the central worktop and untidily stuffed in the ream of papers. 'Right!' he said, clicking down the catch and heading for the door. 'Come on, then! We're running pretty late!'

As he left the room, Alex let out a short cry of disbelief at the incorrigibility of the man, then walked over to the table and gave his mother a kiss on the cheek. '"Ravishing" was the word he used.' He stepped away from her and watched as her cheeks began to colour and a self-conscious smile stretched across her mouth. 'See, I told you that getting someone to live with us would spice up our lives a bit. It's good to see you smile again, Mum.'

Liz got to her feet and reached up and ruffled his hair. 'You'd better be off, darling. I'll see you this evening.'

Picking up a pile of books from the kitchen table, Alex hurried over to the door. 'Okay, but it'll be late. I'm playing golf, so don't bother cooking anything for me.' He opened the door and immediately bumped into the tall figure of the professor as he came back into the kitchen.

'Sorry, Alex! Forgot to mention something.' He turned to Liz. 'How about trying an opera now?'

Liz stared at him, aghast. 'What?'

'Tomorrow night. The opera in Edinburgh. Suddenly remembered I had tickets.'

Liz shook her head. 'Oh, Arthur, that's very kind, but I really don't know if I can—'

'It would be a pity not to use them. And I promise you that if you don't enjoy it, we'll get up half-way through and leave.'

'No, I honestly think that it would just be wasted on me. I'm sure that you must know someone else who'd be more appreciative—'

'How can you tell?' Alex interjected. 'You've never seen an opera.'

The professor turned to his student and nodded in agreement. 'Thank you, Alex. My sentiments exactly.' He looked back at Liz. 'Well, will you come?'

Liz pushed her hands into the back pockets of her jeans. 'I don't really think I should. I just feel that I've been away quite a bit over the past few weeks, and Dad and I are still extremely busy.'

Arthur showed disapproval at her meagre excuse by wrinkling up his nose. 'What? Two evenings is termed as "being away quite a bit"?'

Liz let out a resigned sigh. 'Well, I'll have to speak with Dad.'

Arthur nodded. 'Good. And if you have any problem with him, I shall beat him tonight at cribbage and win the right to take you.'

Liz laughed. 'You might lose, you know.'

'Not even a possibility.' He turned and pushed a grinning Alex out the door in front of him. 'I taught him to play, remember?'

Liz listened to the sound of the Peugeot van fade off as it turned the corner of the steading, then stood with her arms crossed, taking in the comforting and welcome silence in the house. Alex had been right. Since the professor had moved in, their lives had certainly been 'spiced up.' No, that was an inadequate phrase. 'Disrupted' would probably be more apt.

She glanced over to her treasured Rayburn cooker and surveyed what remained of the two identical rubber imprints that had been melted onto the otherwise polished chrome top, a small yet now permanent reminder of the professor's attempt to dry off his hiking boots. That had probably been the worst, but in no way the first indication that he was totally without any idea of house-training. During his first week in residence, he had taken it upon himself to wash a pair of socks in the basin in the upstairs bathroom, even though she had been magnanimous in her offer to add his somewhat threadbare garments to her already burgeoning load. Somehow he had managed to flush them down the lavatory, a misdemeanour that only came to light when the drains began to back up on themselves and the house became permeated with the smell of raw sewage. That, in itself, had almost been enough for her to ask him to pack up his two battered canvas suitcases and leave the house. However, such was the vehemence of opposition to the idea, both from Alex and her father, that she had to recant on her threat, and was left to consider why this man had managed to inveigle his way into their household in such a short space of time. And the more she considered it, the more she began to realize that his attributes far outweighed his shortcomings. The uncertainty of what he was going to do next had created a sense of hilarious urgency amongst her two men, and after her initial negative, and often bad-tempered, reaction to this, she found herself being caught up in the new air of carefree happiness that had descended upon the household. Furthermore, her father had now begun to cast aside his quiet moroseness, his world suddenly stimulated by the intellect and wit of the professor, with whom he had struck up a close relationship. Every evening, they would disappear together into the hitherto unused sitting-room, each carrying a small glass of Jack Daniel's bourbon, and there they would sit, behind closed doors, talking or playing cards until well past midnight. When she eventually took herself off to bed, having enjoyed an hour or two of peaceful solitude in the kitchen, she would hear the laughter from within and smell the rich, heady aroma of the professor's pipe tobacco filter its way into the hall as she passed by.

His presence in the household had also greatly benefited Alex, in that he was able to receive extra German tuition gratis. It had been the professor's idea that, during their journeys to and from St Andrews, the Peugeot van should become a far-flung outpost of the German state, and that only the native tongue should be spoken within its mucky confines. Such was the success of the venture that the bounds of the German state were soon increased by the annexation of the farmhouse, but she and her father, mind-boggled by their unintelligible communications in the kitchen, had managed to exercise their full democratic powers of veto, reclaiming the place as sovereign territory.

And what about her? How would she term the effect that the professor had had on *her* life? Negative? No, that was too strong, but certainly he had managed to throw a sizeable spanner into her seething and grinding works. She had in no way been ready for a man to ask her out, in no way *prepared* for a man to ask her out, especially one who had to be near enough a quarter of a century older than she. But it probably had been that lack of preparation, coupled with the over-enthusiastic, and to what she considered as bordering on downright disloyal, support that the professor had been given by both Alex and her father that had forced her to accept his invitation. Alex had even used the professor's age as a *reason* for her to accept. 'Don't worry, Mum,' he had said. 'You'll be quite safe with him. I mean, just look at his age!' So she had undergone the alien task of 'scrubbing herself up,' as Alex had so tactfully phrased it, and rummaging through her wardrobe for something half decent to wear. Three times she had opened the door of the bedroom to make her way downstairs, and three times she had closed it to change her appearance. First her dress – Laura Ashley or Debenhams' best? Then her hair – brush it or just scrunch it? Then her shoes – flats or heels? She would have probably been quite happy to stay up there all night had Alex not yelled up the stairs that the professor was getting quite agitated that they might miss the first act. So she had gone, totally mismatched, to make an appearance before her 'date,' feeling like one of those dressed-up potatoes with the blue hat, red nose and pink mouth stuck into its skin.

And as she walked into the kitchen, Arthur had turned from viewing the kitchen clock and, after taking one long look at her, had let out a loud, extended wolf whistle. Surprisingly, her reaction to that had not been one of anger, but one that precipitated a stream of quite feeble, self-conscious mutterings. 'Oh, you're just doing that to be kind, aren't you? I'm afraid that I just have nothing to wear. Everything that I have on is *at least* ten years old. I just hope you don't mind spending the evening with someone who looks like *this*!' And that was when the anger kicked in – not with him, but with herself – for being so wet, for sounding like a simpering, downtrodden wife and making these excuses, for even giving a damn what she was wearing! But Arthur had just shrugged his shoulders and said, 'Well, you can think that if you like – but I think you look bloody wonderful, and I'm going to be proud to have you as my companion for the evening – even though you are at least twenty-five years too young for me!'

And that was what had broken the ice. She had thought to herself, Liz, my girl, I think that this man understands how you're feeling. Alex is right. He's no threat to you, so why not just go out and enjoy yourself?

And they had done so – even though she had found the play so highbrow that she had lost track of the plot somewhere in the first act.

But now it was becoming more complicated. She didn't want these evenings to become a feature of her life, nor an intrusion into it. Even though it had only been a case of going to the theatre and coming straight back home again, they had talked in the car and over their interval drinks, and she had fallen victim to his obviously kind but inquisitive nature, telling him about her upbringing, her marriage and the subsequent disaster that had befallen that. And as she had done so, she'd realized that she wasn't ready for any man to have this depth of understanding of her situation. She was still knotted up inside in the knowledge that his gender was the perpetrator of the brutal hurt she was experiencing, and consequently she wanted to dislike and distrust every man that she met. But, with Arthur, she had found it difficult to keep up this brittle reserve. She had therefore adopted an alternative and finely balanced strategy of trying not to talk directly to him or look at him in the house so as not to raise suspicions in her father or Alex of there having been a fall-out, in the hope that it would discourage Arthur from proffering further invitations. Still, she didn't want to alienate herself from the friendship that he showed, not only to herself but to her father and Alex. And she did like him.

But this *had* to be the last time. They would go to the opera in Edinburgh and she would make a concerted effort not to be drawn into talking either in the car or over their drinks. Thereafter, she would have a quiet word with Alex and her father and ask them to support her in her decision not to go out with him any more. In that way, surely nobody would get hurt.

It wasn't she who made the decision to leave. She was really quite enjoying the whole new experience of opera and the atmosphere engendered by the ornate grandeur of the cavernous auditorium, even though she was completely at sea as to what was happening on the stage. This was demonstrated to her by the fact that, at a point just before the close of the first act, when she thought everything was going just perfectly for everyone concerned, the woman in the seat next to her began to dab at tear-filled eyes with a handkerchief. However, as the curtain fell and even before the house lights had come up, Arthur jumped to his feet and stated in an embarrassingly loud and carrying tone that the heroine had a voice like a bullfrog with laryngitis and that he really didn't want this to be Liz's first taste of opera. So, without even waiting to down their preordered interval drinks, Arthur took her arm and ushered her down the stairs and out into the street.

'Sorry about that. That was a complete waste of time.'

'It wasn't at all. I was really quite enjoying it.'

Arthur scratched at his head. 'Ah. Right. Well, that just shows how selfish a person I am. Would you like to go back in? I suppose I could just about bear another . . .'

Liz shook her head. 'No, I'm quite happy not to.'

'All right.' He stuck his hands into the pockets of his raincoat and blew out a decisive breath. 'In that case, I think that the least I could do is to take you somewhere for a bite to eat.'

'No, really . . . thanks.' She heard her voice sound sharp in response. 'I mean, that's a very kind thought, Arthur, but I don't feel that hungry. Anyway, we've got a fairly long journey in front of us.'

'Nonsense! An hour would get us home. What's more, I'm feeling pretty hungry. What do you say to just finding a pizza place or something like that?'

Liz let out a short sigh of resignation, realizing that his persistency would far outlast hers. 'Okay, then, but as long as we can find somewhere that will serve us quite quickly.'

There were two reasons for them not finding anywhere for the next hour. Firstly, the time of night, and secondly, their joint lack of knowledge of Edinburgh. Having walked half the length of Princes Street without finding a suitable establishment that didn't have a queue for tables, they returned to the theatre to pick up Liz's Land Rover. While she collected it, Arthur went into the theatre to ask advice as to where best they should try, but in waiting for him outside, Liz thought to suggest that they should just cut their losses and head for home. The opportunity, however, never arose, as Arthur came bounding down the steps and, with a jubilant cry of success, jumped into the car and directed her towards the west end of town.

The restaurant was only half-full, and Liz could only surmise from the assembly of welcoming waiters in their full-length white aprons, the razor-creased pink table-cloths and velvet-covered gilt chairs that the place was probably far beyond the financial budget of most people. One of the waiters detached himself from the smiling bunch and came forward to take Liz's coat. 'Have you a reservation, sir?' he asked Arthur.

'Yes. Kempler.'

'Of course, Mr Kempler,' he sang out as if now recognizing Arthur as a regular customer. He quickly relieved Liz of her coat, and its speedy disappearance suddenly made her feel exposed and underdressed in front of the other diners. She pushed down self-consciously at the side seams of her black dress, having experienced great trouble earlier that evening in finding something different to wear and discovering that she was certainly a little plumper since the last time she had worn that particular garment. She turned and gave Arthur a half-smile. 'Are you sure this is all right? I mean, it's not exactly a pizza place.'

Arthur took off his raincoat and handed it to the waiter, and she immediately took comfort in the fact that her dining companion had obviously made no special effort to dress for the evening other than to add a clean shirt to his customary attire of hairy tweed jacket and stringy knitted tie. 'Well, it's Italian, anyway. If you really want pizza, I'm sure that they could rustle one up.'

'I didn't mean that. I just thought that . . . well . . . they might take quite a long time to serve us.'

He stood aside so that Liz could follow the waiter first to the table. 'Just don't worry about it. I'll make sure that we're as quick as possible, but hey, you won't turn into a pumpkin if you're not home by midnight.'

The waiter seated them with theatrical flourish, flicking open their napkins with such force that they cracked like whips before setting them with accomplished humility on their laps. He handed them the menus, and Liz swallowed hard in an effort not to gasp in shock at the prices.

Arthur laughed as he studied the menu. 'My God, you'd think we'd had enough of the Italian language for one evening, wouldn't you? Still don't understand a word of it.'

'I thought you were a linguist.'

'If being a linguist constitutes knowing more than one foreign language, then I'm no linguist.'

'So why only German?'

Arthur shrugged. 'My native tongue, I suppose, in a manner of speaking.'

'Oh? Why is that?'

The waiter came back with a wine list and stood by Arthur while he gave his order. Liz sat back in her chair and watched him. Here's your chance, girl, she thought to herself. You ask *him* about his life, you get *him* to talk. In that way, you won't have to talk about yourself. Just don't let him get a word in edgeways.

He glanced over to Liz. 'A bottle of white all right for you?'

'Yes, but I'll only have one glass, seeing that I'm driving. Could I have some mineral water as well?'

Arthur slapped the covers of the wine list together and handed it back to the waiter. 'A bottle of number twenty-one, please, and a glass of mineral water.'

Liz leaned her elbows on the table and looked intently at her dining partner. 'Well?'

'Well what?'

'Why is German your native tongue, "so to speak"? I thought you were Canadian.'

'Well, it does happen to be a multinational country. Have you never heard of French-Canadians?'

'Of course! But not German-Canadians.'

The waiter came back with a copper tub brimming with ice, from which he took the bottle of wine and poured a little into Arthur's glass. Arthur waved his hand.

'Just go ahead. I'm sure it's fine.'

'So, are you a native German-Canadian?' Liz asked, persisting with her questioning, enjoying the fact that she, for once, had control of the conversation.

Arthur shook his head. 'No. I'm not. I'm Canadian now, but I was born in Germany.'

'Really? When did you leave?'

'In 1939.'

Liz nodded slowly, understanding the relevance of the date. 'Right. Just before the . . .'

'The war. Yes.' Arthur took a drink from his glass. 'My father was, like me, an academic, a physicist to be precise, and also vice-president of the Technical Institute in Stuttgart. When "Führerprinzip" was introduced in 1933, all members of staff at the Institute who were of Jewish descent were immediately fired. In other words, all my father's most erudite friends. Mr Hitler was particularly hostile to any scientific advancement that originated from a Jewish brain, and it has even been mooted that that was why, during the war, Germany lagged behind the rest in the development of the nuclear bomb. Anyway, my father stuck it out for the next six years in the hope that he could help keep up the student numbers, but they declined fast, regardless of his efforts. So you can imagine that when he began to express his sentiments towards all this rather too openly, he was never going to be first in line for a popularity award. Having a wife and three small sons, I being the youngest, he understood only too well the direction in which things were going and he thought that the risk was too great in staying in the country. So, one night, he took what he could carry from the house, bundled us all into his car, and we made our escape. As it turned out, only just in time. My father heard many years later of the fate that befell many of his fellows at the Institute.'

'So you went straight to Canada?'

'Yes. In the salubrious elegance of a Dutch tramp steamer.'

'How old were you?'

'Two, I think.' He smiled at her. 'There you are. You can work out my age now.'

Liz let it pass without comment. 'So what did your father do when he got to Canada?'

'Not a lot to begin with. We were housed in a sort of refugee camp for about four months, and then my father had an opportune meeting with a friend from the university who had emigrated ten years beforehand. It was he who really saved our lives. Within two months, the guy had pulled enough strings to strangle an elephant. We were given Canadian nationality, the man found us a small house in Toronto and a job for my father in a high school there.'

'That was a bit of a come-down, wasn't it? I mean, going from a university to a high school?'

'You're right. But beggars couldn't be choosers. He just knuckled down and did his job. But what with the problems in Germany and the fact that he missed his friends and the mental stimulation of working in research, things didn't go well for the old boy. I don't think that I ever remember him being in any mood other than deep depression. He died almost ten years to the day after we arrived in Canada.'

Liz bit at her lip. 'I'm sorry.' It was a falter, but she had to keep pressing on. 'And what about you? What did you do?'

'I went to the high school and then on to the University of Toronto.' He laughed. 'And that's when my story begins to have certain parallels to yours.'

Liz's back straightened, relinquishing her relaxed position, and she felt her screen of defence begin to shut down on the conversation. With opportune timing, the waiter came to the table to take their orders.

'Now, what are you having?' Arthur asked.

'I think just cannelloni as a starter, please, and that'll do me.'

'What about sharing a green salad with me?'

'All right then.'

Arthur looked up at the waiter. 'So, that's one cannelloni starter and a lasagna verde, and we'll have a green salad to share.'

The waiter wrote quickly on his pad, and with a gracious bow left the table and hurried away to the kitchen. Arthur smiled at Liz. 'Go on.'

'What?'

'Go on with your questioning. You're doing well.'

Liz let out a quiet laugh at the intuition of the man. He knew exactly what she was doing. 'I can't remember where we'd got to.'

'I said that my life had parallels with yours.'

'Ah. Yes. Right, then – in what way?'

'I got a girl pregnant. She was a fellow student – I was nineteen, she was eighteen. It was almost regarded as criminal in those days, so I married her. Actually, it turned out to be a pretty good marriage, even though, to begin with, we lived on air. It lasted twelve years, during which time we both graduated, both got jobs, and we had three children, two girls and a boy. But then I . . . well . . .' He paused, twisting his mouth to the side as if finding it difficult to continue.

'You did what?'

Arthur held out his hands, as if already submitting to her reaction to his confession. 'I left them.'

Liz's brow furrowed. 'For what reason?'

'Because I was selfish, impulsive, bored, wanting to make a success of my life. You think of every bad reason for me to walk out on my family and I can guarantee you that it would have gone through my mind.'

Liz said nothing. What could she say? Here they were talking about him, but she could not pass comment without making it seem to be a direct reflection on her own circumstances.

She picked up her wineglass and took a sip, then, catching in his eye an inquiring look to see her reaction, she picked up her mineral water and took a sip from that as well.

'It's pretty shocking, isn't it?' he said eventually.

She nodded. 'Yes. It is.'

He leaned forward on the table. 'I wasn't having an affair at the time, you know. There was no one else – if that makes it any easier for you to understand.'

'Not really.'

'No. I can quite see that. Anyway, I have started, so I shall keep on going. My wife and I eventually divorced, but I continued to keep them financially, which was pretty hard on the salary that I got. That was probably the main reason why I never married again. Okay, I had some passing affairs, but none that lasted. It was always myself that broke them off. Not because I didn't want them to work. It was just that I never really trusted my instincts ever again.'

'But you kept seeing your family?'

'No, I didn't, because there was obviously great animosity between my wife and myself and she didn't want me anywhere near the house, so I just thought it best if I got out of their lives. I took a job in Vancouver and ended up living there for twenty years. However, about five years ago, I had this great impulse to find the children. Don't know what brought it on. Probably approaching my sixtieth year. I found out where each of the girls lived – luckily they were both still in Toronto – and I visited them on the same day, because I didn't want one to put the other one off from meeting me. And there they were, married with children – my grandchildren – and we talked – and we made up – eventually.' He paused. 'It was the hardest thing I ever had to do in my whole life. For a week, I found myself teetering along a rotting rope bridge over this gaping chasm of rejection, with the haven of acceptance never seeming to get any closer on the other side.'

'But you made it.'

'Eventually.'

'And what about your son?'

'I'm still on the bridge – I think. It could quite possibly be broken.'

'How do you know? Did you meet him?'

'Yes, I did – thanks to Angela, my eldest daughter, who filled me in on what he was doing and how to get in touch with him.'

'And?'

'He's young – and he's powerful – and he's dead-set against marriage.'

'Because?'

'You can probably hazard a guess.'

'Yes, I suppose I can. So what does he do?'

'Oil. He's in oil. Everywhere in the world where they speak Spanish, he's in oil.'

'Another linguist, then?'

Arthur laughed. 'Again, if you consider being fluent in another language qualifying one as a linguist. Doesn't speak a word of German.'

'So where is he based?'

'Everywhere. Philippines, South America, Spain, London, Aberdeen . . .'

'Aberdeen?'

'Not very Hispanic, is it? But he does come up here quite a bit. He's in exploration. And that's the real reason that I came over here to Saint Andrews. I had to find a place that I could wait around to meet him, and as you can imagine, I can't afford to do that without working.'

'And what happened when you did meet . . . what's your son called?'

'Will. Wilhelm, actually, after my father. Well, just let's say it didn't go off so well as with the girls. Angela had given me his mobile phone number, and through the wonders of modern technology, I eventually managed to track him down in Spain. The great thing about the telephone is that it's pretty difficult to think of an immediate excuse when you're taken unawares, so I managed to arrange a dinner meeting with him for the next time that he was in Aberdeen. It turned out to be pretty disastrous, because despite my consuming more humble pie than was good for my egotistic appetite, he tore strip after strip off my guilt-ridden body. Thank God not physically. You can imagine what he looks like, having worked hands-on in oil exploration. But the one thing he inherited from me was an academic's brain, so he managed to reduce me to pulp within the first hour of our meeting.'

'So the rope bridge collapsed.'

'I don't know. I'm hoping that it's still hanging by a slender thread.'

She looked down at her finished plate, not having realized that she had been served her meal, let alone eaten it. She put her knife and fork together and sat back in her chair.

Arthur looked at her. 'Okay. My turn to ask a question. What would you say that you have really missed in your life?'

'In what way?'

'Well, you got married and had Alex when you were pretty young. There must have been times when you were cooped up in the house, bathing him or feeding him, when you said to yourself, "Gosh, I wish I could be doing *that* right now."'

Liz considered this for a moment, then shook her head. 'No. I can't think of anything. I was quite happy with my lot, and I probably didn't have too high expectations for myself anyway. I suppose I did have some regrets in not going on to college, but that was some time ago.' She paused. 'What about you? What have you really missed?'

'I didn't think that I had missed anything until I met my children again. That's when I realized that I had really lost out.'

'Don't you think that you deserved to lose out?'

'Yes, I did – but you didn't.'

Liz did not reply, but instead concentrated on making sure that the smile did not slide from her face.

'So,' Arthur continued, leaning forward on the table, 'I shall slightly rephrase my original question. Looking at your life as it is now, what do you feel that you have missed out on?'

Liz felt trapped for an instant as she struggled for an answer. Looking at her life as it was now, she could only think of what her wants were at that precise moment, and they were all overloaded with negative intent. She did not want to see the golf course built, she did not want to stop farming, she did not want to see Gregor again. But they were all irrelevant to his question. Then something extraordinary happened in her brain. As she concentrated anew, a chink appeared in the hitherto impenetrable layer of bitter resolve, and through it shone a thin but bright light of happy recall.

'Riding!' she exclaimed, a broad smile suddenly bursting onto her face.

Arthur nodded in appreciation of her answer. 'Riding.'

'Yes. Dad bought me my first pony when I was eleven, and he used to take me to all the pony-club events in the area. Looking back on it, it was all quite embarrassing, because there were always these smart trailers pulled by Range Rovers, and we used to turn up with a battered old Land Rover and the sheep trailer. Sometimes, if the place where the event was being held was close by, he'd even take the tractor. Anyway, I became quite good at it – I mean, I didn't compete or anything like that, but I used to go out quite a bit with the local hunt and charge all over the county on horseback.' She sat back in her chair, a contented smile on her face at the recollection. 'Yes, that was fun.'

'But you didn't exactly miss out on it, did you?'

She shook her head. 'No, you're right. I didn't. But when Alex was born, I had no time to ride any more, and Dad said that it was unfair for my horse to be standing around in a field all day not being ridden, so we sold him.' She paused and focused her eyes on the palm of her hand, and began tracing small circles on it with her forefinger. 'And along with him went my childhood . . . and I was nowhere near ready to lose either.'

'No, I dare say you weren't,' Arthur said quietly. He clapped his hands together, as if to dispel the mist of melancholia that was beginning to descend upon the proceedings. 'Right! Riding. I'll make a mental note of that one. Anything else?'

Liz sat forward on her chair and rested her elbows on

the table. 'Erm, let's think now . . . travel! I've always wanted to travel.'

'Where in particular? The Far East? Africa? America?'

'Don't mind. Just anywhere out of this country. I was going to go to Austria with some friends just after we finished school, but, well, I became pregnant and my mother wouldn't let me go. I don't know if it was supposed to be for the baby's sake or just my punishment for being such a wild young girl. Anyway, holidays thereafter were few and far between. That's the problem with coming from a farming family. You're either too busy to take holidays, or, when you're not, it's always at a time of year when the weather is telling you that it's the wrong *time* to take a holiday.' She laughed. 'I remember when Alex was about five, we spent a whole week in a café on the Isle of Mull drinking coffee and watching the rain teem down outside. The kind old lady who owned the café realized we were having quite a time controlling Alex, so she pulled a chair over to the one-armed bandit, stuck him on it, gave him a cupful of tokens and told him to do his best. It could have been the start of a dreadful addiction.'

Arthur smiled. 'You know, you should do that more often.'

Liz giggled. 'What? Go to the Isle of Mull?'

'No. Laugh like that. It suits you. Your whole face lights up.'

The smile slid from Liz's face.

'Oh, dear, I've embarrassed you.'

'No – no, you haven't really,' Liz replied quietly. 'It's just that I don't, well . . .'

'Don't what?'

Liz looked at him. You can't say it, you know. You can't say that you don't think that he should be saying those kind of things to you, that he's too *old* to be saying those kind of things to you. 'It's just that I don't believe in compliments like that any more.'

'Well, you should, because I wouldn't waste my time saying it if I didn't mean it. Anyway, if you weren't embarrassed before, you might well be after I've finished my next statement, so I'd be grateful if you would hear me out, because it might just turn out that it's me that ends up embarrassed.' He leaned back in his chair. 'Right, are you ready for it?'

Liz laughed weakly, in trepidation of what was to follow. 'Go on, then.'

'Okay. In two weeks' time, I'm heading off to Spain – to Seville, actually, for Holy Week, or Semana Santa, as they call it. I've yet to witness it myself, but it is supposed to be one of the most phenomenal and spirit-lifting experiences that one can imagine. I thought that it would be an ideal trip for Will and me to do together, hoping that he might be able to coincide it with a business trip, so I went ahead and booked it up about three months ago. When I met him that time in Aberdeen, I was going to put the idea to him, but the whole evening was such a disaster that I just thought that it was the wrong time to ask. So when I returned to Saint Andrews, I sent him the itinerary and the plane ticket and told him to take time to think about it before he made a decision. Unfortunately, I received the ticket back by return post with a letter enclosed saying that he had meant what he said during our dinner together – that he never wanted to see me again. So I have this spare ticket – and I was wondering if you might consider coming with me.'

Liz gulped before trying to make a reply. 'Arthur, I—'

'I'm not finished yet. I know that I probably should be, but I'm not. Liz, Gregor is a fool. I know that because I did exactly as he did. I left my wife and children – in your case, a child. But you cannot brood on it forever. It would be a waste for someone with your attraction, with your humour, with your beauty, to just slip into a life-style of self-rebuke and misery. I know that I am quite a bit older than you, but I know that I can help—'

'That's just it, Arthur.'

'I'm sorry?'

'You're too old for me. You are nearer to my father's age.' Liz pushed back her chair and got to her feet. 'It just wouldn't seem right.'

Arthur looked up at her. 'Look, sit down for a minute.'

Liz remained standing, casting her eyes around the restaurant so that she didn't have to look at him. She noticed that the occupants of the neighbouring table were staring at them.

'Please?'

With reluctance, Liz resumed her seat.

'Listen, I just want to say that I know how you're feeling. I know that probably the last thing you want to think about at the minute is making any form of commitment with another man – and I find that totally understandable. I didn't actually get my phraseology worked out too well, but what I wanted to say was that it's our difference in age that is the key to the whole thing. I'd be no threat to you, Liz. You wouldn't have to be fighting me off' – he let out a low chortle – 'which is more the pity for myself, but I promise you that you would have to make no effort other than to enjoy yourself.'

Liz was silent for a moment before letting out a settling breath. 'I'm sorry I said that – that thing about your age, Arthur. You're right. I'm probably too defensive for my own good at the minute.'

Arthur tilted his head to the side in recognition of her state of mind. 'So, what do you say? Will you at least think about it?'

'No, Arthur, I can't. Maybe if you were to ask me the same kind question a year from now, I might give it thought, but there's just too much going on at the minute, too much to sort out – what with the farm, with the golf course, with my family . . . and with Gregor. I would feel as though I'd be running away from my own problems.'

'I wouldn't say that. More like you would just be distancing yourself from them. It might give yourself the chance to see them more clearly, to see them more in perspective.'

'No, I don't think so.' She got to her feet again. 'If you don't mind, Arthur, can we just leave it?' She paused. 'Listen, I really value your friendship, as does everyone in my family, so please, can we just leave it at that?'

Arthur brought his hands down on the table and pushed himself to his feet. 'All right. But I'd have kicked myself for not trying. I'll go ahead and get the bill.'

Liz nodded. 'Okay. And I'll go and get the car.'

She walked towards the door of the restaurant, where their waiter, who had witnessed her first attempt to leave, was already waiting to help her on with her coat. She walked out onto the street and took in a deep inhalation of fresh air. Then, as she turned to make her way to where the car was parked, she glanced at her wrist-watch. It was ten past twelve. She had already turned into a pumpkin.

CHAPTER 10

Eleanor Bayliss Hamilton took in a deep breath, catching the rich aroma given off by the abundance of flowers that decorated the chapel. Not wishing to witness the final moment, she gripped hard at her husband's hand and looked up high into the airy coolness of the crematorium roof as the priest said the final words, sending the coffin slowly along the soundless conveyor belt before disappearing forever behind the purple velvet curtains. Above the muted organ tones, she heard her elder sister, who sat on her other side, let out a series of short, stuttering sobs as she fought hard to stifle her emotions, and without looking at her, Eleanor felt for her hand and gave it a reassuring squeeze.

Good thoughts and happy memories. It was on these that she had been trying to concentrate throughout the service in an effort to stop herself from crying openly. And it really hadn't been difficult. Her father had had many attributes and few shortcomings. Throughout his life, he had been kind, gentle, supportive to his whole family, and she had had to search hard through her memory bank in order to recall a time when he had ever rebuked them as young children. It had always either been left to their mother, or, if one of their frequent misdemeanours was thought so appalling that his judgement was deemed necessary, he would do little more than chew pensively on the leg of his reading glasses before uttering something quite ineffectual, such as, 'Well, I wouldn't bother doing it again, if I was you.' Then it would be back to reading the sports section of the newspaper to find out who had won a golf tournament in some far-flung corner of the world.

Yet this disinterest in their discipline was more than matched by the enthusiasm and affection he showed for his daughters, never taking the easier option of treating them as a unit, but always making sure that each received the special encouragement and praise to develop her own individual character and interests. And throughout his ninety years, he had never stopped doing that.

But even as she thought about all the happy times in the past, and recognized the fact that she was truly blessed in having had a loving father for all those years, it was not enough to dispel the emptiness she felt in knowing that he had gone forever. It had all happened so fast, too. The young consultant who had been looking after him in the hospital had said that the heart attack was most likely the follow-on to a mild stroke which had gone undetected. So nobody was to blame – least of all poor Bobby. It had only been three weeks since her own sixty-fifth birthday party, when she had talked so fiercely to her younger sister about her own concerns for her father's well-being. Since then, his health had declined so suddenly that he and Bobby had never set foot together on a golf course again.

The completion of prayers was heralded by a general movement amongst the congregation, accompanied by a short ripple of emotion-clearing coughs. The priest stepped down from the pulpit and moved to the centre of the chapel, directing a kindly and reassuring smile towards the family pew. Opening up his prayer-book, he took out a piece of paper which he settled across its pages. 'My friends, I would usually think it appropriate to end a service at this point. However, it was Simon Bayliss's own express wish that we should not bring proceedings to a close on a sad note, but rather on one that celebrated the triumph of his being able to survive for ninety glorious years in God's presence on this planet.' A reserved murmur of amusement ran through the congregation. 'I would ask you therefore to lift your voices in unison one last time in celebration of his life by singing together "Jerusalem" – number 578 in your hymnals.'

The organ came to life with a loud blast, almost cutting off the last few words of his sentence, and the packed chapel rose to their feet as one. Gordon cupped his hand under his wife's elbow and helped her up, and as she steadied herself, Eleanor leaned forward to glance past him to where Roberta still remained seated beside her mother. Although it may well have been construed other-wise by those who stood in the pews behind, there seemed little sign of mutual support being given, for while her mother bowed her head, Roberta stared hard at the purple velvet curtains, oblivious to all that was happening about her. Her face showed no sign of sadness or loss, but was set in a fixed expression of utter disbelief, her whole comportment making it appear as if she had made up her mind to freeze-frame her life at the point that her father's coffin disappeared from sight. Eleanor looked down at her hymn-book, now feeling the tears begin to prick at her eyes. Oh, Bobby, she thought to herself, I *knew* that this was going to be unbearable for you. I said as much to myself that day in Nielsen Park, but I had no idea that you were going to have to deal with it so soon. And you still have the worst to come.

The family had sat in silence around the dining-room table in her parents' house the night before as the lawyer went through the will, but Eleanor had been unable to hold herself back from letting out a cry of incredulity when he had read through the final paragraph. He could *not* ask that of Bobby. She had immediately launched into a full riposte, pointing out the impracticalities and needlessness of the request, but it was Bobby who had held up her hand to stop her in mid-flow, saying that if it was her father's wish, then she would do it.

But it was to happen so far away. To Eleanor, it was the only unthinking, unreasonable thing that her father had ever asked of any of them.

She pulled Gordon's hand towards her mouth and gave it a kiss, and he turned and gave her a broad smile of love and support. Thank goodness she still had him. She could never imagine what it would be like to lose him.

CHAPTER 11

The eighth hole on the proposed Balmuir Championship Course was 420 yards in length. It dog-legged at a good drive's distance from the tee around a natural outcrop of scrub-covered granite before sweeping down into the hollow to where the white-staked outline of the green nestled itself against the rocky backdrop of the shoreline. From this high vantage point, Jonathan Davies and Michael Dooney, the course architect, surveyed the topography of the hole, struggling to hold open a copy of the plan in the gusting wind.

The tall American grabbed at the flapping sheet as a particularly strong blast threatened to take it off seaward. 'Let's try putting it on the ground. Doesn't matter if it gets dirty.'

Stretching it tight between them, they laid it out, placing a large stone at each corner to hold it secure before squatting down on their haunches to inspect it.

'Do you think we're making it tricky enough?' Davies asked, looking up from the plan and squinting in concentration as he tried to imagine the layout of the hole in the open fields.

'Yeah, I think so. Remember from down there, the hole is blind – you can't see it from the tee because of this lump of rock that we're standing on. What's more, it follows a pretty difficult par-five, so it does fit into the general pattern of the course, putting an easier hole after a testing one.' He stood up, placing both hands on his hips to stretch out his back. 'Anyway, this is only a computer generation of the basic layout of the hole. I can always see how things turn out and bring the rough in from the left a bit or stick a couple of pot bunkers down there by the fence where the dog-leg comes into play.'

Davies pushed himself to his feet and carefully dusted from his suit trousers a couple of bright yellow petals that had blown off the flowering gorse. 'That'll rather penalize the big hitters, don't you think?'

Dooney flashed his wide, piano-key smile. 'It's to be a championship course, you know. The big hitters should know how to avoid them.'

Davies nodded. 'Okay. If you say so.'

Dooney delved into the inside pocket of his wind-cheater and took out a notebook and pen to jot down his observations on the hole, glancing down at the plan and looking out across the hole as he did so. 'That fence,' he said, pointing out the half-mile line of rickety posts that stretched from the bottom of the field up to the road. 'That's the boundary between the two farms, isn't it?'

'Certainly is.' Davies let out an exasperated laugh.

'Maybe the front line of battle would be a more apt description of it.'

Dooney shot him an inquiring glance. 'I take it then that you're no further forward with your negotiations.'

'No, not yet.' The venture capitalist flicked the stones from the plan with the toe of his rubber boot, then bent forward and picked it up and began to fold it carefully along its creases. 'I sometimes feel like spouting out the old cliché about "of all the places in all the world, I had to pick this one."'

'Yeah, I get your point. But take comfort from the fact that you have chosen the minutest corner of the earth on which I think God had always intended golf to be played.'

'Oh, I know that. It's the Garden of Eden, as far as that's concerned. But then God did also create Adam and Eve.'

Dooney chuckled. 'Of course.' He became serious. 'So you don't think she'll budge?'

'It doesn't look that way at the moment. I mean, all you have to do is look around. Every field's got some damned crop growing in it. Does it look to you as if it was ever intended that a golf course should be laid out here?'

'Well, I think, on that point, you have to give them their due. If the financial packet had been in place, they might not have felt the need to cover their backs by growing crops this year.'

'I'll grant that that may be true of Gregor, but I wouldn't think Liz had any intention other than to see all the crops on Brunthill harvested.' Davies took off his narrow tweed cap and swept a hand across his thinning hair. 'I don't like being beaten for an answer, Mike, and, to be quite honest, I'm really beginning to despair of this whole project. Here we are, ready to go at a moment's notice, and I still feel as if I'm juggling at least three balls in each hand, trying to get the finance raised and trying to get those two to agree with each other.' He paused, letting out a resigned sigh. 'A couple more weeks. That's all I can afford to give it, Mike, regardless of the fact that we're going to lose thousands on it. A couple more weeks, and then we head Stateside.'

Dooney slapped his notebook closed and slid it back into his inside pocket, the action making it look as if he felt it was worthless to take any more notes. 'When do you plan to tell *them* that?'

'Tonight. I have a meeting with Liz and her father in the pub, and I'm just going to take the bull by the horns and invite Gregor to join us.'

'The final show-down, then?'

Davies began to pick his way down the narrow path, his wax jacket rasping against the jagging gorse-bushes. 'That's it, Mike. The final showdown.'

As Dooney began to follow on, the shrill ring of a mobile phone sounded out. He stopped and dug his hand into his pocket. 'Mine or yours?'

Davies pulled out his phone. 'Mine.' He pressed the 'speak' button. 'Hullo? . . . yes, this is he . . . oh, hullo, Lionel, how are you? . . . good . . . yes, I can speak, but can you hang on a minute? The reception's not very good here.' He turned and began to retrace his steps up the slope. As he passed Dooney, he put a hand on the

American's arm and gave it a tight squeeze. 'Fingers crossed, Mike. This could be it.' He continued on to the top of the outcrop and bent down behind a clump of gorse to shelter from the wind . . . 'Hullo, Lionel? Yes, that's better, so what's the situation? . . . right . . . okay . . . and you're one-hundred-per-cent sure that's firm . . . right . . . and what about conditions? . . . well, that's great news, Lionel . . . absolutely, it's really lifted my spirits . . . okay then, we'll speak soon.'

He pressed the button on his mobile phone and held wide his arms as if in triumphant praise. 'You were absolutely right, Mike. God does want a golf course built here after all.'

Dooney smiled up at him. 'You mean you've got the finance?'

Davies bounded down the slope to where he stood. 'Yup. Every last penny – signed, sealed and delivered.'

Dooney let out a loud rodeo whoop. 'Well done! Now all you have to do is deal with Adam and Eve.'

'Well, I have the incentive. It's now just a question of finding a tempting-enough apple for both to bite into.' He reached up and placed his arm around the shoulders of the course architect. 'But right now, my friend, I would suggest that we might hedge our bets a little and put those diggers on stand-by.'

Liz stared out of the kitchen window, aware of the two distant figures moving across the farthest field on the farm, but her mind was too preoccupied for their presence to register any small measure of concern or inquisition.

157

She glanced down at the sheet of letter-head on the kitchen table, then bent forward and picked it up. Once again, she read through its precise wording, her head filled with a mixture of bewilderment and fury as to why news of such overpowering consequences should be imparted in the form of a computerized print-out.

The door of the kitchen opened and her father walked in. She hurriedly folded the letter and moved across to the work island, where she tucked it under the pile of otherwise unopened mail. Taking the cap from his head, Mr Craig spun it through the air with a deft flick of his wrist. It came to rest only a few inches from where she had secreted the letter. He looked at her concernedly. 'You all right, lass? You look a bit washed out.'

Liz shook her head. 'No, I'm fine. Just seem to have a bit of a headache.'

'Take a couple of aspirin, then.'

Liz shook her head, but it was more to acknowledge the fact that that seemed to be his answer to all ailments. 'It's just come on.'

'Right. Well, could you just make a wee note somewhere that we're needing a couple of bags of hen-feed? The last one's just finished.'

Liz put both hands on the work surface and gripped hard at its edges, her father's innocent-enough request seeming, at this point, to be as demanding as a child moaning endlessly for sweets in a shop. She felt anger and emotion grip tight at her stomach as the fight and resilience that had been hitherto fired by her break-up with Gregor and her subsequent efforts to keep the family farm intact began to ebb from her body. It would seem now that it had all been for nothing.

'Dad, we cannot afford to buy any more damned hen-feed!' she blurted out through clenched teeth, her eyes brimming with tears of hopelessness and frustration.

The farmer gave her a lengthy stare, his expression registering both concern and a guarded understanding of the reason for her outburst. 'What's the matter, lass?' Liz did not reply. 'Is it the bank?'

Liz slipped out the letter from the bottom of the pile and handed it to him. 'They're going to foreclose on us, Dad,' she said quietly, slipping her fingers into the front pockets of her jeans. 'So no more hen-feed – no more of anything.'

She watched as her father read once through the letter, then, with the slightest nod of acceptance, he folded it up and placed it gently back on the worktop.

Liz stared at the letter, incredulous at his reaction. 'Is that it, Dad? Do you not understand that that letter effectively ends a hundred and fifty years of our family having farmed here?'

Mr Craig walked towards his daughter and encircled her shoulders with his strong lean arms, pulling her tight against him. 'Lizzie, I can't allow that thought to pass through my mind, because it would be no use. We have done everything that we possibly could, and I'm that proud of you for giving so much of yourself in trying to keep the place going.'

Liz pushed herself away from him. 'But you can't accept it that easily, can you? Surely if we asked the bank, they would give us a little time to come up with some alternative?' She turned from him and began to pace back and forth across the kitchen floor, her face a study of concentrated intent, as if she were trying to come up with one last desperate escape plan from a condemned cell. 'What about a sale and leaseback? Bob Maclure did that with some pension company about ten years ago, didn't he? That would raise sufficient capital to clear the overdraft.'

'Pension companies aren't that interested any more in land, Lizzie. Anyway, by the time we cleared the overdraft, there'd be little left for working capital and we'd just be back to square one in no time at all – this time as tenant farmers.'

Liz's eyes widened at another thought. 'Well, what about Andrew in Australia? Why don't we ask him to buy the farm? I'm sure that he would help if he knew . . .'

'I've no wish to get Andrew involved in this. He made a decision many years ago that he wanted nothing to do with the farm, and I think it would be unfair to ask him.'

'Well then, what about . . . ?'

'Lizzie, stop!' He took hold of her shoulders and guided her towards the kitchen table, then pulled out a chair. 'Now would you please, for a moment, just sit down there and be quiet, because I want to say something. All right?'

For a moment, Liz showed every sign of resisting his request, but then, with a sigh of resignation, she slumped down onto the chair. Her father swung one around for himself and sat down, leaning his elbows on the table and rubbing a hand over his gaunt cheeks. 'Listen, lassie, we're not the only farming family to have these problems, you know. It's not unique to us, so we don't have to feel guilty or feel that we have failed in any way. There's a good few others like us. I read about them every week in the newspaper or in *The Scottish Farmer*. It's just the way things are in the industry at the minute. But what you have to realize is that many of these families have nothing to fall back on, so they end up just throwing the keys of the farmhouse onto the bank manager's desk and walking off the land.' He paused, folding his fingers together and pressing them to his mouth. 'I don't want to be forced into doing that, Lizzie, and I'm afraid that we would be if we kept hiding away from the truth any longer. We're lucky enough to have an alternative. It's all there, set in place, even though I know you're not too keen on the idea.'

Liz's eyes narrowed. 'You're not meaning the golf course?'

'I am.'

'But we can't—'

Her father cut short her objection. 'Yes, we can – and we're going to!' he exclaimed, a hint of vehemence in his voice. 'I'm running out of energy, lass. I'm tired of farming and tired of having to cope with this financial millstone that we have to carry around our necks all the time. But what is of much greater concern to me is that I think it's the only way that we'll have any chance of laying bare those defence barriers that you've been setting up all about yourself.' He reached across and touched the side of her hand on the table. 'Lizzie, I know what's been driving you for the past six months, and even though I can quite understand it, I don't like it – and neither does Alex. We've all had to suffer great upheaval in our lives recently, but we have to keep trying to make the best of things. You *have* changed, lass, and quite a bit, too. Both Alex and I see it, and I have to say that sometimes it quite frightens us. I've never wanted to tell you this before in such a blatant way, because I know that you've been hurting that badly. But I see no sign of you getting any better, and I think that it's time that you're given a wee push in the right direction.'

Liz let out a choking breath and clasped tight the hand that touched hers. 'Oh, Dad!' In one movement, she slid off her chair and onto his lap, putting her arms around his shoulders and pressing her face into the nape of his neck, exactly as she had done to seek comfort as a small child. 'I'm so sorry, Dad. It's just that I miss everything so much. I want everything to be as it was.'

He patted her back gently. 'I know you do, lass. I know it too well, and if it were in my power, I'd change it all back for you.' He pushed her away so that he could look up into her face. 'But things *are* different now and you've got to make a wee bit of an effort – for all our sakes.'

Liz nodded slowly and wiped away the tears from her cheeks with the back of her hand. 'I know. You're right. I do feel bitter – and angry, not just about Gregor, but Mum as well. I just felt that all our lives had been shattered, and I wanted to hold on to whatever was permanent and safe in our lives.'

'I know that – and I don't blame you for trying.'

She smiled at him. 'So what do you think we should do?'

162

'Well, firstly, I would suggest that you go to the meeting in the pub tonight and tell Jonathan Davies that we will give his project our full support.'

'Don't you want to come?'

'No. I think that I'd better be going into Saint Andrews to see the bank manager, and I'll tell him what we've decided to do. And then I'll just head on over to Cupar to see if I can fix up a date for a farm sale with the auctioneers.'

'Already?'

'Yes, already. If we're to stop, then I don't want it dragging on forever.'

Liz nodded in agreement. 'So that's the first thing. What's second?'

The farmer laughed. 'Aye, well, secondly, could you please get off my lap? My old legs are about to collapse.'

CHAPTER 12

The barman of the Doocot Arms sat swinging his legs over the edge of the stainless-steel work surface in the small kitchen that linked the public and lounge bars, throwing back his head in laughter at the joke that the corpulent young chef had just told him. Half-way through the story, he had thought of one himself that would be a perfect follow-on, but just as he launched into telling it, he heard the heavily sprung double doors of the lounge bar bang shut. He held up a finger, listening for a moment, then jumped down off the side. 'First customer of the evening, I think.'

Four quick steps took him to his position behind the bar and he fixed a smile on his ruddy features as the sprucely dressed man approached him. 'Good evening, Mr Davies. How have things been today?'

Jonathan Davies thumped the thick cardboard file that he had been carrying down onto the polished surface of the bar. 'Fraser, I think that I can say in all honesty that things have gone rather well today.'

'Glad to hear it. So, what will it be?'

'Just a half-pint of lager, please.'

The barman reached up and took down a glass from the rack above the bar. 'So what's the latest on the golf course?'

'Things are progressing.'

That was as much as he was prepared to say. He had always been careful not to discuss the project too openly in front of the locals, other than with those who were directly involved or when he was keeping to a strict agenda at a public meeting, and he certainly wasn't going to start discussing it with Fraser, the barman. He had learned that lesson the hard way, having once let slip the merest titbit of confidential information to the man, which not only reached the ears of every resident in a five-mile radius within a time span of about four hours, but did so with an appalling degree of distorted embellishment. He had also the strongest suspicion that it had been Fraser's gossiping bar-talk that had provoked the affront that Liz had suffered at the last meeting.

So he simply smiled a thank-you to the grinning barman, picked up the glass of beer and his file, and moved over to one of the tables to await the arrival of the others.

With a synchronous jerk at each trouser leg, he settled himself in his seat and took a sip of beer. Then, flicking the bands off the file, he took out a printed sheet of paper and began to give its contents a final run-through.

Even though it hadn't taken him long to work out what his tempting 'apple' was going to be, he still felt a pang of anxiety about the impending meeting. It wasn't so much that he felt that the offer was insufficient, but more that he had begun to have second thoughts about inviting Gregor, thinking, in retrospect, that it may have been more tactful to approach both parties separately. But then, this was crunch time. At this stage, he couldn't afford to appear kind and considerate, even though it went against his better nature. If nothing even remotely began to swing in his favour during this meeting, he would be left with no alternative other than to inform them of his plans to pull out.

But what a bloody waste of time and effort that would be, not least taking into account the resources that his consortium had already ploughed into the project to cover the research and development, the marketing and planning. He had always been able to keep quite upbeat at investors' meetings, because invariably there had been new progress to report, and he had always been able to skirt around any issue that related to the owners of the land. However, if the project were to fall through at this advanced stage, then challenging questions would be asked of him about why he had chosen not to bring these problems to light beforehand, and at that point his integrity and business capability would no doubt become the subject of debate.

He scanned the sheet of paper again. He could offer no more. He simply could not *afford* to offer more. It was crunch time for everyone.

The door opened and closed with a bang, and he looked up to see Liz walking towards him. She was dressed in a short brown corduroy skirt and yellow cotton shirt that she had tucked loosely into a broad silver-buckled belt, and a large leather handbag hung by a long strap from her shoulder. The trailing fringe of her otherwise short blonde hair was swept to the side, held in place above her right ear by a small gold clasp, the full effect being one of wholesome simplicity rather than alluring sophistication. There was no doubt that he found her attractive, but it was more in a protective nature, always being aware that there was an expression of deep hurt and acute vulnerability ever-present in her hazel-brown eyes. She gave him a faint smile of greeting as she approached, and he quickly slipped the sheet of paper back into the file and rose to his feet to greet her. 'Liz, how nice to see you.' He gave her a kiss on either cheek. 'Come and sit down. Is your father on his way?'

Liz slid the handbag from her shoulder and hung it on the back of a chair opposite to the one that he had been occupying. 'No, I'm afraid not. He had things to do.'

'Oh dear. That's a pity.' He made no effort to hide the disappointment in his voice. 'Well, what can I get you to drink?'

'Just an orange juice, please.'

He walked over to the bar, noticing that Fraser was sidling a glance past him at Liz, a half-laughing sneer of disdain on his face. 'One orange juice.' He missed out on the 'please' on purpose. Leaning both hands on the bar, he watched vacantly as Fraser went about his business. Dammit, this was going to be a disaster. He had been counting on the presence of Liz's father to temper the whole meeting. Now, not only was he going to have to try to sell the addition to his financial package, but he was also going to have to tread as carefully as a bloody marriage counsellor. Hell, why was he worrying about *that*? As soon as her husband walked through that door, Liz was probably going to get up and leave anyway.

The door swung open and Gregor's square, muscled figure appeared. Davies turned, pressing his back against the bar and glancing quickly from one to the other, as if about to witness an almighty shoot-out in a Western saloon. Liz had seen him now – but she made no movement to leave. In fact, she still had that same smile fixed on her face. It was Gregor who looked more ill at ease, taking what seemed like an eternity to walk the short distance from the door to the table, never taking his eyes off Liz, as if he fully expected some show of hostility at his appearance. But nothing happened. Davies turned back to the bar and quickly paid for the orange juice so that he could return to the table to mediate.

'Gregor, thanks for coming,' he said, his voice sounding jolly to cover for his uneasiness. 'What can I get you to drink?'

'Don't worry. I'll get myself something.' He was still looking at Liz as he spoke. He nodded at her. 'Liz?'

'Hullo, Gregor.' Her voice was calm, almost resigned.

Davies gave an inward sigh of relief. So far, so good. He placed the orange juice in front of Liz and sat down opposite her.

'I didn't know Gregor was coming,' she said quietly.

Davies pushed back his chair, then leaned forward,

resting his elbows on his knees. He linked his hands and began to turn his thumbs nervously around each other. 'I know you didn't. I'm sorry if it upsets you, but I just—'

'It doesn't upset me.' Her tone hadn't changed.

Davies nodded and smiled at her. 'I'm glad.'

Gregor pulled out the chair next to him and sat down, placing his pint of beer on the table. Davies slapped his hand down on top of the file. 'Well, I think that we'll just get started, shall we?' He opened up the file and took out the sheet of paper. 'Right. I'll start with the good news. I received word today that we have the full complement of money necessary for the project.' The news was greeted with silence from both parties. Davies let out a short cough of apprehension before continuing. 'Anyway, so we are now in the position to move forward – that is, if we can come to some sort of agreement. Now . . .' he followed on quickly so as to give Liz or Gregor little chance of interrupting, '. . . I have drafted out here a codicil which I would add to the purchase agreement, copies of which you will both have already.' He handed each a sheet of paper. 'It states that The Balmuir Sports Development Company would be willing to give you full market value of growing crops in all fields which have been designated for development.'

'That's my whole farm,' Liz murmured, almost inaudibly.

'Yes, I do understand that, Liz.'

'Are you talking about market price at time of harvest, or just cost of production?' Gregor asked.

'No, full market price at harvest, taking a mean average

of yields in the area. Now I think that this is a fair offer, and one that my consortium should quite rightly put forward, considering that we did not have our financial package in place at the time of sowing.' Out the side of his eye, Davies caught Gregor slowly nodding his approval. 'So, at this precise time, we are ready to move, and all we need now is your acceptance of the offer.'

He sat back and crossed his arms. That was it. He'd said it. Now it was up to them. Either they agreed, or he would have to start telling them of his alternative plan.

Gregor glanced across at Liz, then back to Davies. 'Well, you know my answer.'

Davies nodded. 'Liz?'

Liz picked up her glass of orange juice and drained it, and as she got to her feet and slung her handbag over her shoulder, the two men watched open-mouthed, like children who had had newly opened presents snatched away from them. She saw this and smiled in amusement. 'Don't worry. I'm not going to disappoint you both. We'll agree to it.'

Davies's mouth fell open even further. 'What?'

'Are you sure, Liz?' Gregor asked, a measure of concern in his voice.

'Yes. Both Dad and I are sure.'

'My word!' Davies couldn't believe that it had been that simple. 'Well!' It was on. The project was going ahead. He slapped his hands down hard on his knees and jumped to his feet. 'In that case,' he exclaimed, now making no effort to control his excitement, 'I think that we should bust open a bottle of champagne right now.'

Liz held up her hand to refuse the offer. 'Thank you, Jonathan, but it's not really a moment of celebration for my father or me. We heard today that the bank has foreclosed on us and, well, that's the reason why we felt that we had little option other than to accept your offer. But thank you, anyway, and if you will excuse me now, I think that I'd like to go home.'

'Of course,' Davies replied, recovering his decorum.

Liz smiled at him, then cleared her face of all expression and nodded a farewell to Gregor. She turned and walked out of the lounge bar without looking back.

The two men stood in silence, their eyes fixed on the door of her departure. Gregor turned and picked up his pint glass and quickly drained it. 'Give me a moment, Jonathan.'

Liz slid into the driving seat of the Land Rover and put the keys into the ignition, then sat back and let out a long sigh. She caught sight of her face in the rear-view mirror and closed her eyes, not wanting to look at the person who had betrayed her ideals, who had given up the fight. It's finished, she thought to herself, you've capitulated – and what on earth are you going to do with yourself now?

She turned the key and the old vehicle spluttered to life. She reversed quickly and spun the wheel, looking to the front in time to see Gregor jumping aside to avoid her. She stopped abruptly. Déjà vu. This had all happened before. She sat watching him for a moment as he made no move to approach her, then slowly she reached forward and turned off the engine.

Gregor walked tentatively over to her door and opened

it, and rested his shoulder against the side of the vehicle, his body facing in towards her. 'I was just wondering . . .'

She turned to face him. 'What?' she asked aggressively.

'If you were all right.'

She sniffed out a derisive laugh. 'No, not really. Would you be?'

'No. I mean, I'm not – either. I got a letter, too.'

She looked straight ahead through the windscreen, fixing her eyes on the lettering of the pub sign. Anything rather than to have to look at him. 'From the bank?'

'Aye. They've foreclosed on us too.'

Us. That was a good one. She paused before replying. 'So that meeting was make or break for you too.'

'For all of us, I think.' He dug his hands into his pockets and cast a nervous glance about him. 'I'm sorry that it had to end this way, Liz.'

'What are you sorry about?'

'The farms – that they both went to the wall.'

Liz nodded. Ah, that, she thought to herself. For a moment, I thought you were apologizing for something else. 'So what are you going to do now?'

Gregor shrugged. 'Don't know. I suppose I'll have to start looking for a job in farm management.'

'Around here?'

'Not specifically. There's nothing much to keep me around here.' He bit at his lip, realizing what he had just said. 'Sorry. I didn't mean it that way.'

Liz nodded.

'How's Alex?' he asked.

'Fine.'

'I'd like to see him sometime, Liz.'

'I'll tell him.'

'I mean, I really would like to see him.'

She understood his meaning. Well, why not? Things were different now, especially if he was going to be moving away. There was no reason to deprive her son of a father, or vice versa. After all, what was it her own father had said about having to start to make the best of things the way they were? She turned to look at Gregor. 'I'll ask him if he would come over to see you.'

Gregor smiled at her. 'Thanks.'

There was another uneasy silence. No need for any more, Liz thought to herself. She turned the ignition key.

'I never knew you liked the theatre.'

Her hand froze on the key. 'What?'

'The theatre.' There was a brightness to his voice; she couldn't tell whether it registered inquisition or just interest.

'How did you know about that?'

'Jonathan Davies told me. He came around to your house that night you went out.'

'Ah, right. Well, in answer to your question, yes. I do like the theatre – and the opera, for that matter.'

'That's good to hear.' He let out a long breath. 'And this is, erm, Alex's professor that you've been going with.'

'Yes, it is.'

'Nice man, is he?'

Liz turned to look at Gregor. He stood now with his back to her, his face looking down, and she leaned forward enough to see that it was a six-inch nail that he must have had in one of his pockets that he now turned over and over in his fingers. Why was he asking these questions? He's not – no, surely he's not *jealous*.

'Yes, he's *really* nice.' Go on, girl, overplay it. See what happens when you dig in the knife a bit. 'He's funny. He's wonderful to talk to. In fact, he's just great company.'

Gregor nodded. 'I'm glad. I think you, well, deserve it.'

Liz turned the ignition key and started the engine. 'Yes, Gregor, so do I.' She closed the door of the car, and in doing so felt a rush of exhilaration flood through her body for the first time in countless months. She pressed her foot on the accelerator and took off, glancing back in her side mirror at Gregor. What was he doing now? Why was he running after the car?

He pulled open the door, forcing Liz to stop abruptly. As she did so, a small Mini Metro pulled into the pub car-park. 'You won't forget to ask Alex, will you?'

Liz did not answer. Her eyes were fixed on Mary McLean as she got slowly out of the car. Gregor turned to follow her line of sight.

'Gregor?' Mary asked. Liz was sure she could detect a tremble in her voice.

'Hi, Mary,' he replied quietly.

'What are you doing here?' Yes, there was a definite tremble.

'We had a meeting – with Jonathan Davies, that is.'

'Why didn't I come?'

'Well, I . . .'

'I think I'll leave you two to sort this out between yourselves,' Liz cut in. She closed the door and drove out to the edge of the car-park, and having checked the road she swept out, catching a glimpse in her rear-view mirror of both Gregor and Mary standing at a distance from each other and staring at her departing vehicle.

Anyone who might have happened to witness her driving through the village and up the hill and around the corner to the farm road might well have thought she was under the influence of drink, because she laughed uncontrollably the whole way at the thought of Mary McLean's simpering hurt. And what made the pleasurable ache in her stomach even more acute was the fact that she *had* been seen. Miss Mouncey, Balmuir's nervous little spinster, had been scuttling along the pavement on her way back from the church, her little basket no doubt containing her tin of Brasso and an abundance of polishing cloths, when Liz had driven past at speed. The sight of her jumping like a frightened mouse and diving into a shop doorway to conceal herself had nearly been enough to cause Liz to steer the Land Rover into a parked car.

She made it to the end of the farm road and stopped, and slowly began to bring herself under control. That had been quite *wonderful*. If she had tried to stage-manage that herself, it could not have turned out more perfectly. She imagined what it must have been like for Mary seeing her boy-friend running after his ex-wife's car and yanking open the door.

What on earth could she ever think he was doing, other than proclaiming undying love for his estranged wife? She laughed again at the thought. Perfect retribution without an iota of malice on her part. And what about Gregor? It *had* to have been some kind of jealous pang that had fired those questions. There could be no other explanation.

She suddenly felt a comforting sense of well-being again, of self-control, of self-confidence. She put her foot down on the accelerator, but then immediately took it off as her eyes focused on the farm in front of her, the green fields sweeping down to the shoreline, and a small dark cloud of nostalgia and loss rolled across her bright sun of new-found elation. It was gone. Nothing could save it now – and as Gregor had said, there wasn't much to keep them around now. The glint came back to her eyes. No, there wasn't, was there? And why not? Even Gregor had said that she deserved it.

She slammed shut the kitchen door behind her, catching Leckie as he bounded towards her and jumped into her arms. She made her way through to the hall and opened quite forcefully the door of the sitting-room and walked into a thick cloud of pipe smoke. Her father and the professor sat opposite each other each clutching a fan of cards, two small glasses of Jack Daniel's placed on the carved oak coffee-table between them. Both gave her a look as if they had just been caught red-handed in some illicit speakeasy. Then the farmer saw the expression on his daughter's face and a wide smile spread across his wrinkled cheeks.

Liz let out a long breath. 'Arthur?'

The professor pushed himself out of the sagging sofa, his expression of guilt now turning to one of consternation, as if he might be trying to work out what new household misdemeanour he could have committed. 'Yes?'

'I was wondering if you had found anyone to go with you to Seville.'

Arthur's shoulders dropped quite visibly in relief. He shook his head. 'No. Actually, I haven't bothered to try. Why do you ask?'

'May I come with you?'

The two men glanced at each other and Liz detected the merest sense of conspiratorial triumph in their eyes. The professor turned and gave her a gentlemanly bow. 'Liz, I would be delighted if you came! And I promise you that I would adhere to all our conditions.'

She smiled at him, then looked down at her father, whose face had not yet lost its Cheshire-cat grin. 'Hullo, lass,' he said.

CHAPTER 13

The contractors moved in on the last work-day of the second week in April, two days before Palm Sunday. Their heavy machines lumbered down the road to Brunthill, their tyres so wide that, in one pass, they reduced the grass verges to the same level as the road, and when they found that they were unable to make the tight turn around the steading, they took down twenty yards of the roadside fence to gain access to the fields. There was no one at the farm to witness this event, nor to see later, in the bottom field directly below the house, the lush green carpet of malting barley that had shown such promise of yielding a bumper crop being unceremoniously scraped away and thrown into great heaps by the gleaming blades of the bulldozers.

Mr Craig stayed with Liz and the professor at Edinburgh Airport until he had seen them through to the security section, the latter never giving a backward glance as he disappeared into the screened-off area, his constantly worn raincoat flapping out behind him. Liz, however, turned and gave her father a final wave and he knew from the look on her face that she felt both trepidation and excitement at the thought of her incipient holiday. But she managed a smile and blew him a kiss and then was gone.

He turned and walked slowly back along the wide stone-floored arcade, glancing in at the shops that sold vacuum-packed smoked salmon and ties and pieces of designer luggage, none of them being of any interest to him. He stopped briefly at the newsagent's to buy a paper, then descended the stairs and walked out of the terminal building and across the road to the short-term car-park.

The weather in the earlier hours of the morning had promised much, but now the wind had freshened and the sun was allowed only moments to radiate its warmth as high broken clouds slid endlessly across its face in the pale-blue sky. He held hard to the door of the Land Rover as he clambered in, then closed it with a jarring clatter and threw the paper onto the passenger seat. He did not start the vehicle immediately but sat back to watch the endless movement of people around him, every one industrious in his pursuit, whether it was trying to work out how to cram various pieces of luggage into a too-small boot or making a mad dash to catch a soon-departing plane with ticket clamped between teeth so that hands could juggle with brief-case, overnight bag and car keys.

But there was no hurry for him. For the first time in his whole life, there was absolutely no hurry. He had arranged for Bert, the tractorman, to feed the few orphan lambs that were still dependent on the bottle, there being little else left for the old boy to do. That had been a sad moment, bringing to an end his thirty years of loyal stewardship, but he was past retirement age at any rate and it had not been difficult to tell, by the beady glint in Bert's eye, that the news of one month's notice was more than assuaged by the mention of a healthy redundancy payment. However, there was no more tractorwork to be done. The big John Deere and his own trusty Fordson Major, along with all the implements and all the livestock, everything right down to the broken-shafted fencing mallet, would be sold at public auction the week after Liz returned from Spain. He had tried to arrange for it to happen beforehand, but the auctioneers had been unable to come up with an earlier date. So time was his own. There was certainly no need to go back to the farm straightaway.

He parked three-quarters of the way up the Royal Mile and made his way slowly up the cobbled street to Edinburgh Castle. He stood high on the battlements, craning over to look down on Princes Street and its two parallel thoroughfares, George Street and Queen Street, then far out across the intricate layout of the New Town to the river Forth and beyond to Fife. He waited there until he had witnessed the ceremony of the one o'clock gun being fired, and then set off back towards his car, stopping in at an old lead-windowed pub for lunch. He sat in the corner with a half pint of beer and a plateful of haggis and mashed turnip and read his newspaper, feeling quite out of place in his old market suit amongst the gaudily dressed tourists and the casual refinement of the townsfolk. And it was that sense of not belonging that suddenly made him feel quite lonely, and he thought of Kathleen, his dear, sweet, quiet wife, and wished that she could have been there, to watch and to discuss the people about them as they had done countless times before. He folded his paper and got up, leaving his beer and food half-finished, and once outside the pub he felt that he had had enough of the hustle and bustle of the city and decided to start making his way home.

Although the traffic coming out of Edinburgh was light, he took his time in driving back to the farm, criss-crossing Fife on a nostalgic journey along a multitude of B-roads which took him through parts of the county, past farms and properties, that he had not seen for many a year, parts that he had never seen without Kathleen by his side. On numerous occasions, when a memorable view would come into sight, he would pull over into a lay-by and sit for a time just looking – and thinking. Consequently, when he did eventually walk back into the farmhouse kitchen it was evening, the clock on the wall making its last movements towards eight o'clock.

Alex turned as he entered, a cooking pot in his hand. 'Hi, Granddad, I was expecting you to be home long before me.'

The cap came off the farmer's head and was discarded with customary precision onto the central worktop. 'Aye, well, I just thought I'd take my time.' He walked past his grandson, glancing in at the contents of the pot. 'Baked beans, eh?' He let out a chuckle. 'That should get you going.'

Alex gave him a sheepish look. 'Is that all right? I'm afraid that I'm not much of a cook.'

Mr Craig crossed over to the table and sat down. 'Don't worry about me tonight, lad. I had a big lunch. Anyway, I think we might just go down to the pub for something to eat in future, don't you think?'

'Well, it would certainly save you from being poisoned by me.' He paused as he stirred the pot. 'Only thing is, Granddad, that I did say to Mum that I might head across to see Dad a couple of times.'

'Of course you did, Alex. That's a good thing to do.'

'So, did they get off all right?'

'Aye.'

Alex laughed. 'Poor Mum. I reckon that if she had known the state that she was going to get herself into over her passport and trying to find clothes to wear, she might have given the whole thing a second thought.'

'Aye, well, I think she did on more than one occasion. But I'm sure that she'll have a rare old time once she's out there.'

Alex ladled out his beans onto a plate. 'Did you see the state of the road fence on your way in?'

'I did. I suppose that's something that we're just going to have to start putting up with.'

Alex carried his supper over to the table and sat down next to his grandfather. 'They've started already, you know. Down in the bottom field. It doesn't look that attractive, either.'

'No, I don't suppose it does. I think I'll just leave it to the morning before I go to have a look at it myself.' He leaned his elbows on the table. 'So, what's been happening with you today?'

Alex swallowed a mouthful of beans and bread. 'I've been caddying on the Old Course all day.'

His grandfather looked surprised. 'Have you now? I thought that you weren't going to start that until the summer holidays.'

'I wasn't, but I don't have much work on at the minute and I'm in dire need of a few extra pounds in my pocket, so I just went down to the caddymaster's office on spec. He said that there were plenty of golfers needing caddies, and told me to roll up whenever I had time on my hands.'

'So it was worth it, was it? Got some big tips?'

'Well, to start with, I thought it was going to be a disaster. I went off with a Japanese foursome at just after ten o'clock, and we took all of five hours to get round. They were in and out of bunkers, taking photographs of each other, and the time that they took to line up putts! You'd think that every one was to win the Open! But, to be quite honest, it wasn't that funny. We were holding up play behind and the course rangers kept giving me and the other three caddies stick for not getting them to move faster. And then, of course, none of the Japanese knew how to speak English – or they pretended not to know – and they never took any notice of our efforts to get them shifting. I mean, even on the eighteenth green, they spent about five minutes bowing to each other and shaking hands after they'd finished.'

Mr Craig shrugged. 'Och, well, I suppose one can

understand them wanting to savour the moment. It probably was the highlight of their lives, like Muslims visiting Mecca.'

'Yes, Granddad, but there is a code of conduct, you know.'

He grinned at his grandson's admonishment. 'I'm sure there is, lad. So that was it, I take it. You got no more work after that.'

'Well, I decided to hang around for a bit, even though the other caddies had decided to finish, and just before a quarter to four the caddymaster called me over and asked if I could do a round with a single person on the Jubilee. So I did – in three hours dead.'

'Heavens! You must have been fair hurrying the poor man.'

'Well, for a start, it wasn't a man. It was this very small, fairly old Australian lady, and I tell you that I had to stop myself from bursting out in laughter when I first saw her, because she was standing there with this enormous Titleist bag beside her that just about dwarfed her. Anyway, I said to the caddymaster that I would take her out, even though I had a strong suspicion that we would still be playing at midnight.'

'And you were proved wrong.'

'And how! She turned out to be a terrific golfer! She had this huge swing, which is pretty amazing for someone of her age, and she could hit the ball for miles. She sort of defied all those laws of physics that have anything to do with size and power. She actually ended up going round the Jubilee in only nine over par.'

Mr Craig cocked his head to the side. 'Must have been some lady.'

'She was. Actually, I didn't know if I was going to like her, to begin with. She didn't speak much other than to ask about club selection and distances. I put it down to her being a little off-hand at first, but as we played, I began to realize that she just seemed . . . well . . . a bit sad, as if she might have been widowed recently. She didn't wear a golfing glove, though, so I could see that there was no wedding ring on her finger. Anyway, I thought I'd make an effort to break the ice a bit, so I told her about how I was at university in the town, and after that she really opened up and showed genuine interest in what I was doing. The long and the short of it was that, because of the way she played and the amount of talking we did, the time went past really quickly, and at the end of the round she handed me a tip that was twice the size of the one I got from my Japanese guy.'

'So it was all worth it, then?'

'Yes, it definitely was. In fact, I was just thinking that I might do it again tomorrow and then get back to studying on Monday.'

Mr Craig pushed himself to his feet.

'What are you going to do?' Alex asked.

His grandfather laughed. 'What? Now, or for the rest of my life?'

'No, I meant now.'

He walked towards the door that led into the hall. 'Well, I thought that I might just get myself a wee tipple of Jack Daniel's, and then teach you how to play cribbage.' He turned to look at his grandson. 'That is, if you've got nothing else to do.'

Alex shook his head. 'No. You can bring me a "tipple" too, if you like.'

Mr Craig flicked his head to the side and let out a resigned sigh. 'Aye, well, I suppose you're of that age now.' He opened the door, and as he entered the hall, Alex heard him laugh. 'All these bad habits have been introduced by your professor, you know,' he chortled in the distance.

CHAPTER 14

The moment she slid open the balcony window of her bedroom on the fourth floor of the Hotel Cazaral, the sterile frigidity of the air-conditioned room was invaded by the comforting warmth of Seville's night air. It carried on its breath the aromatic cocktail of watered vegetation mixed with a slight hint of drains and petrol fumes, the latter emanating from the grumble of traffic that moved unceasingly along the wide Avenida de Menéndez y Pelayo below. Liz stepped out onto the balcony and stood for a moment taking in the city's sultry air before moving forward to the iron railings and opening the street map that she had found on the bedside table. Directly in front of her, she could just make out the dimly lit paths of the Murillo Gardens stretching along the backbone of the avenue, the spiky silhouettes of its palm trees only just distinguishable against the dense backdrop of foliage that secreted the Alcázar Palace from view. Beyond that in the distance, scraping at the very roof-top of the city, the cathedral's vast, ornate mass and towering Moorish spire stood out against the night's horizon, fixed in fiery illumination. She glanced to her left and watched as the traffic merged around the Plaza Don Juan de Austria before breaking free of its constraints down the Avenida del Cid. She stretched her hands along the railings, becoming aware at that point of the unaccustomed smile of contentment that transfixed her face. This was different. This was exciting. Less than one full day away from Scotland, and already distance had begun to create a new perspective in her mind, the whole cultural change and the upsurge in temperature squeezing the rancour from her spirit and overriding the problems and worries that had engulfed her over the past months.

Yet she was fully aware of the fact that the day had not started on such a carefree note. When she had left her father that morning at Edinburgh Airport, she had been a jangle of nerves and of mixed emotions, both at the thought of flying for the first time and by recriminations at leaving him to deal with all the legal papers involving the sale of the farm. Consequently, from the moment that she had turned to give him a final wave and had seen him standing alone and altogether quite vulnerable, she had been totally uncommunicative towards Arthur, the whirlwind of thought that had spun through her brain quite wrongly blaming him for enticing her away from her father and away from home. But, to give him his due, Arthur seemed to have understood this immediately, and his blustering passage through the security channel had been the last solo act that he had carried out. Thereafter, he had been constantly at her side, never making demands on her company or trying to chivvy her along with jolly remarks about adventure and intrigue, but just being there, silently supportive. Then, after white-knuckling the armrests of her seat during take-off, she had sat by the window and watched as the landmarks grew smaller and the fields became nothing more than a quilting of green. It was at that point that she had been suddenly gripped by the exhilaration of it all, the size of the world fast diminishing below her and, along with it, the insignificance and unimportance of her own rankled existence.

The five-hour wait at Gatwick Airport for the Seville flight had been much longer than was normally necessary, but Arthur had admitted that he was always nervous of missing connections and had thus booked it with a safe, though maybe, in retrospect, excessive turn-around interval. Liz had bought a couple of postcards, one of Buckingham Palace and the other of a punk rocker with a bright green Mohican haircut, and had sent them to her father and to Alex, respectively. Then, over a coffee and Danish pastry, Arthur had pulled out a heap of guidebooks on Seville from his brief-case and had proceeded to pick out passages that were relevant to Semana Santa. Glancing at her over his smudged reading spectacles and puffing away on his momentarily lit pipe, he had read them out in a voice that could quite easily have indoctrinated everyone in the restaurant.

It was the thought of the Danish pastry that suddenly made her realize that she was feeling extremely hungry, having had nothing other than that and a few mouthfuls of plasticky airplane food to sustain her during the day.

The flight to Seville had been on time, but with the add-on of an hour for time difference, they had not landed until a quarter to ten at night. Consequently, by the time the taxi had dropped them off at their hotel, both she and Arthur had decided that they could wait until the morning before eating. But now, looking out from her balcony at Seville, she found that her appetite and energy had been rekindled.

Going back into the room, she picked up the telephone on the bedside table and dialled Arthur's room number. It rang without reply. Puzzled by this, she opened the door and walked along the corridor to his room. She knocked. Again, there was no reply. She lifted her fist to repeat the action, but at that moment the door sprang open. Arthur stood there in a pair of striped Viyella pyjamas, the top of which was buttoned up to the neck, with a tooth-brush protruding from the side of his mouth.

'Lij! Whashamatter?' he mumbled.

'Nothing. I was actually wondering if *you* were all right. I called you on the telephone, but you didn't answer.'

Arthur took the tooth-brush from his mouth. 'Sorry, I was in the bathroom. I didn't hear a thing. Why were you calling?'

'No reason in particular. Only I was just going to suggest that . . . well, never mind.' She paused and gave his attire a quizzical glance. 'Arthur, aren't you feeling quite hot in those pyjamas?'

'No, I'm bloody well not. I'm freezing. I can't find the control switch for the air conditioning.'

'Have you tried ringing reception?'

'Yes, but I couldn't make myself understood to the night porter. He doesn't speak any English.'

'Oh. Right. Well, do you want *me* to have a look?'

The expression on Arthur's face registered all too clearly his thought that if he had been unable to get to the root of the problem himself, then there was very little hope of Liz's working it out. Nevertheless, he moved aside to allow her entry before returning to the bathroom to continue brushing his teeth.

Liz stood in the centre of the room and surveyed the walls, but there was nothing obvious, other than the usual light switches. She walked over to the built-in wardrobe. 'Have you tried in here?'

Arthur appeared at the door of the bathroom, rubbing his face with a towel. 'Sort of.'

Liz pulled open the double doors and pushed aside Arthur's clothes, which he had already, quite uncharacteristically, hung up. The control box with the LCD read-out was on the back wall. She pressed the 'off' button and immediately the whirring fan slowed down and eventually stopped. She closed the doors. 'There you are. You know where it is now. At least for the time being, you won't feel as if you're back in Scotland.'

Arthur nodded. 'Thanks.'

Liz started to make her way back to the door of the room. 'Well, sleep well, then. I'll see you in the morning.'

'Wait a minute. You never told me what it was that you were wanting.'

'Oh, nothing. It wasn't very important.'

'Tell me anyway.'

She turned and smiled at him. 'Well, I was going to suggest that we might go out to get something to eat.'

'Oh, I see. But I thought that . . .'

'I know. I did say that I wasn't hungry, but I am now . . . anyway, it doesn't matter.'

Arthur held wide his hands and looked down to appraise his own dress. 'Well, I suppose I could change, but I don't know if we'd find anywhere at' – he glanced at his wristwatch – 'half past eleven.'

'Oh? I didn't gather that from your Spanish guide-books. You read out that they were "a nation of late eaters," and on a Friday night, I would have thought that they'd have eaten later than usual.' Arthur's reluctance to accept her idea was clearly displayed by the way that he puffed out his cheeks and screwed up his face and scratched at the back of his head. 'Anyway,' she continued quietly, 'please don't think any more about it. I can quite easily wait until the morning.'

Arthur's face lightened. 'Are you sure? You don't mind?'

'No, of course not.'

He moved forward and opened the door for her. 'I'm glad. To be quite honest, Liz, I'm feeling really flaked out. Travelling seems to take it out of me nowadays. But just you wait and see,' he exclaimed keenly, giving her a light, boys-together punch on the shoulder. 'I'll be right as rain in the morning.'

Liz smiled at him. 'Good night, Arthur.'

'Good night.'

Liz shut the door of her bedroom behind her and sat

down heavily on the edge of her bed. That was that, then. A good idea fallen flat. She could always call room service and order a sandwich, but then she might just get embroiled in an unintelligible conversation with the night porter. Anyway, that really had not been her initial impulse. She wanted to continue the day, to relish this new change in herself. Of course, she could still go out and try to find somewhere for herself, but she had no idea in which direction to go or even how to ask, and Arthur might quite easily be right in saying that it was too late. She picked up the television remote and flicked through the channels, but all the programmes seemed to have a political overtone and all were in Spanish. She turned it off, went over to her suitcase and took out a wedge of shirts and placed them on a shelf in the cupboard. She stopped, her hands still resting on the pile. Come on, she thought to herself, you're behaving like a spoilt schoolgirl. He *is* a bit older than you, although most things about him belie the fact, but you can't expect him to go burning the candle at both ends. And after all, he's been nothing but supportive of you all day, so he's more than entitled to call the tune for a change. In fact, why not try to do something you've been reluctant to do since the first time you met him? Why not just give the man a chance?

CHAPTER 15

Stopping at the bottom of the grassy bank, Mr Craig leaned both hands on the top of his carved ram's-horn crook and stood for a minute to catch his breath, watching as the Jack Russell flew past him and raced up the slope towards the house. Without hesitating in his stride, Leckie leaped up onto the stone wall that encircled the front garden and turned to watch the farmer, his cocked ears and quivering tail willing the old man to follow at a similar pace.

Mr Craig laughed and shook his head. 'You'll have to hold on a wee bit, Leckie. I canna quite keep up with you.'

He set his crook firmly in the ground and began to push himself slowly up the bank, digging the toes of his steel-capped boots into the soft ground to give himself better purchase, but even in doing so, there were a couple of times during the ascent when he had to grab at well-rooted grass tussocks to stop himself from tumbling backwards down the steep incline. When he had made it to the top, his feat was immediately acclaimed by Leckie with a furious round of congratulatory barking before he launched himself off the wall and into his master's arms.

'Canny now, wee lad!' he exclaimed as he fought to steady himself on the narrow plateau. 'You'll have me down at the bottom again if you carry on like that.' He turned, tucking the wriggling animal under his arm, and leaned against the wall to look back over the route just covered on his early-morning walk. Alex had been right. Even in one day, the contractors had managed to change the whole aspect of the landscape. The cut that they had made through the length of the bottom field stood out in blackened shadow against the verdancy of its surroundings, as brutally administered and as painful to observe as a razor slash on a human face. He let the dog drop gently to the ground and took from the pocket of his overalls the aging Instamatic camera with which he had already begun to record the metamorphosis of his farm. He held it to his eye and lined up the shot, but before he had time to click the shutter, a renegade cloud in the otherwise clear azure sky muscled its way in front of the sun, obliterating the shadow in the excavation and blending it in with the existing contours of the land. Mr Craig took the camera from his eye and squinted up at the cloud, a wry smile cracking the seriousness of his features. Maybe that's a sign from the Almighty, he thought to himself. Maybe He's saying to me, 'Look, don't bother taking a photograph of it looking like that. How about I just move this cloud a wee bit this way? There you are, that's not so bad now, is it?'

He curled the cord around the body of the camera and slid it back into his pocket, and, picking up his crook, he pushed open the gate and walked up the overgrown path to the front door. He turned once more to look out across the fields. The cloud had passed away from the sun and the shadow had reappeared. He reached into his pocket again for the camera, but then stopped and slowly withdrew his hand. No, he thought, it's not worth recording – not in this transitional stage, at any rate. You know yourself that your soul is deep-rooted enough in this piece of land to love it, regardless of its cosmetic appearance, so just be excited about what is to come, and not sad or reproachful about what has been. The vision of what it *was* like is instilled into your very being, so just turn your eyes from it all until such times as you can look down from this vantage point and see the tall fescue grass that will soon cover those stark brown banks waving in the breeze and the morning sun dance those shadows across the undulations of the newly grassed fairways. And be thankful to the Almighty that you'll still be in this house to enjoy it.

He kicked the mud from his boots and opened the front door and made his way as lightly as he could through the hall to the kitchen, knowing that his action of entering by that door while still wearing his working boots had been sacrilege in the eyes of his wife and a ruling still vehemently upheld by his daughter. He took off his cap and flicked it onto the central worktop, then stood surveying the kitchen. In the twenty or so hours of losing its female control, the room was fast coming to resemble a bachelor's residence, the sink brimming with unwashed dishes and the table still strewn with the previous day's newspapers. He took off his coat and hung it on the back of a chair, then set about clearing the surface of the table, folding up the newspapers and placing them on the pile of other reading material on the window-seat. He picked up the used cereal bowl and the half-full bottle of milk, and realized, at that point, that Alex must have already had his breakfast. He added the bowl to the tottering pyramid in the sink, then walked over to the refrigerator, noticing as he passed the worktop the hastily scribbled note half-hidden by his cap. He wiped his hands on the seat of his trousers and picked up the note, holding it at a distance so that he could focus on the writing.

> Granddad,
> It's 7:30 and I'm heading off. I want to get out early on the course and try to fit in three rounds today – make a bit of serious money. So don't hold back supper for me, because if I'm not too late, I'll probably drop in to see Dad on the way home. Anyway, I've made up a mountain of ham sandwiches, which should keep me going for the day. So I'll see you when I see you.
> Alex

'Good on you, lad,' the farmer said quietly to himself, balling up the note in his fist. He moved towards the rubbish-bin and then stopped, eyeing the plastic bag that stood on the worktop. He tipped the lid of the bin and discarded the note, then pulled the bag towards him and looked inside. It contained a large bottle of water and Alex's supply of sandwiches.

He shook his head. 'Alex, you dunderhead!' He pulled the handles of the bag together and tied them in a knot, then walked over to the back kitchen door and hung it on the latch. The Jack Russell, who had been lying on the window-seat, sprang down and ran towards the door, eagerly anticipating another action-packed walk, but his ears drooped in disappointment when the farmer turned away from it.

''Fraid not, Leckie,' he said, rolling up the sleeves of his shirt. 'And I'm afraid that you're going to have to stay here while I go into Saint Andrews. I'm not sure how long I'm going to be. But first,' he gave his hands a decisive rub, 'I'd better get this place sorted out.' And, moving across to the sink, he began running scalding water onto its overcrowded contents.

Having lost the morning to clearing up the house and to fleeting visits to the supermarket and the bank, Mr Craig did not arrive at the caddymaster's office until the gold-painted hands on the clock of the Royal & Ancient Golf Club had just clicked into alignment at midday. He took his place at the office window behind a small, immaculately dressed Japanese man in the pork-pie golfing hat who appeared to be having great difficulty with his limited knowledge of the English language in getting himself fixed up with a caddy whose credentials matched his specific requirements. Eventually, after a great deal of slow talking and multitudinous hand signals on the part of the caddymaster, the little man gave him a bow of gratitude and walked away with a smile of bemusement on his face. The farmer walked forward to the window, seeing the caddymaster let out a long sigh of relief. He smiled at the man. 'Having a bit of a trauchled day, are you?'

The caddymaster raised his eyebrows. 'No more than usual,' he replied morosely. 'I think sometimes, though, that this job would be more suited to some multilingual high-flyer rather than a mere mortal like myself. Anyway, how can I help you?'

'I was looking for my grandson. He's working for you at the minute. Alex Dewhurst.'

'Oh, Alex. Right.' He scanned his book. 'No, you've missed him. He came in about half an hour ago, but then went straight out again.'

Mr Craig clicked his tongue. 'That's a pity.' He held up the plastic bag. 'He forgot his lunch this morning.'

The caddymaster glanced at the bag in his hand. 'If you want, you could leave it here for him. Mind you, I don't think that he'd be much further than the third hole, if you want to get it to him quicker. It's getting quite slow out there on the Old Course now.'

The farmer nodded. 'In that case, I think I'll just take myself a wee walk. It's a good enough day for it.'

He thanked the caddymaster and turned to walk down the Tarmacked path that ran adjacent to the first hole. As he did so, the starter's voice sounded out over the loudspeaker. 'Next match play off, please.' He stopped and looked over to the first tee, where a brightly dressed golfer had already begun to settle himself into his shot. With a fearsome swish of his club, he let fly at the ball, and the farmer squinted his eyes in an effort to follow its path through the air. He lost it for a moment, then saw it land far up the fairway, but over to the right, dangerously close to the nearest point of the Swilken Burn. There was a loud guffaw from the other golfers on the tee as the shot was cheerfully castigated, and Mr Craig smiled to himself at the good humour of the whole proceedings. He turned and walked over to the bench that stood in the lea of the caddymaster's office and sat down, deciding that he would stay for a bit to watch the buzz of activity that surrounded this great arena. He was in no hurry, and he was sure that Alex could wait a further half-hour for his lunch.

As the golfers left the tee and began to make their way down the first fairway, he leaned back on the bench and crossed his arms, thinking to himself how easy it was, in living so close to St Andrews, to take for granted a view that would probably rank as the most famous in the golfing world. Behind the first tee, the imposing building of the Royal & Ancient Golf Club of St Andrews, with its pale stone walls, roof-top balustrades and ever-watched-through windows, stood proud sentinel over the great links course. At the far side of the broad fairway the deceptively sloping eighteenth green tucked itself hard in against the lattice-fenced bank, defying entry to its inner sanctum like a stag at bay, its front apron guarded by the Valley of Sin, the hidden dip in the ground which captured all those who displayed too much caution in hitting their approach shots to the heart of the green. Beyond that, creating the southerly wall of the rectangular amphitheatre and running almost the entire length of the eighteenth fairway, was the narrow road known as The Links. Its border was lined with an ill assortment of buildings, some whitewashed, others natural stone, some tall and austere, others small and pleasantly faced: shops, private dwellings, hotels and golf clubs clustered together with no regard to size nor shape. Farther out, where the course began to widen without the hindrance of buildings, the Swilken Burn meandered its way across the fairway, its diminutive width spanned in front of the eighteenth tee by the small, stone-arched Swilken Bridge, the definitive foreground for any photograph taken of this great golfing vista. And then, out still farther to the monolithic Old Course Hotel that fringed the seventeenth fairway, its magnificent position on the site of the old railway sheds affording its rooms the prime panorama of the Home of Golf. Aye, he thought to himself, there's many a human being on this planet who would sell his soul to be sitting where I am right at this minute.

He watched the next two foursomes tee off before deciding that it was time that he made a move. Picking up the plastic bag, he pushed himself to his feet and was about to move off down the path when he heard the sound of a woman's voice drifting around the corner from the caddymaster's window.

'Good morning. I was wondering if I could get a caddy to take me out on the New Course.' The farmer recognized the rounded tones of an Australian accent.

'I'm afraid that we have no one available, madam,' the caddymaster's voice replied. 'All the caddies are out on the Old at the minute.'

'Oh, *no*!' There was despondency, almost a hint of desperation in her reaction to the news. 'What do I do then?'

Mr Craig looked through the windowed front of the office to see if he could get a glimpse of the woman, but the caddymaster's body obscured his view.

'All I can suggest, madam, would be for you to go down to the starter at the New and he'd be able to fix you up with a trolley.'

'But I don't want a trolley. I can't manage one, and anyway, I don't know the course. I really do need a caddy.' The caddymaster offered no reply to this, and the farmer heard the woman let out a deep sigh of despair. 'Listen, I went out late yesterday afternoon on the Jubilee with a young caddy called Alex Dewhurst. If I waited until later, do you think that he might be available?'

Mr Craig nodded. He thought that that was who it was. He took a step forward and glanced around the edge of the building. She was dressed in a pale-blue polo shirt and Black Watch tartan trousers, and the arms of a yellow sweat-shirt were draped around her shoulders. The upper part of her face was hidden under a white sun visor, the top of which displayed a head of cropped greying hair. She wasn't as small as he had imagined – maybe about five feet three – but what certainly made her seem more diminutive was the enormous black Titleist golf bag that stood at her side.

The caddymaster let out a laugh. 'Ah, young Alex again, is it? He seems to be a popular lad this morning. His grandfather was here earlier on looking for him. I'm afraid

Alex is out on the Old at the minute, but if you'd like to come back . . .' The farmer moved behind the woman, into the caddymaster's line of sight. 'Oh, look, there's the gentleman behind you.' He addressed him. 'Did you catch up with Alex, then? This lady was wanting him to caddy for her later on in the afternoon.'

The woman turned and tilted back her head so that she could view the farmer from under her visor. He smiled at her. 'No, I've yet to go out. I've just been having a seat around the corner.'

The woman turned to the caddymaster. 'So you've no idea when he'd be available?'

'Sorry, madam. It could be three hours, it could be four. There's no easy way of knowing.'

She bit at her bottom lip, then shook her head in resignation. 'Well, I suppose it had better wait for another day,' she said quietly, almost to herself. She put her arm through the carrying handle of the golf bag and heaved it onto her shoulder and, with her body bent almost at right angles under its weight, she began making her way slowly up the path towards the clubhouse, her white-studded golf shoes clicking on the solid surface as she went.

Mr Craig nodded a quick farewell to the caddymaster and walked hastily after her. 'Excuse me.'

She stopped and turned around, letting the bag slip from her shoulder. 'Yes?' she said in a clipped voice that made her frustration all too apparent.

'I was just going to say that I'm about to head out across the links to meet Alex.' He held up the plastic bag. 'The lad forgot his lunch.'

'So?'

'Well, I was wondering if you would like me to carry your bag. I'd be quite happy to.'

The woman studied him for a moment before a smile came across her face. 'That's very kind of you, but don't worry yourself. Anyway, it's a pretty heavy bag.'

'Och, I'm sure I've carried heavier bags than this in my time.' And before she could open her mouth in objection, he took the bag from her and hoisted it onto his shoulder, his steely frame hardly bending under its weight. 'There you are, you see? I may be old-looking, but I've still got a bit of muscle left on me.'

The woman let out a quiet laugh. 'I didn't say that you were old-looking.'

Mr Craig gave her a wink and patted the side of the bag. 'Well, I just thought that you might be thinking that I looked a wee bittie ancient to manage this.'

'Not at all. The only reason I hesitated was that I know that Alex is out on the Old Course, and I want to play the New.'

'Aye, but they run parallel on the way out to the turn.'

She nodded. 'Yes, I'm aware of that.'

'Well then, there's a chance that I might catch up with him there, so I'd just nip across to the other course and give him his lunch.'

The woman gazed out across the links, contemplating his offer. 'Are you sure you wouldn't mind? I mean, do you have the time?'

He let out a laugh. 'Right now, I have all the time in the world.' He turned and began retracing his steps down the path, and if anyone, at that precise moment, had been looking out of one of the windows of the Royal & Ancient, they might have been quite amused at the sight of the tall, angular figure, formally dressed in a tweed jacket and cap, striding away down the side of the first fairway of the Old Course with the enormous golf bag on his shoulder, while, at his side, the short, stout woman half-walked, half-ran to keep up with his progress.

The New Course starter had been right in saying that play was fairly clear out in front of them because they managed to cover the first three holes in just over half an hour, mainly because the woman never seemed to hit a shot that deviated from a central line down the fairway. Mr Craig had begun to enjoy his walk, although he was surprised that any effort to make conversation with her was met with monosyllabic answers, and there had been no attempt at any form of introduction. At first, he had put it down to her being a tough little Australian with a somewhat off-hand manner, having witnessed at the outset of the round her terse refusal to the kindly invitation proffered by two elderly male golfers for her to join them on the course. But as she played he tempered his judgement, understanding that she was probably more content to be in her own company and to be able to lose herself in concentration on her own game. And then he remembered what Alex had said to him the night before, and he realized just how intuitive the boy had been. There was something sad about this woman, an aloofness, a need to be alone yet finding it hard to deal with her own loneliness. There was no doubt in his mind that those symptoms pointed to some acute loss in her life, for he himself recognized them all too well. But what was her loss? It certainly wasn't a husband. He didn't need to look at her hand to tell that. After forty-five years of married life, he just knew – just felt it in the way that she was, in the way that she acted. Yet it really was not his place to ask questions of her, and at any rate he was quite happy just to be out there on this warm, breezy day, running his errand for Alex and enjoying his impromptu exercise.

They played on to the fourth hole without hold-up, then walked through the narrow gorse-lined path to the fifth tee where, for the first time, they caught sight of the players in front of them, pacing the green 180 yards up the closed-in fairway. As they putted out and replaced the flag, the woman stood with her hands on her hips, contemplating the hole. She turned to look at him, her mouth squinted in pensive uncertainty. 'Well, what do you think?'

Mr Craig stared at her for a moment. 'What do I think?' He looked up the fairway to the hole. 'Well . . .' He placed the golf bag on the ground and walked over to stand beside her. He took his cap from his head and rubbed at the puckered wrinkles on his forehead. 'I would say,' he continued slowly, 'that it would look a good bit shorter – and probably even a good bit narrower than the holes we've played so far.' He nodded in finality. That was all he could think of saying about the hole. Nevertheless, he felt quite pleased with himself in being able to formulate what he hoped she would consider a constructive judgement on something about which he knew very little.

He replaced his cap and walked back to the edge of the tee and picked up the golf bag. When he turned to look at her, she was standing, still with her hands on her hips, observing him with her mouth hanging slightly open.

'When I asked the question "What do you think?" I was hoping that you might be able to tell me what club I should use.'

He frowned. 'Ah. Right.' He studied the clubs in the bag for a moment, then pulled out her driver, removing the soft velour cover to expose its gleaming head. He held it handle-out towards her, but she made no move to take it.

'But that's my driver.'

'Aye, well, it's the club you've used for your first shots up until now, and I would say that you're doing a pretty good job with it.'

The woman came towards him, a light smile stretching the corners of her mouth. 'You don't know much about the game of golf, do you?'

He shook his head. 'No. Not a thing.'

The woman laughed. 'I'm sorry. I was under the impression that your grandson must come from a long line of caddies.'

He looked at her quizzically. 'Now, what would make you think that?'

'Well, you seem to know the layout of the courses well enough – and then, when we started, you said that you'd carried heavier bags than mine in your time.'

Mr Craig's mouth opened in realization. 'Ah, well, then it's myself who should be apologizing. I had no wish to mislead you. I do know about the courses because I've walked around them a number of times with Alex. He's a fair golfer himself, you know. And as for the bags, well, I'm afraid that I was referring to fertilizer bags and the like. I've been a farmer all my days, you see.'

'A farmer!' the woman exclaimed, her voice breaking into a laugh. 'Oh, my word, I had no idea. I am sorry. What a mix-up.'

'I should have said something earlier maybe, but I didn't think that there was any need.'

'Of course there wasn't! I just naturally thought . . .' She paused for a moment. 'I am sorry. You must think me pretty dreadful.'

'I wouldn't say that.'

'Well, I would. I'm afraid that I've never been too communicative when playing golf at the best of times, especially—' She stopped talking abruptly and dropped her head, clenching her bottom lip between her teeth. Being unable to see her eyes under the sun visor, Mr Craig could not tell whether the action was to stop herself from saying something that might offend him, or to halt a break-out of emotion. His instinct told him the latter, and he therefore thought to diffuse the moment immediately with a cheerful act of friendliness. He took off his cap and held out his hand to her.

'Well, might I ask for whom do I have the honour of caddying?'

She tilted back her head and smiled at him. He had been right. He could see now that her eyes were glazed with tears. She reached out and took his hand. 'Roberta Bayliss.'

He felt the strength of her grip in his hand and gave it a solid shake. 'I'm very pleased to make your acquaintance, Miss Bayliss.'

'Roberta . . . please. And you are?'

'Craig's my name.'

'Well, Craig, it's a pleasure to meet you too.'

The farmer smiled. No doubt her immediate surmise was that Craig was his first name, thinking that he would be carrying the same surname as Alex. There seemed little point in putting her right. It might just cause another flurry of embarrassment, and he was sure that he could last out the round with the pretence. Besides, he had never been too enamoured with the Christian name that his parents had bestowed upon him. He glanced back up the fairway to the hole. 'Well now, Roberta Bayliss, let's get back to our game of golf. What do you reckon we should be using here?'

Roberta smiled at his inclusive remark. 'I think, Craig, that *we* should be using a four-iron.'

And so they continued the round of golf, conversation between them thereafter coming a little easier when her concentration on playing would allow. Nevertheless, the farmer was always aware of the marked reservedness in her nature, almost an unwillingness to offer any information about herself, and the questions she asked of him appeared quite forced, as if stemming from an obligation to be polite, rather than a need or desire to form any degree of friendship. However, in giving his answers as they walked, he had ample opportunity to study her features without giving rise to any affront on her part. She wasn't beautiful or pretty in the classic sense – she was too small and too solidly built for that – but there was a naturalness about her, a youthfulness that made it difficult for him to judge her age. Fifties? Yes, he thought, probably mid-fifties. Her face was untouched by make-up, yet it was remarkably smooth and unlined despite the fact that he could tell from the healthy glow of her skin that she was not one to spend many hours indoors, away from the heat of the Australian sun. When asking a question, she would tilt back her head to look up at him and he could make out below her visor a pair of striking blue eyes which he knew at one time must have sparkled with laughter and wicked humour, but now seemed filmed by dullness, like a metal that had lost its lustre.

Once free of the dense gorse-bushes that chevroned away from the eighth tee, the fairway of the long par-5 widened out to touch with the farthest reaches of the Old Course, at that point affording a close view of the players on the four 'loop' holes. Having waited until Roberta Bayliss had played her second shot, Mr Craig walked over to the fringe of rough grass that separated the two courses and, shielding his eyes against the glare of the sun, scanned the area for Alex. There was no sign of him. He glanced at his watch and made a quick mental calculation, working out that there was no way that he could have gone farther than this. He turned and made his way up the fairway to where Roberta was already standing by her ball, working out her next shot. She turned as he approached. 'Did you see him?'

He shrugged the bag off his shoulder. 'No! I doubt he's yet to reach here.'

Roberta was silent for a moment, her eyes drifting off to the left of the line that she would be taking for the next shot. She raised her arm and pointed. 'Would you think that's the furthest outward point on the Old Course over there?'

He followed her line of sight. 'Aye, it would be.'

She let out a sigh that seemed to quiver with trepidation. 'Well, in that case, I am going to want to excuse myself there for a bit, so I'm quite happy for you to wait until Alex arrives.'

'Will you not mind the gentlemen behind coming through?'

'No. I'm in no hurry.'

In playing out the hole, Mr Craig witnessed for the first time Roberta missing a shot, her third scuttling no more than twenty yards along the ground, and once she had made it to the green, she walked over to her ball and picked it up without bothering to putt it into the hole. She came over to him and put the ball back in the bag, then unzipped one of the larger pockets and took out what appeared to be a large, silver-topped Thermos flask.

She looked up at him, cradling the flask in both hands. 'Where will you wait for Alex?'

'I'll have a wee seat over there,' he replied, pointing to the bench that was positioned high at the back of the eighth tee on the Old Course.

'All right. Well, I'll just come to get you when I'm through.'

She turned and walked up onto the dunes and he stood watching her progress until she disappeared from sight.

He hefted the golf bag onto his shoulder and set off across the rough grass to the eighth tee on the Old.

The timing of their meeting could not have been better planned, because as he made it over to the bench he could see Alex approach the seventh green, skirting around the large bunker that stretched across its front. His grandson stopped and pulled a club from the bag and handed it to the golfer, and in casting a glance towards the hole, he caught sight of his grandfather. After a brief moment of uncertainty, he raised his hand in greeting, then, having watched the golfer play his ball to the green, he exchanged club for putter and walked across to where his grandfather was now seated on the bench.

'Hi, Granddad! What are you doing out here?'

Mr Craig held up the plastic bag. 'You left this on the kitchen table.'

'Oh, thanks, you're a star!' he exclaimed, taking the bag from him. 'I hadn't realized that I'd left it all at home until I parked the car in Saint Andrews.' He frowned in puzzlement when he caught sight of the golf bag that leaned against the bench. 'What are you doing with those?'

His grandfather chuckled. 'You'd wonder, wouldn't you?'

Alex dropped the golf bag that he was carrying to the ground and went over to take a closer look at the clubs. 'I know them. They belong to that Australian woman I caddied for yesterday afternoon.'

'Aye, they do. I saw her at the caddymaster's office and recognized her from your description. She wasn't able to get a caddy for the New Course, so I thought to kill two birds with one stone and volunteered my services.'

'Good for you. I hope she's paying you well.'

Mr Craig squinted the side of his mouth in dubious consideration of his grandson's remark. 'Well, if reward is based on knowledge of the game, I think I'd probably end up having to pay her!'

Alex laughed and turned to survey the area around them. 'Where is she, then?'

He pointed a thumb over his shoulder. 'Up behind there on the dunes. She wanted to excuse herself.'

'Ah, right. So she's playing by herself again.'

'Aye, she is.'

'Not much fun for her, is it?'

'No, I wouldn't think it. I would guess that she's quite a lonesome person.'

The large group with whom Alex had been caddying – four Americans with their respective camera-laden wives and three other caddies – had finished on the seventh green and were making their way across to the tee. Alex stooped to pick up the golf bag. 'Well, I suppose I'd better go and make myself useful.'

'Aye, you do that, lad, and I'll see you later on this evening.'

Alex nodded. 'All right, and thanks, Granddad, for bringing out my lunch.'

Mr Craig winked at his grandson. 'No bother.'

He watched the four Americans drive off, each of their shots making the green and being met with loud whoops of congratulations from the four wives, and as they set off down the short fairway, Alex turned and gave his grand-father a brief wave. He reciprocated, then settled back to wait for Roberta Bayliss.

There was still no sign of her by the time the second group of golfers following Alex's game had played from the tee, and at that point he began to feel a small measure of concern about her well-being. He glanced at his watch and worked out that he had been there for nearly forty minutes. Surely whatever she had to do wouldn't take her that long? He got to his feet and picked up the golf bag, and walked back onto the New Course and across to the edge of the last green that she had played. He laid down the bag in the short rough at the back of the green, then began to climb up onto the dunes, pushing aside the spiky reeds to clear a path for himself. Every ten steps or so, he stopped and called out her name – he thought, in this case, that it would be more fitting to address her as Miss Bayliss – but there was never any reply.

At the top of a large dune, he stood scouring the long ridge for any sign of her, his eyes sweeping round to take in the wide Eden Estuary, stretching across to the RAF air base at Leuchars on the other side. The tide was on the turn, the currents sweeping away at an alarming rate around the Out Head and into St Andrews Bay. He felt a knot of apprehension grip at his stomach as his mind raced back over his own assessment of her apparently sad demeanour.

'Oh, my word, lass!' he said out loud. 'I hope you haven't gone and done something foolish.'

He took a step nearer to the edge of the high bank and

once more scanned the ridge. Something caught his eye fifty yards over to his left, a splash of bright yellow against the pastel background of the dunes. It was the woman's sweat-shirt, laid out on top of the reeds as if to dry. He made his way towards it, moving as quickly as he could over the rough ground. And then he saw her, sitting on the pebbled beach below him, her back against the stone breakwater, staring blankly out across the estuary. He walked to within twenty yards of where she sat, then stopped, concerned that she might be still occupied in doing something to which he should not be witness.

'Miss Bayliss?' he called out quietly, so as not to startle her. 'Are you all right?'

She did not seem to hear him. He stood for a moment before making the decision to move closer. He moved down to the bottom of the bank and crunched noisily across the pebbles, hoping that the sound of his footsteps would warn her of his presence. He walked up and stopped directly in front of her. She had taken the sun visor from her head, and her cropped grey hair was ridged at both sides from where the band had held it tightly in place. She sat motionless, resting her chin on her knees, her hands clasped around her legs. The Thermos flask was wedged between her feet.

'Miss Bayliss, I don't mean to disturb you, but I was just getting a wee bit concerned. Are you all right?'

Still she neither answered nor made eye contact with him, and the farmer, taking this as a clear indication that he was intruding on her privacy, turned to leave. 'Well, I'll just away back and wait for you by the green.'

'Craig?' She spoke quietly, a choking falter in her voice.

He turned. 'Aye?'

'Please don't go.' She placed her hand on the ground beside her. 'I wouldn't mind having some company.'

Mr Craig eyed the place that she had indicated, thinking to himself that it offered a mite less comfortable seat for his bony posterior than it did for her own. 'All right, then.' He took off his jacket and, folding it up to afford himself some degree of padding, he walked across and placed it next to her, then slowly lowered himself to the ground, glancing across at her as he did so. He could tell from the puffed ruddiness of her cheeks that she had been crying. 'So what's been happening to you, lass?'

She turned and smiled at him, then let out a short laugh that immediately subsided into a tremble of emotion. 'Lass. If only. I'm nearly sixty-one, you know!'

Plucking out a white-bleached twig that lay caught between two large pebbles, the farmer drew up his long legs and rested his elbows on his knees, and began twiddling it between the thumb and forefinger of both hands. 'Well, you'd hardly think that.'

Without looking at him, she reached across and brushed her balled fist across his shirt-sleeve. 'Thanks for that.'

They sat together in silence, looking out across the estuary, a stretched arm's distance apart, but their adopted positions mirroring each other, the only sound being the swish of the light wind in the reeds above them and the rippling sweep of the waters being carried away on the tide. It was he who eventually spoke. 'So, Roberta Bayliss, what are you doing here so far from home?'

Roberta glanced down at the large Thermos flask that she held between her feet. She reached forward and picked it up. 'Do you really want to know?'

'Aye, if you want me to.'

She undid the top of the flask and handed it to him. He looked inside. There was no trace of liquid, but a light covering of grey dust clung to its cream-coloured plastic interior. He looked at her inquiringly.

She reached over and took back the Thermos, and having replaced the lid, she gripped the bottom of the flask in the palm of her hand and held it out in front of her, her elbow supported on her knee. 'That was my father. He is now no more. That's it.' She carefully placed the flask back between her feet. 'I brought him all the way from Sydney,' she continued, casting her eyes about her, 'and now he's where he wanted to be, blowing about in the wind on the furthest point of the Old Course at Saint Andrews.'

Mr Craig nodded slowly, everything now becoming clear in his mind, all the thoughts and theories that he had had about her suddenly beginning to fall into place. He wondered if he should say something, some standard form of condolence, but then felt that it might sound too glib or even too familiar. Better to remain silent and allow her to do the talking.

'He loved this place, you know. Of all the courses in the world that he had played, this was the one he loved the best. And probably the proudest moment of his life was when he was made a member of the R and A. It didn't happen until he was sixty, but by golly, from then on, he was over here whenever he could find reason, that usually being either the Spring or the Autumn Meeting. It was really the only time during the year that I didn't travel with him. He always said that it wouldn't be much fun for me, because when he wasn't playing golf, he'd spend his time sitting in the Big Room in the clubhouse, and as you probably know, women don't go in there.' She shook her head and let out a heavy sigh. 'Pretty ironic, isn't it? This is the only time I've ever got to come here with him.'

'And I would think,' the farmer said slowly, 'that it must have been an awful hard thing to do.'

Roberta smiled wistfully at him. 'Too right, it was. I had absolutely no idea that this was what he had planned until the lawyer read out the will to us all. My two sisters were really opposed to the idea. They said that it was too much to ask of me, having to come all the way over here and then having to play a round of golf during which I was to scatter his ashes.' She paused. 'But I knew I had to do it. It was my duty. You see, he wasn't only my father, Craig, he was my best friend as well.'

'Could you not have got someone to come with you?'

'No, not really. My two sisters are married and have their own families to worry about, and Mum's too old to take on such a huge trip. Anyway, Dad and I were always together on the golf course, so it just seemed right that we were together here.'

Mr Craig flicked the twig into the air and watched the

freshening wind take it off. 'So you'll now be having to make the long journey home?'

'Not until Tuesday week. I managed to get a cheap air ticket, but it meant staying quite a bit longer than I had intended. So I'll just be killing time until then. I might play a few holes of golf, if I feel like it.'

'Are you staying in the town?'

'Yes, in some guest house. It's run by a pretty pernick-ity widow called Mrs Winterbotham.'

Mr Craig laughed. 'Och, her! I know of her!'

'Do you?'

'Well, not personal-like. But I have a good friend who's had the displeasure of receiving the rough side of her tongue.'

There now being a coolness to the wind, Roberta got to her feet and pulled down her sweat-shirt from the bank. She put it around her shoulders before resuming her seat. 'Tell me about your family, Craig,' she said quietly.

He pushed out his legs and turned to lean his weight on his elbow. 'Well, to begin with, I have a son who lives in your country.'

'Really? Whereabouts?'

'Oh, a good way from you. Over on the west coast, in Perth. He's been out there for twenty-three years now. Married an Australian girl and they've got two kids, both at university.'

'Do you see them at all?'

'Just once in the last five years. Andrew has his own engineering business, so he's kept pretty busy. But then I have a daughter back here.'

'Alex's mother?'

'Aye, that's right. She and Alex live with me, seeing how's her marriage broke up last year.'

'And your wife?'

'I'm afraid that she passed away last year as well.'

Roberta turned to look at him. 'I'm sorry. What a horrible year you must have had.'

'Aye, well, things got kind of bad, but we're beginning to pick up the pieces and get on with our lives.'

Roberta gazed once more out across the estuary. 'Right now, I can't ever imagine myself being able to pick up the pieces.'

'Aye, you'll be thinking that at the minute, but you will do eventually. I felt the same way for a good few months after my wife died, but then different things began happening about us, and they all helped to bring a new focus into my life. It's a bit like driving for hours on a main road, and then turning off onto one that runs parallel and finding the scenery completely different, even though you're still heading more or less in the same direction. But you do need guidance to pick the right turning – if you like, someone who can do the map-reading for you. It won't happen any other way.'

There was a moment's silence before Roberta spoke. 'That's all very well, Craig, but in my life, my father was both the driver and map-reader, and I'm afraid that there's no one waiting in the wings to take over from him.'

Mr Craig pushed himself to his feet and stooped down to pick up his jacket. 'Well, I wouldn't be so sure about that. When you get back home, you try putting out your indicator for a time, just to show that you're ready to make the change, and I think that you might be surprised at who's waiting in the shadows to take over.' He held out his hand. 'But right now, we'd better be making a move before someone gets the idea that you've given up on golf and decides to walk away with your clubs.'

Roberta reached down to retrieve the flask and her sun visor, then took his hand and found herself pulled effortlessly to her feet. She smiled up at him without relinquishing her grip on his hand. 'Thanks, Craig, for your time. I have to say that I'm glad that I met you today.'

The farmer found himself quite nonplussed both by this physical contact and by the degree of affection in her voice, so he broke the moment by giving her hand a firm shake, as if being introduced to her for the first time. 'And that goes for myself as well, Roberta Bayliss.'

He stood aside to allow her to walk in front of him along the beach, and as she passed him by, she stopped. 'Craig, would you mind if we didn't play on the way in? I don't really feel like it any more.'

He nodded briefly. 'Aye, that's fine by me. That'll give me time to hear more about yourself.'

They took the most direct route back to the town, following the track that cut through the gorse-bushes between the two courses. Occasionally they stopped, either for him to drop the golf bag to the ground and to rest his shoulder for a while, or to allow players to drive off from a tee without distraction. Roberta talked animatedly as they went, recounting stories of her life in Sydney and of the travels that she and her father had experienced in visiting golf championships throughout the world, her only regret being that she had never once attended a British Open with him. They walked in at an easy pace, so much so that when they eventually passed by the caddymaster's office, the clock on the R&A clubhouse was fast approaching five o'clock.

The guest house where Roberta was staying was a good distance from the course, so Mr Craig was insistent that he should give her a lift, saving her from carrying the golf clubs any farther. They collected the old Land Rover from the car-park that lay adjacent to the Golf Museum, and then cut up through the town to her destination. Roberta pointed out the house as they approached, and he pulled the vehicle over to the side of the road beside the black wrought-iron railings. They both got out and he opened up the back door of the vehicle and took out her golf clubs.

'I can manage from here, Craig,' Roberta said, offering out her arm for the clubs.

'I wouldn't hear of such a thing,' he retorted, slinging the bag up onto his shoulder. 'A few more yards won't hurt me.'

Roberta smiled at him. 'Thank you.' She turned and walked up the steps to the front door and rang the doorbell. It was a full minute before the door was opened by a thin, austere-looking woman wearing a pink nylon housecoat and a pair of turquoise fluffy-toed slippers, her pale, powdered face set as expressionless as a death-mask. She stood in the doorway, as square as her meagre frame would allow, making no effort to move to the side.

'Have you not got your key with you?' the woman asked, glowering at Roberta through narrowed eyes. Mr Craig was amazed that she could utter a word with her mouth set in such an admonishing manner. He felt a smile come to his face. If there was ever a hen's arse of a mouth, that woman was the proud possessor of it.

'No, I'm sorry, Mrs Winterbotham,' Roberta replied, sounding like a schoolgirl who had just been reprimanded by her teacher. 'I'm afraid that I left it in my room.'

The woman folded her arms and stood aside. 'Well then, it's lucky for you that I was in the house.'

As Roberta made to enter the house, the woman glanced down at her feet and immediately stepped in front of her to deny her access once more. 'Those wouldn't be golfing shoes you have on, by any chance?'

Roberta looked down at her shoes. 'Yes, they are.'

The woman let out a petulant groan. 'Well then, if you had taken time to read the pamphlet in your room, you would have noticed that I have banned golfing shoes from being worn in my house. They do untold damage to my carpets. So please kindly take them off here on the doorstep.'

Roberta turned away from the woman and raised her eyebrows at Mr Craig, then sat down on the top step and began to unlace her shoes. He gave the golf bag a quick shrug-up onto his shoulder, then strode up the steps and, pushing past the woman, entered the house. 'Where can I put this?' he asked abruptly, a tremor of anger in his voice.

The woman made a show of rubbing at her elbow where the end of golf bag had lightly brushed against her. 'What do you . . . ?'

The farmer pointed to his feet. 'Listen, you crabbit besom, these are not golf shoes, so where do you want me to put this?'

There was a snort of laughter from Roberta as she bent over to pull off one of her shoes. The woman heard it and shot a lasered stare at the back of her head. She turned to Mr Craig and gave him the benefit of the same look. 'How dare you call me—'

'Och, woman, if you've got nothing nice to say, then don't bother saying anything at all.' He leaned the golf bag against the radiator shelf in the hallway, pushing aside a small figurine of a 'Shepherdess with Lamb in Arms' to make room for the club-heads. As he walked out of the door, the woman turned away, muttering to herself, and picked up the golf bag and started to struggle with it up the steep staircase.

Roberta pushed herself to her feet, golf shoes in hand, the expression on her face registering both mirth and nervous apprehension. 'Golly, Craig, I hope she doesn't throw me out after you saying that to her.'

He shook his head. 'No, she wouldn't dare. She's the kind who's all a-bluster until she gets challenged. Anyway, it just doesn't seem right that people come here to Saint Andrews to have a good time and then get confronted with someone like that.'

Roberta sighed. 'I know, but at least the place is cheap

and she does keep it spotlessly clean.' She passed her golf shoes over to her left hand and held out the other. 'Craig, I won't hold you up. I can't tell you how much I have appreciated your company today. You've really helped me through something that I've been dreading for ages.'

Mr Craig took her hand and shook it. 'Aye, well, people meet sometimes when they shouldn't and sometimes when they should, and I think that we've probably both been on a lucky streak today.'

'So do I.' She walked up the steps and into the house, then turned, her hand on the door. 'And please give my kindest regards to Alex, and say how much I enjoyed meeting him.'

'I will do.' He watched as Roberta gave him a final wave and closed the door.

He made his way down the steps and around the back of the Land Rover, waiting there until a car had passed by on the narrow street. He opened the driver's door and clambered in, and sat with his hands resting on the wheel. Up until the moment that they had arrived at the house, he had felt only deep sorrow for Roberta Bayliss, having made the long, lonely journey from Australia to scatter her father's ashes. But now guilt seemed to play its part in the equation, and he felt a responsibility in allowing her to be abandoned for over a week in that unfriendly household with that dragon of a woman who just happened also to be his fellow countryman. He thought back over what he had said to Roberta out on the golf course, and wondered if he had been stupidly insensitive in saying that someone might step out of the shadows when she got home. Having heard her story, he realized now that there had been no one else in her life besides her father. She would be returning to nothing, except a deep void that would never be filled.

He started up the Land Rover and put out his indicator to turn onto the street, and the very action in doing it and the clicking sound that emanated from somewhere behind the stark display panel made him stop the vehicle abruptly. He sat for a moment staring straight in front of him, then slapped his hand hard against the centre of the steering wheel. Dammit, he thought to himself, you're a stupid man. You couldn't see the wood for the trees, could you? You were so busy expounding your naïve philosophies on life, all about finding a map-reader and putting out an indicator, that you couldn't tell that her indicator was already out. If there was ever a time that Roberta Bayliss needed help, it was right now, and she was a hell of a lot more likely to benefit from it in this country than when she returned to her empty, pointless life in Australia. You've got the time, man, and so does she.

He sat for a further five minutes, his mind churning with thought, then he got out of the Land Rover and made his way up the steps to the house and rang the doorbell. The woman took less time to answer it, but her reception was decidedly more frosty.

'What do you want?' she asked curtly.

'I'd like to see Miss Bayliss, please.'

Without uttering a word, the woman closed the door on him. He waited for a full minute, and had just about come to the conclusion that she had ignored his request, when the front door opened and Roberta appeared. Her face lit up when she saw him. 'Hullo, Craig. Did you leave something in the golf bag?'

He shook his head. 'No, nothing like that.' He took off his cap and scratched at the back of his head. 'I was just wondering if you'd ever heard of Carnoustie?'

Roberta looked at him quizzically. 'Of course I have.'

'What about Gleneagles?'

'Yes.'

'Troon?'

Roberta laughed. 'Of course.'

'Well, I was sitting in the car just then, and I thought to myself that I didn't have much to do over the next week, and I wondered if you would like to go and play them. I mean, I would just drive you and carry your clubs. I couldn't play or anything like that.'

The sparkle that he sensed had been lost from Roberta's eyes suddenly returned. 'Are you being serious, Craig?'

He nodded. 'Never more so. I am in need of a bit of a distraction myself at the minute, and I just thought that it might be nice to see those places.'

'Well, in that case,' Roberta replied, her voice now alive with excitement, 'I would love to do that.'

'Good. I'm glad. There is another thing, though. I reckon that we'll have to be starting off quite early each morning, so I think it would be best if you saved me the trip into Saint Andrews by coming to stay with Alex and me out at the farm.'

Roberta shook her head. 'Oh no, Craig, I couldn't—'

'Aye, you could. It's part of the package. You can't have the one without the other.'

Roberta bit at her lip. 'But what would I say to Mrs Winterbotham?'

'Let's deal with one thing at a time. Do you want to take up the offer?'

She nodded eagerly. 'Yes, I'd love to.'

'Right.' He walked up the steps and into the house. 'Well then, in that case, you just leave Mrs Winterbotham to me.'

CHAPTER 16

Mary McLean leaned forward over the dressing-table and studied her face carefully in the mirror, rolling her lips together to make sure that her lipstick was applied evenly. Satisfied that there were no obvious smudges, she distanced herself slightly from the mirror and gave herself a final viewing, at the same time placing everything back in her make-up bag and fastening the zip. She glanced at her watch. It was ten past seven. If she didn't get a move on, she was going to be late. She lobbed the little bag into the hold-all on the floor and, jumping to her feet, scooped it up without bothering to close it. She walked quickly towards the bedroom door, stopping for a moment in front of the full-length mirror on the wardrobe to get the overall effect. She was pleased with what she saw. Her blonde hair was held back off her face by a pair of Calvin Klein sunglasses that perched on the top of her head, and her well-proportioned figure was perfectly complemented by the new Nike track suit, its pale yellow looking demure yet sporty against the tan she had acquired courtesy of the sun-bed at the games club. Okay, so she might not be as good as the rest of her playing partners at badminton, but she certainly could knock spots off them when it came to appearance.

She hurried down the stairs and made her way along the corridor to the kitchen, starting in surprise at the sound of a dish crashing to the ground in the larder as she passed by. A loud expletive followed. She stopped and looked in to see Gregor standing with his check-shirted back to her, one hand on his hip, the other rubbing at the back of his head, as he perused the splintered ashet on the ground, framing the remains of the roast lamb as if it were some obscure piece of modern art, while a mud-slide of gravy oozed slowly across the stone floor.

'Gregor? What on earth are you doing?'

He swung around to face her. 'I'm looking for the beer. What have you done with it?' His voice was edged with nervous irritation.

'I've put it in the fridge, where I always put it.'

'I didn't see it.'

Mary let out a sigh and walked across to the fridge, putting down her hold-all on the table as she passed by. She opened the door and removed a large tub of margarine and a carton of orange juice, revealing the cans of lager, still attached by their plastic ring holder, at the back of the rack. She stood aside and, with a sweep of her hand, invited Gregor to take a look for himself. 'There you are. Six cans of beer.'

He thrust his hands into the pockets of his jeans and shook his head. 'Well, I didn't see them,' he mumbled.

Mary smiled and walked towards him and gave him a kiss on the cheek. 'Don't get into such a state, Gregor. It'll be fine. He's your son, after all. Just be natural with him.'

Gregor flicked back his head. 'I thought I was the last time, but it just ended up with him walking away from me.'

Picking up her badminton racket from the sideboard, Mary put it in the hold-all and did up the zip. 'Well, the difference is that this time he called *you*, so he obviously wants to see you, and what's more, he hasn't got his mother around to poison his mind against you.' She paused, leaning her hands on the top of the hold-all as she looked at him. 'Listen, I have to get going, otherwise I'll be late.'

'When will you be back?'

She picked up the bag and moved over to the kitchen door. 'Not sure. I might stay and have something to eat afterwards.' She opened the door and turned back to look at him. 'Anyway, it's better I'm out of the way. It'll be easier for you to talk things through without me being here.'

Gregor nodded. 'Aye, I think you're probably right.' He walked over to her and planted a kiss on her cheek. 'Thanks, love.'

Mary gave him a smile. 'And while you're waiting for him, you can clear up the larder.'

He laughed. 'Thanks, love.'

For once in his life, Gregor was pleased that there was a mountain of paperwork to be cleared in his office. He worked his way methodically through the outstanding bills of the farm, paying off those which had final reminders, then moved on to updating his stock records on the sheep, making sure that all was in order for the farm sale that was scheduled in two weeks' time. Glancing at the clock on the wall at a quarter to nine, he closed his battered notebook and turned off the computer and sat back in his chair, wondering if Alex had had second thoughts about coming to see him.

He picked up the copy of *The Scottish Farmer* from the desk and began to leaf through it, and a feeling of dark despondency came over him at the thought that the information which was contained within its pages, and which had hitherto been integral to his life, was now irrelevant and unimportant. New sheep vaccines, new machinery developments, market reports on livestock and cereal prices – they would be of no use to him in the future. He flicked through to the end page and scanned the employment section. There were a number of jobs for casual tractor drivers, a few for hill shepherds, and one for a sales representative with a mineral-supplement company. But there wasn't one for a managerial position. He discarded the magazine onto the desk, and linking his powerful, calloused hands behind his head, he breathed out a long sigh of discontentment. What the hell was he going to do now? Two years off his fortieth birthday and he was out of a job. No, not just out of a job – out of a way of life. He knew nothing other than how to farm. He stared through the window as the setting sun gathered in its crimson rays, draining colour from the sky through the corrugations in the high, static cloud formation. Well, be thankful for small mercies, he thought to himself, at least for once the weather's on your side. You'd feel a lot worse if your depression were matched by the elements.

He heard the car change down a gear as it came around the corner of the steading, and the engine screamed mercilessly for a second before it came to a skidding halt on the loose chips in the courtyard. He got up quickly from his chair and walked through to the kitchen just as the back door slammed shut. Alex appeared, his face aglow both from his day on the golf course and the adrenaline rush of a hurried journey.

'Sorry I'm late,' he said, standing on the threshold of the kitchen door as if waiting to be invited into the house.

'You're not at all,' Gregor replied. 'I mean, you didn't have to rush back for me. I was just going to expect you whenever.'

Alex nodded. 'Right.' He cast an eye around the kitchen. 'Is Mary in?'

Gregor let out a grunt of a laugh. 'No, you'll be all right. She's gone out to play badminton.'

'Oh, I didn't mean it in that way! I was just, well, asking.'

Gregor moved over to the refrigerator and opened the door. 'Do you want a beer?'

'Yeah. That would be great.'

He took out two cans and lobbed one over to his son. The ring-pulls came off simultaneously. 'So, how did you get on today?'

Alex took a drink from the can and wiped the back of his hand across his mouth. 'Good. I managed to fit in three rounds, which all goes to help the bank balance a bit.'

'That's pretty fast going. What time did you finish?'

'Well, it was getting pretty dark. I'd say just before eight o'clock.' He paused. 'But then I bumped into a friend from university, and she insisted that we go to have a drink.'

Gregor raised his eyebrows and a teasing smile tilted the side of his mouth. 'She sounds keen.'

Alex dismissed the remark with a shrug of his shoulders. 'Not really. She's just a friend in the same German tutorial group as me.'

'So she's from Saint Andrews, then?'

'No. Down south. I think she lives somewhere near Swindon.'

The smile remained on Gregor's face. 'And she sort of stayed up here for the Easter break so that she could see you.'

Alex blew out derisively. 'No, she did not. She wanted to do some extra study before next term, so she got a part-time job waitressing in a restaurant in town.' He looked hard at his father. 'Look, it's no big deal. She's just a friend. Anyway, I think it's pretty dumb for anyone to get caught up in any kind of "heavy commitment" at this time.'

Gregor nodded slowly, realizing that his attempt at generating some sort of easy banter between them was beginning to falter, and the guilt that he still felt over his break-up with Liz hit at a paranoic nerve, and he wondered if Alex's last remark was not aimed directly at their own failed relationship. It was he now who was more eager to end that particular conversation. 'You're quite right,' he said quietly, 'I think that's a wise thought.' He moved towards the door that led out onto the paved terrace. 'How about we sit outside for a bit? I think it's warm enough.'

The breeze had died down with the ebbing of the tide, and an airy coolness had settled over the barley field in front of the house, extracting from the green tillers of the growing crop a sharp pungency that struck at the senses more effectively than a powerful decongestant. Feeling goose bumps rise on his forearms, Alex placed his beer can on the small cast-iron table and took his jersey from around his waist and pulled it over his head. They dragged out metal chairs and sat down, Gregor tilting his onto its back legs and putting his feet up onto the low stone wall that surrounded the terrace.

'So how are you and your grandfather getting on without Mum being around?'

'All right. Neither of us are that brilliant at cooking, though, so we might quite easily starve by the time that she gets back.'

Gregor took a sip of his beer. 'Have you heard anything from her?'

'Not yet. Mind you, she wouldn't have arrived in Seville until late last night, and then I was out of the house first thing this morning.'

'Of course.'

'Granddad might have by now, though.'

Gregor nodded but didn't reply.

'He was out on the New Course today.'

Gregor turned to look at his son, a frown on his face. 'Who?'

'Granddad. He was out caddying.'

Gregor laughed. 'Never.'

'Yup. I'd left my sandwiches at home this morning, so he brought them out to me, and on the way he just happened to bump into this Australian lady whose bag I'd carried yesterday and whom I had told him about last night. Anyway, he recognized her from my description, and seeing that she couldn't get a caddy, he thought that he'd just kill two birds with one stone and help her out.'

Gregor cocked his head to the side. 'Well, good for him. Obviously there's still life in the old dog.'

Alex silently acknowledged his father's witticism with a smile and looked about him. On the small patch of lawn on the other side of the wall the old swing stood in retirement, its four tubular legs surrounded by tall clumps of dead grass, while, on its swinging chains, rust had taken hold where the black paint had peeled away. Beyond that, over by the vegetable patch, he noticed that a section of wood on the rectangular box that his father had embedded into the ground to serve as a sandpit had succumbed to wet-rot, and lay, white with fungus, where it had broken off. All monuments to a past childhood. His childhood. He felt a surge of nostalgia weigh heavy in the pit of his stomach. This place had been his home, and now it had been made alien to him. He turned back to look at his father, who had his chair tilted even farther back and was gazing straight up into the clear, but as yet starless, sky.

'How's Grandpa and Grandma?'

His father contemplated the question for a moment, then kicked his feet off the wall and sat forward in his chair, placing his can of beer on the table. 'They're well enough, I think.'

Alex watched him. 'Meaning?'

'Meaning I haven't seen much of them recently. I'm not exactly the most popular person in their world at the minute.'

'Because of having to sell the farm?'

Gregor looked at him and smiled. 'No, Alex. They can understand the reasoning behind that. It's over you and your mother.'

Alex nodded. 'Right.'

His father let out a deep sigh. 'You know, Alex, no matter what age you are, it's a pretty hard thing to take when you can't speak to your parents – especially your father. Dad was always a much better farmer than me, so I miss him a lot, for his advice and support, especially at the minute.'

Well done, you, Alex thought to himself, that's quite a clever angle. He drained his can of beer. 'Maybe then you should take time to go to see him too,' he said quietly. 'Just have a conversation with him, like we're doing now.'

Gregor scrutinized his son's face, hoping that he was on the verge of a breakthrough. 'And you think it would help, Alex?'

'Yes, I think so, once everyone has accepted the fact that the situation isn't going to change.'

'And have you?'

Alex pushed himself to his feet. 'To be quite honest, not really. But life's too short, isn't it?' He picked up his empty can and made his way over to the door. 'Do you want another?'

Gregor sprang to his feet. 'Look, you sit down. I'll get them.'

'No, don't bother. I can do it.'

They came together in the doorway, Gregor's powerful shoulder accidentally knocking the taller yet slighter frame of his son against the doorpost. Both stood back, two feet apart, to let the other enter the kitchen first.

'I'm sorry,' Gregor murmured.

Alex shook his head. 'No bother. It didn't hurt.'

'No, Alex. I mean I'm really sorry – for everything. I'm sorry that both you and your mother ever got caught up in my life, and that you've both been so badly hurt by it.' He rubbed hard at the back of his head. 'Shit! Listen, Alex, I'm not a great man with words and I don't even know if I'm putting this across the right way, but—'

'Look, Dad,' Alex cut in. 'Let *me* put it across for you. If I hadn't got caught up with your life, I wouldn't be here. It's as simple as that. You're my father. You could be dead, or you could have run off with Mary to the other side of the world. But you're still here – and we're still talking, and I would guess that you're probably still quite concerned about Mum and me. Okay, so you're right in saying that you've hurt us both really badly, but you're not, as you think, the most loathsome bastard that this world has ever produced, so please don't give yourself the pleasure of being that hard on yourself.'

Alex's voice had risen in volume so much throughout his statement that his last syllable echoed around the farm buildings. The two looked hard at each other and Alex watched as his father drew in his breath. He had seen him do this before, when he was about to lose his temper. But this time he just snorted out a laugh.

'Yes,' he said, nodding his head slowly. 'That was probably what I was going to say.'

Alex spun the empty can into the air and caught it. 'But if it makes you feel any better, I still think you're a bit of a bastard.'

Gregor smiled and reached out and gripped his son's forearm and guided him towards the door. 'Well, I think on that point, we might have come to some sort of an agreement.'

The car swept around the corner of the steading and came to a halt facing them, catching them both in the blinding glare of its headlights. Gregor put up a hand to shield his eyes. 'Now who the hell could that be?'

The engine was cut and the lights went out, and before they could accustom their eyes once more to the falling darkness they heard the door being opened and slammed shut and the sound of footsteps approaching them.

'Good evening, Gregor.'

He recognized immediately the clipped English tones of Jonathan Davies.

'Jonathan! This is a surprise. I didn't expect you.'

By the time Gregor had finished his half-hearted welcome Davies had sprung up onto the terrace wall and had come down into the weak pool of light that shone from the lamp above the kitchen door. He was dressed casually in a maroon cashmere jersey and yellow corduroy trousers, sporting at his neck a neat blue cravat instead of his customary tie. In his hand he carried a large plastic bag, the contents of which had clinked noisily as he had executed his hurdle. 'Oh dear!' he said, grimacing as he looked from Gregor to Alex. 'I hope I haven't come at a bad time.'

Gregor shook his head. 'No, not at all. You know Alex, don't you?'

Davies smiled at Alex and shot out a hand. 'Indeed I do. How are you, Alex?'

Alex clasped his hand. 'Well, thank you, Mr Davies.'

'Jonathan – please.'

Gregor turned to go into the kitchen. 'We're just about to have a beer, Jonathan. Will you join us?'

Davies held up the plastic bag. 'Well, I was wondering if I could interest *you* in the contents of my bag. We haven't really celebrated the start of work on the golf course yet, and seeing my wife has gone down south to visit her mother, I thought that tonight might be quite opportune.'

Gregor laughed. 'And what, may I ask, do you have in your bag?'

Davies put it down on the table and delved in it to produce a magnum of Taittinger champagne, two packets of Kettle potato chips and a box of Havana cigars. He stood back so that both Gregor and Alex could feast their eyes on his booty. 'So what do you think?'

Gregor scratched slowly at the side of his face, making

it look as if the decision were a hard one. He looked over to his son. 'Difficult to judge, isn't it? Beer or champagne.'

Alex gave his head a quick shake. 'No competition,' he said, making his way quickly into the kitchen. 'I'll get the glasses!'

Mr Craig picked up his mug from the kitchen table, then reached across for the one that sat in front of Roberta, his action being prompted by his house guest stretching her arms above her head and letting out a loud yawn.

'I'm sorry, Craig,' she said, pushing herself to her feet. 'That was pretty rude. I think that I must still be suffering a bit from jet lag.'

'Och, it's hardly surprising that you're tired,' he replied, walking over to the sink and washing out the mugs under the tap. 'You've had a pretty exhausting day, what with one thing and another.' He glanced at the kitchen clock and his mouth opened in horror when he saw that it was a quarter past eleven. 'Heavens, what am I thinking about, keeping you up to this time? I had no idea that it was that late. You should have said something before now.'

Roberta took a dish-towel from the rail in front of the Rayburn, and picking up one of the mugs from the draining-board, she began to dry it. 'Not at all. I wouldn't have wanted to turn in any earlier. I haven't had the opportunity to talk so much for goodness knows how long.'

'Well, I hope I didn't bore you,' he said, taking the mug from her and hanging it on a hook on the dresser. 'My life has been fairly humdrum in comparison to yours.'

'I wouldn't say that for a minute! I found it all fascinating, especially those new plans for the golf course. I can't wait to have a look at it in the morning.'

'Well, you'll be able to get a good view of it from your bedroom window. Not that there's much to see at the minute, what with them just getting started.' He took the other mug from Roberta and hung it up. 'Now, I would suggest that we just play it by ear tomorrow. If you're still feeling a wee bit tired, we can give the golf a miss and you can just have a lazy day here.'

'No way!' Roberta exclaimed. 'I'll be fine! I wouldn't give up the chance of playing Carnoustie for all the tea in China.'

He smiled at her. 'Good. In that case, I'll knock on your door at, say, eight o'clock, and we'll have a bite to eat for breakfast and then leave here around nine. How would that be?'

'Perfect,' Roberta replied, trying to stifle another yawn. 'By Jiminy, I really have got the gapes.'

'Well, get yourself away to bed then. You know where everything is?'

Roberta nodded. 'Yes, thanks.'

'Right. In that case, I'll just get the dog put out for a minute before I turn in myself.' He opened the door that led into the hall and stood aside for Roberta, but they were both beaten to it by the Jack Russell, who muscled his way between their legs and stood panting in eagerness at the front door.

'Goodness, I wish I had that much energy,' Roberta

sighed, walking to the bottom of the stairs and beginning to climb them quite laboriously.

Mr Craig laughed. 'I think it might be spurred on by the fact that he knows he's taking a loan of me. He knows full well that he's not allowed to put so much as a paw into this part of the house when my daughter's here.' He turned the heavy key in the lock. 'Go on then, you wee devil, I'll let you get out here this time.' Giving the door a sharp tug, he immediately jammed its underside on the doormat, but it left a wide-enough gap for the dog to squeeze through and disappear outside, barking frantically. Mr Craig bent down and pulled away the mat, then opened the door fully and looked outside. He stood there for a moment, gazing out at the night, then turned and took a pace back to the bottom of the stairs. 'Are you away to bed yet?' he called out.

Roberta appeared at the bathroom door, tooth-brush in hand. 'No. Why? What's the matter?'

'Nothing. I just think it's worth you coming down to have a wee look out here.'

She came down the stairs and they walked out into the garden and stood side by side on the small stretch of lawn. The moon was full and perfectly formed, hanging in the star-lit sky like an anchored balloon above the distant sea, its light so intense that it was possible to make out the movement of water in its reflection. The fields below the house were bathed in an ecliptic glow that picked out every contour of the land as far as the eye could see, and the air was so still that all that could be heard was the muted sound of the waves tumbling idly against the rocks on the shoreline and the eerie hoot of an owl which, although perched somewhere in the trees away down by the gully, sounded as clear as if it had been sitting on the garden wall.

'Craig, this is *so* beautiful,' Roberta whispered, as if she felt that her voice might introduce an alien sound to the tranquillity of Nature's night.

'Aye, it is.' He paused for a moment to allow the owl to hoot unchallenged. 'It always is.'

'And look at the lie of the land. It really will make the most wonderful golf course.'

'Do you think that?'

'Oh, without a doubt! It's a natural.' She cupped her hands around her eyes to shield off the glare of the moon. 'I hope the guy who's designing the course knows what he's doing.'

'Aye, well, he seems to. He's an American lad. Done quite a number all over the world.'

'Yes, but even I can see that this is going to be a completely different challenge. This'll be a links course, not a manufactured one. It'll have to be treated with such delicacy.'

Mr Craig turned to look at her, a grin on his face. 'You give me the impression that you're a bit of an expert yourself.'

Roberta shook her head. 'Not me. Dad. It was always his dream to design a golf course. He read every book possible on the subject. His idea was always that one shouldn't *build* a course, one should sculpt it. He said that, wherever possible, it should blend in with the physical layout of the land, and that could be simply matching the existing undulations or even creating lines that mirror the hills on the horizon.' She let out a deep sigh as she once more swept her eyes across the glowing landscape. 'My word, he would have fallen in love with this place.'

The farmer cocked his head to the side. 'Well, he'd be a man after my own heart then.' He saw Roberta give an abrupt shiver and she folded her bare arms across her chest to ward off the cold. 'Come on,' he said, moving back up the garden path, 'let's get inside. It's getting quite fresh out here.'

On reaching the front door of the house, he turned to see that Roberta had yet to move, her eyes now transfixed on something in the direction of the neighbouring farm. She raised her arm and pointed a finger. 'There's no road over there, is there?'

'No. Just a track that links this farm with the next.'

A puzzled frown wrinkled her brow. 'Well, there seem to be headlights coming this way.'

The farmer could now hear the sound of a diesel engine blowing out noisily through a cracked exhaust pipe. He took a few steps down the path and looked out in the same direction as Roberta. 'Well, I never. That's Gregor's fork-lift.'

They watched the lights slowly approach, and as the vehicle got nearer they were able to make out, above the grumble of the engine, the sound of voices singing in what seemed like a tuneless descant. The fork-lift momentarily dipped into a hollow, then reappeared, and at that point the farmer realized that they had not been listening to the rendition of one song, but two, both being belted forth at full volume, as if those who were performing them were trying to compete for air-time.

Roberta let out a laugh. 'It sounds to me as if a party's just been had. Who is it?'

The farmer smiled and shook his head. 'I'm not sure at the minute, but when you get to hear "Flower of Scotland" and "Swing Low, Sweet Chariot" being sung together like that, it usually means that there's a Scotsman and an Englishman having a wee bit of a musical difference.'

They moved forward and leaned on the garden wall and watched as the fork-lift pulled to a halt at the bottom of the bank. The two singing figures were sitting in the bottom of the grain-bucket, only their heads visible above its steel rim, on to which both clung hard, having been transported the half-mile along the bumpy track high up in the air. The driver slowly lowered the bucket to within three feet of the ground, then tipped it forward, and the musical duet immediately slid up-scale into a cry of protest as the two figures were unceremoniously dumped out. The engine was cut and the driver clambered with what seemed like infinite care from the cab, only to have his true colours shown when his wavering foot completely missed the final step and he swore out loud as the serrated metal rasped against his shin.

Roberta let out a short laugh but immediately stifled it with her hand when she saw the farmer hold a finger to his lips. He cleared his throat. 'And *what* do we have going on here?' he called out, his voice sounding as stern as that of a disgruntled schoolmaster. The two figures scrambled unsteadily to their feet and, now joined in line by the limping driver, all three stood peering up at Mr Craig and Roberta. One of them detached himself from the group, took a couple of steps back and ran at the bank, only managing to make it to the top on his third attempt.

Alex swayed slightly as he stood in front of them, an inane beam on his ruddy features. 'Hullo, Granddad.'

The farmer acknowledged the greeting with a brief nod of his head. 'Alex. You know Miss Bayliss, of course.'

Alex grinned at Roberta. 'Hullo, Miss Bayliss. What're you doing here?'

'You'll get an explanation of that later,' the farmer cut in, 'once I've heard yours.'

Gregor now made an appearance at the top of the bank, still rubbing at his aching shin, and Alex cast him a glance as if requiring immediate moral support. Gregor noted the farmer's look of disapproval and made an effort to appear as compos mentis as he possibly could. 'Well?' That was all he could manage in greeting.

'Gregor. This is Miss Bayliss. Miss Bayliss, this is Alex's father.'

Gregor came forward, wiping his hands on the seat of his trousers. He shook Roberta's hand. 'Pleased to meet you, Miss Bayliss.'

The third figure appeared now at the top of the bank, blowing forcefully with the effort of the climb. Jonathan Davies took a silk handkerchief from the pocket of his soil-streaked corduroy trousers and wiped his brow, then came forward and tripped over a clump of grass, only managing to break his fall by splaying his hands out on the wall.

'And here we have Mr Davies!' exclaimed Mr Craig, turning to Roberta to hide the fact that he was now finding it quite hard to control his own laughter. 'Miss Bayliss, this is the gentleman to whom we have entrusted the task of turning this farm into a championship golf course.'

Davies looked up at him, a pained expression of embarrassment on his face. 'Good evening, sir,' he said quietly, keeping one hand on the wall to steady himself and putting out the other to the farmer. It was shaken with force. 'Mr Davies, may I introduce you to Miss Bayliss – from Australia.'

'How do you do?' he said weakly, shaking Roberta's hand.

Mr Craig clapped his hands and rubbed them together. 'Right! Now that we have the introductions out of the way, let's hear what you've all been up to.'

There was a general casting of looks between the three before Gregor took the lead. 'We've just been over at Winterton having a wee celebration . . .'

'Oh, a *wee* celebration, was it?' the farmer remarked, rubbing interestedly at his chin.

Gregor cleared his throat before continuing. 'Well, Alex and I were just having a beer together when Jonathan here arrived with some champagne . . .'

'Ah, champagne. That's nice, though.'

Davies pushed himself away from the wall and looked

as if he were about to fall over. 'Would you mind awfully if I sat down?'

'Not at all, Mr Davies. You go right ahead.'

Davies walked as if on rubber legs over to the top of the bank and slumped down on the damp grass, his legs dangling over the edge.

'So, have you been enjoying anything other than champagne then?'

Gregor looked across at Alex. 'Well . . .'

'Havana cigars,' Alex interjected, the smile that remained transfixed on his face making him seem utterly pleased with himself.

'Ah, then. Champagne and Havana cigars.' Mr Craig shook his head. 'Well, lad,' he said, looking at Alex, 'I would say that you're in for a real humdinger of a hang-over in the morning.'

The statement seemed to be sufficient to wipe the smile from Alex's face. He dug his hands into his pockets and looked down at his feet, and began scuffing at a loose stone with the point of his shoe.

Gregor rubbed a hand across his mouth. 'Listen, I'm sorry about this. It was my fault. I shouldn't have maybe let him drink so much.'

'Ah, well,' Mr Craig started slowly, 'maybe you shouldn't have. Keep in mind, Gregor, that I have a responsibility for him too, while his mother's away.' He let out a long sigh. 'On the other hand, a wee tick of grease is sometimes needed if one wants to get rusty machinery to turn easy again.' He smiled at them both. 'I'm glad that you two are on course once more.'

Gregor nodded. 'I didn't let him drive.'

'I can see that.' The farmer flicked his head in the direction of the fork-lift. 'Mind you, it's a toss-up as to which would have been the safer mode of transport.'

Gregor scratched at the back of his head. 'Yes, well, I think that Alex and I could have walked, but we were a bit concerned about Jonathan over the . . .' He had turned to look to where Davies had been sitting, but stopped abruptly when he realized that the bank was now unoccupied. He walked quickly to the edge and looked over. 'Oh, for goodness' sake!' He disappeared down the bank. Mr Craig pulled open the garden gate, and both he and Roberta hurried over to stand next to Alex. They watched as Gregor examined the body that lay curled up in a foetal position at the bottom of the bank.

'How is he?' Mr Craig inquired, a note of concern in his voice.

Alex looked up and let out a short laugh. 'Sleeping like a baby.'

There were sighs of relief at the top of the bank. The farmer turned to his grandson. 'You'd better get down there and give your father a hand to bring the man inside. I don't think he'd survive a homeward journey in that grain bucket.' Alex's fixed grin returned and he slid down the bank to help his father.

Mr Craig put his hand on Roberta's arm and guided her back through the gate. She stopped and turned to him. 'You're a pretty understanding man, aren't you?'

He shrugged. 'Och well, there's no harm done. I'm quite sure that it won't become a habit. I remember when

I was a wee bit younger than Alex, I had a few too many pints of beer at the Harvest Home and was sick as a dog all night. The headache that I had the next morning was a great help in teaching me to act in moderation from then on.' He paused for a moment. 'I hope you're not feeling too off-put by all that's gone on tonight. I can vouch that it's not a regular occurrence.'

Roberta smiled at him. 'You know, Craig, I don't think I've had so much entertainment for, well . . . ever!'

'Good,' he said, as they walked together up the garden path. 'I'm glad that you see it that way.' He opened the front door and ushered Roberta into the house.

CHAPTER 17

The *paso* (large platform), that bore El Señor de la Presentación, a massive eight-figure display portraying the presentation of Jesus to the people by Pontius Pilate, swayed its way up the narrow street. Its forward motion seemed imperceptible as the *costaleros*, who remained hidden from view beneath the embroidered side canopies, shuffled forward with the immense weight of the float upon their cushioned shoulders. Myriad candles bordered its ornate plinth, sending up a plume of smoke into the cool night air that drifted unbroken past open windows and crowded balconies, their railings draped with fringed rugs or interwoven with an abundance of flowers that would eventually be dispersed by the unfelt breeze swirling softly about the roof-tops. In front of the procession, ordered lines of *nazarenos*, members of the fraternity to whom the *paso* belonged, cleared a way through the thronging crowd, their identity concealed beneath full-length white robes and tall purple conical hoods. And behind the float came the masses, an ever-changing multitude who joined the procession from side streets or doorways or bars as others left for rest or much-needed refreshment.

Liz concentrated hard as she followed on amidst the crowd, her own movement being regulated by the uneven pressure on her upper body exerted by those behind and in front of her. Despite the freshness of the night, she felt hot and sticky from the heat generated by so many people in such close proximity to one another, and her eyes smarted from the constant waft of cigarette smoke that hung like a rain-cloud about their heads. Desperate to keep her balance in the jostling crowd, she fought an unseen battle for space on the ground, endlessly stepping on toes and smiling apologetically at those who she thought might be their owners. On many an occasion over the past three days, her own feet had fallen victim to this painful, yet unavoidable, abuse, and she had resorted to buying a pair of heavy leather boots, both to protect her feet and to help them cope with the many miles that both she and the professor had walked through the streets of Seville.

But sore feet was a pittance of a price to pay for the pleasure of actually being there, being part of this incredible happening. She had never been particularly religious in her life, but she now found herself captivated by the contrasting atmospheres of reverence and cele-bration engendered by the colourful parades, the *pasos* depicting the Passion of Christ that she had followed or watched pass by during the course of Semana Santa now giving a tangible meaning to a story that she had known since she was a little girl. She felt closer to it all than she had ever done before, and sometimes wondered how little difference there must have been in her watching events unfold before her eyes here and actually having been in Jerusalem all those years ago, and following Him through the streets and on to Golgotha, and watching Him being nailed to the Cross.

She looked around to see if she could discover the whereabouts of the professor, eventually catching sight of his tall figure ten yards behind her. He had taken off his jacket, revealing a pair of bright-yellow braces which, worn over a dark blue shirt, contrasted quite irreverently with the funereal dress of those about him. He was attempting to stand still in the jostling crowd so that he could read about some point of interest in his guidebook, whilst emitting from his pipe a cloud of smoke that was adding quite effectively to the general tobacco smog. He looked up, catching her eye, and gave her a fixed grin which seemed to register more desperation than contentment, then began to push his way through the crowd towards her. As she watched him approach, Liz found herself once more reflecting on how selfish she had been towards him when they had first arrived, because, as it had turned out, he could not have been a more perfect companion and guide, having demonstrated from the outset both an unrelenting energy that belied his age and a ceaseless enthusiasm during all their sightseeing quests.

Together they had marvelled at the Moorish splendour of the Reales Alcázares, become hopelessly lost in the maze of streets that made up the Barrio Santa Cruz, and imagined the fiery atmosphere in the Plaza de Toros de la Maestranza. They had stood at the top of the towering

Giralda, high above the cathedral, looking out over the roofs of the city, and away to the north, beyond the many bridges that spanned the waters of the Guadalquivir River, to where the foothills of the Sierra Morena pimpled the horizon. They had taken a horse-drawn carriage along the tranquil avenues of the Parque María Luisa and had had their photograph taken by their sombre coachman on the semicircular esplanade in front of the Plaza de España. And then they had stood patiently outside basilicas to witness the first sighting of one of the flower-bedecked *pasos*, the images greeted with whoops of joy and cries of admiration, before following on in the procession, walking for hours through the narrow labyrinthine streets of the city. And never had there been a moment when she had needed to ask a question on who, why, or wherefore, because the professor was always there with his guidebook, keeping up a constant yet engrossing commentary, tinged with his own dry humour, on whatever they were seeing.

He squeezed his way between the short, stout Spanish couple who stood directly behind her in their Sunday-best attire, and blew out with exertion when he arrived at her side. 'My God, I'm hot!' he exclaimed, taking a red-spotted handkerchief from his trouser pocket and wiping the glistening beads of sweat from his forehead. 'Listen, there's a street just coming up on the left. What do you say if we just dive down there and go find somewhere quiet to get a drink and some tapas?'

Liz stretched up on her toes and peered over the heads of the crowd to where the platform was being carried, seventy yards ahead of them. 'What about waiting until it gets to the end of this street?'

He followed her line of sight. 'That's another four hundred yards! It could take at least another hour to get there.' He made to wipe at his forehead again with the handkerchief, but in doing so in such a confined space his elbow caught the side of the mantilla-covered head of the small Spanish señora whom he had just passed. He gave it such a healthy blow that her finely arranged bouffant hair-do slipped to the side, making the black lace shawl that covered it now resemble more a badly erected tepee.

'I'm sorry!' he said, instinctively grabbing hold of the woman's arm to steady her. 'I mean, er, *lo siento*.' The woman pulled her arm from his grip and gave him a look that could kill. He turned to Liz and pulled a grimace that barely disguised the fact that he was about to burst out laughing. 'My word, what a way I have with women!'

Liz closed her eyes tight with embarrassment. 'I think you're right, Arthur. Time to beat a hasty retreat.' She began pushing her way diagonally through the crowd, making for the refuge of the little street that the professor had pointed out.

They had just extricated themselves from the worst of the throng when the sound of a deep baritone voice rang out across the street in a long, warbling wail. Liz walked to the edge of the pavement and looked up to the balcony where the singer stood, directly above the *paso*, his arms outstretched in mournful supplication.

'Oh, for goodness' sakes!' the professor groaned. 'Not another bloody *saeta*.'

'Come on, Arthur,' Liz said reproachfully, giving him a bump with her elbow, 'they're wonderful. I think they're really moving.'

'Which is more than the crowd will do for the next fifteen minutes.'

Liz gave him a bewildered look. 'What's the matter? You're not being your usual bright self.'

He let out a long sigh. 'I know. I suppose it's just the heat – and all these people. I'm just beginning to feel a bit tired and crabby.'

'Come on, then,' Liz replied, taking him by the arm. 'Let's go. I think we've probably done enough for tonight.'

'Listen, I don't want to be a killjoy,' he said, pulling away from her grasp to allow clear passage for a woman and her two small daughters to hurry up the street to join the parade. 'We could have a quick drink and then catch up with it all later.'

Liz glanced at her wrist-watch. 'No, it's a quarter to twelve. I'm quite happy to call it a day, if you are.'

Arthur nodded. 'Glad you said that. My legs are beginning to feel decidedly wobbly. I don't think I've quite recovered yet from our climb to the top of the Giralda.'

'Right. Well, let's get back to the hotel then – if we can find our way.'

'Just leave that to me!' he exclaimed, his good humour seemingly restored by the prospect of returning to the hotel. He stopped to peruse the street map in the back pages of his guidebook. 'Now, if we go down here, turn left, then right, then left . . . then right again, we can cut through the Barrio de Santa Cruz and out by the Jardines de Murillo.' He smiled at Liz. 'How does that sound to you?'

Liz shrugged. 'I'm afraid you can't ask me, Arthur. I still don't have a clue about this place. If it wasn't for you and your map, I'd probably be lost here forever.'

He slapped shut the guidebook and took hold of her arm. 'In that case, stick close to me and I will guide you through the wilderness.' He moved her off down the street at a jaunty pace, his head held high in a display of exaggerated smugness. 'Oh, how wonderful it makes me feel to be considered so important!'

They lost their way after the third turning, having come to a small junction from which five narrow streets led off, and subsequently choosing one that took them in the opposite direction to their planned route. A quarter of an hour later, they regained their bearings outside the Iglesia de Santa Cruz, by which time their camaraderie was under severe duress, the professor now furious at the fallibility of his own map-reading skills and becoming quite desperate to get back to the hotel.

'Thank God for that! Come on, this way!' he called out, waving his guidebook like a flag. He had begun to walk at such a frenetic pace that Liz had to break into a jog to keep up with him. She stopped for a moment to catch her breath, but seeing him disappear around the corner of the church and frightened that she might lose him, she set off after him.

The cry was loud enough to bring the crowd's babbling noise to a momentary silence, then people started moving quickly down the street from where it had sounded out. Liz found herself caught up in the hurrying masses, and as one man ran past her he slipped and grabbed at her arm to steady himself. '¡Cuidado, señora!' he laughed. 'Hay mucha cera aquí.'

Liz smiled at him, not understanding a word that he had said, but thinking it better to make some sort of reaction to his joking comment. She stepped off the pavement and her foot immediately slid out in front of her, and she too found herself having to grab at a passer-by to maintain her balance. She looked down at the cobbled surface of the street and noticed that its length seemed to be glistening in the lights that shone out from the shops. She scuffed her shoe against a cobble and noticed a whitish residue build up in front of her toe. Bending down, she brushed a finger against it, then smeared it with her thumb, realizing immediately that it was wax, deposited there by the hundreds of candles that had been carried up and down the street.

'Don't try to get me up, you fool!' Liz heard Arthur's voice cry out from the centre of the crowd that had gathered farther down the street. 'Can't you see the bloody thing's broken!'

'Oh, no!' Liz muttered to herself in horror. She made her way as fast as she dared to the back of the crowd and began pushing her way to the front. 'Arthur?'

'Liz! Where the hell are you?'

The crowd moved aside to allow her through, and she found Arthur leaning heavily on one elbow in the middle of the street. His feet were splayed out in front of him, his face ashen-white, and his lips were drawn back to reveal teeth clenched in pain. Liz looked down the length of his body and immediately saw the impossible angle at which his left foot stuck out from his leg. She dropped to her knees beside him. 'Arthur, what have you done?'

'What the hell do you think I've done? Some stupid bastard has sprayed the street with bloody candle-wax! My sodding foot's broken!' He let out a loud moan. 'Oh, God, it hurts!'

Liz got to her feet and looked desperately around at the crowd, who just stood eyeing Arthur as if he were some kind of unclean being. 'Can someone not call an ambulance?' The onlookers turned to each other and shrugged their shoulders. Liz tried again. 'Ambulance!' She held out her hands, trying to think of some word that might resemble the Spanish equivalent. '*Ambulante?*'

A tall young man, impeccably dressed in a light blue linen suit, pushed his way through to the front and, delving into the inside pocket of his jacket, produced a mobile phone. '*Ambulancia, señora. El quiere una ambulancia.*'

'Yes!' Liz nodded frantically, 'Yes, please – and quickly!' She knelt down beside Arthur again and took hold of his hand. She felt his grip tighten like a vice around her own, and she knew then that he was in desperate pain.

'I'm sorry, Liz. What a stupid bloody thing to do! This was *not* what was planned.'

'Don't worry. Please don't worry. The important thing is to get you to a hospital as quickly as possible.'

'I know, I know, but what are you going to do now? How are you . . . ?'

'Just don't worry about me, Arthur. I'll be fine.' She felt

260

a hand on her shoulder and turned to look up into the face of the young man.

'The ambulance comes now, señora. She comes now.'

Liz smiled at him. 'Thank you so much.'

'*De nada.*' He turned and began to push his way through the crowd.

Liz pulled her hand free from Arthur's grasp and stood up. 'Excuse me!'

The man turned. 'Señora?'

'Do you speak English quite well?'

He smiled. 'No.' He held a thumb and forefinger millimetres apart. 'Only a very little.'

'Well, that's enough.' She gave him her most pleading look. 'Do you think you could just stay with us until the ambulance arrives – please? Neither of us understands a word of Spanish, and I have no idea what to say when it comes.'

The young man held out his hands in apology and cast a glance towards the bar at the side of the street. Liz followed his gaze to where a girl sat at a table, her dress expressing sophistication, but her features little humour. She watched the commotion with only a modicum of interest and raked back her long dark hair with fingers that also held a newly lit cigarette. 'I am sorry, but I cannot. It is – how do you say? – my first time?'

Liz let out a long sigh. 'I think you probably mean your first date.'

The man laughed, understanding the subtlety of her point. 'Yes, you are right. My first date. Now you understand how bad is my English.'

Liz nodded. 'Well, thank you for your help, anyway.' She turned around to find that the majority of the crowd had dispersed, and an old woman in a black dress had come out of one of the adjacent houses and had kindly put a blanket around Arthur's shoulders and one across his legs. She now stood beside him jabbering her heart-felt condolences in Spanish. Liz walked over quickly to his side and knelt down. 'Why the hell do all the Spaniards smoke so much?'

Arthur managed a querying look through his pained expression. 'What?'

Liz shook her head. 'Nothing. Just give me your hand.'

The ambulance took fifteen minutes to reach them, but once the two paramedics had given Arthur a pain-killing injection and had carefully placed him onto the stretcher and loaded him into the back of the vehicle, it took only a further seven to get to the hospital. Liz sat beside him on the way, holding hard on to his hand as the ambulance sped through the crowded streets, its siren wailing like a banshee. Her concern now was not only for him, but also because even she could tell that the direction in which they were travelling was taking her farther away from the hotel.

Swinging off the road into a narrow service lane, the ambulance came to an abrupt halt under the brick-pillared entrance of the hospital. Quickly opening up the back doors, the two paramedics wheeled Arthur out, and having been given no indication as to what she should do,

Liz followed on as they pushed the trolley through the frosted-glass swingdoors, above which was written the word URGENCIAS in dark red letters. There was a turmoil of activity inside, the long hallway crammed with doctors in green fatigues trying to organize and administer to the hordes of patients in need of attention. Young children with pallid faces sat quietly in oversized wheelchairs, whilst mothers monopolized the showing of grief, stroking fiercely at their child's head and dabbing theatrically at their own tear-filled eyes with the edge of a handkerchief. An old woman, dressed in a black shapeless dress, moaned in pain as she was helped slowly to her feet. She clutched fiercely at her rosary beads and struggled to cross herself as her arms were clamped in support by medical staff who, emitting quiet words of sympathy, began to move her off at a snail's pace along the corridor. There were others who appeared to be there for no reason apart from the show, leaning unconcernedly against walls with their hands in their pockets, and murmuring to each other every time another trolley was wheeled in through the entrance doors.

Liz was threading her way through the melée in pursuit of Arthur when one of the paramedics turned around and noticed that she was following. He waved a finger at her.

'¡No aquí, señora!'

'Could I perhaps come with you?' Liz asked.

He came back toward her, and taking her by the arm, guided her back to the double doors. He opened one and pointed at the words NO PASAR that were written across the frosted glass. Liz held out her hands, signifying to the man that she didn't know what she was meant to do. He pointed at a plate-glass window behind which was the reception desk, and beyond that, a stark waiting room with lines of green chairs anchored together on long metal tubes. He walked out of the door and pointed to one that was adjacent. '*La entrada está allí.*'

Folding Arthur's jacket over her arm, she went into the waiting room as directed and sat down, and watched through the plate-glass window as the paramedics wheeled Arthur away down the corridor.

The two women who sat behind the reception desk eyed her momentarily, then spoke furtively with each other before one came through from the office and approached her with a clipboard. She gave it to Liz, along with a pen, and made a writing motion with her hand to indicate that she wanted the admittance form that was clipped to it filled in, then left her and returned quickly to the office. Liz cast an eye over the form. It was all in Spanish. She could make out a few of the headings, and began filling in the professor's name and a sparse address – Hotel Cazaral, Seville – being unable to remember the name of the street on which it was situated. But that was as much as she could do. She got up and walked over to the office window and handed across the clipboard. 'I'm sorry, but I can't understand the rest.' The woman looked at the form and smiled at her. '*¡No se preocupe! Es suficiente.*'

For one and a half hours Liz sat in the waiting room, watching people come and go. Complete families, all with worried faces, entered the reception area, where they would fret over the condition of one of their own with the two receptionists. Then, having received much mollification and reassurance, they would come to sit on the seats next to Liz and continue their overwrought banter. On many an occasion, Liz found it difficult to work out exactly which of their group was requiring the urgent hospital treatment, so melancholy was their joint demeanour.

She was watching an old man, dressed in a pair of worn corduroy trousers and drooping cardigan, a black Basque beret set rakishly forward on his bristling grey head, as he shuffled slowly along the corridor with the support of a heavy cane walking-stick, when a young doctor with black-rimmed glasses came into the waiting room and approached her, the white coat that he wore over his green fatigues flapping open as he walked. He held in his hand the clipboard that she had given back to the receptionist.

He smiled at her. '¿Señora, no habla español?'

Liz shook her head.

He sat down beside her and took a pen from the cluster that was clipped to the top pocket of his coat. 'My English is no good, but we try, yes?'

Liz sighed with relief on hearing words that she could understand. 'How is he?'

The doctor scratched at the back of his head with the pen. 'He is all right, but it is not a good break. We have to give him . . .' He paused as he searched for the word. '. . . sedativos?'

'Sedatives.'

'Yes, we have to give him sedatives to pull the foot straight.'

'Can I see him?'

'Not yet, señora. First, I must ask you some questions.' He studied the form on the clipboard. 'Now, has he . . . *alergias?*'

'Allergies?

'Yes.'

Liz shook her head. 'I don't know. Can't you ask him these questions?'

'No, señora. He sleeps.'

'Well, I'm afraid that I don't know these kind of things about him. He's just an acquaintance, a friend.'

The doctor nodded slowly in realization. 'Ah! So the señor is not your husband, then?'

Liz let out a short laugh. 'No, he's not! He's just my tenant.'

'Tenant?' the doctor asked, looking perplexed by the word.

'He lives with me.'

'Ah, he *lives* with you, then.'

'No! I mean, not like that!'

The doctor shook his head in confusion. 'Señora, I am sorry if I do not understand, but I must have a *firma* . . . to give permission to do the operation.' He held out the clipboard and pen. 'Can you please do this?'

Liz took them from him and sat for a moment with the pen poised above the consent form. She *supposed* he was all right. After all, he had managed to storm his way through life this far, smoking his wretched pipe and drinking quantities of bourbon. And anyway, there was no doubt that he needed to undergo the operation. She signed the form and handed it back to the doctor.

'Thank you, señora.' He got to his feet.

'Do you think that I should wait to see him?'

The doctor glanced across at the clock on the office wall. 'I think not. We will operate now, but then he will not be awake until much later. I think you will be better to go back to where you stay and return in the morning.'

'All right.' She stood up and slung her handbag onto her shoulder. 'Could you then tell me the name of this hospital?'

'La Macarena.'

'What? As in the Virgin?'

The doctor smiled. '*Exactamente*. As in the Virgin.' He turned to leave.

'Just one more thing,' Liz called after him.

'Yes?'

'Have you any idea how I get back to the Hotel Cazaral?'

The doctor thought for a moment. 'I'm not very sure of this hotel, señora. I am from Córdoba.' He held up his hand. 'But please wait. I shall ask.' He walked over to the office window and handed back the clipboard, and engaged one of the women in a few seconds' animated conversation, during which there was much hand-waving and reaffirmation of directions. He came back over to her. 'Right, señora. It is quite good. I take you to the door.' He walked beside her to the entrance. 'Ah, yes, I forget to ask! Can you bring some clothes and tooth-brush for the señor in the morning?'

'All right. And by the way, he's a professor.' She

thought it best to tell him this, in the hope that it might save Arthur from getting needlessly rankled in his efforts to explain.

'Ah, he is a teacher.'

'No, he is a professor. It's his title.' The young doctor looked none the wiser. 'In a university.'

'Ah!' he declared, appearing now to understand what she was saying. 'A *catedrático*. A very clever man, then?'

Liz sighed, realizing that her attempts to explain were bearing little trace of enlightenment. 'Yes, I suppose so. A very clever man who can't walk down a street without falling over.'

'I'm sorry?'

Liz shook her head. 'Never mind.'

They walked out through the door, and Liz immediately felt a considerable decline in the temperature since she had entered the place. Taking her jersey from around her waist, she pulled it over her head as she walked with the doctor across the service lane and out onto the pavement.

'Now, señora, you go up to that street there,' he said, indicating the fast-moving carriageway to her left, 'then go to the right for two hundred metres, and then to the left, and when you are there, you do not leave this road. It is very big all the way to the Avenida de Menéndez y Pelayo, and your hotel is there.'

'Right. And how far is it?'

'I believe about three kilometres.'

'Three kilometres! I didn't think it was that far! I'd be better getting a taxi.'

The doctor let out a sigh. 'You want to take a taxi now?'

'No, don't worry,' she replied, realizing from his tone that she was fast becoming a nuisance to him. 'I'll just walk. And thank you for all your help.'

The doctor gave her a smile, then made his way quickly back to the entrance, dodging around a newly arrived ambulance as he crossed the service lane. Liz watched him until he had disappeared through the double doors, then turned and set off on her way back to the hotel.

The walk across the city was, as the doctor had suggested, quite straightforward, and there was never a moment when she felt uncomfortable in being out alone at that time of night because the streets were as busy as they had been during the day. On countless occasions, she had to step off the pavement, finding her path blocked by swarms of children who played like puppies around the street-side tables at which their parents sat. She would return a smile if she caught the eye of a doting mother, but that was as far as she could go in communicating with anyone, and it was this inability and the fact that she now had no one with whom to interact that made her start reflecting on her own isolation and loneliness. Other than Arthur, she knew absolutely no one in this vast, humming city. Thinking about it, she knew no one in this *country*! She couldn't talk to anyone, she had no idea of how to get around the place by herself, and she now realized how much she had come to rely on Arthur for the companionship and security that he offered. She felt an aching knot tighten in her stomach as the alien sensation of homesickness engulfed her, and all she wanted to do now was to return to Scotland, to see her father and Alex, and to talk with them. Yes, that was it! Just to talk to someone without having to help others search for words, or for herself to try to understand this wretched language.

By the time that the vertical blue-lit sign on the side of the Hotel Cazaral came into view, she was almost running, desperate to get back to the haven of known territory. She pushed through one of the heavy glass doors and entered the foyer, and even though the pale-green marbled décor was as warmly welcoming as an unfilled swimming pool, she breathed out a sigh of relief at the familiar sight of the two sludge-brown armchairs, incongruously positioned to draw attention to the hotel's ornate wall-hanging and the model of the Spanish galleon in full sail that stood below it on the corner of the carved pine chest.

A man was standing at the reception desk, his luggage clustered around his feet as he talked animatedly in Spanish with the young girl who manned the desk, and whom Liz had not seen before. Her fingers danced in stuttered bursts over the keyboard of her computer, and a look of puzzled anxiety creased her forehead. The man reached across the desk and swung the screen around so that he could look at it himself, and the girl took a pace back and nervously twiddled her pen in her fingers as she watched for his reaction to what he was viewing. He slowly shook his head and spun the screen back to face her, and came out with a short expletive that, judging from the look on the receptionist's face, Liz understood to be a particularly potent swear-word. The girl took a deep breath and spoke to him in a thin, wavering voice but he cut in, his raised tone resounding around the marble walls of the foyer. He held up his hands as if admitting defeat and gave each of his suitcases a hefty dunt with his foot, making them slide across the highly polished floor towards one of the armchairs. He turned and followed their path and slumped down into the chair.

Liz walked forward to the desk, hoping to take advantage of the momentary lull in their heated debate. She was feeling tired and low-spirited and she didn't want to have to witness any more of this haranguing match. 'Excuse me,' she said, giving the girl a wide smile to assure her that she was going to be friendly.

The girl continued to punch the keyboard, but lifted one hand to stop Liz from speaking further. '*Un momento, señora. Tengo que asistir a este caballero primero.*'

Liz turned and looked across the foyer to where the man was sitting, resting an elbow on the arm of the chair and rubbing at his eyes with his fingers. He was probably in his mid-thirties, broadly built, and was dressed in a light fawn corduroy jacket, white open-necked shirt and jeans, and although he was tanned, he certainly did not have the colouring of a Spaniard. A tangled mass of sandy-blond hair curled over his collar, and the cuffs of his jacket were drawn back enough to reveal a profusion of freckles covering his wrists and hands. He sat with his legs crossed, showing off a pair of high Spanish riding boots with crossed ankle-straps under his jeans. He dropped his hand to the arm of the chair and looked straight at Liz, fixing her with a pair of startlingly blue eyes. He pulled down the corners of his mouth and held out the palms of his hands, as if to signify that matters were out of his control.

'*¿Señor?*' the girl called out to him.

The man made no move to leave the chair. '*¿Sí?*'

'*Lo siento, pero yo tendré que llamar el gerente.*'

'*Si cree que es necesario, pero primero quisiera una copa.*'

'*Desde luego. ¿Qué quiere usted?*'

'*Whisky, un whisky doble, y una botella de agua con gas.*'

The girl smiled at him, relieved that he seemed to be becoming better-humoured. She made to move from behind the desk, then, as an afterthought, turned back and looked towards Liz. '*¿Señora?*'

'Thank you . . . yes. Could I have the key to room four hundred and ten, please?' She blurted it out quickly, longing just to get to her room and go to bed.

The girl looked perplexed, not having picked up what she had said. '*¿Llave?*'

Liz let out a long sigh and shook her head. 'I don't know!' She pointed towards the rack of keys that hung behind the girl. 'Key – for room four hundred ten.'

'The Spanish for key is *llave*.' The voice, slanted in an American accent, came from behind her.

She turned and looked at the man. 'I'm sorry?'

'The girl asked you already if you wanted your key.'

Liz bit at her lip. 'I didn't know that. I can't speak any Spanish.'

The man shrugged. 'Well, you shouldn't expect everyone here to speak English, then.'

'I don't,' she replied, giving him a look of bewilderment at his rudeness before turning back to the girl.

'Well, then, ask for it in Spanish. The word is *llave*.'

Liz felt her cheeks flush with anger, not only because of his attitude, but because, for some stupid reason, she realized that her eyes had begun to well up with tears. Dammit, she thought to herself, what the hell are you doing? You've gone through worse emotional moments than this over the past few months. You can cope with this. She brushed fiercely at a cheek to wipe away an escaping tear. On the other hand, why on earth *should* she have to cope with this? She was tired and alone and all she really wanted to do was to go to bed now, and having longed to hear just one English word spoken to her for the past hour, when it did eventually materialize, it was just . . . so unfriendly.

'Go on, try it. The word is *llave*.'

Liz spun round and glared at the man. 'Why don't you just shut up?' The quiver in her voice made the rebuke totally unconvincing.

She noticed the expression of self-amusement drain from the man's face the moment that he caught both her intonation and her look. She turned back to the receptionist, willing her to find the key so that she could get away, but the girl just cast bemused glances from one to the other, her hand poised over the rack of keys, in the hope that someone would give her verification as to which she should hand over.

The man appeared at Liz's side. '*La llave para la habitación cuatrocientos y diez.*' The girl quickly took the key from the rack and gave it to Liz.

'Thank you.' She turned and lowered her head as she passed him, but he took her by the arm to stop her.

'Listen, I'm sorry. I didn't mean to be rude.'

'Well, you were,' Liz replied curtly, focusing on the hand that clenched her arm. She glanced up at his face, narrowing her eyes, and realized that his tan was mostly made up of an abundance of freckles. 'In fact, I think you still *are* extremely rude.'

He let go of her arm immediately and held out his hands. 'Look, I've just apologized. What more do you want?'

Liz gave him what she hoped was her most sardonic smile. 'Nothing at all.' She broadened the smile momentarily, then made her way towards the lift.

'Okay, I really, really am sorry.' The man continued to walk by her side. 'I was just being bloody-minded. I don't want you to go off thinking I'm a first-rate bastard, because I'm not. The fact is that I was meant to be here five hours ago, but my plane from Madrid was late, and I've just got here, and, well, I don't really want to be here, but now that I am, they don't have a damned room for me, and . . . I'm sorry, but I just suppose that I took it out on you.'

Liz stopped abruptly and turned to look at him. 'And I also have had a horrible night. My friend has broken his ankle, he is now in hospital on the other side of this . . . city, and I . . . just want to go to bed.' In saying this, her emotions seemed now to get the better of her, and for the first time she was conscious of tears running unguarded down her cheeks. She made her way quickly up the stairs and around the corner to the lift and pushed hard at the button. The man came after her.

'How about joining me for a whisky or something?'

Liz shook her head.

'What about a coffee?' he said quietly, his voice almost pleading.

As the lift arrived, Liz suddenly remembered the doctor's request. She turned to the man. 'No . . . thank you, but if you want to be helpful, you could maybe ask at reception for the key to my friend's room. I have to take some of his clothes to the hospital tomorrow.'

'Of course. What's his room number?'

'Four hundred eighteen.' She shook her head. 'No, it's not.' What *was* the number? She hadn't been to his room or had reason to contact him there since the first night. 'Maybe it's four hundred twenty.'

The man smiled at her. 'Look, there's no problem.' He began to make his way back to the reception desk. 'Just give me his name.'

'Professor Kempler.'

He stopped dead in his tracks and slowly turned to look at her, the friendly smile visibly sliding into a questioning frown. 'Professor Arthur Kempler?'

Liz took in a breath of surprise. 'Yes, that's right,' she replied, her voice suddenly bright in the comforting realization that Arthur might be a common link between them. 'Do you know of him?'

'Arthur Kempler is your friend?'

'Yes,' she replied, her moment of elation turning to one of puzzlement as she viewed the stony expression on his face. 'Why do you ask that?'

The man shook his head slowly. 'My God!'

'I'm sorry?'

The man walked two paces to the wall and leaned his back against it, folding his arms across his chest. 'The man is incorrigible! He's completely *insatiable*!'

Liz walked over and stood in front of him. 'Listen, I'm sorry, but I don't know what you're talking about. How do you know Professor Kempler?'

He let out a mocking laugh. 'So you're the new woman in his life, are you?'

'I beg your pardon? No, I am not the . . . look, I don't need to explain myself to you! Who are you anyway?'

'Who am *I*?' The man shook his head again. 'Well, madam, I just happen to be his son.'

The word hit Liz as if a church bell had been sounded too close to her ear. It rebounded from one side of her head to the other, the resonance of his tone thrashing around in her brain as if desperate to escape from its confines. She just stood staring at him with her mouth open. 'You're . . .' She gulped to try to bring some moisture into her mouth. 'You're Will?'

A cynical smile spread across the man's face. He looked down at the ground. 'Of course. You would know all about me, wouldn't you?'

'Well, yes, I do, but only because Arthur told me that you weren't going to be coming out here with him. I wouldn't be here otherwise.'

'That'd be right,' he murmured.

'Yes, as a matter of fact, it is!' Liz exclaimed. 'It's absolutely right! You told Arthur that you didn't want to come. In fact, I think that your exact words were that you never wanted to see him again.'

This obviously struck a delicate chord. He paused before replying. 'Well, that's between him and me, isn't it? That's for a father and son to sort out.'

'Of course it is. I have never wanted to get involved in Arthur's affairs.'

'Oh, Arthur's affairs!' He let out a scoffing laugh. 'That's an extremely apt choice of words. Well, I can tell you that there have been plenty of them.'

Liz swallowed hard, realizing that she had said completely the wrong thing. She felt her face colour with embarrassment at the line of conversation and she didn't want to be drawn into it any further. 'I wouldn't know about that,' she said quietly. 'That's none of my concern.'

'Oh, isn't it?' he replied, looking hard at her, his blue eyes afire with contempt. 'Maybe you just wouldn't *want* to know.'

This final innuendo hit hard at Liz. She let out a short cry and shook her head in disbelief. 'You think I'm having an affair with your *father*?'

The man shrugged. 'And why should I not think that?'

'Well, for a start, he's about twenty-five years older than me!'

'Age difference has never bothered him before.'

'*Him?* We're not talking about him! We're talking about *me*! It would bother me. I don't need to go chasing

after older men. I have a husband . . . or *had* a husband.'
She shook her head. Her argument was becoming
confused. 'Anyway, why am I saying all this? I don't have
to prove anything to you.' She paused for a moment,
wondering if it wouldn't be better just to leave things
right there, but then decided to set the record straight
once and for all. 'Listen, I'll explain the situation to you,
so please get this into your extremely suspicious mind.
Your father is my son's German tutor at Saint Andrews
University, and as he had nowhere to live, my son
persuaded me to allow him to come to lodge with us on
our farm. He has become a good friend of *my* father, and
also to us as well. Now, our farm has just gone bankrupt
and we're having to sell it, and that is after five generations of our family having farmed it. As you can imagine,
that is quite a devastating blow for us all. What's more,
my husband has just walked out on me. So to get a little
distance between myself and the place, I accepted your
father's *extremely* kind offer to accompany him out here –
and to be quite honest, the longer I spend here, the more
I wish that I had never, *ever* set foot in this wretched city.'

She looked away from the man, her eye caught by the
appearance of the young receptionist. She glanced from
one to the other, a look of fear on her face as she held up
her hands in an attempt to quieten their incomprehensible and hostile exchange. 'I'm sorry,' she said quietly to
the girl. She took in a deep breath and looked back at
him. 'Now, if you'll excuse me, I am very tired and I'm
going to bed.' She put her hand on the lift door and
pulled it open.

'What about the old man's clothes?' the man asked, his voice subdued.

She glared contemptuously at him. 'I shall get the *llave* tomorrow morning and collect them then.' She entered the lift and pressed the button for the fourth floor.

He quickly came to stand in front of her. 'And what about him?'

'I don't know,' Liz answered as the inner door closed in front of him. 'Isn't that for you to decide?'

Letting herself into her room, Liz walked straight over to the bed and sat down heavily upon it. She put the palms of her hands against her brow and rubbed it hard in an attempt to relieve the throbbing in her head. 'Oh, my goodness, what *is* going on?' she said out loud, then fell back on the bed and closed her eyes, and in feeling its longed-for comfort beneath her, the last vestiges of resistance to sleep quickly drained from her body.

CHAPTER 18

Jonathan Davies rounded off the address on the envelope with a precise underline, gave the ink a quick blow, then replaced the top on his fountain pen and picked up the folded letter from the desk and tucked it inside. He bent over the flap to seal it, but then paused, having second thoughts as to whether its contents had said enough. He took out the letter and reread it.

He hadn't had to write many letters of apology before. He had always prided himself on his own decorum, his naval training having instilled in him a discipline of courtesy and gentlemanly behaviour. He therefore understood how appallingly he had let himself down at the farmhouse the other evening, not only embarrassing himself but also the farmer and his lady guest. And what was more, his inability to hold his drink had resulted in his forcing his presence on the household for the whole night. And dammit, he had come to respect that family so much, in the way that they had been able to handle the countless adversities that had been heaped upon them. Yet throughout his association with them, they had always remained friendly and accommodating toward him at a time when they could quite easily have regarded him as the enemy.

The contents of the letter, he decided, could never humble himself as much as he would like, but it would just have to do. He replaced it in the envelope and sealed it, then, getting up from his chair, he made his way over to the door of his office. The telephone on the desk rang. He tucked the letter into the inside pocket of his jacket and retraced his steps and picked up the receiver.

'Jonathan Davies . . . yes, hullo, Lionel . . .' As he listened to the words spoken to him he felt the colour drain from his face and the sting of adrenalin ran up his nerve ends to explode in his brain. '. . . You can't be serious! . . . but you *assured* me that they were going to back the project! Had they not signed the agreement? . . . Yes, but the work's well under way, Lionel! The earth-movers are working right at this minute! . . . Well, it's all very well for *you* to suggest that we stop them, but don't you understand what this means? . . . No, it is *not* a temporary hitch. We now do *not* have the complete package in place at the time of commencement, and that was the condition upon which the American consortium insisted. Did they give any reason for pulling out? . . . Oh, come on, Lionel, that is a technicality! I think they're acting in a totally unprofessional manner. They shouldn't be in the business of lending money if that's their policy . . . I dare say you won't be recommending them again, Lionel, but that's no help to us. Do you realize that this will probably spell the end of this project? . . . I'm afraid that's no help. I could never continue on such a speculative basis . . . Yes, I know I have little choice. You don't have to point that out . . . All right, one week, that's all I can afford to give you, and in the meantime, I'm going to have to suspend all work . . . Right, well, you do that and just keep in touch.'

He replaced the receiver with force, then slammed his fist down on the desk. He slumped back into the chair and covered his face with his hands. This just could not be happening, he thought to himself, this is a complete nightmare. What the hell was he going to do now?

He had been raising capital for this project for the past four years, so there was really no hope of raising a sixth of the full amount within the space of a week, *and* he had an interim progress meeting with the principal backers in ten days' time.

Maybe he shouldn't bother waiting the week. Maybe it would be better just to pull the plug on the whole project right now. It seemed to have been dogged with bad luck from the moment of its inception, and he really could not afford to take on any more of the capital burden himself. He had already funded the research and development by taking out a double mortgage on his house, and his own assets within the venture-capital group were also tied up as collateral. So there was nothing left on which to fall back. He couldn't afford to go on and he couldn't afford to stop.

He reached across the desk to pick up the telephone to call the contractor, and as he did so the envelope in his inside pocket crinkled gently. He took it out and leaned back in his chair and studied the address. *What* was he going to say to them? How on earth could he break the news? All he had really succeeded in doing was leading them down the garden path with his grandiose ideas. Okay, so Gregor's farm was still intact, but how could Liz and her father ever begin to market their farm in its present condition? And there was simply nothing left with which to help them reinstate it.

He picked up the receiver and dialled a number. 'Willie? Good morning, it's Jonathan. Listen, what are the boys doing at the minute? . . . Well, you'll have to stop them . . . I know, Willie, but there's been quite a major hiccup, so just get them to stop for now. Is Michael Dooney on site? . . . Right, well, could you ask him to wait there until I come over? . . . probably in about an hour. I have to go to Winterton first to see Gregor, and then Mr Craig at Brunthill, but after that I'll just walk down to see you both . . . all right. Thank you, Willie.'

The farmyard at Brunthill was still wet following the cloudburst that had occurred during the previous night, and a deep, muddy puddle stretched the length of the flight of steps that led up to the back door. Jonathan Davies skipped over it, took a deep breath, then climbed the steps and gave two sharp knocks on the door. He heard first the muffled bark of a dog from the depths of the house, then someone allowed it through to the back kitchen, where it stood yelping and scratching on the other side of the door. It opened and the small dog, taking little notice of his presence, ran past him down the steps, hurdled the puddle at pace and disappeared off into the steading.

'Mr Davies!' The farmer stood in the doorway, his quite conservative attire of tweed jacket, cavalry-twill trousers, checked Viyella shirt and knitted tie being incongruously offset by a pair of white trainers and a dark green baseball cap with GLENEAGLES emblazoned above its peak in gold lettering.

'I'm sorry, Mr Craig. Is this a bad time? Are you just going out?'

'Shortly, but not quite yet. Come on in.' He stood aside to allow Jonathan to walk in front of him to the kitchen. 'Now, you remember Miss Bayliss, don't you?'

The diminutive woman had just entered the room by the door leading from the hall. She was carrying a small suitcase. 'Of course,' said Davies, his hand outstretched as he approached her. She put down the suitcase next to the set of golf clubs that leaned against the kitchen sideboard, then turned to greet him.

'Hullo, Mr Davies. How nice to see you again.'

He cast an eye over the luggage. 'I'm sorry, I should have rung first. I see that you *are* both going out.'

'No, not at all,' replied the farmer. 'I'm a long way from being ready to leave yet. Would you like a cup of coffee?'

'No, please don't bother yourself.'

'It's no bother. We're about to have one.' Mr Craig tipped back the lid of the Rayburn and placed the kettle on the hot plate.

Davies slid his hands into the pockets of his suit jacket. 'Right, well, that's very kind,' he said quietly, feeling quite ill at ease. 'So . . . where are you off to today?'

Leaning back against the Rayburn, Mr Craig crossed his arms and smiled broadly at Roberta Bayliss. 'Well, we're heading westward, Mr Davies. We've played Carnoustie, Gleneagles and Rosemount, so we've decided to ring the changes and go off for a couple of days to play some of the courses on the other side of the country.'

Davies tried to show interest in what was being said to him, but his mind was more occupied in working out how best he could break the news. He flashed the farmer an apprehensive smile. 'Well, what a good idea!'

Mr Craig walked across to the sideboard and took down three mugs from their hooks. On his way back to the Rayburn, he was intercepted by Roberta. 'Listen, I'll make the coffee,' she said, taking the mugs from him, 'and then you and Mr Davies can have a talk.'

'Well, that's very good of you, Roberta!' He turned and placed his hands on the central worktop. 'So, Mr Davies, I might well be wrong, but I'd say that you're looking a wee bit worried about something.'

Davies let out a short laugh. 'You could say that, sir.'

Mr Craig nodded. 'Then we'd better hear it, hadn't we?'

Davies cleared his throat. 'Well, for a start, I had written you a letter this morning concerning my behaviour the other night.'

The farmer frowned in puzzlement, yet it did little to disguise the smile of amusement that wrinkled the sides of his mouth. 'The other night? I don't recall there being much amiss with your behaviour the other night.'

Davies shifted edgily on his feet. 'That's kind of you, to see it that way. However, I believe there was, and I hope very much that both you and Miss Bayliss will forgive me for appearing at your house in such a state, and also for my unscheduled overnight stay.'

Mr Craig shook his head. 'In my mind, there's nothing to forgive, Mr Davies. It was a pleasure to have you stay under my roof.' Pushing himself away from the worktop, he walked over to the fridge and opened it and took a bottle of milk from the door-shelf. 'So you can now stop looking so worried about life and just enjoy your cup of coffee.'

'I would very much like to, Mr Craig, but I'm afraid that I have some other quite distressing news.'

The farmer turned and slowly began to unscrew the top, his eyes fixed on Jonathan Davies. 'And what might that be?'

Davies took a deep breath. 'I'm afraid that one of the backers has pulled out.'

His hand did not make even the minutest waver as he poured milk into the three mugs. 'And what exactly does that mean, Mr Davies?'

'It means a suspension of work. An indefinite suspension of work.'

Mr Craig came over and handed him the mug of coffee. 'And have you broken this news to Gregor yet?' he asked.

Davies nodded. 'Not yet. I've just been over to Winterton, but he wasn't there.'

The farmer carried his mug over to the window and stood with his back to Davies, staring out across the fields. 'So you would be reckoning,' he said slowly, 'that this golf course won't get built.'

'I don't know, Mr Craig. I spoke this morning with our business consultancy in London, and they're going to see if they can raise the shortfall in the City over the next week.'

'And do you hold out much hope for that?'

Davies paused before replying. 'I have to say that I'm afraid I don't.'

Roberta Bayliss had been standing by the Rayburn, listening intently to the conversation but feeling uneasy about her presence while such dire news was being imparted. 'Excuse me,' she said quietly, 'I realize that it is probably not my place to speak, but I just wondered if you were a golfer yourself, Mr Davies.'

Davies smiled at her. 'I'm afraid I'm not, Miss Bayliss.'

'Well then, as a keen golfer myself, I hope you don't mind my saying that it would be a crying shame if that golf course wasn't built. It is probably one of the most beautiful sites I have ever seen, and I can tell you, Mr Davies, I've seen some of the world's best.'

'I am fully aware of this, Miss Bayliss. Michael Dooney, the course architect, agrees with you wholeheartedly on that point. But we have strict conditions in place, one of them being that if we don't have the full financial package at the due date of commencement, then our major backers in America wish to pull out and redirect their money into a new golf course over there.'

Roberta nodded, understanding his problem. 'They're frightened of speculative ventures, right?'

'Exactly.'

'And you've already started.'

'Yes.' Davies looked towards the lean figure of the farmer, silhouetted against the window. 'I'm so sorry about this, Mr Craig. I don't know what else to say.'

The farmer turned and let out a long sigh. 'No, I appreciate that, Mr Davies, and I appreciate you coming to tell me. I can see that it must be very hard for you too. You've put a good deal of your own money into this project as well, haven't you?'

'Yes, I have.' He drained his mug and placed it on the sideboard. 'I know that Liz is in Spain at the minute, Mr Craig, but I hope very much that when you speak to her, you'll pass on my heartfelt apologies to her.'

'Well, I won't be telling anyone just yet, Mr Davies, and I would hope that you might take my advice in doing exactly the same. Not even Gregor.' He turned to Davies. 'Let's just give it the week. Something might turn up, and then hopefully we can just forget that this conversation ever took place.'

Davies shook his head. 'I'll have to tell the contractor, Mr Craig, and Michael Dooney.'

'If you haven't told them yet, I wouldn't bother doing so. If you have to hold off construction for a wee while, I'm sure that you can think of an adequate excuse. Remember that this farm has served my family for five generations, Mr Davies. A week in the life of this place is very short, and it could quite easily result in its future being made secure. I would like to think that we owe it that at least.'

Davies contemplated this for a moment. 'All right, I'll try to come up with something.'

'I'd be most grateful if you could do that,' Mr Craig replied, making his way towards the door that led into the hall, 'because if I don't get myself ready for this trip, we'll never get off.' He put out his hand to Davies as he passed him. 'Goodbye, Mr Davies. We'll just keep our fingers crossed.' He looked quickly in the direction of his house guest. 'Maybe you could show Mr Davies to the door, Roberta.'

Roberta smiled at the two men. 'I'd be glad to.'

He hadn't been away from the house for so long that he could not remember even if he still owned a suitcase. He went though every cupboard on the upper floor of the house, eventually tracking down a dusty object with a handle in the roof-space above the back bathroom. He carried it carefully to his bedroom, opened the window and gave it a few solid whacks against the side of the house, then, laying it on his bed, he stood back to appraise it, hands on hips. It wasn't the most salubrious piece of luggage he had ever seen, definitely not as smart as Roberta's, but it had two good catches, even though they were slightly rusted, and what's more, it wasn't filled with junk. He threw back the lid, then opened his cupboard door and scratched at the back of his head as he considered which of his meagre supply of clothes would be most suited for the trip.

Half an hour later, he came down the stairs with the burden of a severely overfilled suitcase to hand, the cover of a *Farmer's Weekly* flapping out of one of its bulging sides. Ripping it off, he crumpled it up and put it into his jacket pocket, then quickly made his way through to the kitchen. As he entered, he heard Roberta saying words of farewell to someone at the back door. She closed it and came back into the room.

'Sorry I was so long,' he said, dropping the suitcase by Roberta's luggage and trying to position himself in such a way that she didn't see it. 'I'm a wee bit out of practice in knowing what to take on a trip like this.'

Roberta smiled at him. 'That's all right.'

He looked towards the back door. 'Who was that you were talking to?'

'Oh, only Jonathan Davies.'

'What? He's only just gone?'

'Yes, well, we got talking about Australia. He'd been to Sydney once when he was in the navy.'

'Had he now?' He took hold of the strap of Roberta's golf bag and swung it onto his shoulder, then picked up a suitcase in each hand. 'Right, are you ready to go?'

Roberta made no move towards the back door. 'Listen, are you quite happy to go – under the circumstances, I mean?'

Mr Craig nodded. 'Aye, perfectly. We can gain nothing at all by worrying about it at present, so I suggest that we follow the party line and have no mention of it for the next week. So let's away and enjoy ourselves.'

'All right. Did you leave the note for Alex?'

'It's on the table.'

'Okay then!' She walked through to the back kitchen and opened the door, standing aside to let him out with his load. 'He's pretty old-fashioned, isn't he?'

'Who?'

Roberta dropped the snib on the door and pulled it shut behind her. 'Jonathan Davies.'

He heaved the luggage into the back of the Land Rover. 'In what way?'

'Calling you Mr Craig.'

He slammed the door of the vehicle shut and rattled the handle to make sure that it was closed properly. He then leaned his elbow against it and took off his baseball cap and smoothed back his hair. 'Well, maybe I should confess something to you.'

Roberta gave him a quizzical look. 'What?'

'Craig is my surname.'

Roberta looked aghast. 'You're joking!'

'Not at all.'

'Do you mean to say that I've been calling you by your surname all this time?'

'Aye, you have.'

'But that's . . . that's dreadful! I mean, why didn't you tell me earlier?'

'Well, just because you started calling me that and I thought it would be an embarrassment to us both if I was to enlighten you, and, well, as it happens, I'm not awful partial to my Christian name in any case.'

'And what might that be?'

He laughed. 'I'd just rather you called me Craig.'

'Come on, tell me your Christian name.'

A pink flush rose to his cheeks and he crossed his arms, then unfolded them and scratched at the back of his head. He took a pace towards Roberta and whispered something in her ear, then stood back to watch for her reaction. The expression on her face, however, registered surprise rather than the hilarity that he had anticipated.

'I don't see anything wrong with that name,' she said.

The farmer smiled. 'Well, it's never been one that I've ever got used to. It was always considered a bit out of the ordinary around here. When I was at the school, it left me open to all sorts of nicknames.'

Roberta nodded. 'I've got a pretty silly nickname too back home.'

'Have you now?' he sang out, his eyebrows raised in interest. 'And what might that be?'

'Bobby. Stupid, isn't it? It's a boy's name.'

'Aye, but it's a good name. I had a sheep-dog once called Bobby.'

Roberta let out a cry of astonishment. 'A sheep-dog!'

'Aye, and an awful loyal one at that.' He put his fingers to his mouth and let out a shrill whistle to call in the Jack Russell.

Roberta laughed. 'Well, I think that it would be best if we gave that name a miss, just in case you get tempted to start whistling me up!'

Mr Craig opened up the passenger door of the Land Rover for her. 'Aye, well, there might be a good chance of that happening. And I think we'll just stick to Craig as well, shall we?'

Roberta climbed into the vehicle. 'Are you sure you don't mind?'

The farmer waited for the dog to scuttle in beside Roberta's feet before slamming the door closed. 'Nothing would make me happier.'

CHAPTER 19

Liz entered the dining-room of the Hotel Cazaral at exactly eight o'clock the following morning and was surprised to find that, even at that relatively early hour, it was almost full to capacity. As she was shown to a table in the corner of the room she cast an eye around those who were having breakfast and sighed inwardly with relief when she realized that he was not there. She had no idea – nor did she care – whether he had managed to get himself a room in the hotel, but she was taking no chances, her plan being to get away from the place before he put in an appearance. Consequently, as she sat down at the table, she immediately ordered coffee and toast before the waiter had the chance to leave her.

Realizing that she was now going to have to cope with being alone for the duration of her stay, she had been up early that morning to give herself time to go through her Spanish phrase-book, writing down on a piece of hotel letter-heading some sentences that she felt might be of some use to her. She was studying these, head resting in her hands, when a shadow fell across the paper and she looked up with a smile of anticipated gratitude on her face, expecting it to be a waiter asking her if she wanted anything more. But there *he* stood before her, a hold-all in his hand and a watchful look of uncertainty upon his face.

He faced the palm of his free hand towards her and held up two fingers. 'Can we declare a truce?' His voice hit a momentary silence in the dining-room, and Liz looked around, noticing that a large family seated three tables away from her own had overheard the remark and were now watching them with intent, having obviously understood his remark. She really did not want him anywhere near her, but on the other hand she didn't want to cause a scene. She gave a brief nod.

'Can I join you?' he asked, pointing to the empty chair at the table.

'If you must, but I'm not going to be here for much longer. I have to summon up my courage to go and ask for a *llave*.'

The man twisted up his face, as if he had just received a hard slap on the cheek. 'Ouch! I reckon I deserved that.' He pulled the chair out and sat down, placing the hold-all beside him. 'Actually, as it happens, you don't have to ask for that any more.'

'Why not?'

He pointed to the hold-all. 'I've been to his room and got everything for you.' He paused, scrutinizing her reaction to this. 'I hope you don't mind?'

Liz shrugged. 'Why should I mind? You're his son and I'm just a friend.'

He leaned forward across the table. 'Listen,' he whispered furtively, 'can we just get rid of this hostility bit? I really am trying my best to make amends.'

Liz drained her cup of coffee and sat back in her chair, staring at him for a moment. 'Could you answer me just one question?'

'Sure.'

'What are you doing here?'

He considered this for a moment. 'I don't really know.'

'That's no answer.'

'Maybe, but it's the truth. I was in Madrid on business and I had a couple of days clear, and I knew that my father was in Seville for Semana Santa, so I thought I'd just make a trip down here.'

'Because you wanted to see him again.'

'Well,' he replied, making a gesture of indecision with his head, 'let's just say that I was going to leave my options open.'

'That's a bit of a change of heart, isn't it? Arthur said that you had returned your plane ticket and that you had said that you didn't want to see him again.'

'Yeah, I did say that,' he drawled, 'but in retrospect I think that it was a pretty childish thing to say.'

'But how did you know that he was here in this hotel? You returned everything to him.'

'No, not everything. He'd sent me an itinerary along with the plane ticket, and for some reason I held on to that.'

A waiter appeared at their table and Arthur's son ordered coffee and toast for himself. He asked Liz if she wanted anything else, but she declined the offer.

'Anyway,' he continued, 'even after I'd finished my business in Madrid, I was still of two minds as to what I should do. So I just sat in the coffee shop at the airport staring out the window at the planes taking off, trying to work out whether I really wanted to see him again or just forget the whole idea and take a flight back to London. And then I decided that it was pretty dumb going through life not knowing one's father when there was an opportunity of getting to know him, even though he had done irreparable damage to the lives of everyone in my family.' He paused for a moment and glanced at Liz. 'Maybe you don't know the whole story.'

Liz nodded. 'Yes, I do. He told me, and I have to say that he did make himself out to be the villain of the piece.'

He blew out derisively. 'Well, if he told the story straight, he wouldn't have been able to make himself turn out anyway else.'

The waiter made his way over to their table, a tray held aloft on his upturned hand. He placed a laden toast-rack on the table and poured out a cup of coffee for the man. '¿Algo más, señor?'

He held up a hand. 'No. Nada más.' He took a sip of coffee, then rested his elbows on the table, linking his hands together. 'So, after much deliberation, I booked a flight to Seville. The only trouble was that it was five hours late, and I arrived tired and angry, mostly because I'd had time to churn things over in my mind and, as a result, had begun to doubt my initial judgement. You know, all those things about a leopard not being able to change its spots.' He sat back heavily in his chair and pushed his hands into the pockets of his jacket. 'And that was why I jumped to the wrong conclusion with you last night – and if it helps any, I am still *very* sorry for what I said.'

Liz bit at her lip, not knowing what to say, his explanation having been so succinct that she now understood totally his reaction to their meeting. She cleared her throat. 'So where did you stay last night?'

'Here.' He let out a quiet laugh. 'Actually, I nicked the old man's room.'

'They allowed you to do that?'

'Once they'd studied my passport and seen the names were the same.' He leaned forward, his hand outstretched. 'Talking of which, I'm Will Kempler.'

Liz looked at the hand for a moment, then reached out and took hold of it. His grasp was firm, the palm of his hand surprisingly rough. 'And I'm Liz Dewhurst.'

He let out a sigh of relief. 'Well, Liz Dewhurst, I have to tell you right now that I have been up half the night, cursing my own stupidity and ignorance, and wondering if I would ever get the chance to find out your name.'

At that point, they both became aware of someone standing at their table and looked up to see the father of the family which had shown such interest in their initial interchange. He grinned inanely at them, an expression that was mirrored on the faces of the other members of his family, who had all been making moves to leave, but now stood in the centre of the dining-room, gawking in their direction. He craned forward over their table as if he were about to take them into his confidence, and clasped his hands tightly between his knees. 'I do hope you don't mind my coming over,' he said quietly in a twanging English accent, 'but my wife and I couldn't help but notice that you were having a bit of a hard time, and we just wanted to say how delighted we both are that you seem to have made amends, because Seville is just too beautiful a place at the minute to have one's differences.' He stood upright and held out his hands. 'Now you don't have to say anything, but my wife and I *and* my whole family would just like to let you know that our prayers go with you.' He turned to his family, raising his eyebrows to signify a successful mission and bathing them with a smile of self-benevolence before he moved over to where they stood. Then, straddling an arm around the shoulders of both his buck-toothed wife and a stringy teen-age daughter, he led his flock out of the dining-room.

Will screwed his head round to watch them for a moment, then turned back to face Liz. She continued to track them, her mouth open in amazement, as they descended the stairs and walked through the small seating area before disappearing around the corner to the hotel entrance.

Will chuckled. 'Wow! That was a bit deep, wasn't it?'

Liz snorted out a laugh. 'Deeply embarrassing, more like.'

'Oh, well,' he said, throwing up his hands dismissively. 'Each to his own.' He took a drink of coffee and leaned forward on the table. 'So, Liz, what are we going to do with Arthur?'

The smile left her face on hearing the word 'we.' She had never thought for a moment that she would be having to consider the 'we' situation. 'Well, erm, I . . . I don't really know. I mean, well, what are your plans?'

Will shook his head quite forcefully. 'I don't really know either.'

There was a moment's uneasy silence. 'Maybe,' Liz said eventually, 'it's for you to decide. You are his son, after all.'

Will let out a grunt. 'Yes, I was afraid you'd say that.'

'What did you expect me to say?'

'No, no, I mean I agree with you entirely. It's just . . . quite difficult.'

There was another silence. They both opened their mouths to speak at the same time.

'Sorry.'

Liz shook her head. 'No, you go on.'

'Well, I was going to suggest that we should both go to see him, and then . . . take it from there.'

'Don't you have to go back to work?'

'Yes, I do – eventually, but under the circumstances, maybe I shouldn't.' He scratched at the back of his head. 'Listen, I'm sorry, I'm not being very decisive about this, but the ridiculous thing is that you, as a friend, know him much better than I do, as a son!' He continued his display of uncertainty by pulling hard on his ear-lobe, then suddenly brought his forefingers down hard on the table and beat out a quick drumroll. 'Come on, we'd better try to be methodical about this. When is your return flight booked for?'

'Next Tuesday.'

'Right. Well, I would reckon that he'd probably be able to fly home by then, so maybe the best idea would be for me just to stick around and fly back with you. After all, I think it's going to be pretty important that you have someone around who can speak Spanish.'

'That's exactly the point that I was going to make. Only my feeling is that now you *are* here, it might be better all round if I just flew home straightaway.'

Will shook his head. 'That is not a good idea.'

'Why not?'

'Because I am fairly sure that Arthur will have booked early to get a discount rate, and if that's the case, your ticket will be non-transferable. If you do change flights, you'll have to pay a hefty surcharge.'

Liz felt her heart sink at this news. She had been hoping that this would be considered the optimum idea, not through any disloyalty to Arthur on her part, but because she realized that if she did stay, there would be little alternative other than to spend time with this man whom she really didn't know and of whom she was still quite uncertain.

'And also what has to be taken into consideration,' Will continued, 'is that you are my father's friend. I think that if you did take an earlier flight home, it may be construed that I'd forced you to do that, and I can tell you that my father and I certainly won't be needing to look for reasons to fall out.' He let out a short laugh. 'And that's the other reason I don't want you to go. Both my father and I may well need the services of a friendly ombudsman.'

Liz looked long at her hands clasped tight together on her lap. There was little alternative. She was going to have to make the best of the changed circumstances, regardless of what they might throw up. She let out a long sigh. 'All right.' She discarded her napkin onto the table. 'Well, maybe we should go to see him.'

'Okay!' Will exclaimed, pushing back his chair and getting up. 'But before we go, do you have your plane ticket?'

'No, Arthur does. They could be in his room, though.'

'I wouldn't know where to look. Can you remember what airline you travelled with?'

'GB Airways.'

Will nodded. 'Well, my reckoning is that they probably have only one flight a day. I'll have to warn them that they have a passenger with a broken leg, so they can arrange for him to have a row of seats to himself.'

Liz took in a long breath. 'Goodness, I never thought of that. Do you think that'll be possible right after Semana Santa?'

'No idea.' He gave her a wink. 'But I can be very persuasive.' He picked up the hold-all. 'So I'll meet you down in reception in a quarter of an hour.'

'All right.'

Liz got to her feet and began to follow him out. He had only taken a few paces when he stopped and turned, and she could not avoid bumping into him. He smiled at her. 'I really am sorry about last night.'

She nodded slowly. 'Well, let's hope that we don't have to mention it again.'

Arthur was feeling disgruntled. Things were beginning to annoy him intensely, especially the man in the bed next to him. Having regained consciousness after his general anaesthetic, he had been wheeled into his room at four o'clock in the morning, and had hoped that his drowsy state would allow him to continue sleeping. However, it was not to be, because the man, who appeared to have no visible sign of injury or illness, took one look at Arthur's heavily plastered leg and immediately took it upon himself to demonstrate to his new companion that he was the one in much greater need of medical care and attention. Arthur had therefore spent the remaining hours of the night listening to his neighbour turning constantly in his bed, each move being accompanied by a long moan or a loud groan. The noise, what's more, was further exacerbated by the vociferous, though no doubt comforting, tones of his middle-aged and quite unattractive daughter, who was having to stand night-time vigil over him, snatching at rare moments of rest in the discomfort of what looked like an un-upholstered dentist's chair.

Besides all this, he had begun to feel quite alone – and quite bored, and even though he was being fed a regular supply of pain-killers his leg still ached, and he was becoming increasingly conscious of an itch that had developed under his plaster-cast, somewhere just up from his fourth toe. He also missed his pipe sorely. He knew that it was sitting in his bedside cabinet, but he could neither reach it nor was he allowed to smoke it. The nurse who had assisted in the operation to set his leg had made this abundantly clear to him when she had wrestled it from his clutches in the operating theatre, giving him express instructions by way of sign language not even to think of putting a match to it in the hospital.

Nevertheless, of all his concerns, his greatest was for Liz. He hadn't realized that she wasn't with him until he had woken up just before they took him down to the operating theatre. He had become quite agitated about her whereabouts, but the young doctor, who bore a somewhat disconcerting resemblance to Buddy Holly, had explained to him in pretty poor English that he had suggested that she should return to the hotel. When he had then let slip that he had given her directions to walk, Arthur had blown up, asking why the hell he hadn't thought of getting her a taxi, because she was incapable of finding her way to the bloody cathedral in Seville, let alone her hotel. This had obviously been the wrong simile to make with the young man, because at that point he had walked away from Arthur without response, only returning to administer an injection with about as much delicacy as a bayonet thrust.

He now lay prostrate on the bed, staring at the blank white walls of the room. There was no chance that he could go back to sleep, the man next to him now snoring away quite contentedly. He pushed himself up awkwardly to a sitting position and turned around as far as he could to try to rearrange his pillows, but in doing so he caught the blanked-off needle that stuck out of the vein in his forearm. 'Damnation!' he cried out in pain. 'What the hell is this thing doing in my arm anyway?' The man's daughter looked across at him, a pleading look on her face as she held a finger to her lips. She pointed to her slumbering father. 'Oh, that's a good one!' he mumbled to himself. 'It's a damned pity you can't make *him* shut up for a minute.'

At that point a well-built nurse, dressed in a white uniform that strained across her ample frontage, came bustling into the room and unclipped the chart from the bottom of his bed.

'Excuse me,' he asked, his voice edged with irritation. 'Could you tell me why is it so necessary for me to have this thing in my arm?'

The nurse did not reply, but simply smiled at him, replaced the clipboard and left the room.

'Oh, for heaven's sakes!' he exclaimed in a loud voice. 'Why can't anyone speak English around here?'

'Well, if there's anyone in this hospital who does, they'll no doubt have heard you by now.'

He turned to see Liz smiling at him in the doorway. 'Liz! Am I glad to see you! I was wondering whether you'd ever made it back to the hotel or not.'

'Arthur, don't you think you should talk a bit more quietly?' she said, glancing at the sleeping man as she walked around the bottom of his bed. 'You'll wake him up.' She cast a sympathetic smile at the woman who sat beside him, clutching his hand.

'Good riddance, too. He's kept *me* awake ever since I got in here.'

'Arthur!'

'Don't worry! Neither he nor his daughter can understand a bloody word I'm saying.'

'Maybe not, but I'm sure that she can understand from your tone that you're not being over-friendly.' Liz eyed the plastered leg, supported by a cantilevered bracket above the bed. 'So how is it this morning?'

'Bloody sore.'

'I'm sure it is. Are they giving you pain-killers?'

'Yes, but I don't think they're strong enough.'

'What? Not up to Jack Daniel's, then?'

Arthur grunted a laugh. 'Certainly not!' He leaned forward towards Liz, a furtive look in his eye. 'Talking of which, you don't think you could . . .'

'Not on your life, Arthur! Just wait until you come out!'

'I thought you might say that,' he groaned, slumping back against his pillows. 'So that's it – the holiday period's over, is it? You now change back into being the Scottish schoolmistress.'

Liz reached a hand slowly forward towards the needle that protruded from Arthur's arm. 'Do you want me to give that a not-so-gentle turn in your arm?'

'Don't you touch that!' he cried out, covering the needle with his hand.

'Well then, don't be so grumpy, and don't go taking your misfortunes out on me. Anyway, there's someone here to see you that might cheer you up a bit.'

'Who?'

'I'm not telling you. It's a surprise.'

'Male or female?'

'Male.'

Arthur raised his eyebrows. 'Hell's teeth, I break my leg, end up in hospital, and you go off picking up stray men all over the place.'

'My word, you *are* feeling sorry for yourself, aren't you? As a matter of fact, I did not pick him up. He was at the hotel when I arrived back there last night.'

'Good-looking, is he?'

Liz laughed. 'Arthur, he is devastating! But I have worked out that it's probably in his genes.'

'That's all I need,' he droned. 'Some dark-eyed Spaniard coming to ogle over my . . .' He turned around when he became aware of the figure that stood in the doorway, clutching a hold-all in both hands, and the gloom lifted like a veil from his eyes when he saw who it was. 'My word! Will! What on earth are you doing here?'

Will entered the room and came to stand at the bottom of Arthur's bed. 'How are you feeling?' he asked, putting down the hold-all beside the bed. When he straightened up, Liz could tell that the smile on his face was forced.

Arthur pushed himself up in the bed. 'Fine! Fine! Never better.' He looked at his son, shaking his head in disbelief. 'Well, this is wonderful! I wasn't sure whether . . .' He trailed off and reached for the glass of water on the bedside cabinet and took a drink.

Will frowned. 'You weren't sure whether what?'

Arthur fixed a broad grin on his face. 'I wasn't sure

whether it was you at first in the doorway. But how marvellous that you've come.'

'Well, it was an on-the-spur decision,' Will replied with little animation in his voice. He looked down at Arthur's leg. 'So how is it? Nothing too trivial, I hope.'

Liz saw immediately from Arthur's open-mouthed expression that the remark was hurtful. 'Will,' she said guardedly.

Will let out a quiet laugh. 'It's all right. It was meant as a joke.' He placed both hands on the rail at the bottom of the bed. 'So, what's to be done with you?'

Arthur shook his head. 'Not a lot, I wouldn't think. I have no idea how long I'm going to be here.'

'Three days at the most,' Will replied, pushing himself away from the bed. He leaned back against the wall and folded his arms across his chest.

Arthur's eyes widened at the news. 'How did you find that out?'

'I've just been to see your doctor. He wants you out of here as soon as possible. He says that you're too much of a liability.'

'I am not! I've been a model patient so far.'

'Oh, yeah? And model patients try to light up their pipes in the operating theatre, do they?'

Arthur bit at his lip to suppress a grin. 'Well, I was slightly disoriented.'

'I'm sure you were.'

'Listen,' Liz interjected, trying to balk any chance of a confrontation between the two men. 'Now that we know that Arthur will be out of hospital by the weekend at

308

least, maybe we should think about what we're going to do.'

Will screwed up the side of his mouth as he considered the scant alternatives to hand. 'Well, we can't do much other than get him back to the hotel, and kill time there until we fly home on Tuesday.'

Arthur shot a querying look from one to the other. 'We?'

Will unfolded his arms and dug his hands into the pockets of his jeans. 'Yes, well, I didn't think that it would be fair for Liz to struggle back with you by herself, so . . . I've rung the office and told them that I'm going to take a week off.'

'Right,' Arthur said quietly. 'Well, that's very kind of you, Will.'

'Don't mention it. I couldn't very well abandon a sinking ship, now could I?'

There was a definite note of provocation in his final delivery. However, the need for an answer was avoided by the appearance of the busty nurse, who sailed into the room and cleared a space around Arthur's bed without issuing any form of command, relying solely on her considerable size. She stuck a thermometer under Arthur's tongue, unhooked the notes from the bottom of his bed, squeezed the big toe of his plastered leg until she saw him wince, wrote something down, withdrew the thermometer and wrote down the reading, then replaced the clipboard and walked out of the room, saying something in passing to the sleeping man's daughter, who sniggered and turned to look at Arthur, making no attempt to hide the smile of amusement on her face.

'I bet that nurse said something about me,' he said out of the corner of his mouth, his eyes narrowed in suspicion at the woman.

Will laughed. 'Yes, she did, actually.'

Arthur glanced up at his son. 'Dammit, of course! I was forgetting you speak this language! What did she say?'

'You wouldn't want to know.'

'I certainly would.'

'All right. She said that she was sorry that this woman here had to suffer being in a room with two grumpy old men.'

'She never did!'

'God's truth.'

Arthur humphed. 'What nerve! I'm at least ten years younger than him.'

'I think that we should get back to talking about the plan of action,' Liz cut in, not wishing to give Will the chance to needle his father, even though it was being done ostensibly with humorous intent. 'Are you happy with what's been suggested, Arthur?'

He turned to gaze out the window as he contemplated Liz's question. 'No, not really.'

'What do you mean, not really!' Will exclaimed, frustrated at his father's apparent belligerence. 'There's no altern—'

'I know! I know!' Arthur broke in, holding up his hands defensively. 'Please just let me explain before you bite my head off!' He paused, watching Will closely. 'All

I was just wondering,' he continued in a slow, reasoning voice, 'was whether we couldn't get away from Seville for a bit. If I go back to the hotel on Friday, I doubt I'm going to get much rest at all, what with Semana Santa coming to its climax. And there's surely going to be a great many more people around over the weekend.'

'Maybe we should consider first what Liz wants to do. She might still want to see it all.'

The two men looked in her direction, awaiting her reply. She shook her head. 'What I want to do is the least of our considerations. Arthur has to be the priority now.'

Arthur smiled at her. 'I'm sorry about all this, Liz. It's really mucked everything up, but you do still have until Friday. If you do want to go and join in with the parades, I'm sure Will would accompany you.' He glanced at his son. 'Wouldn't you, Will?'

'Of course.'

Arthur brought his hands down on the bed, as if he had successfully put an auction lot under the hammer. 'Good! That's decided then.'

'But have you any idea where we would go?' Liz asked, 'or, more to the point, *how* we would go? You're not going to be fit for travel, are you?'

'I don't see why not. I'd have to get back to the hotel somehow, so I'm sure an extra few hours in a car wouldn't harm me.'

'But we don't have a car.'

'I'm sure we could hire one, couldn't we, Will?'

Will nodded. 'I would think so. It would have to be a

pretty big one to allow you to get stretched out in it.'

'Great! In that case, fix it up, could you? I'll pay for it and claim it back on my travel insurance.'

Liz laughed. 'But we still don't have a clue where we would go!'

'No, we don't, do we?' Arthur scratched pensively at the day's growth of stubble on his chin. 'You know Spain, Will. Do you have any ideas?'

'None at all, I'm afraid. I don't really know around here too well. Madrid's been my stamping ground.' He pushed himself away from the wall. 'But I'm sure that the hotel would be able to recommend someplace. Liz and I could go back there now and make some inquiries.'

A dark expression of gloom came over Arthur's face at this suggestion. 'You don't both need to go, do you?'

'What?' asked Will. 'You want Liz to stay here to hold your hand?'

'I don't mind staying,' Liz said quickly.

'Look.' Will bent down and picked up the hold-all and placed it on the bottom of the bed. He undid the zip and took out two paperback books and threw them into Arthur's lap. 'Those should keep you entertained.'

Arthur held one of the books at arm's length as he viewed the title. 'My goodness! Mickey Spillane! I haven't read one of these for ages.'

Will shrugged his shoulders. 'Well, I don't remember much about you, but I do recall there always being a pile of those books by your bed.'

Arthur looked up at his son, wide-eyed in wonderment. 'You remember that?' He laughed. 'Not the most auspicious memory for a son to have of his renegade father, but nevertheless, I am deeply touched that you can recollect anything of me at all. Thank you.' He reached across to the bedside cabinet for his reading spectacles and put them on, then opened the book and began reading immediately.

'So do you want me to stay?' Liz asked him.

Arthur glanced at her over the top of his spectacles. 'What?'

'I asked if you wanted me to stay.'

'No! No!' Arthur replied, finding it difficult to drag his eyes away from the book. 'It'd be much better if you went with Will. He'll probably need a hand choosing a place to stay.'

Liz laughed. 'So we have your permission to leave you.'

Arthur had gone back to reading the book. He looked up. 'Of course, of course!' he said, waving his hand in dismissal. 'You head off.'

Will gestured to hurry her away before Arthur changed his mind. She gave a friendly smile to the daughter of Arthur's room-mate in passing as she and Will walked quickly to the door.

'You will come back, I trust?' They both turned simultaneously to look at Arthur. His eyes still hadn't left the book. 'These won't keep me amused forever, you know.'

Liz caught Will raising his eyes heavenward. 'No, Arthur, we'll be back later.'

'And when would that be?' he asked, this time looking up at them.

Liz opened her mouth to reply, but Will pre-empted

her. 'When we have everything sorted out, all right? Probably this evening.'

Arthur nodded. 'Good. I'll see you then.'

Will pressed the button on the lift and stood back to watch the lights above the door flash out the changing floor levels. 'So what do you feel like doing today?'

'Not a great deal, to be perfectly honest,' Liz replied, leaning her shoulder against the wall of the corridor. 'I'm feeling quite washed out after all the goings-on over the past twelve hours. If you wouldn't mind, I think that I might just go to bed and try to catch up on some sleep.'

The lift doors opened and they both entered. He pressed the button for the ground floor. 'Well, that suits me fine. I've got a bit of work to do anyway, *and* I'll have to try to find somewhere that we can all stay.' The lift clunked to a halt and the doors opened. They made their way along the corridor towards the main entrance. 'I would suggest that we maybe meet up later this evening and go get something to eat.'

'What about seeing Arthur?' Liz asked, stopping momentarily to allow the automatic doors to open up in front of her.

'We don't have to make it that late. Anyway, I'll take on visiting duties. I'm going to have to spend the night with him, at any rate.'

'Is that necessary?'

'So the doctor told me. Seemingly, it's the way the system

works over here. They look after him during the day, but at night, it's over to the family.'

They had reached the pavement beside the bustling Ronda de Capuchinos, and Will walked over to the edge of the thoroughfare and looked both ways for a taxi. Liz went to stand beside him. 'I could do that, if you like.'

Will shook his head. 'No, I think you deserve to take it easy tonight.' He turned and gave her a wide grin. 'Besides, it'll give us an opportunity to do a bit of father-son bonding, and no doubt we'll get on a hell of a lot better if he's asleep for most of the time!' He let out a shrill whistle and waved his hand at a taxi that was approaching them on their side of the road. They watched as it veered across from the central lane in a heart-stopping manoeuvre before coming to a standstill beside them. He spoke briefly to the driver and opened the door for Liz, and they had hardly the time to settle themselves in their seats before the man took off again, pulling out into the street without a backward glance, his actions resulting in a sickening squeal of brakes behind them and the furious pumping of at least three car-horns.

Will was silent for a moment, then blew out a sigh of relief. 'Okay, so if we're lucky to make it back to the hotel in one piece, what time do you want to meet up this evening?'

Liz did not reply immediately, but stared out of the window at the passing traffic. She turned to look at him, a half-smile on her face. 'Listen, please don't feel that you have to take me out, just because of the way things are at the minute. I can understand that it must be quite awkward for you . . . as it is for me.' She paused for a moment, but continued when she saw that he was about to speak. 'You see, I'm not very good company right now, as you can probably guess from what I told you last night. I was all right with Arthur, because he knew . . .'

'I'm looking forward to taking you out.'

Liz cast him a querying look. 'Why?'

'Because I need to talk, and I think that you probably need to talk as well.'

She shook her head. 'I have nothing that's worth saying any more. I mean, not just to you . . . to anyone. To go over the same old ground again would just be self-indulgence.'

'Great! So let's be self-indulgent! Maybe it's fate. Maybe we've been thrown together in this far outpost to be self-indulgent together.'

Liz laughed. 'I think that you could be manipulating the path of destiny just to suit yourself.'

'I know! It's fun, isn't it? So, I shall ask you again. What time tonight?'

'I don't know,' she replied quietly.

'What? I don't know, you don't want to come; or I don't know, you don't know what time to make it?'

Liz smiled at him. 'The second, I suppose.'

He nodded at her, a triumphant grin on his face. 'Good! In that case, we'll meet at seven o'clock in the bar.'

'I don't have much to wear; I mean, for going out.'

He cast an eye over her from head to foot. 'I'm sure you'll look just fine.'

*　*　*

At a quarter to seven that evening she was looking anything but just fine, due to the fact that she had slept as if comatose throughout the day and had forgotten to set her alarm clock. It was only Alex's telephone call at half past six that had woken her, and when, during the course of their conversation, he had announced in quite a matter-of-fact way that he was alone in the house because his grandfather had gone off to the west coast with an Australian woman to play golf, she had questioned him for much longer than time allowed. She now ran around the bedroom in her bra and knickers, her mind buzzing with mixed emotions about the inexplicable antics of her father, while at the same time wondering why it was that every time she had to go out in the evening she went through this palaver of trying to decide what she should wear. She pulled her meagre supply of dresses from the wardrobe one by one and held each up in turn in front of the full-length mirror on the wall before discarding them onto the bed, at the same time rubbing hard at her wet hair with a towel. They all seemed so unsophisticated, so . . . country-bumpkin-like. When the wardrobe was completely devoid of articles of clothing she went through the process in reverse, eventually settling for a pale-blue short-sleeved summer frock, more out of desperation than choice. She pulled it on over her head and contorted her arms around the back to pull up the zip, then gave the wrinkles a forceful brush-out with her hands. She found a lamb's-wool cardigan that was as good a match as she could muster, then made her way quickly through to the bathroom to put on her make-up.

Having made a hurried job on her mascara and eye-liner, she screwed out her lipstick and puckered up her lips, but then stopped with it held inches from her mouth and stared at her reflection in the mirror. Her pursed mouth matched perfectly the look of contempt in her eyes. What on earth did her father think he was doing? His wife, her mother, had only died less than a year ago, and surely theirs was now a happy and complete-enough household without some other woman being introduced into it. Heavens, she'd only been away for five days and he was already gallivanting around with some person that she'd never met! She stopped her thoughts there, suddenly realizing how much she was distorting the truth, beginning to understand that she herself was the source of her anger and frustration. She slowly let her hands fall to the edge of the basin and lowered her eyes to avoid looking at her own reflection. Why are you reading into this something that you know full well isn't there? Just think on what Alex took time to explain, you stupid, embittered woman. Your father was doing this out of the kindness of his heart, to help someone who was in need of friendship, of company, of solace. You're resentful of his selfless nature, jealous of his ability to carry on with life, while you cannot cope with what you have lost. She looked back up at the mirror and saw the freshly applied eye make-up run in blackened streaks down her cheeks. She coughed out a sob, and then felt other sobs take hold, juddering her body and gripping her stomach as fiercely as birth-pains. She bent down and laid her face on her hands. Oh, Dad, I'm so sorry. I'm so sorry. I didn't mean to

318

think that of you. My mind is just so twisted, so resentful. She bent up her head so that she was looking at her poor, pathetic reflection in the mirror. Oh, Gregor, why did you do this to me? Why – did – you – do – this – to – me?

The telephone rang insistently in the bedroom. She listened, but made no move to answer it. It kept ringing. She pulled a long strip of lavatory paper from the roll and wiped her eyes, then blew her nose as she walked through to the bedroom. She picked up the receiver. 'Hullo?' she asked, her voice croaky.

'Hi. It's me. Will.'

'Oh, hullo,' she replied, trying to lighten her tone to sound as if she were pleased to hear from him. It came out thin and wavery.

'It's ten past seven. Just wondered how you were getting on.'

She took in a deep breath to try to steady her voice. 'Will, would you mind if we didn't go out tonight?'

There was a silence at the other end of the line. 'Are you all right?'

She cupped her hand over the receiver and cleared her throat. She brought it back to her mouth. 'Yes, I'm fine. I'm just not feeling very well.'

There was another silence. 'Okay,' he said quietly. 'There's always another night.'

She replaced the receiver and sat down on the bed and covered her face with her hands. Well done, she thought to herself, there's one more missed opportunity. No doubt you'll be making those kind of feeble, stupid excuses for the rest of your sad, lonely life. She gave her nose a hard blow on the piece of lavatory paper and got up and walked slowly back to the bathroom, taking off her cardigan as she went. She chucked it over the towel-rail and turned on the hot-water tap in the basin, and cupping her hands under the steaming flow, she threw water onto her face, caring little for the fact that it was almost too hot to bear. She took a towel and rubbed hard at her face, looking in the mirror to see if she had managed to remove every stain of make-up from her cheeks. She had been successful on that account, but what proved indelible were the puffed eyes and red nose. She shook her head. How attractive. How wonderfully, bloody attractive.

There were two sharp knocks on the door of her room. She stood with the towel pressed against her mouth and listened. Whoever it was would go away again if she didn't answer. She walked quietly through to the bedroom and stared at the door. There were two further knocks. '¿Señora?' The voice seemed extraordinarily high-pitched, but she was sure it was male. She took two steps towards the door.

'Yes?'

'Servicio de habitaciones, señora.'

Liz threw the towel onto the bed. 'All right. If you could just give me a minute, please.' She gave each eye a rub with the back of her hand, pulled in a long sniff and walked over to the door and opened it.

Will stood with the side of his head in his hand, his elbow resting on the door-frame. 'Hi. I thought you might not answer the door if you knew it was me.'

Liz looked at him. His hair, still wet from his shower, was swept back sleek across his head, and she noticed that the collar of his corduroy jacket was damp where the mass of sandy blond curls touched it. He was dressed no differently from when she had seen him last, but his shirt and jeans were freshly laundered. She lowered her head, so that he couldn't see her face and so that she didn't have to look into his piercing blue eyes. 'Will, I really meant what I said. I'm not feeling very well.'

'Right. So that's why you've got yourself all dressed up, is it?'

'I am not dressed up. This . . . thing is as old as the hills.'

'It doesn't matter how old it is. It's how you look in it, and I think you look pretty good.'

She heard a rustle as he moved his position, and felt his hand cup under her chin. He lifted her face to look at him. 'What's happened, Liz?' he asked quietly.

The kindness in his voice was too much for her to stand. She felt the misery well up inside her again, and her face crumpled. 'I just feel so . . .' She could say no more, the convulsive sobs returning.

He put an arm around her shoulders and pulled her close into his body. 'Hey, hey, hey,' he said soothingly. 'Come on, things can't be that bad.'

'Can't they?' she sobbed. 'How would *you* know?'

'Okay, okay, so maybe I don't know.' He took her arms and put them around his body. 'But how about a hug between friends to get things on the right road?' He held her tight to him. 'There, that's better, isn't it?'

The feel of his body was too familiar. The taut muscles in his back, the squareness of his frame, the power of the arms that enfolded her. Only the height and the smell, some expensive aftershave that Gregor would never dare or afford to wear, were different. She pushed herself away from him and stood back, knowing that the look she gave him was filled with contempt. He read it well, and took in a deep breath, placing his hands on the small of his back. 'I'm sorry,' he said quietly. 'I didn't mean to—'

She held up her hand to stop him. 'No. It's not for you to apologize. Only maybe now you realize what kind of wilting flower you're dealing with.'

'I don't think you're a wilting flower. You may be a deeply hurt person, but you're no wilting flower. But, on the other hand, maybe you understand now how I feel about my father – someone whom you love deeply, whom you trust, who one day just . . . gets up and walks out of your life.' He stuck his hands in the pockets of his jeans. 'I know what you're talking about, Liz. I've been there. The circumstances may be different, but it never stops hurting.'

Liz turned to look at him. 'But you're all right. You're not like me.'

'Really? I have a job that takes me all over the world. Why? Because I don't want to settle down. Why don't I want to settle down? Because I don't want to meet a girl and marry her. Why don't I want to marry? Gadzooks! The problem has just been solved.' He paused for a moment and cast his eyes around the room. 'You can never get away from it all, you know, but you sure as hell have to make the best of what you've got.' He walked across to her and took hold of both her hands. 'Tell me, what was your husband called?'

She looked up at him. 'Why do you want to know?'

'I just want to know his name.'

'Gregor.'

'Well, in that case, *fuck* you, Gregor, and *fuck* you, Dad.' He looked at her, a broad smile on his face. 'You should try saying that – not about my dad, that's my prerogative, but you can say that about your husband.'

Liz shook her head. 'No, I couldn't. I've never said that about him.'

'But I sure as hell know that you felt like saying that about him.'

Liz lowered her head to hide the smile that had unwittingly come across her face. Once again, he cupped his hand under her chin and pulled it up so that she was looking directly into his eyes. 'Go on, say it.'

She paused, finding it difficult to stop the smile creasing her face. 'Fuck you, Gregor,' she said quietly.

'No, no.' He considered her delivery like a stage director might rehearse one of his star actors. 'Not enough feeling. Try it again.'

Liz didn't know if she was laughing or crying. 'FUCK YOU, GREGOR!'

'Good for you,' he said quietly. He put his arms around her shoulders and once more pulled her close to his chest. She pushed her face against the lapel of his jacket, feeling the tears run down her cheeks, yet knowing there was a broad smile on her face. It slipped slowly away when her eyes focused on the open door of her bedroom. She pushed herself away from Will and made a gesture with her eyes for him to look behind him. Will turned and together they stared out into the corridor. There stood the family – the father, the buck-toothed wife, the stringy teen-age daughter, and all the rest of them. Will turned to Liz and bit on his lip to stop himself from laughing. He looked back at the family and gave them a wave with his hand. 'Hi, there,' he called out in a cheery voice.

The father did not reply, but gave them both an icy stare before walking away, his body bowed in dejection. Only the wife flashed them an uneasy smile before they all scurried off after their leader.

'Oh dear,' Will said slowly. 'I think that we two lost souls are just about to become the "intrigue" of the hotel.'

Liz blurted out a laugh. 'It's your fault if we are.'

Will shrugged his shoulders. 'Yeah, I suppose it is.' He let out a deep sigh. 'But that's what happens when I get hungry. I get all sort of tensed up and say outrageous things.' He smiled warmly at her. 'So, how about joining me for something to eat, so nothing more outrageous can be said?'

Liz hesitated for a moment. Go on, she thought to herself, get on with life. Don't be such a miserable idiot. She nodded. 'Well, you'll have to give me time to put on some make-up.'

'Don't you know,' Will said, leaning back against the wall and folding his arms and crossing one leather riding boot over the other, 'that time means very little in Spain?'

*   *   *

From the outside, there was no way of knowing that it was a restaurant, save for the small glass cabinet that housed the menu, handwritten in Spanish on pink paper, which was attached to the wall at a height that deemed it only readable by someone over six feet tall. Will opened the heavy, riveted wooden door and ushered Liz into a small high stoned-walled courtyard, the length of which was lined with round white-clothed tables, each lit by a single candle held within a bulbous and ornately engraved glass hurricane lantern. A wooden pergola stretched the full length of the terrace, laden with an unruly twist of vines that drooped so low in places that the black-waistcoated waiters had to dodge their heads to the side as they hurried between the kitchens and the farthest tables, where the majority of those already dining were seated. At the other end of the courtyard open French windows led inside to a small room that only had space for four tables, all occupied.

Will glanced in at the crowded area. 'Are you going to be all right eating outside? It's not that warm, is it?'

Liz looked around the restaurant. 'This is wonderful. I would hate to eat inside. There's so much . . . atmosphere out here.'

A grinning waiter approached them, deftly flicking his white dishcloth over his shoulder as he walked. '*Buenas noches, señores.*'

'*Buenos noches. He reservado una mesa.*'

'*Vale. ¿Su nombre, señor?*'

'*Kempler.*'

'*Por supuesto. Sigame, por favor.*'

He led them to a table half-way along the terrace, an

agreeable distance from the main cluster of diners. He pulled out a chair for Liz.

'*¿Es un poco frío esta noche, verdad?*' Will remarked.

The waiter laughed. '*Sí, señor, pero no aquí. Tenemos braseros.*' He bent down and lifted up the white table-cloth and the thick woollen blanket that lay beneath it. A wooden deck, matching the size of the table-top, was attached to the legs of the table just above ground level, and a hole had been cut into its centre to accommodate a large cast-iron pan that brimmed with glowing embers. '*¡Hay mucho calor aquí, señor!*'

Will smiled at him. '*Muchas gracias.*' He pulled out his chair and sat down opposite Liz.

'That's a bit dangerous, isn't it?' Liz remarked furtively, once the waiter had left them.

'Not if you work it right. Pick up the blanket, stick it over your knees and put your feet up on the platform.'

Will watched Liz as she did as he had suggested, and saw the comforting smile come over her face as she began to feel the heat from the brazier. 'That is remarkable!'

'Well, in rural areas of Spain, it's still the main heating system for many of the houses. That's why so many Spaniards suffer during the winter from frost-bitten faces and chilblained knees.'

'They don't really, do they?'

Will laughed. 'No, I doubt it. I think it's what one might call an old wives' tale.' He caught the waiter's eye and beckoned him over to the table. 'Now, what would you like to drink?'

'I think, er, just a glass of white wine, please.'

'Well, let's go mad and have a bottle.' He glanced up at the waiter, who had come to stand beside their table. '*Una botella de vino blanco de la casa.*'

'*Sí, señor.*' The waiter turned to go, but spun round when Will called him back.

'*Y queremos comer pronto.*'

'*Vale. Les voy a traer la carta.*' He turned, ducking his head instinctively to avoid the trailing vine, and headed off quickly towards the interior restaurant.

Will pulled his chair forward and leaned his elbows on the table. 'So where have you been eating with my father while you've been out here?'

'Nowhere like this. We usually just grab something in a tapas bar, and then head off again to join in with the processions.'

Will nodded and let out a sigh. 'I'm sorry about all this happening. It's rather ruined your reason for being out here. If you want, we could always go out after dinner and see what's happening.'

'No, thank you!' Liz replied, holding up her hands in refusal of his offer. 'I can tell you, it's quite a relief not having to walk the soles off my shoes for one night.'

The waiter brought over the menus and the bottle of wine and poured a splash into Will's glass, who waved his hand for the wine to be poured without being tasted. Then, picking up his glass, he held it forward to the centre of the table. 'So, what shall we drink to?'

Liz waited for her wine to be poured, then picked up her glass and gave his question a moment's thought. 'Arthur's speedy recovery?'

'Good one.' He reached over and clinked Liz's glass. 'Arthur's speedy recovery . . . and starting over.'

She gave him an inquiring look. 'What do you mean?'

'Well, I think it's probably time that we all stopped living in the past, and tried to make the best of what life will deal out for us in the future, don't you?'

She slowly lowered her glass to the table and averted her eyes from his. 'That's a difficult one.'

'I know it is, but we all have to start somewhere, don't we?'

She looked up. His glass was still raised. She smiled at him and held up her glass. 'I suppose so.' They brought their glasses together once more.

'So, Liz Dewhurst, what about telling me your life story?'

Liz shook her head. 'There's not much to say, other than what I told you in my garbled version last night. I'd much rather hear about you. Arthur told me that you were in oil.'

'For my sins, yes.'

'Why do you say that?'

Will shrugged. 'Well, things change. What I do now is a world apart from when I first joined the industry.'

Liz settled her arms on the table and watched him intently. 'In what way?'

'It's not very interesting, you know.'

'And neither is my story.'

Will laughed. 'All right, if you insist. Where do you want me to start?'

'At the beginning?'

328

'Okay. Well, I was brought up in a suburb of Toronto with my mother and two elder sisters – and no father, of course.'

'Was your mother blonde?' Liz cut in.

'No.' He smiled and ran his fingers through his hair. 'Ah, you're wondering about my colouring, aren't you? I don't know where that came from. Somewhere in the hidden depths of my family background, no doubt. When I was young, I remember my father saying that it was the milkman, and being pretty naïve at that tender age, I always thought that the milkman had changed the colour of my hair by pouring milk all over my head when I was a baby. It wasn't until I was quite a bit older that I realized what he really meant. Anyway, to continue, I went through high school there, and at the age of eighteen – I was just about to go to a local college when the last of my sisters got married – it was then that I decided to leave home.'

'Why then?'

'Well, I didn't want to be the only one left at home, and it seemed a better time than any. My mother had just met up with this man who made her as happy as she had been since my father left her. He then became a sort of fixture in the house, and seeing that I didn't get on too well with him, and the feeling was obviously reciprocated, I thought it best if I wasn't around to rock the boat.'

'So what did you do?'

'I managed to wangle myself an American work permit and headed up to Alaska, where I got a greenhorn job as a right-of-way inspector and surveyor on the oil pipeline that linked Prudhoe Bay on the Arctic Ocean with the terminal at Valdez. I was up there, freezing my butt off for nine months, before a whole squad of us were moved down to Argentina to work on a new oil development project that was starting up there.'

'That sounds a little more exciting.'

'It was, and also pretty educational. That's where I learned to speak Spanish. Anyway, after six months there, I was assigned to the drilling division of the company as a surveyor. We worked way down in the south of the country in the Comodoro Rivadavia area on wild-cat exploration, which means that we carried out high-risk investigation of prospective development sites. We became quite a tight-knit team, all hands-on, and because of the nature of our work we were treated with a healthy respect by the other rednecks who worked the routine development wells and work-over rigs. When we went on leave to Rio or Buenos Aires, we'd walk into a casino and the regulars would stand aside and allow us unhindered passage to the bar. No one messed with us. Mind you, it was probably because we all stank after a month of wild-cat drilling.'

Liz laughed. 'So, what happened then?'

'Well, a number of things. The oil prices crashed a couple of years beforehand, the economy was up the creek and corruption was rife. So my company decided to stop all further exploration in Argentina, and we were packed off to new pastures.'

'Did oil production stop completely there?'

'No way. It's still going strong. There was a wave of

privatization in Argentina a few years ago, and quite a number of Spanish companies returned there in force. That's why I come out to Spain so much now. Most of our Argentinian operation is handled from Madrid.'

'So where did you go then?'

'The North Sea for eight years. Based in Aberdeen.' He juddered his shoulders. 'God, that was cold work! And then we went over to the Philippines.'

'Now, *that* must have been considered a cushy number!'

'You'd think so, wouldn't you? As it happened, it was, and still is, a difficult *and* delicate assignment. When we first arrived out there, offshore oil exploration was in its relative infancy, but nevertheless, by this time "the environment" had become a buzzword, and we found ourselves having to carry out lengthy negotiations at every level – provincial, regional, national, governmental – before we were able to do so much as lift a finger.'

'Why there so much?'

'Because the Philippines happen to have one of the most pristine physical environments on earth. Each of the seven thousand islands is surrounded by coral reefs and phenomenal marine life.'

Liz gave him a knowing look. 'And you would rather have just gone in and drilled.'

'No, actually, I have to say that that is the fallacy! Contrary to what everybody thinks, oil companies are pretty careful when it comes to protecting marine environment. In fact, I sympathized so much with the conservational aspect of it all that I always found myself saying the right thing in front of the governmental officials, and they got to like me – and trust me. And all this came to the attention, or maybe was *drawn* to the attention, of the big brass in the Madrid head office, and before I could say "oil boom," I was made Chief Negotiator on Environmental Issues for the company.'

'And that's what you are now.'

'In a way.' He grimaced. 'Only now I have a grander title. Health, Safety and Environment Manager of Kalmex Oil Exploration, Inc.'

'Wow!' Liz looked suitably impressed. 'But you said earlier on that things had changed. In what way?'

Will shrugged. 'Because I don't drill any more. I am a negotiator, an ambassador, a corporate diplomat, and I'm pretty good at all of it, if you can excuse me for blowing my own trumpet. But I'm a harder and more knowledge-able man than I was back then. I have to be. And some-times I don't like myself for it. I'd rather be back working with the team.'

'Are they still together?'

'A few of the diehards are. I caught up with them the other day in Aberdeen, and having a couple of days to kill, I went out with them to one of the rigs. It was pure nostalgia. For the first time in goodness knows how long, I got my hands dirty again.' He stretched the upturned palms of his hands over the table for Liz to view them. At the base of each finger and across the lower joints was a multitude of broken blisters. 'And sore.'

Liz laughed. 'Yes, I can see those are worker's hands.'

She found herself totally unprepared for his next move.

332

He reached across and took hold of the hand with which she had been supporting her face, turning it so that the palm faced upwards. He brushed a finger across its surface. 'And so is that.'

The physical, almost intimate contact hit her like an electric shock. Abruptly, she pulled her hand away from his grasp and sat back in her chair to distance herself from him. 'Yes, well, needs must,' she said curtly, glancing around the restaurant, anywhere to avoid coming into eye contact with him.

Her moment of embarrassment was broken by the waiter, who came to stand by their table, a smile on his face and a pen poised expectantly over his pad. Will picked up the menu.

'Right. So what do you feel like having?'

Liz shook her head. 'I'm not sure.'

Will glanced quickly at the fare. 'Okay. In that case, do you like pork?'

'Yes.'

'Good. Well, that's a safe bet around here.' He looked up at the waiter. '*Dos solomillos.*'

'*Vale, señor. ¿Con patatas y verduras?*'

'*Sí.*'

'*Gracias, señor.*' He whisked the menu from Will's clutches and headed off towards the kitchen.

Will leaned forward on the table and watched Liz closely. He had noticed in the instance before she had averted her eyes from his that they had registered a completely different reaction to the one he had witnessed in her hotel bedroom. There was no contempt this time, only a profound fear. 'I'm sorry. That was an insensitive thing to do. I think it's probably because I've been in male company too long. I don't get much chance to understand the finer points of life.'

Liz shook her head in dismissal of his apology. 'Have you never had a girl-friend?'

He gave the question thought before replying. 'No. Not really. I've had the occasional fling in different parts of the world, but that's all they were. I'm just too busy to get caught up in any long-term commitment, and because I'm never in one place for more than a couple of days, I don't think that it would be fair.'

Liz let out a sigh. 'Well, it's a good excuse, anyway.'

Will laughed. 'Yes, it is, isn't it?' The smile slid slowly from his face, to be replaced by a frown of serious contemplation. 'I've seen it happen all too often before, the offspring from a split marriage ending up in a mirror situation. Working in the oil industry turned out to be the best way to avoid it all.'

'And you have no regrets?'

'Not really. Well, maybe a bit, but I think that's just me getting a bit more sentimental with age. Anyhow, I've been on my own for so long now that I reckon I'm far too self-centred and set in my ways to impose myself on anyone.'

'So what's all this about "starting over" again, then?'

He grimaced. 'Ah. Well, I was really meaning with my father. I don't think that I'll be introducing any other discipline into my life.'

The waiter glided across the paved courtyard towards

them and slid the brimming plates onto their place-mats with practised aplomb. '*¡Qué aproveche, señores!*' He gave a short bow, then turned and left.

'Goodness! I don't think I've eaten as much as this since I've been here,' Liz exclaimed, studying the mountain of food on her plate.

'Well then, I would suggest that it's time you started filling yourself up a bit. The best way to curb emotion is to fill your stomach, and what better way to do it than with a good chunk of Iberian pig.' He took a mouthful of food. 'By the way' – he stopped talking until he had swallowed – 'I found a place for us all to stay.'

'Did you? Through the hotel?'

'No. I thought it best not to get them involved. I borrowed a map, though, then picked an area and found it on the Internet.'

'How did you do that?'

'I have a laptop with me all the time. It's invaluable for keeping in touch.'

Liz sliced through the tender meat as easily as a hot knife went through butter. 'I'm a complete dunce when it comes to the Internet. Alex, my son, tried to teach me once, but I found it all far too confusing. I've only just learned to master doing the farm accounts on the computer. So, go on, where is this place?'

Will put his hand in his inside pocket and produced a piece of hotel letter-heading. Liz saw that there were a few handwritten notes scribbled upon it. 'Well, it's a small private hotel in the Sierra de Cañareas,' he read out, talking as he was eating, 'about one hour and a half north of here. It's set in one hundred acres of chestnut and cork trees, and every room commands a wonderful view, which, on a clear day, can mean seeing right across to the next province.'

Liz laughed. 'How far is that? About two hundred metres?'

'Probably! Anyway, what sold me on the place is that it's run by an English couple, so you won't have to scramble for your phrasebook every minute of the day, and my father won't need to lose his rag at not being able to understand what's being said to him.'

She raised her eyebrows. 'Yes, well, that'll be a good thing. Did you tell them about him?'

'What? Losing his rag all the time?'

'No!' She smiled at his joke. 'About his leg.'

'Yes. They said that that was fine. The whole house is built on one floor and they have one bedroom which is set up for wheelchair access. So, the long and the short of it is that I've booked ourselves in there from Saturday until Monday. We have to get Arthur back to hospital on Monday afternoon so that the doctor can make sure that he's all right to fly on Tuesday. Seemingly there can be the risk of deep-vein thrombosis if one flies too soon after sustaining an injury like that. So we'll just drive down here on Monday morning and get him checked.'

'And you've managed to get a car as well?'

'Yes, all fixed. I called around the hire companies and explained our problem, and eventually tracked down a vehicle called a Seat Alhambra. The guy said that it had seven seats, and if there were only going to be the three of us, he could take out the middle row, so that the old boy could stretch his leg out in the back.'

'Well, that all sounds perfect.'

There was a lull in their conversation while they ate, only broken by the occasional utterance of appreciation about the food. As soon as Liz had laid her knife and fork together, the waiter appeared at their table and whisked away the empty plates. '*¿Algo más, señores?*'

'Do you want anything else?' Will asked.

She shook her head. 'No, thanks, I'm fit to burst. That was delicious, though. Thank you.'

Will looked up at the waiter and smiled at him. '*No, nada más. Solamente la cuenta.*'

'*Por supuesto, señor.*'

As the waiter left them, Will studied Liz intently. 'So, you mentioned your son Alex earlier on. I'd like to hear about him – and everything else, for that matter.'

Liz placed her napkin on the table. 'No, not tonight. I'm not feeling like telling that story tonight. Maybe another time . . . maybe.' She glanced at her watch. 'Anyway, if you don't go to see Arthur soon, he might "lose his rag," as you put it.'

Will nodded and pushed himself to his feet. 'Okay, but I will hear it, even if I have to negotiate it out of you, and as you know, I'm pretty good at that.'

Liz got to her feet. 'We'll see.' She began to walk towards the wooden door in the wall, but then turned and looked up at him as he followed. 'Thank you, Will, for tonight.'

'Not at all. It was a pleasure having dinner with you.'

'I didn't mean that so much as, well, just acting as a friend.'

He gave her a wink. 'I wasn't acting.'

CHAPTER 20

The cold west wind blew in hard from the Atlantic, whipping up the dark waters of the sea loch into angry waves that beat heavily against the boulders on the shoreline, throwing a frothy spray across the wide green verge to leave large rippling puddles on the uneven Tarmac surface of the road. Mr Craig pulled hard at the door of the red telephone-box in an attempt to shut out the rain hurled in stormy gusts against the window-panes. However, sometime in its more recent history, either a heavy-handed person or a previous storm had wrenched the door from its top hinge, making it impossible to shut. He bent forward in the confined space and screwed up his eyes to focus on the zip fastening of his waterproof jacket, and, once connected correctly, he pulled it up to his neck. Delving into the pocket of his trousers, he took out a handful of change and placed it on top of the telephone. Once again he strained his eyes to read through the operating instructions, just to refresh his memory on its use. He picked up the receiver, dropped a pound coin into the slot and dialled the number.

It rang four times before being answered quite unexpectedly. 'Hullo?'

'Alex, is that you?'

'Hi, Granddad, how are you? How's the caddying going?'

The old man chuckled. 'Och, I'd say that I still have a lot to learn. Why are you not away out today? I was getting myself all ready to speak to that wretched answerphone.'

'Well, I did go out early this morning, but the weather turned bad and I got soaked, so I just came home and had a bath. How about you? Is it the same where you are?'

'Aye, it's dreadful,' Mr Craig replied, rubbing the sleeve of his jacket against one of the panes of glass and staring out at the elements. A small lobster boat was bobbing its way courageously down the loch towards the Ballachulish Bridge, its square, concrete structure nothing more than a vague outline in the rain-heavy mist. 'So we decided that it was best to give the golf a miss today as well.'

'But it's been all right up until now?'

The farmer stuck a finger in his free ear. 'You'll have to speak up a bit, Alex. It's awful difficult to hear you with this wind.'

'I said it's been all right up until now?' Alex yelled down the line.

'Aye, couldn't have been better. We managed to play around Prestwick on Tuesday afternoon, then Turnberry on Wednesday and Troon yesterday.'

'That's pretty good going! And you had no trouble getting on any of the courses?'

'Och, we had a wee bit of a wait each day, but we were always lucky enough to join up with another game, which made it all the more enjoyable for us both.'

'And have you been staying in first-class hotels?'

Mr Craig chortled. 'No, nothing like that, son. We just made do with a couple of small B and Bs, which I would say were probably just as comfortable.'

'And did Leckie get to go in as well?'

'No, he did not. He was quite happy making a bed for himself on my jacket in the Land Rover.'

'Just as well. So, is this you on your way home now?'

'Not quite yet. Miss Bayliss bought herself a wee book on the golf courses of Scotland, and she's taken quite a shine to the idea of playing Dornoch and Tain, so we're on our way up north.'

'Heavens, Granddad! You'll be away for ages! When does Miss Bayliss have to fly home?'

'Not until Tuesday, but she's awful keen to be back in Saint Andrews by Sunday evening for some reason or other, so we'll be returning then, come what may.'

'Right.' There was a pause, during which Alex obviously took a mouthful of food, because when he spoke again, Mr Craig could hear that his grandson's words were muffled. 'So, whereabouts are you right at this minute?'

'Just before the Ballachulish Bridge, if you know where that is.'

'I've heard of it. Never been there, though.'

'Well, we've just had a pretty miserable journey up

from Crianlarich and through Glencoe, and the weather's that bad that I think we'll just get to Fort William, and stop off early for the night.'

Alex grunted a reply which the farmer knew from past experience meant that his grandson was either being distracted by the television or simply wanted to end the telephone call. He had more questions to ask, so he persisted with the conversation.

'And have you heard from your mother at all?'

'Yeah,' Alex replied, his voice sounding quite bland. 'I called her a couple of nights ago. Oh, wait!' A tinge of humorous excitement lifted his tone. 'You'll never guess what's happened.'

'Tell me.'

'The professor's broken his ankle.'

'Ach, never!'

'Yup, he has, and quite badly, too.'

'How did he do that?'

'Slipped on some candle-wax in the street.'

The farmer clicked his tongue. 'Och, that's awful bad luck.' He paused for a moment, giving quick thought to this new development. 'Maybe I shouldn't go north then. They'll no doubt be coming straight back.'

'No, they're not. The professor's son said he'd fly back with them—'

'The professor's son!' the farmer broke in. 'So he *did* get out there.'

'Seemingly. Mum said that he turned up at the hotel just after it happened, so he's going to arrange for them all to fly back on Tuesday.'

'Well, then, it sounds as though they have everything under control. So you don't think there's a need for us to change any of our arrangements?'

'No, not at all. And by the way, talking of your arrangements, she didn't half fire questions at me about you and Miss Bayliss.'

Mr Craig laughed. 'Aye, I can well imagine that she did. I hope you gave a true account of what's been taking place now, Alex.'

'Of course I did. She got into a bit of a tizz about the whole thing, so I had to!'

'Good for you, lad. Now one more thing before you go . . .' The telephone started to signal the need for more money. 'Hang on . . .' He put in another pound coin. 'Alex? Are you still there?'

'Yes.'

'Listen, lad, the main reason for my calling is just to explain something to you. You may have noticed that work has stopped on the golf course. Now, I'm pretty sure that it's only a temporary measure, so when you next speak to your mother, I don't want you to bother even mentioning it, all right?'

There was a silence at the other end of the line. 'I don't know what you mean.'

'Well, I'll explain it all when I get home, but in the meantime, if you could just keep it quiet from your—'

'But, Granddad,' Alex interjected, 'work hasn't stopped.'

'I think you'll find that it has, Alex,' Mr Craig replied quietly, taking his grandson's remark as a pleading objection to the idea.

'But it hasn't. I know that for a fact. Dad and I were down there yesterday afternoon with Michael Dooney and Jonathan Davies. Michael even asked me for my thoughts on his easing out the dog-leg on the fifth hole. That doesn't sound as if work's been stopped, does it?'

Mr Craig breathed out a long sigh of relief, feeling a huge burden of worry lift from his mind. 'Well, I'm awful glad to hear that, Alex. Things must have been sorted out much quicker than we had all anticipated.'

'That's good, then,' Alex replied, his tone dropping once more, denoting a further waning of interest in their conversation. 'Is there anything else, Granddad?'

'No, I don't think so.' He paused. 'So, what's on television?'

Alex laughed. 'Football. Scotland's playing Sweden in a World Cup qualifier.'

'Ah, well, lad, I won't hinder you. I'll call you from Dornoch.'

'All right, Granddad.'

Mr Craig replaced the receiver, scooped up the remainder of his change and pulled up the collar of his jacket in readiness to meet the storm. He opened the door carefully, wary that one good blast could well separate it altogether from the telephone-box, and hurried across to the lay-by where he had parked the Land Rover. He had left the engine running in an attempt to keep Roberta warm, but in doing so, the windows were misted with condensation on the inside, there being only one pin-point of clarity where, in searching for its master, the Jack Russell had been pressing his nose against the glass. Mr Craig opened the door and clambered in as quickly as he could, the small dog jumping across onto Roberta's lap to make way for him, and then leaping back onto his as soon as he was settled in his seat.

'All well?' Roberta beamed at him. She was dressed as if setting off on an Arctic expedition, and the knitted hat that had been just one of her many purchases in the factory shop on the edge of Loch Lomond was pulled down over her ears so that her small bright eyes were just visible beneath its woolly brim.

'Aye, all well. He hasn't burned the house down yet.' He took hold of Leckie and returned him to Roberta's knee. 'I'll tell you the best news, though,' he said, turning to her with a broad smile on his face. 'Work's still going ahead on the golf course.'

'Oh, that's wonderful!' she exclaimed, giving her hands a single triumphant clap, the sound being deadened by her gloves. 'You're right, that is the best news. I couldn't think of anything worse than knowing it would never be completed.'

'And those are exactly my own sentiments.' He put the vehicle into gear and slowly moved out of the lay-by and onto the road. 'Right then, let's go! Fort William next stop!'

They spoke little during the remainder of their journey, Roberta knowing that her travelling companion was finding it difficult enough to concentrate on driving in the appalling conditions without her adding to his problems by asking questions on points of interest. So she contented herself in gazing out at the mist-shrouded countryside, directing any comment that she had to make on its stark and untamed beauty to the dog. She didn't mind the silence. It gave her time for her own thoughts, to consider the extraordinary change of circumstances that had come about in her life over the past week. When she had first arrived, she had felt that there was little left to be happy about, yet now she was aware of the smile of contentment that seemed to be fixed permanently upon her face. And it was all due to this extraordinary man, someone whom, in her closeted existence back in Australia, she would have more than likely passed in the street without giving him a second thought. His wisdom, though simply portrayed, was deep and understanding, and his attitude towards life and death, through his own experience, had helped to pierce the dark and hopeless despondency she had felt since the loss of her father. It was a friendship, an easy companionship that she could never have imagined existing again in her life. And that's all it would, or could, ever be. They were too old, too different and their geographical distances too great for either even to consider a permanence between them.

Roberta turned in her seat to track the progress of a small ferry that pushed its way across the choppy waters of Loch Linnhe. She let out a long sigh, realizing immediately that it was one that tingled with excitement, not regret. For she knew now that the special bond that had formed between them would never be broken, even though they were to live the rest of their lives on the opposite sides of the world to each other.

The rain became marginally lighter as they drove along the side of the loch and into Fort William. Though the wind remained strong, clouds still clung low to the surrounding hills, shrouding the upper reaches of Ben Nevis and diminishing its usual towering presence over the town. As they made their way along the main thoroughfare, Roberta looked out at the drab line of shops that bordered both sides of the street. Grim-faced pedestrians hurried along the pavements, clutching at coat-necks with hands that were white with cold or struggling with umbrellas to keep them from turning outside in. Mr Craig slowly edged the Land Rover past a vociferous contretemps between a meek-looking traffic warden and an irate young businessman who had displayed a bullish disregard of parking laws by leaving his large four-wheel-drive vehicle on a double yellow line outside the bank. A major traffic snarl-up had ensued, which impatient motorists were beginning to celebrate by leaning hard on their horns or rolling down their windows and shouting out in biased support of the young man.

At the far end of the street, Mr Craig pulled into a large car-park which was empty save for three identical tour coaches, recently arrived from Glasgow. They were in the process of disgorging their passengers, a profusion of white-haired ladies in thin summer mackintoshes who sought shelter from the cut of the wind by huddling together at the front of the coaches while struggling to secure the ties of plastic fold-away rain-hats under their chins. There was, however, obviously a strict timetable for the day's outing, because, besides the weather, they were having to cope with the impatient and quite hostile attentions of one of the bus-drivers, a sour-faced man with an incipient moustache and a white-shirted beer belly that bulged well beyond the fastening capabilities of his maroon blazer. Waving his arms in the air as though herding unwilling sheep into a dip-tank, he edged them away from their refuge towards an aging clapboard café where a sign with fading illustrations of multicoloured ice lollies was all that enticed them into its gloomy interior.

Roberta looked around at her companion, who sat chewing at the side of his mouth as he stared out the window.

'Makes me feel cold just looking at that sign over there,' Roberta said quietly.

Mr Craig nodded slowly. 'Aye, I was thinking that myself.' He leaned back in his seat and thumped the palm of his hand down on the steering wheel. 'Not really what we're used to, is it?'

Roberta laughed. 'No, it isn't. I'm afraid that I have to say that I find it all quite depressing. Those poor old dears over there really make me feel my age. I mean, some of them couldn't be that much older than me.' She paused as she watched one of the ladies attempt to return to the bus to collect something that she had obviously forgotten, only to have her arm taken by the driver and forcibly marched back to the café. 'You don't think that *we* look like that, do you?'

'No. But if we stay here any longer, we could be running the risk that others might think that of us.'

'So what should we do?'

Mr Craig looked at his watch. 'Well, it's only two o'clock now, so I suggest that we just keep going. We should be able to make Dornoch in two to three hours.'

'But what about you? Will you be all right to drive all that way?'

He craned his neck forward to look up at the sky. 'Och, it's not so bad now. I've an inkling that it might start clearing as we head up the road.' He took a last glance around him before crunching the Land Rover into gear. 'Anyway, I think it would be a better option, don't you?'

He had been right about the weather. By the time they had driven the length of Loch Ness, the wind had abated to such an extent that its waters now mirrored the reflection of the surrounding hills in glassy calmness. Sunlight, as weak as a luminous watch that had been starved of light, broke through the dwindling clouds and bathed the countryside in a shadowless glow. And when, in the late afternoon, they passed by the war memorial and drove down the gentle slope into the main street of Dornoch, the sky above the dark slate roofs and smoking chimney-stacks was a cloudless blue, and the sun, now recharged but defeated by the passing of the day, thrust forward a last defiant burst of light that cast out before them the lengthy shadow of the Land Rover, a harbinger of their arrival.

The small, stone-built villa stood back from the main street in its own carefully tended garden. Protruding over its boundary wall was a dark green sign with gold italic lettering that announced it as 'Craig-na-Fhalde, a bed-and-breakfast establishment that has been Highly

Recommended by the Scottish Tourist Board for the past four years.' Below the main sign, hung on brass cup-hooks for easy detachment, was a smaller one on which was written in similar script: 'Vacancies.' Mr Craig turned into the short gravelled drive and pulled to a halt as close to the crocus-filled flower border as he could, allowing room in case another car had to park alongside the Land Rover.

He turned off the engine and leaned forward to survey every aspect of the property through the windscreen. 'Now, would this seem all right to you?'

Roberta, however, had already opened the door and was clambering out of the vehicle. 'It looks absolutely perfect. Come on.'

He got out and shrugged off his jacket, placing it on the driver's seat as a bed for the dog, then walked around the back and took out their two cases. Together, they made their way the short distance to the arched front porch, where they found that the door had already been opened to them by an elderly couple.

'Hullo and welcome!' they said in unison, both sporting enthusiastic grins. The woman took over. 'We heard you arriving.' She rubbed her hands briskly together. 'Oh, my word, the chill's fairly come down, now that the sun is away. Come on, let's get you inside.'

They were shown into a narrow hallway, cluttered with unmatching, though neatly arranged, pieces of furniture. A staircase, lined with small water-colours depicting Scottish landscapes, rose steeply to the upper floor. There was a comforting warmth about the house, and the smell of pine logs burning in an open fire seemed to complement the welcome that they had been given by their hosts.

'Now, first things first,' the woman said in an airily organized voice as she closed the front door behind her. She turned to the small half-moon table that sat next to a burgeoning coat-stand and opened up a leather-bound visitors' book. 'Would you mind just signing your names here before I show you to your room?'

'It would be two rooms that we require,' Mr Craig stated quickly. It was not the first time that he had had to say this, but he still felt his face colour, more for the embarrassment that it might cause Roberta rather than for himself.

'Of course it would be,' the woman replied without altering her tone. 'My apologies.' She handed a pen to Roberta. 'Now, might I ask if you've eaten tonight?'

Mr Craig shook his head. 'No, not yet.'

'Oh, now that's a pity, because we usually do offer our guests an evening meal, but I'm afraid that both my husband and I are going out to a *ceilidh* tonight. However, there are some good places to eat in Dornoch, and we'd be more than happy to point you in the right direction before we go.'

Roberta stopped writing in the book and looked up at the woman. 'Can I ask what a *ceilidh* is?'

It was the first time that Roberta had spoken, and the woman reacted to her Australian accent with a kindly eagerness. 'A *ceilidh*! Well, it's just a party where we have a bite to eat and sometimes a wee bit to drink, and dance a few Scottish reels.'

'That sounds really good fun!' Roberta replied, smiling at the woman before she continued to write.

Mr Craig had caught the twinkle in Roberta's eye, and a frown of consideration came over his face. 'Now, would this ceilidh be a private function?'

'Oh, not at all!' the woman replied. 'It's just being held at a local hotel as a fund-raiser for our local branch of the Women's Rural Institute, so everyone who turns up is more than welcome.' She glanced at her husband, wondering whether she had been correct in her reading of the farmer's question. 'Of course,' she continued in a tentative voice, 'if you would like to come, we'd both be more than delighted to take you with us.'

The farmer glanced at Roberta. 'What would you feel about that?'

'Well, it sounds a wonderful idea. Only problem being that I haven't got a thing with me that I could wear to a party.'

'Oh, it's not that smart at all!' the woman declared. 'Just a simple dress would do.'

Roberta bit at her lip. 'That's what I mean. I don't have a dress.' She looked apologetically at the farmer. 'I didn't even bring one with me from Australia. I didn't think I'd be needing one.'

'Och, it couldn't matter less,' he said, smiling reassuringly at her. He took the pen from her and began to write his name in the book.

Roberta noticed that the woman cast a brief look at her from head to foot, as if sizing her up. However, it was more than apparent that anything her hostess had to offer would be too slim-fitting for her own plump figure.

'I suppose it would be too late to buy something, wouldn't it?' Roberta asked.

'Well, I didn't want to have suggested it myself, but' – the woman held her finger pensively to the edge of her mouth – 'let's just see what we can do, shall we?' She took the telephone receiver off its wall mounting and dialled a number. 'Hullo, Jean? . . . It's Isla here . . . Aye, we're fair looking forward to it. Now, Jean, I know that you'll have closed up for the night, but we have some visitors here, and they were considering coming to the *ceilidh*, but unfortunately the lady doesn't have a dress. Would it be an awful imposition if I brought her along, just to see if you had anything that might be suitable? . . . Are you sure, Jean? . . . Well, that's very kind of you, dear . . . Yes, very good . . . Right, in ten minutes . . . Thank you, Jean . . . goodbye.' She replaced the receiver and turned to Roberta with a grin of success. 'Well, that's settled then.'

'That's so kind of you,' Roberta said, taking hold of the woman's arm and giving it an affectionate squeeze. 'It's Isla, is it?'

'Yes.' She turned to her husband. 'And this is Gordon.'

'Well, it's really good to meet you both. I'm Roberta, and' – she glanced at the farmer, a broad grin on her face – 'this is Craig.'

There was a general shaking of hands before Isla held up a finger to command attention. 'Now, I don't think we should keep Jean waiting at the shop, so I suggest that Gordon quickly shows you to your rooms, and then

Roberta and I can nip down the road to see if we can find her something to wear. How would that suit you?'

'That would be perfect,' Roberta replied. 'Can I ask at what time we would need to be ready?'

'We should be trying to get there for seven-thirty,' Gordon answered, 'if we want to get a good place to sit.' He glanced at his watch. 'That would mean leaving here in about two hours.'

'More than enough time,' Roberta exclaimed, grabbing hold of her suitcase and readying herself to follow Gordon up the stairs.

'Please, Roberta!' Isla gasped. 'Gordon can quite easily manage that!'

'She won't let you, you know,' the farmer said with a wry smile on his face. 'I can carry her golf clubs, but not her suitcase.'

A polite tingle of humour buzzed about them before Gordon, taking note of the farmer's comment, began to climb the stairs empty-handed. 'So you're here for the golf, then?'

'Yes, we are,' Roberta replied as she followed on behind.

'And have you played Dornoch before?'

'No, never. This is the first time.'

'Well, if you like, I'd be more than happy to join you on the course tomorrow and show you the way round.'

'Are you sure?'

'Of course. It would be my pleasure.'

'In that case, thank you, Gordon. We'd love that.' Roberta turned to look at Mr Craig, who was two steps below her on the stairs. 'A party *and* a golf game organized,' she said quietly. 'Who says we're getting old?'

He flicked his head to the side. 'Not me, lass.'

Even though he had had the heater on in the Land Rover, Mr Craig had begun to feel a painful stiffness in his back and shoulders due to the persistent dampness of the day and his many hours of being at the wheel. Consequently, once he had seen Roberta off on her shopping trip with Isla, and having fed the dog and taken him for a short walk, he returned to the house and ran himself a hot bath, knowing that he had enough time to have a long, self-indulgent soak.

And so he lay there, with the water lapping under his chin, feeling his eyes grow heavy as the ache in his body succumbed to the comforting heat.

'Hullo, Nathaniel.'

The voice came to his ear as quiet as a whisper, yet its pitch was as clear and as recognizable as the call of a songbird on a frosty morning. He turned and looked across to where she sat on the lid of the small white chest by the window, her back upright, her legs together and her thin hands resting upon her knees. She was wearing her floral apron over the faded green woollen dress, her white hair neatly permed, and her pink spectacles, still with the piece of Sellotape binding on one of the legs, perched on the edge of her pretty, fine nose. A wistful smile touched at the corners of her mouth, and she watched him with tenderness in the eyes.

'Hullo, my darling,' he replied in as quiet a tone as her own. 'How are you?'

'All is well with me. All is well.'

'I miss you so much.'

'I know you do, and I miss you.'

'I talk to you all the time.'

'And I hear you.'

'You're always with me.'

'And you with me.'

'I'll never forget you. You know that, don't you? Whatever happens, I'll never forget you.'

'I know you won't. You're a good, gentle man, Nathaniel Craig. That's all I wanted to say. You're the best man I ever knew.'

He woke with a start, feeling immediately his skin prick with goose bumps in the cooling water. He turned to look at the small white chest in the window, but there was no one there. Only his neatly folded towel, which he was sure that he had thrown down on the bathroom floor, occupied the space.

An hour later he descended the stairs, running a finger around the collar of his shirt in an attempt to relieve its tightness. He stopped in front of the mirror in the hallway and gave himself a last once-over. Even though he had had the tweed suit since his twenties, it still fitted him well enough, but the lapels were slightly frayed at the edges and the years had knocked most of the coarseness from the material. He was just smoothing down his unruly white hair with the palm of his hand when the door adjacent to the mirror opened and Gordon appeared, resplendent in a kilt and tweed jacket, his green-stockinged legs criss-crossed with the long tasselled laces of a pair of dancing pumps.

'Craig! I thought I heard someone coming down the stairs.' He stood to the side of the door and held out a hand to invite the farmer into the room. 'Come away in and we'll have a wee dram before we go. There's no telling how long the ladies are going to be.'

They entered the small sitting-room, where the farmer felt the heat of the roaring fire hit him immediately.

'Now, take a seat over there,' Gordon said in his melodious Highland voice, pointing to the deep armchair that was drawn up to the fire. He walked over to a tall cabinet that stood against the back wall and opened its doors with a flourish, then gave his hands a single clap and rubbed them together as if meaning business. 'Right. What will it be?' He surveyed the abundance of bottles on the shelves. 'I have our local tipple Glenmorangie, or there's Glendurnich, which is a Speyside, or maybe it's an Islay you prefer, in which case it would be Laphroaig.'

'You'll think me an awful heathen, Gordon,' Mr Craig said as he sank back into the armchair, 'but I'm not really much of a drinker.'

'Are you not? Oh dear. So I won't be able to tempt you with anything?'

Mr Craig detected from the despondent tone in

Gordon's voice that it could quite easily be taken as an affront if he didn't accept something. Pushing himself to his feet, he made his way over to the cabinet. 'Well, let's see now,' he said, studiously appraising his host's supply. 'Would that be a bottle of Jack Daniel's you have at the back there?'

Gordon raised himself onto the toes of his dancing shoes and peered into the cabinet. 'My word!' he sang out, reaching for the black bottle. 'I'd clean forgotten that that bottle was there. I think that it was given to me by an American couple who came to stay with us last year.' He held the bottle out at arm's length to read the label. 'Jack Daniel's. Well, I never! That's exactly what it is.' He twisted off the top. 'You'll have one of these, then.'

The farmer judged this to be more command than question. 'Just a wee one by itself would do me fine.'

The measure poured was much greater than he could cope with, so he was quite relieved when Isla eventually entered the room to interrupt their fireside chat. 'We'd best be going, Gordon, otherwise we'll be late,' she said, pulling on a fleece-collared coat over her party dress.

Gordon drained his glass. 'Is Roberta ready yet?' he asked.

'She's on her way.'

Mr Craig followed them out into the hall. 'And did you have some success at the shop?' he asked.

A door slammed shut upstairs and Roberta appeared, making her way quickly down the stairs. Isla smiled up at her. 'You two can judge that for yourselves.'

The long-sleeved dress was ochre-yellow and spotted all over with a blue design that resembled sea-gulls in flight. It was meant to be worn closed at the neck, but Roberta had chosen to leave the top two buttons undone, folding back the flaps into narrow lapels. A dark blue belt gathered the dress at her ample waist, and on her feet she wore a new pair of shoes, their uncreased leather the same colour as the belt. The farmer watched her closely as she descended the stairs. It was no remarkable transformation. She hadn't suddenly become a beauty. If anything, the dress was slightly unflattering to her fuller figure, but the expression on her face made up for any minor faults, being filled with girlish enthusiasm and excitement at the prospect of the party.

'You look fine, Roberta,' Mr Craig said as she came to stand in front of him in the hall.

Roberta looked down at the dress. 'I don't feel it. Not that there's anything wrong with the dress, only I just look a frump in it.' She let out a long sigh of resignation. 'I'm afraid that I've never seen eye to eye with dresses.'

'Absolute rubbish,' Isla clucked admonishingly. 'It suits you perfectly.'

'Aye, it does,' the farmer agreed. 'You look very . . . elegant.' He wasn't quite sure if that was the word for which he was searching, but Roberta seemed pleased enough with the compliment.

'You two men look very handsome as well,' she said, looking both him and Gordon up and down. She focused on Gordon's neatly laced pumps, then turned her eyes to view the farmer's well-polished but heavy black boots. 'Are you sure you're going to be able to dance in those, Craig?'

'Of course. Like you, I didn't bring anything else other than these, but that doesn't mean I can't skip about a bit.'

'Come on then,' Isla said, opening the front door. 'Let's away and see you prove that.'

The hotel function suite, which stuck out from the back of the main building, was one of those suspect structures that looked as if economy rather than longevity had been the more important consideration at the time of construction, and the musky whiff of damp in the long, low-ceilinged room confirmed this to Mr Craig on entering. Nevertheless, it was pleasantly warm due to the abundance of electric heaters that were strategically set about the place and the throng of people, already laughing and drinking, that filled it. Gordon led them to the bar, exchanging greetings with those who stood aside to allow his party through.

'Right! What's it to be?' he asked.

'No, no! I'll not hear of it,' Mr Craig retorted, delving into the inside pocket of his suit jacket for his wallet.

Gordon held up a hand. 'Plenty of time for you to buy a round, Craig. Now, Roberta, what would you like?'

If anything, the smile of excitement on Roberta's face had grown even wider since entering the room. 'Oh, I don't know.' She turned to her hostess. 'What are you going to have, Isla?'

'I think just a small glass of wine.'

'Okay. I'll have one too.'

'Two glasses of wine coming up!' Gordon exclaimed,

holding up a ten-pound note between his fingers to attract the barman's attention. He turned and gave the farmer a wink. 'And I know what you like, Craig, don't I?'

'Not for me, thank you, Gordon. One is quite enough for me for one night. An orange juice will do me just fine.'

'All right. Now, you lot clear away and get a table, while I order these up.'

By the time that the two-man band had readied their instruments – an accordion and fiddle – their little party had finished their meal of meat-loaf and stovies, something at which Roberta had initially cast a sceptical eye before being informed that it was nothing more exotic than potatoes and gravy mixed together. Then, with a long and somewhat squeaky chord, the band brought silence across the room.

'Ladies and gentlemen,' the fiddler announced into the microphone, then turned briefly to play with the knobs on the amplifier to get rid of the ear-splitting feedback. 'Ladies and gentlemen, please take your partners for a Gay Gordons.'

Gordon and Isla joined others in jumping to their feet. They took their place on the small parqueted dance floor beneath the multicoloured glare of the revolving disco globe. With hands and feet poised in the correct position, they readied themselves.

'Right!' Mr Craig declared, slapping his hands on both knees and getting to his feet. He held out a hand to Roberta. 'Come on, let's see what we can do.'

'No, not just yet, Craig,' Roberta said, shaking her head and holding her hands firmly together on her lap.

'There's nothing to it,' he replied in quite a forceful tone. 'All you have to do is watch the couple in front and allow me to guide you through it.'

'Is it not really difficult?'

'No more so than swinging a golf club. Come on!' He pulled Roberta to her feet and all but dragged her onto the dance floor. 'Now, put your right hand up to your shoulder – that's it – and take my other hand with your left in front. Well done. Now, we're set to go.'

'Do I walk or skip?'

'No, no, just walk through it for now. We'll leave the pas-de-bas to the experts.'

The band played another resounding introductory chord and then they were away. At the first turn, Roberta was so tense that she resisted her partner's guidance to turn and they bumped head-on into the couple who had been in front of them and who were now coming back towards them. However, there was no anger or animosity at the clash, just a hoot of laughter from the couple.

'Just relax!' the farmer shouted to her above the volume of the jigging music. 'I'll take you through it.'

After that, they were away, Roberta closely watching the movements of the other dancers and responding to Craig's verbal commands and to the guidance of his hands. 'This way! Good! Now turn! That's it! And now birl!' And he would spin her around, holding her right hand aloft, forcing her to go faster and faster. By the time they were into the second rendering of the dance, she had it perfectly and his commands stopped, and she now began to take note of his neat little steps as he rocked gently from side to side up and down the floor. She became aware of the coarseness of his calloused hands rubbing like sandpaper against hers as he spun her around, and then, when she came out of it, giddy enough to fall over, he would pull her to him and they would circle in a fast polka step, he keeping her inches away from the couple in front. And then it dawned on her that this was the first physical contact that she had had with this man, the first physical contact she had had with *any* man since . . . well . . . since she could remember.

The band brought the dance to a close with a final chord and everyone clapped, the couples on either side of them giving special praise to Roberta for picking up the routine so quickly. She beamed at them, her face flushed with both the effort and the elation of having mastered the dance. She turned to Mr Craig, who stood looking down at her, a gentle, proud smile on his face. On impulse, she reached up and put her hands on his shoulders, and pulling his head down towards her, she planted a kiss on his cheek.

'Thank you, Craig, that was wonderful fun!'

The farmer's face coloured as he put his hand up and rubbed at the place where she had kissed him. 'Oh, well, we've only just started, Roberta,' he said, giving his head a questioning flick to the side, though there was a teasing glint in his eyes, 'which leads me to wonder what my reward might be once you've mastered the more difficult reels.'

Which, during the course of the evening, she did. They always started at the bottom of the dance set to give her an opportunity to watch how it was done, but by the time it came to their turn, she had studied the others with such intent that she went through the complicated movements without hardly putting a foot wrong. There were only a couple of occasions when Mr Craig had to give her a gentle push to guide her in the right direction. She had even been able to work out the basic rudiments of the pas-de-bas, practising the steps below the table during dances that he had deemed, quite disparagingly, as being 'nothing more than just a stupid kerfuffle' and 'not worth getting up for.' By the end of the evening, the intricacies of the Duke of Perth, the interweaving complications of the Eightsome Reel and the arm-wrenching frenzy of Strip the Willow were now emblazoned upon her mind. As they made their way home in Gordon's car, she sat silently in the back while the others chatted away, her feet aching gloriously and her head pulsating with the lingering sound of the music to which she happily kept dancing away in her mind's eye.

'Who's for a nightcap, then?' Gordon asked as they entered the house and he helped his wife out of her coat.

'Not for myself, thanks, Gordon,' Mr Craig replied, stifling a long yawn with his hand. 'It's been a pretty long day, so I think I'll just go and let my dog out of the car for a minute and then head up to bed.'

Isla turned sharply from hanging up her coat. 'Oh, my word, I never realized you had a dog with you! Do you want to bring it in for the night? Gordon and I wouldn't mind if you did.'

He shook his head. 'No, no. Leckie's happier sleeping in the car. He kind of treats it as his own territory.'

Isla smiled at him. 'Well, if you're quite sure.'

He turned the wooden knob of the front door and was about to open it when it occurred to him that his hosts might well have retired by the time he returned. He stopped and looked back at them. 'I would just like to thank you both for taking Roberta and me with you tonight.'

'Me, too,' Roberta followed on immediately. 'Without any doubt, I think that it has to be the highlight of our little trip.' She beamed at the farmer. 'Don't you, Craig?'

He nodded in agreement.

'Don't even mention it,' Gordon replied. 'It was a pleasure to have your company.'

'And I second that entirely,' Isla said, taking hold of her husband's arm. 'Now, just before we go our separate ways, maybe we should have a quick discussion about breakfast. When do you think you'll be wanting to play golf?'

Roberta held out the palms of her hands. 'Well, if Gordon would really be kind enough to join us on the course, then we'll go along with whatever he thinks.'

'It would probably be best in the morning if the weather's good,' Gordon replied, 'so maybe a nine-o'clock breakfast? Would that suit?'

Roberta glanced at the farmer. 'Is that all right for you, Craig?'

'I'll fit in with whatever's going on.'

'Right!' said Isla. 'Nine o'clock it is! And we'll see you both in the morning.'

* * *

Leckie shot out of the Land Rover as soon as the door had been opened for him, and immediately sniffing out the back wheel, he lifted his leg for such a lengthy period of time that Mr Craig thought that he might keel over as relief set in. Eventually he finished and then set about accomplishing his next priority of greeting his master.

'That was awful unfair, wasn't it, wee laddie? I shouldn't have left you for so long.' He picked up the dog by the scruff of the neck and tucked him under his arm, and then allowed him to lick enthusiastically at the side of his face.

'Is he all right?'

He turned to see Roberta standing on the front porch. Her arms were folded across her chest and she rubbed at the sleeves of her new dress to ward out the chill of the night.

'Aye, he's fine. Just a bit desperate to relieve himself.'

Roberta walked over to stand beside him and looked up at the clear, starlit sky. 'What beautiful nights you have over here,' she said quietly.

He followed her gaze. 'Well, *you've* certainly been blessed with them over the past week. It's not always like this.' He looked down at her and noticed that she was shivering. 'Come on.' He opened the door of the Land Rover to let the dog jump back in. 'Let's get back inside before you catch your death.'

Roberta shook her head. 'Don't worry about me. I'm fine.' She paused until he had locked up the vehicle. 'Craig, thank you for tonight.'

'You've got nothing to thank me for.'

'Yes, I do. I've got everything to thank you for.' She

paused for a moment, then let out a little laugh. 'Do you know that when I came over here from Australia, I was as naïve and as vulnerable as a little child? You see, I'd been protected all my life, and there was never the need to grow up because I always had my father with me. I lived in a time warp. But since being here in Scotland, with you, the extraordinary thing is that I don't feel vulnerable any more. In fact, I feel more confident, more alive than I have ever done before. I really think that now I'll be able to cope with whatever crosses my path in the future, Craig, and it is entirely your doing that I feel this way. I know that our ages probably aren't that different, but I was always aware that maybe, inwardly, I was just treating you like another father-figure, relying on you for your capability, and your calmness, and your kindness. But I know now that that is not the case, because everything you have said to me, everything that you have discussed with me has given me strength. And I cannot thank you enough for that.'

The farmer said nothing for a moment, then folded his arms across his chest and gave her a wink. 'Well, the same goes for me, lass. I never thought that I'd ever jig again.'

Roberta let out a quiet laugh, then, walking over to him, she once more pulled his head down towards her, this time giving him a kiss on both cheeks. She stood back and looked up at him. 'You're a good, gentle man, Nathaniel Craig. In fact, besides my father, I think you're probably the best man I've ever known.'

And as she turned and walked back towards the house, the farmer simply stood and watched her go, aware of the comforting sense of inner peace that gently swept its way through his being, because he knew, from that moment on, that everything would be all right for both of them.

CHAPTER 21

'Will you two speak up?' Arthur shouted from his semi-supine position in the back of the Seat Alhambra. 'It's pretty lonely being back here, and I can't hear a word that you're saying to each other.'

Will glanced at him in the rear-view mirror. 'We're not saying anything of great interest, you know,' he called back over his shoulder. 'We're just looking at the map and trying to work out where the hell we're going.'

Arthur was silent for a moment. 'Well then, maybe you can put on some music.'

'No, we cannot. We need to be able to hear each other.'

Arthur let out a long sigh of discontent. 'I don't see why you had to get such a stupid vehicle. In a normal-sized car, I'd have been able to hear you as well.'

Will turned around and glared at his father. 'Come on, if we had a normal-sized car we wouldn't have been able to get you in. Now just let us get on with finding out the right route, or I'll turn round and take you back to the hospital.'

'Will, watch out!' Liz yelled.

He turned back in time to see that he was heading straight towards an articulated lorry coming from the opposite direction. He veered back onto his own side of the road, causing the wheelchair that was folded up in front of Arthur to shoot violently across the floor and thump hard against the rear passenger door, missing his outstretched plastered leg by a matter of inches. The lorry flashed past, its airhorn blaring.

'Steady on! Remember you've got an invalid in the back here . . .' His voice trailed off when he saw Will look back from the driver's seat, his face ashen with shock and anger. He watched as his son took in a long breath through clenched teeth, ready to let fly at him, but Liz premeditated the outburst by putting her hand on Will's arm and saying something that was once more indiscernible. She turned, a smile on her face. 'Listen, Arthur, we *will* speak to you once we know which way we're meant to be going. It's just a bit difficult at the minute.'

Realizing that Liz had probably saved him from a forceful reprimand, Arthur thought it best to heed her plea and keep a low profile for a while. He turned in his seat and looked out of the window at the wide rolling plains that spread away to the cloudless horizon, their sparse-looking crops beginning to yellow prematurely from lack of rain, and even to his unagricultural eye, he was amazed at how much farther on they were in comparison to the crops that he passed by on his way back and forth between St Andrews and Balmuir. Few buildings graced the countryside save for the occasional large white-walled farming complex seemingly stuck out in the middle of nowhere, with no visible sign of a road or track connecting it with the main highway. And that, too, was of little interest, a ribbon of black that dipped and swayed and turned on its way north through the empty landscape, its sides falling away into deep ditches that were filled with detritus jettisoned by passing vehicles and the occasional half-decomposed body of a dead animal.

He put his pipe in his mouth but thought better of lighting it. Maybe he had been acting a bit like a bear with a sore head. He had already complained of the speed at which Will had driven through Seville, but everyone agreed that Arthur had had good reason for that. Being taken from the restful security of the hospital and catapulted into the fast-moving mayhem of the city streets had felt as if he had hitched a ride with Michael Schumacher. Nevertheless, he just felt so damned useless, and his leg still ached. He had made light of it that morning, being terrified that they would keep him in hospital over the weekend and that he would have to suffer the consequences of yet more sleepless nights in the company of that wretched man and his daughter. But there again, he hadn't been alone, had he? He had been quite amazed and touched by the fact that Will, of his own volition, had spent every night with him, sitting up in that appallingly uncomfortable chair, even though, after the first two nights, the doctor had told him that there was little reason for him to do so.

They drove at pace behind a Lisbon-bound fish lorry

through a small town, its low, whitewashed houses clustered tight to the sides of the road, as if it were their lifeline to civilization. A frail metal barrier protected their front doors from the speeding through-traffic, and the narrow pavement that ran between them relinquished most of its precious space to a line of sickly looking orange trees battered by the blast of passing vehicles and poisoned by the inescapable breath of carbon-monoxide fumes.

He was confused about his feelings towards his son. He hadn't really expected him to come out to join him in Seville, yet of course he was delighted that he was now with them. He and Liz would have found their situation almost impossible without him. He was also gladdened by the way in which both he and Will seemed to be getting on, and he hoped beyond hope that the time that they had spent together in hospital might finally have put to rest the ghosts of their past. That was, of course, barring that little episode a few miles back, for which he knew that his own irascibility was to blame. But maybe even that was part of his confusion. He knew that he should be intelligent and mature enough not to bother about it, but he could not help feeling a deep pang of jealousy at the way that Will was spending, or, more aptly, was *able* to spend, so much time with Liz. Up until the time he had broken his ankle, it had been *he* and Liz who had been the inseparable unit, but now it was Will and Liz. He felt himself excluded from the party, and no more so than now. Sitting right at the back of this wretched vehicle, he was having to watch them chit-chat away to each other without being able to hear a damned word that was being said.

He took the pipe from his mouth, unable to extract much joy from its smokeless bowl, and discarded it with little care onto the seat beside him. He sighed. It wasn't that, though, was it. This situation was always meant to have happened. As he said, he hadn't expected Will to join them, but that was what he had hoped would be the case. The whole idea had been complete pie-in-the-sky when he had discussed it with Liz's father over one of their nightly games of cribbage. But they had both thought that if his plan was to work out, then it would benefit Liz in forming a new friendship, or even relationship, with someone of her own age outside her own claustrophobic environment. And he had based the whole crazy concept on the fact that Will hadn't returned the itinerary.

Then, in its extraordinary way, fate had played its part, and here they were all together. Not as had been planned, but they were together. And now, in retrospect, he realized that it had been a stupid, irresponsible idea, brought about by two conniving old men who thought that they had the right to interfere in the emotional lives of their children. He laughed derisively to himself. Yes, *old* boy, that's what you are now, and that, in truth, is what is hurting you. You've been able to swan your way through life without care, without baggage, without any tangible measure of your age, and now you have been hoist with your own petard. Liz is not *your* age, she's your son's, a mature woman with a son of her own. How could you think that she might ever have become interested in you?

He came away from his thoughts on hearing Liz utter the words 'All the way to Cañareas,' and he watched as she folded up the road-map and tossed it onto the front sill of the dashboard. She turned round in her seat and smiled at him. 'That's it. I think we know which way we're going. How are you doing back there?'

'All right,' Arthur mumbled.

'How's the leg bearing up?'

'It aches quite a bit.'

She smiled warmly at him. 'I'm sure it does. The movement of the car won't help either. Do you want to stop for a bit?'

Arthur shook his head.

'Right. Well, we're on the Lisbon road now, so we reckon that it won't be much more than three-quarters of an hour from here.' She paused, briefly looking out through the windscreen at the road ahead. She turned back. 'Would you like me to get you a pain-killer?'

'No, it's all right. I'll wait until I get there.'

Liz nodded. 'Okay.' She had now turned her whole body in the seat and was leaning her arms on the back head-rest, looking at him. Arthur's attention, however, was drawn to her tucked-in knees, which brushed against Will's forearm as he drove. Neither seemed embarrassed by the contact, and neither made a move to shift position. 'So what do you want to talk about?' she asked, a teasing laugh quavering her voice.

In that instance, Arthur felt his irritation subside. She

was at ease, she was happy, she was completely different from the woman he had known back in Scotland. He may have been the one who had had the truth thrust upon him, but he knew now that the plan had worked. He blew her a long kiss. 'Nothing. I'm fine. I was just being a grumpy old bastard back there. You look ahead. It's not good for you to turn around in a car like that. There'll be plenty of time to talk once we're there.'

'Are you sure?'

'Of course. Anyway, we don't want to miss any of this, do we?' He held out his arms in a magnanimous gesture as if to embrace the new countryside through which they were driving. And it certainly had changed. Now in the foothills of the sierra, the empty plains had given way to smaller fields that were enclosed by heavy-staked fences or stone walls. Gnarled acorn oaks grew in abundance, amongst which lean Retinto cattle grazed at the lush covering of grass interlaced with an abundant mosaic of wild flowers, while black Iberian pigs rooted around under the trees to escape the unseasonal warmth of the midday sun. Beyond, where the land had begun to rise up to dark-wooded hills, gleaming white pueblos touched colour to their sombre appearance, with houses, like timid children, hugging close to the tall central figure of Mother Church.

The traffic had eased considerably since leaving the main highway north, and Will was now able to drive at a much greater pace. Nevertheless, they were still overtaken, even on blind corners, by a variety of fast cars with Seville number plates, their occupants also escaping the city's Semana Santa crowds for the weekend. Although Arthur found their driving skills quite alarming, his concern was much greater for those elderly members of the local population who had chosen to take their morning stroll along the sliver of asphalt at the edge of the road, and even more so for the two old men with flat caps on their heads who sat, hands resting on walking-sticks, on the crash barrier at a near right-angled corner, idly watching the traffic go by.

'What's that?' Liz exclaimed at a volume that he was able to pick up. She was pointing towards the outline of a huge fighting bull that stood, his head turned towards them as if his attention had been caught by their arrival, on a low hill a mile or so in front of them.

'That's the Osborne bull,' stated Will.

'The what?' Arthur called out from the back of the car.

'The Osborne bull,' Will yelled. 'It's an advertisement for one of the Jerez sherries. You'll see them all over the southern provinces of Spain. I reckon that that one's probably the most northerly that you'll find, seeing that we're just about to leave Seville province and enter Huelva.'

As they drove past the figure, Arthur was amazed at the enormity of it, and he thought about passing comment on certain oversized parts of its anatomy, but then felt that it was maybe not one to make with female company present. So he just said it to himself and laughed quietly at his own joke.

They came across Cañareas quite unexpectedly, rounding a corner at which there appeared to be little sign of urban civilization to reveal the town, bathed in sunlight, sitting contentedly below the new ring road in a deep basin in the hills. It was dominated by a large church and the ancient ruins of a Moorish castle that stood high on the outcrop of rock towering above it. As they approached the first entrance to the town, Will slowed the car down, noticing that there was a large queue of traffic, fronted by a packed bus, waiting in the central slip lane to cross the road.

He turned in his seat. 'I was going to drive through town so that we could have a look at the place, but I think we'll give it a miss. The Saturday market will be on, and then there'll be the parades later, so it'll be teeming with people. What do you think?'

Arthur nodded. 'I'd rather just get to the place that we're staying. I'm beginning to get cross-eyed, if you get my meaning.'

Will put his foot down on the accelerator and shot past the line of traffic. 'Okay. I don't think it's that far now.' He took a piece of paper from his shirt pocket, and unfolding it with the help of his teeth, he laid it across the steering wheel. 'I'd say no more than a couple of miles.'

At the highest point of the ring road, Will turned right onto a wide dirt track that led away from the town, and immediately the full beauty of the mountainous countryside was laid open to them. Steep-faced hills that merged into one another were wooded with wide-leaved chestnut and dark-blooded cork trees, sweeping down to green fertile valleys pockmarked with small white dwellings. In the distance, beyond the lake that nudged its way into view between the hills, the land was in stark contrast to this, soaring to an even higher skyline that appeared as barren and colourless as a desert. They passed by a succession of old men trudging their way back towards the town, some carrying gardening implements and sacks across their shoulders, while others slowly ambled along with their hands clasped behind their backs, every one of them turning to face away from the road to avoid the choking dust that was being whipped up by the tyres of the vehicle. Then, rounding a gentle bend, Will had to brake sharply to avoid ploughing into a muleteer who led his two sad-eyed charges along the centre of the road, their backs burdened by hessian panniers brimming with firewood. In his own good time, the old boy guided the mules to one side of the road, then lifted a hand either in acknowledgement or apology and shot them a roguish grin which spread like a crease across parchment on his weather-beaten face, revealing two widely spaced and perfectly useless teeth.

There was no sign to herald the fact that they had arrived at their destination save for a pair of fading green iron gates hung from rough-built stone pillars, which were prevented from swinging closed by two rocks that had at one time been part of the now crumbling drystone wall that surrounded the property. Will drove slowly through the gates, then stopped with his wheels straddling the wide cattle-grid and once more checked his directions. No one spoke. No one dared to make a remark about what might be at the end of the track. He studied the piece of paper for a moment, then balled it up in his fist and threw it into the well at Liz's feet. He clutched the steering wheel and let out a deep sigh. 'Well, let's see what we've let ourselves in for, shall we?' he said quietly.

The track broke free from the shade of the chestnut trees and swung around the side of the hill, dipping, then rising again into a wide turning circle. Will pulled the car to a halt and turned off the engine. 'Thank goodness for that!' he exclaimed, letting out a long sigh of relief and running the fingers of both hands through his hair. 'For a moment back there, I thought we were going to end up staying in a mountain shack.'

The whitewashed house was cut into the side of the hill, so that where they had parked was at the level of the long, pan-tiled roof, faded pink by the sun. It had been built in an L-shape, but was squared off by a large courtyard enclosed by a high wall, in the centre of which was a heavy studded oak door set into a pan-tiled overhang. In one corner a small pavilion had been integrated into the surrounding wall, and a covered terrace ran around the inner part of the building, giving shade to the main entrance door and to the French windows that opened out onto the courtyard.

'This is fantastic, Will!' Liz breathed out quietly. She opened the door of the car and got out and walked over to the edge of the car-park. She turned, her mouth open in wonderment. 'Come and have a look at this!'

Will got out and stood for a moment with his hands in the small of his back, stretching it out, before walking over to stand beside her.

'Look down there.'

Thirty feet below the house, following the ever-decreasing contours of the land, wide stone steps flanked by ornate urns brimming with crimson geraniums led to a paved terrace where light shimmered on the dark blue waters of a large square swimming pool. Below that, further steps led to another terrace, this one half-moon, that fronted an ancient *casita*, its uneven walls covered with a wild bougainvillaea that crept around the windows and tumbled over the sagging lintel of the entrance door.

'Well done you, Will. This is a wonderful find!'

Will shrugged his shoulders. 'That's the power of the Internet for you.'

'Excuse me!' The voice was muffled behind the closed windows of the car. They turned to see Arthur slowly waving to them, as if accentuating the fact that he was trying to attract their attention. 'I'm still here, you know, and if you don't get me out quite soon, something quite untoward might happen.'

Letting out a gasp, Liz ran back to the car and opened up the door. 'I'm sorry, Arthur.' She clambered in beside him and sat down heavily on the seat next to him.

'Watch my pipe!'

'Sorry.' She bent forward and removed the pipe from under her bottom and handed it to him. 'Isn't this just the most wonderful place?'

Arthur nodded and awkwardly began to push himself forward in his seat. 'I'm sure it is, but at this precise minute, my greatest priority is *not* looking at the view.'

'Ah, yes. I was forgetting about that. Right, well, let's get you out of here.'

It took all of five minutes to extricate Arthur from the car, and once they had managed to get him esconced in the wheelchair, he announced that he couldn't wait and that he wanted to get out again immediately to relieve himself. Liz was quite happy to leave this particular duty to his son and walked around to the other side of the car to wait for them.

The sound of a stone rolling down the car-park banking caught her attention, and she turned to find a tall, lean man with tufts of grey hair sticking out from underneath his camouflage jungle hat standing ten feet away from her, his long, sun-tanned face drawn into a knowing smile as he caught sight of Will and Arthur. He was dressed in a pair of blue coveralls that hung from his body like a clown suit, and he carried in his rubber-gauntleted hands a dismantled set of draining-rods. Liz opened her mouth to speak, but he held up a rubber finger close to his lips to stop her.

'Right now,' Will's voice sounded out, 'just hop back a bit. I've got the wheelchair, so put your hands on the sides and support yourself. Now, just ease yourself down.' There was a thump and a groan of relief from Arthur. 'Well done, you've made it.'

The man dropped the draining-rods to the ground and approached Liz, pulling off his gloves as he walked. 'Well, that was one of the more bizarre arrivals that I've witnessed,' he said in a brusque English voice. He held out his hand. 'Johnnie Harker. Welcome to Finca de Rodrigo.'

Liz took his hand and shook it. 'How do you do. I'm Liz Dewhurst.'

'Nice to meet you, Liz.'

She looked round as the wheelchair brigade approached them. 'Will, Arthur, this is Mr Harker.'

'Johnnie, please.' He shook their hands, then stuck his fists on his hips. 'Well, you poor old devil,' he said, looking down at Arthur. 'What a bugger of a thing to happen! Knackered the old holiday a bit, hasn't it?'

Arthur let out a sigh and nodded. 'I would say so.'

'Well, never mind, once you've stayed here, you'll wonder why you ever bothered going to Semana Santa. All those damned crowds, and Seville can get so wretchedly hot, even at this time of the year.' He looked about him. 'Not here, though. Always a cool breeze, even in the middle of summer.' He let out a contented breath, then lobbed his gloves over to where he had set down the draining-rods. 'Right, Liz, if you can manage to guide Arthur down the slope over there to the courtyard, I'll give Will – it is Will, isn't it? Spoke to you on the phone. Good. I'll give you a hand with the luggage, then show you the lie of the land in the house.'

Liz gave the wheelchair a push towards the slope, but Arthur held up his hand to stop her. 'You weren't once in the army, by any chance?' he asked.

The man looked surprised. 'Yes, I was. Now how on earth could you tell that?'

Arthur gave him a wry smile. 'Oh, I just had an inkling. Guards, was it?'

'Good God, no, old boy! Couldn't give a toss for all that squarebashing. No, I was a Gurkha. That's why I'm so at home in the hills. Trained a hell of a lot in the

Himalayas.' He followed Will over to the back of the car. 'I'll tell you all about it over dinner, if you're interested.'

'I bet you will,' Arthur murmured under his breath and he gave the wheels a hefty push to help Liz get started.

Liz leaned forward as she steered him down the slope and whispered in his ear, 'When it comes to gruffness, Arthur, I think you may well have met your match.'

He glanced round. 'Come on! I'm never *that* bad – am I?'

Johnnie Harker led his guests across the courtyard to the front door, which was set into the right-angle corner of the house. They entered a high pine-beamed hallway, unfurnished except for a round mahogany table that stood in the centre of the rustic-tiled floor, its surface covered with objects as if laid out for a memory game: two videos, one shopping basket, a pair of gardening gloves, countless envelopes (both open and unopened), a man's wallet, a set of car keys and two tin cigar cases, all set around a blue Spode china pot which held a flourishing aspidistra. To one side of the hall a carved wooden railing guarded a flight of steps which surprisingly descended to a lower level, while at the front a full-paned window lay open, revealing beyond an iron grille and over the tops of the chestnut trees a stunning view across the lake and away to the distant hills.

'Right,' Johnnie said, 'easy layout. From here, all bedrooms are to the right through that arch, and living-room, dining-room and kitchen to the left. No need to go downstairs. That's where Annabelle and I hang out, so you can scoot around up here, Arthur, without a care in the world. Right, follow me!'

He strode off along a wide passage that ran the full length of the rear section of the building, its roof so high that it was like walking down the aisle of a cathedral. Rounded arches split the area into three equal sections, each supporting an inverted arch that concealed the only source of artificial light in the passage, while above, sunlight flooded in through three small oblong windows, projecting their focused shapes onto the walls opposite. Below them, the height of the area was cleverly fore-shortened by the hanging of sombre but richly coloured Turkish rugs, except at the far end of the passage, where there was a towering life-sized portrait of a nude woman who clutched in both hands a straw hat, strategically placed to cover her tummy button – and nothing else. Having entered the bedroom opposite, Johnnie turned to give more instructions, but caught Arthur eyeing the painting with interest.

'Good, eh? My fortieth birthday present from Annabelle. Damned nearly twenty-one years ago now.'

'It's wonderful,' Arthur replied, being glad of the chance to view it more closely. 'Good-looking woman, too.'

'Yes. Mind you, she was thirty when it was done, but, by God, she's still kept her figure.'

Arthur spun round to look at him, his mouth dropped open. 'You don't mean that that's . . .' He trailed off, realizing that he had probably just put his foot in it.

'What? Annabelle? Yes, of course it is.' He laughed. 'You don't think that she'd allow me to hang pictures of other nude women around the place, do you?' He turned to assess the room, leaving Arthur speechless. 'Right, Arthur, this is your room. Bathroom over there, with lots of handles with which you can heave yourself about. Easy bed to get into. Bell on the wall in case you fall out of bed, or' – he looked out of the door at the portrait of his wife – 'you suddenly decide that you want to sleep with the door open.' He laughed again. 'So, all right for you?'

'Yes, it's perfect, thank you,' Arthur replied, wishing that he wasn't so disadvantaged by his wheelchair.

'Good. Now, Will, you're in the next bedroom and Liz next door to that.'

He marched briskly out of the room, and before Will and Liz had a chance to follow him his voice once again sounded forth. 'Annabelle, darling! Come and meet our guests.'

Arthur suddenly seemed to become quite eager to reach the door, pushing himself away from Liz's clutches, and making his way adeptly across the room. Annabelle, however, entered before he had completed his manoeuvre, resulting in his catching his fingers in the spokes of the chair as he brought it to a halt inches from her legs. There was no blasphemous cry of agony, no pained expression on his face as he looked up at the tall, slender woman. He found it quite difficult not to glance past her and make comparisons as to how she looked both clothed and unclothed. There was, however, no doubting the fact that Johnnie had been right. She appeared exactly as she did in the portrait, her figure still perfect under the blue-striped butcher's apron, her face smooth and unwrinkled, the only difference being that her long dark hair had now turned a lustrous grey and was gathered up in a loose bun at the back of her head.

Johnnie introduced them in turn, and Arthur was gladdened by the fact that he didn't demean him by making any further comment about his indisposition. Annabelle beamed a smile at them. 'Forgive me for not shaking hands,' she said, holding up her own to show that they were covered with flour. 'You caught me in the throes of getting the evening meal ready, but I thought I must come through and say hello. Anyway, it's wonderful to meet you all. Did you have a good journey up from Seville?'

'Went without a hitch,' Will replied. 'We did wonder, though, if we had the right turning at the top of the road. I didn't quite know what we were going to find at the end of the track.'

'That's Johnnie's idea,' she said, making a face that registered both long-sufferance and humour. 'He thinks that it puts off unwelcome visitors.'

'And so it does,' he retorted. 'Right now, what time is it?' He pulled up the oversized sleeve of his coveralls to glance at his wrist-watch. 'Hell's teeth, it's five past two. I've taken four hours to clear that bloody drain.'

'Did you manage to do it?' Annabelle asked, giving him a look of surprised admiration.

'Course I did. Mind you, it's amazing what you find in drains—'

'All right, darling,' she interrupted him. 'I don't think that we want to hear the grim details.' She turned to her guests. 'Now, you haven't had lunch yet, have you? No, good, because I've made a huge pot of soup which Johnnie and I will never finish in a month of Sundays, so why don't you all get settled into your rooms and we'll eat in about fifteen minutes.'

'Which gives us all quite enough time to have a small refreshment first, don't you think?' Johnnie continued. He took hold of the handles of Arthur's wheelchair and manoeuvred him through the door. 'Come on, Arthur, we'll see if we can't get a quick one in before the others join us.'

They had lunch outside on the large vine-draped veranda that fronted the drawing-room, a leisurely, drawn-out meal that lasted for much longer than it took them to finish off the soup and the slab of locally produced goat's cheese that Annabelle had bought in the market that morning. Arthur was quite content in being placed next to her at the table and, with an enraptured expression on his face, proceeded to engage her in a one-to-one conversation, leaving Liz and Will to be entertained by Johnnie. At first, Liz felt the men's company quite overpowering, finding herself completely out of her depth while the two spoke at length about the oil industry, Johnnie being well-informed on the subject as a result of a year's tour of duty in Oman during his army career. However, just when she felt that she was going to pass the whole meal without opening her mouth, Johnnie abruptly terminated his conversation with Will and, physically turning away from him, directed his attention totally to her.

'Now what about you, Liz? What do you do to keep the wolf from the door?'

Liz took in a deep breath. 'Well, nothing really, other

than being a mother to my son.'

'I wouldn't say that's nothing! Damned difficult job. What age is he?'

'Eighteen. He's in his first year at Saint Andrews University.'

'Good for him. We've got two boys as well, both at different stages at Durham University. We get e-mails occasionally from them, and I sometimes wonder from their content whether they're doing any work at all.'

Liz laughed. 'I'm sure they are. I think that they just find playtime more fun to talk about than work.'

Johnnie raised his eyebrows in consideration of her wise remark. 'Maybe. Let's hope you're right.'

'I don't think Liz is doing herself justice either,' Will cut in, smiling across the table at her. 'She's lived on a farm all her life, so she's probably worked harder than we ever have.'

'On a farm?' Johnnie exclaimed, his eyes sparkling with interest. 'But that's wonderful! You don't happen to know anything about sheep, do you?'

'Well, yes, I do. Quite a bit, actually.'

'My word, you're a godsend! Listen, I've just become the proud possessor of ten sheep and a motley-looking ram, and I know damn-all about them.'

And he proceeded to launch into a barrage of questions about sheep husbandry: how long he should run the ram with the ewes, how often he should worm them and what would be the correct time to clip them. When he realized that every one of his questions was being answered with authority, he called along the table to

Annabelle, telling her to stop talking to Arthur and to listen, because they were lucky to have in their midst a real expert on sheep.

Once he felt that his knowledge was replete, which coincided with a point when the two bottles of red wine lay empty in front of them and coffee-cups sat drained of their contents, Johnnie linked his hands behind his head and leaned back in his chair. 'Well, Annabelle,' he said, grinning at his wife at the far end of the table, 'all I can say is thank God this lot are here!' He turned to Liz and gave her a wink. 'Believe it or not, we get quite starved of intelligent people out here.' He threw himself forward and slammed his hands down on the table. 'Talking of which,' he muttered conspiratorially, 'I think it only fair that you should be warned about our other guests tonight.'

'Johnnie!' Annabelle gasped, a look of consternation on her face. She glanced furtively through the wide French windows into the house as if to make sure that no one had walked into the drawing-room unnoticed. 'You're a dreadful man, you know! You're breaking the cardinal rule' – she leaned forward and put her hand on Arthur's arm – 'which is one should never be rude about one's guests – especially in front of other guests.' She glared back at her husband. 'You've obviously had far too much to drink.'

'Oh, probably,' he laughed, 'but sometimes it's such fun to speak one's mind.'

'Well, you mustn't.' She gave him a crooked smile. 'Now to absolve yourself of this quite appalling misdemeanour, I would like to know what little job you have lined up for yourself this afternoon now that the drains are cleared, because . . .' She drew out the word as if she knew already that what she was about to suggest was going to be met with disapproval.

'No!' he interjected. 'I'm not paying bills today. I'll do them tomorrow. I've got to mend that fence up in the olive grove, otherwise the sheep will end up getting splatted all over the road.'

'All right, but you *must* do them tomorrow, otherwise everyone in the town will start denouncing us.' She turned to her guests. 'Now, what do you all feel like doing for the rest of the afternoon? We don't have dinner until nine o'clock at the earliest, so you've got plenty of time for whatever you want.'

It was Will who spoke first. 'Would you mind if I hooked into a telephone line for a couple of minutes? I'm technically still at work, I'm afraid, and I never got the chance this morning to pick up my e-mail.'

'No problem, old boy!' Johnnie said. 'Just head down the flight of stairs in the hall and turn left. That's my study. A bit of a mess, I'm afraid, but clear a space for yourself and get plugged in.'

'Thank you. I don't reckon I'll be that long. I thought then that I might try to clear my head of your wonderful wine and walk into Cañareas.' He looked across the table at Liz. 'How about it? Do you want to come?'

Liz nodded. 'Yes, I'd like to . . . that is, if you don't mind, Arthur.'

He shot her a grateful smile along the table. 'No, you go ahead. I'll just take myself quietly off to my bedroom and read a book.'

'I'm hoping that you'll do no such thing!' Annabelle retorted. 'There's nothing I like better than being entertained in my own kitchen by an intelligent and quite charming gentleman.'

Liz noticed colour rising to Arthur's cheeks for what she judged to be the first time since he had suffered his accident. 'In that case,' he replied, bowing his head slightly toward his hostess, 'I would be delighted to engage you in conversation for what's left of the afternoon.'

By the time Liz had given Annabelle a hand to clear the table Will had finished his work and, at Annabelle's insistence, they were sent packing from the house, leaving her in the company of Arthur, who seemed perfectly content in cutting up carrots on a chopping board that she had placed across the arms of his wheelchair. It took them no more than twenty minutes to walk into town, beating the same track they had seen taken by the old man when they arrived. Crossing over the main road, they made their way down a narrow cobbled street where housewives wearing bright aprons that contrasted with their black dresses gabbled loudly to each other as they swept clean the pavement outside the doorways of their small houses, the multitude of pot plants that hung from the balconies splashing a profusion of colour onto their white frontages.

The street wound round past an open-fronted greengrocer's shop where both customers and staff seemed more concerned with chatting rather than carrying out any form of transaction, and then swung left into the large paved *plaza major* that lay half in shadow and half in bright sunlight. It was thronged with people who milled about the parallel lines of orange trees or bunched together on the wooden benches that were set against the iron railings surrounding the area. A little girl, dressed in her best party outfit, used those who stood about like traffic cones, weaving in and out of them on her small plastic tricycle. In the far corner of the square a noisy game of football was in progress, being watched by a gathering of teen-age girls with sun-glasses perched, as if part of a uniform, on the tops of their heads. They clustered about the dome-topped confectionery kiosk and screamed in delighted horror if the ball was kicked anywhere near them. Beyond the railings, the road that encircled the square was crammed with parked vehicles or encroached upon by tables and chairs that spilt over from the pavements outside restaurants, making it an almost impossible task for those who tried to manoeuvre their cars around the heavily congested area and up the quieter side-streets that led away from it.

Deciding also that the *plaza* was too overpopulated, Will and Liz wove their way across the square and took a street that rose sharply up towards the church that overlooked the town. Half-way up the hill, the street opened out into another square, smaller and less crowded, where they stopped for a moment to catch their breath.

'How about a cup of coffee?' Will asked, pointing to a small restaurant whose few tables and chairs lay out in a sun-trap in the corner of the square.

'I think that's a very good idea,' she replied, squinting her eyes against the sun to look up at the church that still lay a good six hundred yards up the steep road. 'I don't think that I could make it up there today.'

As soon as they had occupied two of the plastic chairs, a waiter appeared through the bead-curtained entrance of the restaurant at a speed that would have suggested that he had been physically ejected from the place. '¡*Buenas tardes, señores!*' he sang out, giving the surface of the table a quick wipe with his dishcloth. '¿*Qué quieren ustedes tomar?*'

'What would you like?'

'Just a cup of white coffee, please.'

'*Un café con leche y un café solo.*'

'*Desde luego, señor. ¿Y algo a comer?*'

'Do you want anything to eat?'

'No, thanks!' Liz replied, blowing out a breath at the thought. 'I'm still wondering whether I'll have enough room for the meal tonight!'

Will laughed. '*No, nada más. Los cafés solamente.*'

'*Gracias, señores.*' He skipped off towards the door, calling out their orders as he pushed his way through the curtain.

Liz leaned back in her chair and, tilting up her head, closed her eyes to the warming rays of the late-afternoon sun. 'This is real bliss,' she said in a slow, languid voice.

Will watched her. 'Not like Scotland, then?'

'No. Definitely not like Scotland.'

'So what's been happening up there?'

'A bit of sun, a bit of rain, but we never get heat. Not

at this time of year, anyway. In fact, come to think of it, we hardly ever get it at all nowadays.'

'I wasn't really talking about the weather,' Will said quietly.

Liz opened her eyes and looked at him. 'What do you mean?'

Will rested his elbows on the table. 'Well, what's been happening to you? You gave me a garbled account that first time we met in the hotel, and then, in the restaurant, you didn't want to talk about it. So how about now? I'd quite like to hear a fuller version.'

Liz shook her head. 'You wouldn't find it that interesting.'

'Honestly, I'd like to know.'

The waiter appeared from the doorway and placed their cups in front of them on the table. Will ripped open the small packet of sugar and poured it into his coffee. 'Well?'

Liz let out a sigh. 'All right, but if I see your eyes drooping for even a second, then I promise you I'll stop and I won't say a word more about it.'

'Okay. It's a deal.'

During the next two hours, however, his attention never faltered for a moment as she went through every detail of what had happened to her over the past year. She even surprised herself at the apparent ease with which she was able to divulge information hitherto too sensitive to relate. She told him about Gregor's long-standing relationship with Mary McLean and how she had been left with no alternative other than to move herself and Alex back to her parents' house. She found herself choking back tears when she told him about the death of her mother, and then the subsequent demise of their farm. She continued talking once they had left the restaurant and made their way back through the town, avoiding the square where even more people seemed to be gathering early for the town's *Soledad* parade that night. By the time they arrived back at the gates of the *finca*, she had told him about her vehement opposition to the construction of the golf course and how it had nearly led to her being ostracized by the local community, and then how Alex had brought Arthur home to live with them and how he had managed to breathe new life into their otherwise sad, introverted life.

'And that's about it,' she said, as they cut up over the hill to approach the house from above. Will made no reply but continued to walk, his head bowed low as he kicked out at a stone, sending it spinning up the small track. 'You see what I mean now. It doesn't make very good listening. It's all pretty self-pitying stuff.'

He closed the gap between them and, looping an arm around her shoulders, he gave her a tight squeeze. 'I don't think that at all. As a matter of fact, I was just thinking about what a jerk I was to blow off at you like that on that first night we met.' He stopped, pulling her to a halt beside him. He put both arms around her neck and held her tight in a powerful bear-hug. 'Jeez, you *have* had one hell of a year, haven't you? I'm not surprised you don't trust anyone anymore – well, anyone of the male gender, that is.'

Without having to push him away, Liz disentangled herself from his clutches. 'I know,' she said, continuing to walk. 'I try not to make it show, but obviously it does.' She let out a short laugh. 'The funny thing is that Arthur has helped me quite a bit, in his own rather peculiar way. I think I've grown to trust him.'

'And what about Gregor?'

She turned and raised her eyebrows at him. 'That's a pretty silly question. Of course I don't trust him.'

'I wasn't actually getting at that. I mean, what are your feelings towards him?'

'I hate him,' she responded immediately. She stopped and pushed her hands into the pockets of her jeans. 'I think.' She smiled at him. 'Come on, let's get back to the house before you draw anything else out of me that I might regret saying later.'

He reached out and clutched her arm. 'Hold on a minute.'

She looked at him quizzically. 'What?'

He let go and stood back from her, crossing his arms as he looked at her. 'Well, I'm now going to say something which I might regret saying later, but before you go back to that house, Liz, I think that you should know a few home truths about yourself. In my eyes, I think you're pretty fantastic, and I don't mean, you know, just the normal things like your looks. You are an extremely engaging person. Your whole aura captivates me. Now, to break that down into easily digested segments, I find you intelligent, fun to be with and wildly practical, and I can quite honestly say that if I had run across you before in my life, then my high-handed opinion on marital involvement would probably have been blown out the window' – he clicked his fingers – 'just like that.' He paused, noticing that her cheeks were beginning to flush with embarrassment. 'And that's the main reason that I had to get that story out of you, because had I not known that you had been so badly hurt, there is no doubt in my mind that at some time over the next few days, I would not have been able to stop myself from making an almighty, no-holds-barred pass at you.' He moved over to the old drystone wall and leaned against it. 'Now, what I would like to know is how that makes you feel? Are you saying to yourself, "Oh, he's just saying that to be kind," or are you saying, "This man must have gone stark-raving mad!" or maybe it's, "Hell, this man's just trying to get me into bed for his own gratification." Or, as I hope it will be, you are saying, "Wow, I think he means it."' He paused again and swept a hand through his hair. 'Okay, that's it. I've said it all. The ball's in your court now.'

It may have been, but Liz found herself unable to formulate any answer at all. She had no inclination to speak. No one had ever said anything like that to her before. Not even Gregor. There had never been any call for it. He hadn't had to court her in that way, because . . . well . . . because of Alex. They had just fallen into a relationship. Maybe that had been their trouble all along. Maybe they had both bypassed the first stages of love. She looked over to Will and saw herself impaled by his eyes. She had to avoid them. She lowered her head and copied his action of flicking at a loose stone with her shoe. What had he said all that for? Was he just being kind? No, he'd plugged that bolt-hole. In fact, he'd been clever enough to plug *every* bolt-hole. He had pre-empted everything that she might have thought about what he had said. Surely he couldn't mean it? Surely it's not *me* that he's talking about? She looked back up at him. He was pretending to appear unconcerned about her lack of response, averting his eyes from her and whistling nonchalantly. Suddenly, he fixed her once more with his eyes. 'Well, what's your answer?'

She smiled at him, and Will realized immediately that he had made a breakthrough. Her whole being seemed to shed the brittle edginess that had been so apparent before, and the expression on her face encapsulated a new-found contentment. 'I'm afraid that I don't know what to say.'

Will punched his fist into the palm of the other hand. 'Great! That's all I wanted to hear. You are quite simply one of the best, Liz, and never, ever think otherwise of yourself.' He pushed himself away from the wall, then immediately held up a finger. 'Just one more thing that you should know before we forget that this conversation ever took place, and that is that you can trust me, too, Liz. I promise that I would never do anything to hurt you.'

'BUGGER THIS SODDING MACHINE!' The voice rang out from behind the small shed that lay fifty yards above them on the track, its echo ricocheting off the hills on the far side of the valley. They looked at each other for a moment before both burst out laughing.

'I think that sounds as if Johnnie is having a little bit of trouble with something, don't you?' Will said, an analytical expression on his face. 'Maybe we should go to see if we can lend a hand.'

As he set off up the path, Liz stayed where she was, watching his robust figure stride away from her. 'Will?'

He turned back. 'Yes?'

'Thanks – and I'm sorry.'

Will shrugged his shoulders. 'Don't be.' He held out his hand to her. 'Come on, let's go see what's troubling Colonel Gusto.'

They found Johnnie crouched at the side of an old Fordson tractor, his head resting against its bonnet, as he struggled to turn an unseen nut somewhere in the inner-most bowels of its engine. As they silently approached him, he stood back from the machine and threw the spanner to the ground in defeat. '*Bollocks!*'

'Having a spot of bother?' Will asked, his question laced with humour.

Johnnie started suddenly at the sound of his voice and spun around. 'Oh, it's you lot.' He looked back at the tractor and put his hands on his hips. 'Bloody thing's stopped dead on me. I was just on the way back from mending the fence, and then, fart! it just gave up the ghost.' He bent down to pick up the spanner, then turned to Will. 'You must have had some experience of diesel engines in your time. Any idea what could be the trouble?'

Will scratched at the side of his face. 'Sounds like fuel starvation to me.'

'That's what I thought, but I've been pushing away at that little lever on the fuel pump to no avail at all.'

'Have you bled the injectors?'

'As best as I could. The wretched thing is so old that one of them is seized right up.'

'That could be the problem then. Maybe you would be best to get someone out to free it?'

Johnnie flicked back his head. 'Easier said than done out here, old boy. It'd cost me a fortune that I don't have.'

'Could you try turning the engine over for a moment?' Liz asked.

The two men slowly turned to look at her.

'What?' Johnnie asked, his tone almost registering annoyance.

'Just press the starter lever for a moment.'

Johnnie shot Will a glance, then moved forward to the tractor and executed Liz's request. The engine turned slowly, its battery nearly dead from Johnnie's insistent cranking.

'White exhaust,' Liz said quietly. 'I think you might have got water in your fuel system.'

'How the hell could that have happened?'

Liz shrugged. 'I don't know. Do you fill it up from a tank or with jerrycans?'

'Usually jerrycans.'

'Then that's probably what caused your problem.'

Johnnie let out a long sigh, as if uneasy at having his lack of mechanical skills exposed by a woman. 'So is there anything we can do about it?'

'Well, we can start by taking off the fuel filter.'

'Right!' said Will, rubbing his hands together and moving forward to the tractor. 'I'll be your apprentice. How do we do that?'

Liz began rummaging through the tin box in which Johnnie kept his ill assortment of tools and came up with an adjustable Stillson spanner. She unscrewed it to its fullest aperture and handed it to him. 'That should do it. Now, take it off as gently as possible so you don't damage it.'

Will placed it against the filter and began to adjust it to fit.

'Erm,' Liz said softly, 'that's actually the oil filter, Will. The one for the fuel is next to the injection pump.'

Johnnie let out a raucous laugh. 'Bloody hell! We men are really being taught a lesson here, aren't we?'

Having been guided to the right place, Will gave the spanner a slow twist and the fuel filter came free. He screwed it off with his hand and handed it to Liz. 'Right, over to you, boss.'

Liz stood back from the two men and poured its contents onto the ground, then, raising it over her shoulder, she brought it down in a whipping movement to remove all residue from it. 'Have you got any clean diesel, Johnnie?'

'Coming right up!' He rushed off into the shed and returned with a plastic fuel can. 'This should do you.'

Liz filled up the fuel filter from the can and went through the motion of emptying it again. Then, filling it up once more, she walked over to the tractor and screwed it back onto its seating. 'Okay,' she said, wiping her hands on the seat of her jeans. 'You can tighten it up again.'

Will leaped forward to carry out his task. 'Now what?' he said, standing back from the machine.

'We bleed it,' Liz replied. 'Here, give me the spanner.'

The two men craned over to watch as she first turned the bleed screw on the bottom of the lift pump, then the one on the side of the injection pump. Once she had diesel seeping from the small aperture, she told Johnnie to crank the engine once more. 'Right, that's enough,' she said, tightening up the screw. 'Now, we've got to check if there's fuel going through to the injectors.' She eased off those that she was able, and breathed out an inaudible sigh of relief when she saw diesel running down the side of the engine block. Tightening up the holding nuts, she stood back and lobbed the spanner into the tin box.

'Is that it?' Johnnie asked.

Liz nodded. 'I hope so. Does the tractor have a heating coil?'

'Yes.'

'Well, you don't have much power left in your battery, so just give it ten seconds before you fire the engine.'

There was silence as Johnnie held down the button beneath the steering wheel, and Liz found herself crossing her fingers behind her back. 'Right, try it now.'

He pressed the starter lever and the engine turned over slowly, but failed to fire. 'Stop!' Liz called out. 'It's nearly there.'

'How can you tell?'

'You're getting black exhaust now. Just put the heater switch on again.'

They waited a further ten seconds. 'Right, try again,' Liz said quietly, 'but this time, push your throttle fully open.'

Johnnie pressed the starter lever once more, and on the third wheezing crank, just when the battery gave every sign that it was going to die for good, the tractor sputtered into life, sending up a cloud of acrid black smoke into the air.

'You bloody marvel, Liz!' Johnnie exclaimed. 'You are nothing but a bloody marvel.'

She moved forward and shut down the throttle, the tractor ceasing its metal-shaking scream and settling into a steady idle. 'I'd leave it running for an hour, just so that the battery can get charged up again.'

She turned to find the two men standing side by side with blatant admiration written all over their faces. Will shook his head. 'Now where on earth did you learn to do that?'

Liz laughed. 'It's not as good as it looks, you know. My father has one of these at home – forty years old and still his pride and joy. I've just grown up with it. It's almost part of the family, so I know all its idiosyncrasies. Now, if it had been a John Deere or a Massey Ferguson, I'm afraid that I wouldn't have had a clue.'

'Well, I certainly couldn't have done it,' Johnnie said, bending down to gather his tools together. He closed the lid of his box and stood up, a thoughtful frown puckering his forehead. 'In fact, you couldn't teach Annabelle how to do it, could you?'

Liz laughed. 'I don't think so.'

'No, maybe not such a good idea. Better that everyone sticks to their domain, what!' He took the tool-box over to the shed and threw it carelessly inside, then, closing

403

the door, he snapped shut the padlock. 'Right, let's get back to the house and tell the world about your expertise.'

As it happened, Liz's 'expertise' in tractor maintenance turned out to be a perfect ice-breaker at the pre-dinner drinks, as the couple from the Isle of Wight, who obviously had become quite intimidated by Johnnie's brusque manner during their stay at Finca de Rodrigo, now appeared dumb-struck by the arrival of new guests in their midst. Even after having been introduced, they sat together on the sofa at the side of the roaring log fire, clutching their glasses of Oloroso sherry and smiling nervously at each other as Johnnie recounted to all Liz's tremendous feat, his tone becoming more vociferous and more animated as he went on.

It was Liz who managed to draw them into the conversation, at a time when she felt that Johnnie had slightly overplayed the subject and was beginning to sound quite chauvinistic in his appraisal of how unexpected it was to find a woman who could do such a job. 'I don't think that's right at all,' she said quite sharply. 'In certain cases, women can be much more practically minded than men.' She turned to the woman on the sofa. 'What do you think, Valerie?'

The woman shot an apprehensive glance at her husband before replying. 'Oh, well . . .' she stuttered. Then she gave a definite nod with her head, as if taking courage from Liz's remark. 'Yes, you *are* right. Just before we came out here, my dishwasher went wrong and I fixed it myself.'

'Yes, she did,' her husband agreed, smiling proudly at his wife. 'And it was quite complicated, too.'

'Jolly good for you!' Johnnie exclaimed. 'Every time I try to do something with one of those infernal machines, I usually end up having to call out an engineer, and then find out that I've succeeded in making the problem a hundred times worse than it was originally.'

Thereafter, during dinner, conversation flowed between them, so much so that when Annabelle drew their attention to the fact that it was almost one o'clock in the morning, they were still seated around the dining-room table. 'Now just leave everything as it is,' she said, getting up from her seat. 'Johnnie and I will clear up in the morning.'

There was a moment of polite dissent before everyone dispersed to their bedrooms. Liz helped Arthur negotiate his wheelchair past the few obstacles in the corridor, then, leaving him in Will's hands to help him get ready for bed, she made her way back to her own room, only to stop short at the door when she heard the clatter of plates being cleared from the dining-room table. She walked back to find Annabelle there by herself, carrying a heaped tray through to the kitchen, the pale-blue dress that she was wearing now protected by her butcher's apron.

'I thought you said you were going to leave this until the morning.'

Annabelle stopped abruptly in the doorway of the kitchen and turned around. 'Liz!' She grimaced, as if being caught carrying out an illegal act. 'You weren't meant to hear me. Johnnie must have left the hall door open when he went out. You wouldn't be kind enough to shut it for me, would you?' She continued on her way to the kitchen and Liz went over to shut the door.

'You caught me out,' Annabelle laughed, on re-entering the room.

'In what way?'

'I always say that I'm going to leave the clearing up until the morning, because it gives the guests no option other than to go to bed. Then, when I think the coast is clear, I slip back in here and do it myself. So much easier, because I know exactly what has to be done.'

'Would you prefer if I went, then?'

'No! Not at all.' She went around the table, picking up wineglasses between her fingers. 'It's just that I don't ever get much time to myself, so I try to grab every opportunity.'

Liz picked up the salad bowl from the centre of the table. 'It must be a real strain having people in your house all the time.'

'It is, but it's what we do to make ends meet. We've learned over the years how to work around our guests, so that lessens the load a bit.'

Liz took the bowl through to the kitchen and placed it on the draining-board. 'How long have you been doing this?'

'Almost ten years now. When Johnnie came out of the army, he had a series of what he termed "dead-end jobs," working for a time in financial management, and then, when he became sick of that, working as a glorified travelling salesman for a timber company. And then, one miserably wet day, he stormed into the house and blurted out that he had had enough of England, its weather *and* the government, and he wanted to live abroad. And I, for once in my life, agreed with him. So we sold our ugly old house in Wiltshire for an exorbitant sum of money and we were able to buy this little patch of heaven and build the house with the proceeds. And then, one day, when the builders and the painters and the removal men had all left, we sat down on our newly arranged furniture and looked at each other and said, "Right. So what do we do now?" That's when panic set in. We had nothing left, nothing to live off. Then, almost the next day, a friend of mine who worked for a fashion magazine in London telephoned and said that she wanted to use Cañareas as a location and could I provide board and lodgings for six models, a photographer and his assistant and an art director? Since then, we haven't looked back.' She turned the dial on the dishwasher and pressed the button. 'So whenever I have a particularly tiresome set of guests, or I get sick of cooking and the clearing up after people and washing interminable amounts of sheets and towels, I just think back and realize just how lucky we have been.'

Liz sat down on the edge of the kitchen table. 'I still admire you for doing it. I only have one house guest at home – Arthur, as it happens – and although he's pretty unobtrusive, I really find it difficult having someone other than my own family around the place all the time. You can never, well, relax.'

'No, you're right. You can't,' Annabelle replied. She took two large wineglasses from the wooden washing-rack above the sink and split the contents of a two-thirds-empty bottle of red wine between them. She handed one to Liz. 'Can I ask you something, Liz, without, I hope, sounding rude?'

Liz gave her a questioning look. 'Yes, of course.'

'It's just that I'm quite intrigued with your situation, and I was wondering – what it is, really.'

'In what way?'

'Well, with your menfolk. I can't quite work it out.'

Liz took in a breath. 'Well, there's nothing really to work out. I'd like to say that I'm young, free and single, but I'm definitely not young, and at the minute I'm not single, because I'm separated from my husband, which I suppose cancels out the "free" bit. So maybe the best definition would be old, tied up but alone.'

'But . . . what about Will?'

'Will? He's just Arthur's son. I came out here with Arthur for Semana Santa and he turned up a couple of days ago, just after Arthur broke his ankle.'

'So you're . . . you're not with Arthur either.'

'Goodness, no! I'm not with anyone – not in that way, at any rate.'

Annabelle shook her head. 'I'm sorry, I shouldn't have asked. It's just that I was rather confused about how you three all fitted in with each other.'

'And are you any more the wiser now?'

She laughed. 'No, not really.' She took a drink from her glass. 'But if you hadn't made it clear otherwise, I would have suspected that you and Will were an item.'

'Will and I? Heavens, no!' She hesitated for a moment. 'What made you think that?'

Annabelle shrugged. 'I don't know.' A smile spread slowly across her face. 'Probably just the way he never took his eyes off you the whole way through dinner.'

'Ah,' Liz replied quietly. She bit at her lip. 'Actually, we were talking about things this afternoon, and he did say something along the lines of what you've just mentioned, but I don't feel ready to start another relationship just yet, Annabelle. The last one hurt me deeply and put me very much on self-defence.'

Annabelle drained her glass. 'Can I ask when this happened?'

'Last year. He went off with another woman.'

'Last year! Well, in that case!' She went into the larder and came out with another uncorked bottle of wine. She refreshed both their glasses. 'Look, maybe I shouldn't say this, but sometimes a relationship with no ties, with no commitments can be the best therapy for a wounded heart. There can be nothing better than to feel wanted, to be made to feel attractive again. Not that you need to be made to feel attractive. Will wasn't the only one making eyes at you across the dining-room table. I don't think that I've seen my husband in such good form for quite a long time. So, my suggestion would be that while you're out here in Spain, far removed from your problems back home, you should just tuck them away to the back of your mind and let things happen. And if the opportunity arises for you to have a wonderful, rip-roaring affair with a man whom I certainly wouldn't throw out of bed on a cold night, then I would grab it with both hands.' She put her hand across her mouth and let out a short, high-pitched giggle, realizing what she had just said. 'Figuratively speaking, of course.'

Liz laughed. 'Of course!' She watched her feet as she swung them back and forth under the table. 'Have you . . . well . . . ever done anything like that before?'

There was a moment's hesitation before Annabelle replied. 'Yes, as a matter of fact, I have.' She pulled a face. 'My word, the secrets are coming out tonight, aren't they?' Placing the bottle of wine and her glass on the table, she pulled out a chair and sat down. 'When Johnnie left the army and couldn't get a job, he seemed to change beyond recognition and he began to take all his problems out on me. We stopped speaking to each other, we never made love, so, as you can imagine, our relationship was heading straight for the rocks. So I upped sticks and headed off to France for a couple of weeks with a friend, just to get some clear thinking time, and while I was there, I met this man and we had a wonderful time together, and I felt loved again – and wanted again. Then, when I returned to England full of trepidation at what the future might hold, Johnnie had found himself a job and everything just went back to normal again. Only this time it was better, because he, too, had had time to think and he understood that the gulf that had appeared in our relationship was entirely down to him. I never told him about my . . . little affair, not because I wanted to continue to deceive him. I just knew that we would be together from then on and it would have done no earthly good if I had confessed all. But I do know that it works.'

Liz let out a sigh. 'Yes, I can see that it probably would do. It's just that I don't know if I'm quite ready for it. I'm also probably not quite so . . . well . . . liberated as you.'

Annabelle laughed. 'Heavens, how wonderful! You make me sound like a loose woman.' She reached over and placed her hand on Liz's arm. 'Listen, Liz, I promise you that I'm not trying to force your hand on this. I just thought it might help to hear another woman's point of view.'

'Oh, it does, and I appreciate you talking to me about it. I just wonder if it wouldn't make things . . . quite complicated.'

'In what way?'

'Well, I suppose really that my loyalties should still lie with Arthur.'

'Oh, don't bother about Arthur! He's perfectly happy, and he's in no fit state to go spying on your every move. Anyway, you just leave Arthur to me. I think that we've developed quite an understanding ourselves.' She placed her hands on the table and pushed herself to her feet. 'Now, if I don't get to bed quite soon, Johnnie will be through here to find out what's happened to me. So I would suggest that you go off to your room and have your-self some sweet dreams.' She walked across to the sink and rinsed out her glass under the tap. 'Even after ten years of being here, I still feel that this place has an air of unreality about it. It's like Never Never Land. What happens really doesn't exist, so you should just take advantage of it.'

She switched off the lights in the kitchen and together they walked through the sitting-room and out into the hall.

'Good night, Annabelle,' Liz whispered. 'Thank you for your words of wisdom.'

Annabelle moved towards her and gave her a kiss on the cheek. 'Good night, Liz.' She turned and began to descend the stairs. 'And by the way,' she called out softly without looking back, 'Happy Easter!'

CHAPTER 22

The armchair and low coffee-table were not permanent fixtures in the kitchen, nor were they ever likely to become so in the future. Their present positioning successfully blocked up the already restricted floor space and hindered anyone trying to make their way around the central worktop. But then again, Alex wasn't using the room as a place to throw together culinary delights for himself. He had converted it into his living-room, a supremely comfortable area where he had managed to cut legwork to the minimum. He could walk into the house, open the fridge door, take out a beer, make himself his customary life-supporting snack of cheese and Tak's curry-pickle sandwiches, get everything to the coffee-table, flump down into the chair and press the television remote without having to move more than seven paces. It had taken him a good half-hour of back-breaking labour to manoeuvre the two bits of furniture along the narrow corridor and squeeze them through the doorway into the kitchen. However, it had been worth it for the few hours of relaxation that he was able to enjoy every evening after returning footsore from his daily tramp around the golf courses in St Andrews.

The only problem was that the amount of exercise that he was taking, coupled with the heat being thrown out from the Rayburn cooker, provided for a soporific cocktail which had prevented him on more than one occasion from ever reaching his bed. Such was his state of being that night, having sat down to watch the late film and fallen asleep before the titles had even finished, that he would no doubt have been heading for yet another stiff-limbed morning had he not been abruptly awakened by the shrill ring of the telephone. He jumped awake, his flailing hand knocking over the half-full can of beer that had been resting on the arm of the chair.

'*Shit!*' He struggled forward in the sagging armchair, picking up the receiver with one hand while trying to retrieve the can with the other before it had a chance to spill every last drop of its contents on the tiled floor. 'Could you hang on a moment?' he called into the receiver. He got up and threw the phone on the chair, then stood still for a moment with the can in his hands, blinking his eyes to try to clear the disorientation from his head. He placed the can on the worktop, spun off an overindulgence of paper towels and wiped the floor. Lobbing the sodden mass into the sink, he picked up the receiver and sat down heavily once more in the chair.

'Hullo?'

'What on earth were *you* doing?'

'Oh, hi, Dad. Sorry, I was asleep when you rang and

I've gone and knocked over a can of beer.' He let out a long yawn and scratched fiercely at his head. 'What time is it anyway?'

'Quarter to twelve.'

'Hell, you're calling a bit late, aren't you?'

'I know I am, but I've been trying to get hold of you all evening.'

'Ah, right. Well, I'm not long back from Saint Andrews. I met up with a couple of friends after I'd finished work.'

'You weren't drinking, were you?'

'No, Dad, I was not. I'm not a complete idiot.'

'All right, I believe you. Is your grandfather not back yet?'

'No. They've headed up to Dornoch, but he said that they'd be back tomorrow evening.'

'My word, I'd no idea that he was planning to be away for so long. If I'd known, I would have suggested that you come to stay here.'

'No, I'm fine where I am. Anyway, I have to man the telephone in case Mum calls.'

'Have you heard from her at all?'

'Yes, most days. She rang early this morning to say that they were just about to leave Seville and head up into the hills somewhere.' He stretched out his legs and rested them on the coffee-table. 'So, what have you been doing today?'

'Och, just driving about the countryside looking for jobs. I went over to an estate near Comrie this morning for an interview.'

'And?'

'And nothing. It was advertised as a farm manager's job, but I reckon that I'd have been nothing more than a glorified shepherd, working a handful of Blackface ewes on three thousand acres of hill. The house was in the middle of nowhere as well, so I don't think I came over as being that keen.'

'It would be a long way from here too, wouldn't it?'

'Aye, you're right. Those were exactly my sentiments. Anyway, on the way home, I came up with a new idea and went straight round to see Jonathan Davis about it.'

'That being?'

'Well, it was just that I was considering everything, you know, having this house here and my roots being here and you being just across the field, and I thought to myself that I didn't really want to move away. At any rate, I certainly didn't want to end up being stuck on top of a mountain in some dreich farmhouse. So it occurred to me that maybe there was something that I could do around here once the golf course had been constructed.'

'Don't tell me! You're planning to become Balmuir's first golf professional.'

Gregor laughed. 'That'd be right. I'd swing a golf club like a fencing mallet! No, lad, I'll leave that job to you.'

'So what's the idea then?'

'Well, I'm thinking of going back to college.'

'*What?* Where? I mean, to study what?'

'Greenkeeping.'

'*Greenkeeping?*'

'Yes. Why not? I remembered that they ran courses at

the agricultural college in Cupar, so I thought that I'd go and sound out Jonathan about it. He was all for it. He also reckoned that I would probably be able to get a fair-sized grant, you know, for retraining.'

'I wouldn't think it would be that well paid, Dad.'

'Hell, Alex, I'm not a big spender. I don't need huge amounts of money. Anyway, I don't think I've done anything other than *lose* money for the last five years, so getting a cheque of *any* size in my hand would be a step in the right direction.'

'Yeah, I take your point.'

'And once Jonathan's deal goes through and I've paid off the bank, I'll at least have a house with no mortgage, and the golf course is right here on the doorstep. What pleases me most, though, about the whole idea is that in a roundabout way I'd still be working my own land . . .' He paused. 'So what do you think?'

'Yeah, go for it. It's a great idea. What does Mary say about it?'

'She doesn't know yet. She's away for the weekend, playing in some two-day badminton jamboree over near Edinburgh. That's actually the reason why I was calling. Seeing you and I are by ourselves, I was wondering if you'd like to go to the kirk with me tomorrow, you know, for the Easter service.'

Alex sucked in a breath. 'Dad, I can't. I'm afraid that I've arranged to play golf.'

'Have you? Och well, never mind. It was just a thought.'

Alex could hear the disappointment in his father's

voice. 'Listen, we could meet up after I've played and have something to eat.'

'No, I'll tell you what. I won't bother going to the kirk. I'll just come with you and carry your clubs. How about that?'

Alex clenched his teeth at the suggestion. 'Er, well the thing is, Dad, that I already have a caddy – of sorts.'

'Ah. Right.' Alex heard him chuckling. 'It wouldn't be the girl in your German tutorial, would it?'

'It might be.'

'Good for you. Well, then.'

'And her name is Madeleine, before you start trying to wheedle that out of me as well.'

'Madeleine. I like that. That's a nice name.' His father let out a deep sigh. 'Oh, well, have yourself a good time.'

There was silence at the end of the line. Alex shook his head in defeat. 'All right, Dad, if you want, you can come too.'

'Wonderful! That's great, Alex, and I promise you that I won't go putting my foot in it.'

'You'd better not.'

'You can count on me, lad. So what time?'

'I'll pick you up at eleven.'

'Eleven it is. I'll be ready. And, Alex . . .'

'Yes?'

'Happy Easter.'

'And the same to you, Dad.'

CHAPTER 23

Having lived all her days on a farm, Liz had evolved over the years into being both a light sleeper and an early riser. Yet, that next morning, she was completely unaware of the person who entered her bedroom and walked purposefully across to the window. It was only when the heavy wooden shutters were banged open that she woke abruptly and found herself blinking hard at the bright sunlight that flooded into the room. She pulled the top sheet over her face to protect her eyes.

'Come on, madam.' It was Will's voice. 'Time to get yourself into gear. We've got things to do.'

She was about to throw back the sheet, but then realized, in her drowsy state, that she probably looked as if she had been dragged through a hedge backwards, so she kept herself hidden underneath. 'What time is it?' she mumbled, her breath lifting the sheet from her mouth.

'Ten o'clock.'

'What!' She sat bolt upright. 'It can't be!' She glanced over at her clock. 'Oh, God, it is,' she moaned, rubbing at her eyes with the palms of her hand. 'Someone should have woken me earlier. Have you all been waiting for me?'

'No, not really.' She watched him as he made his way back towards the door. 'Everyone seems to have been a bit late this morning. But there's something planned at ten-thirty, so you'd better get your skates on.'

'What kind of thing?'

'That's for you to find out.'

'Oh, Will, that's no help at all! Come on, I'm in a panic. What do I wear?'

'Exactly what you wore yesterday. Just a pair of jeans and a T-shirt. Maybe bring a jersey with you.'

Liz brought her knees up to her chin and gently rested her forehead on them. She let out a groan. 'I think that I've got a bit of a hangover.'

Will laughed. 'You're not the only one. Everyone's pretty fragile this morning.' He opened the door. 'Never mind, what's planned will soon blow away the cobwebs.'

'Have I got time for a shower?'

'Sure. Do you want some breakfast?'

Liz ran her tongue around the inside of her mouth to try to judge if she could stomach any food. Things didn't taste too good. 'Thanks, but no thanks. Could I just have a cup of coffee?'

'It'll be ready in the kitchen when you come through.' He walked out of the room, closing the door behind him.

Liz threw back the sheet and swung her legs over the edge of the bed. Building herself up for the effort, she got to her feet and stood for a moment, her eyes clenched shut as she gave the throbbing in her head time to abate.

She then moved across to the small bathroom and turned on the shower.

When she arrived in the kitchen twenty minutes later, she was relieved to see that there was no great flurry of activity. Annabelle, Arthur and Will were sitting silently around the kitchen table, clutching steaming mugs of coffee in their hands.

'Good morning, Liz,' Annabelle said as she entered. 'How are you feeling this morning, or am I right in thinking that's rather a silly question?'

Liz let out a weak laugh. 'Yes, I'm afraid that I think it is.'

'I know. We're all feeling a bit like that.' She got to her feet and walked over to the sideboard and poured Liz a mug of coffee from the percolator. 'I don't know what kind of wine we were drinking last night. I'm pretty sure that we didn't overindulge that much. I must tell Johnnie to avoid it like the plague in future.'

Liz pulled out a chair and sat down next to Arthur, who was wordlessly slumped in his wheelchair, focusing his eyes on a pepper-pot in the middle of the table. Annabelle placed the mug of coffee and a couple of aspirin in front of her. 'Thanks.' She popped the pills into her mouth, then picked up her mug and raised it to eye-level. 'Well, Happy Easter, everybody.'

There was a forced murmur of amusement from all at the thought that anything could be considered happy right then. The silence was resumed, only broken by the sound of heavy footsteps coming up the outside steps and onto the kitchen balcony. Johnnie entered through the open door.

'Morning, everyone.' His voice reached parts of their

heads which would have been better left untouched. 'What a great day!'

Annabelle sighed as she noticed everyone wincing at his voice. 'Johnnie never suffers,' she said through clenched teeth. 'The man has the constitution of an ox.'

He poured himself a mug of coffee. 'You're all a bit pianissimo this morning, aren't you?'

'Yes, we all are,' Annabelle replied tetchily. 'What on earth did you give us to drink last night?'

'I'm not sure. I think it was something that Fidel in the supermarket recommended.'

Annabelle raised her eyebrows. 'Do you owe him money?'

'Probably. Why?'

Annabelle shrugged. 'Maybe this is his way of giving us a gentle reminder of the fact.'

'Come on. It wasn't that bad.'

'Johnnie, it was appalling, and if you have any left, I would suggest that you take it straight back to him.'

'Oh, all right then. If you insist.' As he sat down next to Will, he brought his hand hard down on his shoulder. 'Are you quite happy with everything – for your day, I mean?'

'Yes, I think so.'

'No questions on your route or anything?'

'No. I think you explained it all pretty well.'

'Good. Well, whenever you're both ready,' he said, looking at Liz, 'you should head off.'

'What?' Annabelle asked, her voice lifting with excitement. 'They haven't arrived yet, have they?'

'Yup.' He nodded his head towards the open door. 'They're waiting patiently at the bottom of the steps as we speak.'

Annabelle jumped to her feet and walked quickly out onto the balcony and looked over the wall. 'Oh, Johnnie, they're beautiful!'

'Yes, they are rather elegant, aren't they?'

Liz looked across at Will, a frown of concern on her face. 'What are we going to be doing?' She looked around the table and suddenly became aware of the fact that all three men seemed to be grinning at her.

'You should maybe ask my father,' Will replied. 'It's all his idea.'

She shot him a querying glance. 'Arthur?'

'Well.' He broke his focus on the pepper-pot, cleared his throat, then lifted his hands as if trying to work out how to start his explanation. 'It was just that I remembered a conversation that we had some time ago, about things that we missed doing, or things that we felt that we'd missed out on. Anyway, during those long nights that Will and I spent together in hospital, we had time to talk and I found out that he enjoyed doing exactly the same thing as you. So I thought that it might be an idea to try to organize something for you both.'

Liz stared at him, trying to remember what it was that she had said. Then a smile slowly crept across her face. 'It's not . . .' She stopped, thinking that she could well be on the wrong track.

'It's not what?' Arthur asked.

'Horse riding?'

Arthur flicked his head to the side. 'Could be.'

'Oh, do stop teasing the poor girl,' Annabelle called out from the balcony. 'Of course it's riding. Come over here, Liz, and have a look at these two beauties.'

Liz sat open-mouthed, glancing from one man to another, then, pushing back her chair, she walked quickly across the kitchen and out onto the balcony to stand beside Annabelle. She looked over the wall and could not help but let out a gasp of wonderment at the sight below her. Two pure-bred Andalusian stallions stood side by side, tethered to the grille of the downstairs window, so similar in appearance that one could have been the reflection of the other. Their black coats gleamed like polished metal in the morning sun and their long, groomed manes fell seductively down the sides of their arched necks. She could hear the tinkle of metal as they champed impatiently on their bits, and from time to time they turned to face each other, flaring their nostrils and tossing their heads as if readying themselves for a confrontation. Across their powerful backs were slung large Spanish saddles, their dark brown leather tooled with swirling patterns and inset with polished buttons, and over their high-backed seats were thrown thick woollen blankets with coloured stripes so vibrant and set so close together that they were dazzling to the eye.

Liz made her way quickly down the steps, then slowed her pace as she approached them, talking quietly as she went, wary in case she frightened them. She smoothed her hand across the neck of the horse closest to her, feeling its powerful muscles tighten at her touch, then, ducking under the tethering rope, she stood between them.

'Hullo, boys,' she said, almost in a whisper. She let them nose her hands, feeling the softness of their muzzles and the gentle warmth of their breath against her skin. Their eyes shone through their trailing forelocks like polished coals as they scrutinized her, vigilantly at first, and then, as they became used to the sound of her voice and the manipulation of her hands, they relaxed their heads and fluttered their long-lashed eyelids open and closed, as if being hypnotized by her actions.

'What do you think of them?'

Liz turned to see that Will had come to stand beside the horse to her left. He reached up and stroked one of its ears.

'They're beautiful. I don't think I've ever seen anything like it before. They just seem so . . . noble. Do you know what they're called?'

'No idea. I suppose we could find out.' He looked up at the balcony. 'Johnnie!' he called out, the sound of his voice making the horses flick back their heads momentarily in alarm.

Johnnie's head appeared over the wall. 'Yes?'

'Liz wants to know if the horses have names.'

'Hmm.' Johnnie looked thoughtful. 'Eduardo's on the left, Carlos on the right.'

Liz craned her head back to look up at him, catching the twinkle of humour in his reply. 'Are you being serious?'

'Er, not really. I actually forgot to ask that question, but

I'm sure they wouldn't mind being called those names for just one day.'

Liz looked back at the horses. 'No, I'm sure they wouldn't. Hullo, Eduardo. Hullo, Carlos.'

Will turned and made his way back up the steps. 'Come on, we'd better start making tracks. Have you got everything you need?'

'Where are we going?' Liz asked as she followed him.

'Around and about. Johnnie has shown me a route on the map which should take us off for most of the day.'

When they re-entered the kitchen, Arthur had not moved from his position at the table, but noticing the look of almost child-like excitement on Liz's face, he settled back, leaning his elbows on the arms of the wheelchair and touching his forefingers against the grin of self-satisfaction that stretched across his mouth. She walked straight over to him and placed her arms around his neck and gave him a kiss on both cheeks. 'Arthur, you shouldn't have done this.'

'I don't see why on earth not. As I said before, it's never too late to start doing all these things over again.'

'I know you did.' Her eyes scanned the plastered leg that stuck out on its metal support on the wheelchair. 'But I just feel bad that you can't join us.'

'Dammit, I've never been up on a horse in my life. In fact, to be quite honest, I hate the wretched animals. If Will wasn't here, I wouldn't have dreamed of organizing this whole day. You'd only have tried to force me into coming with you.'

Liz smiled at him. 'Are you sure you're going to be all right here by yourself?'

426

'He's not going to be by himself, Liz.' It was Annabelle who spoke. Liz turned and watched her do up the buckle of a bulging rucksack that was resting on the table. She handed it to Will, then glanced at Liz and gave an almost imperceptible wink. 'Arthur and I are going to spend a very happy and fulfilling day together, so don't you even think about him.'

Her words jerked at Liz's memory, and she remembered their conversation of the night before. She felt her cheeks begin to flush. 'Right!' she exclaimed, rather too heartily in an attempt to cover for the fluster in her mind. 'Well, that's fine then.' She turned to see Will shrug the ruck-sack onto his shoulders and walk out of the door. 'In that case' – she pointed after him – 'I'd better be off.'

Arthur gave her a double thumbs-up. 'Have a good time.'

'Yes.' She shot him a glance, then looked back at Annabelle. 'Yes, of course.'

As she made her way over to the door, Annabelle came round the side of the kitchen table, took her arm and guided her out onto the balcony. 'How's the head feeling?' she asked as they walked down the steps together.

'Subsiding, gradually.'

'Glad to hear it.' She paused. 'Listen, Liz, I don't want you to go worrying yourself about what we talked about last night. I think, in retrospect, that it was quite presumptuous of me to give you advice of that nature. Probably the wine. It does have the tendency to make me talk too much.'

Liz stopped. 'No. Believe me, it was wonderful to talk

to you. I don't ever get the opportunity to have a . . . female chat like that. I always seem to be surrounded by men.'

Annabelle laughed. 'Wow! *I* should be so lucky!'

'No, what I mean is, my father and my son – and Arthur – and now Will.' She laughed. 'In fact, I think the last time I had a discussion like that was probably in the school playground!' She paused, brushing a wisp of hair off her face and tucking it in behind her ear. 'To be quite honest, it's given me a buzz, and it's made me feel . . . well . . . like a woman again for the first time in I don't know how long.' Her gaze flickered momentarily over the top of the whitewashed wall to where Will was tightening the girths on the saddles of the two horses. 'I can't say if anything . . . *romantic* will ever develop between Will and myself, but I am going to take your advice and just have a good time.'

Annabelle put her arm around Liz and gave her a squeeze. 'You do exactly that, and just see what happens. Nothing need be forced upon you.' She gave Liz a gentle push. 'Now, you get going and we'll see you both this evening.'

Liz made her way quickly down the steps to where Will was now standing with the two horses. He handed her the reins of the one Johnnie had christened Carlos. Whispering reassuringly to the horse, she expertly swung herself up into the saddle without needing to make use of the offered leg-up from Will. As soon as the horse felt her weight on his back, he took a number of high-stepped paces sideways, eager to be off. She kicked her feet into the stirrups and pulled gently on his mouth, bringing him to a standstill.

Will put a hand on the toe of her boot. 'I just judged the stirrups. What are they like?'

Liz stood up in the saddle. 'Fine.'

'Right.' He gathered in his reins and effortlessly mounted his horse. 'Okay, let's get going.'

They set off up the track at a bouncing walk, the two stallions impatient for the chance to rid themselves of pent-up energy. Liz glanced over her shoulder to where Annabelle still stood half-way up the steps. She gave her a quick wave, and Annabelle responded by bringing her hand to her mouth and blowing a kiss.

Before the coming of the motor car and asphalt roads, the remote pueblos that were scattered throughout the hills and valleys of the Sierra de Cañareas were linked by a network of ancient thoroughfares known as *caminos réales*, stone-cobbled tracks bounded by drystone walls, wide enough only to allow unhindered passage for a donkey with its panniered load. In most parts, the cobbles were now hidden below a thin covering of turf, emblazoned with the purple and pink of wild flowers, and the walls had fallen victim to age, crumbling away into adjoining fields. However, the paths were still kept clear of encroaching vegetation by those who came out from the town and used them for access to their small vegetable *huertas*, and by the local parks department, which managed them for the good of the multitude of hikers that visited the area each year.

It was these tracks that Will and Liz followed, one behind the other, the paths being too narrow for them to ride abreast. They wound their way through the countryside in the cooling shade of chestnut trees and cork oaks that leaned out from the side banking, their branches hanging above them like the misshapen arms of some grotesque monster waiting for the right moment to pounce upon them. They passed by small, hidden-away pockets of fertile ground where ordered rows of onions and potatoes and carrots grew, not tended that day as their elderly caretakers would have been at home recovering from the night-long festivities that brought Semana Santa to its climax. Then, as the land began to rise, they left behind them the more ordered low ground and rode up into dense scrubland where the spindly trunks of self-seeded pines grew too close together to afford any view. The horses' hooves struck hard at the ground as they climbed, their powerful shoulders brushing aside the tall brittle cistus plants that grew in across the now no longer tended path. At the top of the gradient, they broke out into open ground and rode side by side along the wide fire-break. They followed the line of the ridge, looking out across the wooded hills that stretched like a ruffled green blanket away to the distant horizon, the unseasonal warmth of the day finally draining their contours of all colour and merging them without a line of demarcation into the pale-blue sky.

The fire-break dipped and rose for more than five miles, and where it eventually petered out they caught sight of a cluster of white houses in the valley. Carefully picking their way down the steep descent towards the village, they entered at its highest point and rode down through a narrow maze of streets hemmed in by houses on whose flat-topped roofs lines of washing swung lazily in the midday breeze. There seemed to be little sign of life anywhere, though voices, intermingled with the clamant strains of television, could be heard through open doorways. They were guided by the church spire, eventually finding their way to the village plaza by way of a lane no wider than the *caminos* that they had been following that morning.

The Café El Borriquero could quite easily have passed as a private house had it not been for the large sign advertising Cruzcampo beer above its open door. They dismounted outside, and while Will disappeared into the pitch-black interior of the establishment, Liz led the two horses to the circular drinking trough that acted as a centre-piece for the paved seating area of the plaza. By the time they had quenched their thirst and Liz had secured them to the hitching rings that were set into the concrete beam above the permanently running water spouts, Will had returned with two glasses of beer, frosted with cold. He set them down at the side of a wooden bench, shaded from the sun by a tall palm tree, and let the rucksack slip from his shoulders.

'It's all very quiet,' Liz said as she approached the bench. 'Where is everybody?'

Will cast an eye around the empty square as he undid the buckles of the rucksack. 'More than likely catching up on their sleep after last night's festivities. We've actually been damned lucky to find that bar open. Easter Day has always been very much a family day in Spain, so I doubt we'll be seeing much action around.'

So they sat together in solitude on the bench, drinking their beer and eating the sandwiches that Annabelle had made up for them, and talking away to each other about their own experiences of riding. There happened to be no real common ground in that, Liz having done most of hers in small pony club events that were organized down to the last detail by a brigade of forceful women. Will, on the other hand, had learned it on a much grander and more liberated scale, working when he was in his mid-teens on a cattle ranch in Manitoba, spending twelve hours a day during his three-month school holiday in the saddle. However, for once Liz did not feel herself immediately belittled or self-conscious about her own lesser achievements, because there had been a time – before she had become pregnant, before she had married Gregor – when she had been just like any other normal teen-age girl, eating, sleeping and talking horses. And now, after so many years, she had returned to that. She felt exhilarated, happy and carefree in the company of this man who talked with as much enthusiasm about it all as she did. What's more, she felt safe with him. Will knew her whole story and had said himself that he would make no move on her. So there was no need, no pressure to take their relationship any further. This was as good a therapy for her, and much less complicated, than what had been suggested by Annabelle.

They would probably have sat there for much longer

had not the sun moved around from behind the tree, and they were dazzled into realizing that time was marching on. They left by the bottom end of the village and followed alongside a river-bed that trickled down the hill-side. Its bouldered starkness was brightened by the crimson flowers of oleander bushes that grew on its banks, relying on lengthy tap-roots to eke out moisture from the parched ground. As they descended the hill, the land became more arid and colourless, and they had to snake their way through huge rocks that lay bare and smooth in their path. They passed by the ruins of a small *casita*, its walls constructed with stones similar to those that were strewn about the place, and Liz wondered to herself how it was possible that anyone could have picked out a living on such an infertile landscape.

They followed the meandering course of the river for an hour, and just when they had begun to express doubts as to whether it was leading anywhere, it suddenly rounded a sharp bend and the land opened out, and the river disgorged its meagre flow into the vast lake that had been visible from Finca de Rodrigo.

It had been Will's intention to explore the environs of the lake for a time, but because of their prolonged lunch he realized that they were running well behind schedule. So, having given the horses five minutes to graze on the lush green grass that bordered the lake, he decided that it would be best for them to take the shortest route back home, and they set off up the winding road that linked the lake with the town of Cañareas. They rode as fast as they felt the tiring horses could manage, the sun's heat now intensified by its absorption into the asphalt surface of the road.

By the time they turned into the gates of the *finca*, the sun was touching the tops of the hills, casting deep shadows through the chestnut trees that fell away below the road. As they climbed the final slope to the house they spotted Annabelle sitting at the bottom of the steps that led up to the kitchen, talking animatedly with a man whom they concluded to be the owner of the horses. She got up as they approached and came forward to meet them.

'My word, you look a healthier person than the one that left this morning!' she said, putting up her hand to stroke the nose of Liz's horse. 'Your face is veritably sun-kissed! How did you get on?'

'It was wonderful!' Liz replied. 'The countryside around here is so . . . different.' She slid out of the saddle, fully intending to continue her eulogy to the day, but was silenced by the sudden sharp pain at the base of her spine. 'Ooh!' She took a couple of stiff paces forward. 'Goodness, I'm not used to that!'

Annabelle laughed. 'Well, nothing that a good soak in a hot bath won't sort out. How did you manage with the horse?' She glanced round at the owner, who had stepped forward to take hold of Will's reins while he dismounted. 'I think Andreas here was a bit surprised to see you back in one piece. He said that there was no way that a woman could keep this big boy under control.'

'She rode him as if she had been on him every day of her life,' Will interjected before Liz had a chance to answer. He pointed at her. '*She* is a true horsewoman. I've seen seasoned wranglers not being able to handle a horse like that.'

Annabelle pulled a face at Liz. 'Well! That's praise indeed.' She turned and said something in Spanish to the owner. He looked at Liz, a broad grin on his face, and taking off his battered straw hat, said something in a high-pitched chatter before giving her a flourishing bow. Will let out a loud laugh and slapped the man on the back.

'What did he say?' Liz asked.

'He apologized for doubting your ability,' Annabelle replied with a chuckle, 'and that he was sure that his horse enjoyed having someone as beautiful as you astride his back all day.'

Liz frowned dubiously. 'How am I meant to take that comment?'

'I'm not quite sure myself,' Annabelle replied, her mouth drawn tight. 'But I think you'd better make yourself scarce before he starts making advances.'

Liz walked over to the man and held out her hand. '*Muchas gracias, señor.*'

He clenched her hand, then brought it up to his stubbly mouth and gave it a kiss. '*De nada, señora, de nada. Es un placer.*'

At Annabelle's suggestion, dinner that night was earlier, seeing that the couple from the Isle of Wight had rung to say that they were going to be spending the night in Seville. Moreover, Johnnie had managed to push

435

Arthur's energy resources to the limit by wheeling him into town and spending the best part of the afternoon drinking copious amounts of Spanish brandy in his local bar before both made their somewhat wobbly way home again.

They ate out on the wide balcony at the front of the house, Johnnie deeming the evening warm enough to do so, and conversation during the meal was occasional but relaxed, all of them feeling pleasantly exhausted after their respective exertions of the day. Liz hardly spoke but sat with a smile on her face, listening with only half an ear to what was being said and allowing herself the luxury of reliving every minute of her day. She couldn't remember the last time she had been able to do exactly that. Over the last eighteen years, she always had to think of other people. Her father, her mother, Alex, Gregor. She began to repeat his name over and over again in her mind, waiting for the clenching knot to tighten in her stomach, for the bitterness to well up from her innermost being. But nothing happened. Only good thoughts came to her, and memories of the past that had hitherto been too powerful and too disturbing to recollect flashed harmlessly before her eyes. And it was at that point that she knew that she had unconsciously turned a corner, and that she was at peace with the past and content with whatever the future might hold for her. She looked around the table, watching individually each of the four people who sat with her, and she realized her deep fondness for them all. After all the shunning and ostracizing that she had suffered over the past year, she was now in the company of friends, *her* friends, and she knew that they took her at face value and liked her for what she was.

'Did you see that?'

'What?' Annabelle asked, following Johnnie's line of gaze up into the sky.

'I've just seen the most incredible shooting star.' He thrust forward an arm and traced its path. 'It went from there right over to there, bright as anything.'

Annabelle got up from her chair and went over to the metal balustrade that surrounded the veranda and placed her hands upon it. She looked up into the sky. 'Goodness, I hadn't realized how clear it was.' She turned back, a sparkle of excitement in her eyes. 'You know, this is a perfect night for star-gazing. Who wants to go down to the swimming pool?'

'Swimming pool?' Arthur exclaimed. 'Not on your bloody life. It's far too cold.'

Annabelle laughed. 'Not to swim, Arthur. To star-gaze. It's the perfect place. We turn off all the lights, and you can just lie down on a sun-lounger and look up into the sky. It's quite fantastic. You don't know just how insignificant you are in this world until you've done it.'

Arthur humphed. 'I don't want to know how insignificant I am. I have enough trouble convincing myself that I'm some kind of worthwhile entity at the best of times.'

His gloomy statement was met with long groans of sympathy from the assembled company, Annabelle emphasizing hers by walking over to him and patting the top of his head as she might have done to a sad dog.

'Annabelle?'

'Yes, Johnnie, my darling.'

Johnnie gritted his teeth. 'I was hoping that we might take advantage of the fact that we'd eaten earlier tonight.'

Annabelle clasped a hand to her chest and stared at him in surprise. 'Johnnie! What a strange thing to say in front of our guests.'

'No, no, not that! I was wondering if you wouldn't give me a hand to finish off paying the rest of the bills.'

Annabelle looked visibly deflated. 'Oh, what a disappointment.' She let out a long sigh. 'All right, I suppose I could.' She began to clear the table. '*Bang* goes the stargazing idea, though.'

'Well, I'm up for it,' Will declared, jumping up from his chair. 'What about you, Liz? Do you feel like giving it a go?'

Liz got to her feet. 'Okay, but only on the condition that we give Annabelle a hand to clear up first.'

'Don't you even think about it!' Annabelle exclaimed. 'You're all paying for the privilege of *not* doing that kind of thing.' She put down her load of plates on the dining-room table and walked quickly out into the hall, returning a few seconds later with two heavy woollen blankets. 'Here, take these with you. It's surprising how much colder it is down there by the pool, even though it's only a few feet lower than the house.'

'Are you sure we can't give you a hand?' Liz asked tentatively.

'Certainly not. I'll cut your fingers off with a carving knife if you so much as touch a plate. Now get going, both of you.' She shooed them away with her hands. 'I'll turn on the pool lights long enough for you to get down there so that you don't fall down the steps.'

They hurried their way through the kitchen and out onto the balcony, then ran down the two flights of steps to the swimming pool, laughing like kids as they tried to get themselves organized before Annabelle switched off the lights. They pulled two sun-beds together and had just wrapped themselves in the blankets when Annabelle's voice sounded out from the house.

'Are you ready?'

'Not quite!' Will called out.

'Too late!' came the response and the lights went out.

'Dammit!' Will laughed. 'She could have waited! I can't see a thing!' He groped around for the sun-bed. 'Where are you?'

'Here.'

'Where's here?'

He felt a hand touch his arm.

'Right. You take the farthest away sun-bed,' he said.

'But I can't see anything either,' Liz replied.

'Well, don't go falling into the wretched pool!'

Liz giggled. 'No, hang on, I've got it now.' She shuffled over to her sun-bed and lay down, and heard the one next to her creak slightly as it took Will's weight. He breathed out heavily. 'Right then, what can you see?'

'Nothing yet. I think we'll need to get our eyes accustomed to it all.'

They lay in silence for a minute, staring up into the sky.

'Wow!' Will said, almost in a whisper. 'Would you look at that! Have you got it too?'

'Yes.'

'That . . . is . . . incredible!' He disentangled an arm from his blanket and pointed up into the sky. 'Look, there's Orion's Belt.'

'Where?'

'There. Can you see it?'

'No, not yet.'

He freed his left arm and put it behind her shoulders. 'Right, come right across and have a look.'

She moved her body over to his and laid her head on his chest and squinted up his outstretched arm, using it like the sight of a rifle. 'Yes, I've got it now.' She made to move back onto her sun-bed.

'Just stay where you are. It'll make it much easier.' He moved his hand across the sky. 'There's the Plough. Have you got that one?'

'Yes.' She felt his chest rise and fall under her head and the soft blowing of his breath on her hair. She let out an involuntary shiver.

'Are you cold?' he asked.

'Yes, I am. Freezing,' she replied, thinking it best to cover up the real reason.

'Well, move for a minute and we'll get rearranged.' He pulled away their two blankets and put them together. 'Right, come in close.' He threw the blankets over both of them and lay back. 'Okay, tuck your side in and resume position number one.'

Liz laid her head back on his chest and felt the warmth of his body next to hers, now conscious of the fact that the whole length of their legs were touching and her hip dug into the hard muscles at the side of his stomach. She didn't know what to do with her hands, so she folded her arms.

'Is that better?'

'Yes, much.'

'Okay, so no talking until we pick out another.'

They lay together in silence, staring up into the sky. 'Can I say something?' Liz asked.

'Not unless it's the name of a star.'

'Well, it's about them. Annabelle was right. It really does make one feel so small and insignificant. I think it has to be one of the most powerful and most beautiful sights that I have ever seen.'

'I was just thinking that myself,' Will replied quietly.

There was something about the sound of his voice that puzzled her. She turned her head and looked up at his face. He was not gazing up into the sky, but looking directly at her. She felt his hand touch the top of her head, and he twisted a finger around a strand of her hair.

'Will.' She felt a constriction in her throat. 'I . . .'

'I know. Don't worry. Nothing will happen.'

She did not turn her face again, neither did she stop him from playing with her hair. For the first time she was conscious of his smell, a mixture of the same musky after-shave that he had been wearing when he had first held her in the hotel in Seville, and the heady pungency of male body. It had been so long since she had lain this close to a man, so long since she had felt the touch of a man. Annabelle was right – she was always right. It was what she needed to be made to feel whole again. And she knew that it was Will – funny, kind, understanding Will – who was the man who could do it for her. She brought up her hand discreetly under the blanket and undid the buttons of her shirt.

Will raised his hand and pointed up into the sky. 'I'm pretty sure that's the Pole Star,' he said quietly.

She reached up and took hold of his hand and slowly pulled it down under the blanket, then, slipping it under her bra, she guided him to her nipple. She felt his body tauten beside her.

'Liz, you don't—'

She put a finger up to his lips. 'I know I don't.'

He was silent, and she could feel his heart thumping like a sledge-hammer beneath her head. Then his fingers began to move slowly on her nipple, and it responded immediately to his touch. He moved his position, and she felt the arm below her back lever her sideways onto his sun-bed and then he was above her, obscuring the stars in the night sky from sight. He remained motionless for a moment, staring down at her face.

'You are truly beautiful, Liz.'

Then he lowered his head, and she felt his lips brush hers. He pulled away again, but she reached up and put her arms around his neck and brought him back to her, and when their open mouths met and their legs entwined, Liz began to feel the long-missed energy of a man flood through her being.

CHAPTER 24

Despite the fact that it was five o'clock in the afternoon after a bright but cold Easter Day, a long line of holiday traffic slowly snaked its way along the approach to St Andrews, stringing back as far as the outer point of the Strathtyrum Golf Course. As the Land Rover approached the rear of the line, Mr Craig blew out resignedly and dropped into a lower gear, jerking out the clutch sufficiently to make the Jack Russell, who had been quivering with excitement on Roberta's knee, scrabble for a foothold. She caught hold of the dog before he was pitched forward into the footwell and looked across at her travelling companion.

'You must be feeling tired.'

He cocked his head to the side. 'Aye, a wee bit, but it's been an easy-enough journey.'

'How long has it taken us?'

He glanced at his wrist-watch. 'Four and a half hours.'

Roberta let out a sigh and looked forward at the line of traffic. 'And now we're stuck in this. So near, yet so far.'

'Och, it won't take that long to clear. I reckon that most of this lot will be heading off in the direction of the beach. Once we're through the town, it'll be plain sailing.'

Roberta bit at her lip. 'Craig, would you mind awfully if we stopped for a minute?'

'What? Right now?'

'No, I mean when we get into town.'

'Surely. Where would it be that you're wanting to stop?'

Roberta pushed the dog onto the centre seat and rummaged in the pocket of her jacket. She took out a piece of paper and unfolded it. 'It's a place called the Scores Hotel.'

'Well, that'll be easy enough. It's just on the way in.' The queue of traffic had begun to speed up and he once more engaged a higher gear. He glanced across at Roberta, wondering why it was that she needed to stop in that particular hotel, and noticed that she suddenly seemed quite agitated. 'Everything's all right with you, is it?'

'Yes, fine,' she replied airily. 'I just have to make a telephone call.'

The farmer chortled. 'Another one, eh? Well, well!'

Roberta reached over and gave his arm a gentle punch. 'What's that supposed to mean?'

'Oh, nothing.' He shot her a teasing smile. 'I was just thinking that for someone who wasn't that well acquainted over here, you've been making an awful lot of phone calls over the past few days.'

Roberta picked up Leckie and replaced him on her knee. 'Oh, I know a few people,' she declared in a self-satisfied tone. 'The important ones, at any rate.'

Three-quarters of an hour later, they turned off the main road and made their way down the bumpy farm-track towards the steading. Mr Craig looked out across the land that had become, over the many years he had been there, the greatest part of his life, knowing every inch of it as well as he knew the back of his hand. But, for once, it was not happiness that he felt at being home. Having physically distanced himself from the place for the best part of a week, he had been able to put to the back of his mind all the problems and sorrow that had been manifest there over the past year. And now the sight of the two bottom fields, their gently undulating topography now changed beyond all recognition, exacerbated his down-heartedness.

'You're not too glad to be home, are you?' Roberta said quietly.

He turned to face her. 'What was that, lass?'

'I've been watching you. You've got sadness written all over your face.'

He gave her a forced smile. 'Aye, well. It's difficult to imagine what it's going to be like never seeing crops growing and sheep grazing in these fields again.' He steered the Land Rover around the corner of the steading and pulled to a halt in the courtyard. 'I really never thought that I'd see the day.' He opened the door, allowing the dog to jump out immediately and disappear into the steading, eager to make up for lost time in the hunt for rats. Mr Craig clambered out slowly, then, placing his hands in the small of his back, he gave it a long stretch before moving around to the rear door to start unloading.

'Hang on a minute!' He felt Roberta take hold of his hand in a powerful grasp, and he nearly lost his balance as she pulled him towards the corner of the house.

He laughed. 'Now where are you taking me?'

'Just come with me,' she replied without turning back. She made her way purposefully around the side of the house and into the small front garden, then marched him over to the garden wall and stood beside him, looking out across the fields below the house. From that vantage point, it was even more obvious how much work had been completed in the time they had been away, and he felt his heart give an extra twist at the sight.

'Do you remember when you brought me out here that night when the moon was so brilliant that we could see every inch of this land?' she asked.

'Aye, of course.'

'Well, what made that so special for me was that I could physically feel your love for this place, in the way that you spoke about it, in the way you seemed so completely in tune with it all. One thing you did that night that I remember so clearly was that you were explaining something to me and you suddenly broke off mid-sentence just to let an owl, away in those trees down there, hoot away uninterrupted. Bet you can't remember that, can you?'

He shook his head.

'Well, there you are then. You do it subconsciously. This farm *is* you, Craig, this land is you, no matter what it looks like. And even if it doesn't belong to you, you belong to it, as do the trees and the birds and everything else that grows and lives here.' She leaned her hands on the top of the wall. 'Don't get despondent by all this. I've seen golf courses under construction before, and they all go through this stage of growth where nothing seems to fit, and then suddenly everything becomes clear, and the ugly duckling turns into the most beautiful swan. You *will* be proud of it, Craig, I know you will, and you will love this land again as much as you ever did before.'

They stood in silence for a moment, then Mr Craig moved towards her and put an arm across her shoulders. 'Thank you, Roberta,' he said, smiling down at her. 'I was needing to hear that.'

'I know you were.' She took hold of his hand. 'Come on, let's go and get those things out of the car.'

He was just pulling the last of the luggage out of the back of the Land Rover when he heard the car changing down a gear as it came around the side of the steading. He stood waiting for it to appear at the corner, clutching Roberta's golf bag in his hand. It was Jonathan Davies. As he pulled to a halt beside him, Roberta came down the back door steps. Davies threw open the driver's door and got out.

'Good to see you back!' he exclaimed heartily, approaching them both and shaking their hands. 'How was the golf?'

'Couldn't have been better!' Roberta replied. 'Every course as beautiful as the one before.' She bent forward to peer through the windscreen of Davies's car. 'Did you meet up with him?'

Davies glanced at his car. 'Yes. He's feeling the cold a bit, I think.'

Roberta hurried over to the passenger door of the car and opened it, then, leaning in, she helped an elderly man with thinning grey hair to his feet. He clutched a briefcase to his portly frame, while at the same time attempting to pull the flaps of his raincoat around him. 'Hullo, Maurice.' She put her hands up onto his shoulders and gave him a smacking kiss on each cheek. 'You really are a star to do this.'

'I've never travelled so far in all my life, Bobby.' He spoke in a soft Australian accent. 'And I don't think I've ever been so *cold* in all my life, either.'

She took him by the arm. 'Come on, then. Let's get you inside.' She guided him across to where the farmer was standing, a look of curiosity on his face. 'Craig, I'd like you to meet Maurice Roache.'

The farmer put forward his hand. 'Pleased to make your acquaintance, Mr Roache.'

The man shook his hand. 'And yours too, Mr Craig.'

The farmer's intrigue was further heightened. How could this man have told, from the way in which Roberta had introduced him, that that was his surname?

'Can we go inside, Craig, before Maurice gets frost-bite?'

'Of course.' He walked over and placed the golf bag with the rest of the luggage beside the steps, then opened the back door and stood aside for the party to enter into the house. 'I'm afraid that you might find the place in a bit of a mess. My grandson has been here by himself for a week.'

'I don't mind what it looks like,' Maurice Roache replied. 'As long as it's warm.'

'Well, I think you'll be all right on that account.'

Mr Craig was pleasantly surprised to find that the kitchen was in an orderly state, although mobility around the room was somewhat hampered by the presence of an armchair and a coffee-table, both of which he recognized as belonging in the front sitting-room. 'Please have a seat at the table, gentlemen,' he said, taking the kettle from the side of the Rayburn and filling it with water from the tap. 'Would anyone care for a cup of tea?'

Roberta walked over and took the kettle from his grasp. 'You go and sit down, Craig. I can do that.'

'No, no, I can . . .'

'Please, Craig. I would *like* you to go and sit down.'

The farmer pulled a face at her. 'All right, I can take a telling.'

As he pulled out a chair and sat down, he noticed that Maurice Roache had opened up his brief-case on the table and was busying himself laying out papers in front of him. He turned and looked questioningly at Roberta, who leaned against the Rayburn, her hands spread along the chrome towel-rail.

'Craig, Maurice here is my family lawyer, and it is to him, and to Jonathan, that I've been making all these telephone calls over the past few days. At my request, Maurice has flown over here from Sydney, and hopefully those papers that he has in front of him will explain why he has made such a long journey at such short notice. Maurice, I think that this might be a good time for you to take over.'

'Certainly, Bobby.' Placing a pair of gold half-moon reading spectacles onto the tip of his nose, he picked up

449

the bundle of papers and knocked them together on the table. He grinned at the farmer. 'Mr Craig, would I be right in thinking that you are unaware of what Bobby is intending?'

He looked up at Roberta, who beamed a smile at him. He shook his head. 'No idea at all.'

'In that case,' the lawyer continued, 'it would probably be best if we started at the beginning.' He took up the top sheet of paper. 'Right, then. Roberta Josephine Bayliss, who happens to be here in our presence, is the third daughter of one Simon Anthony Bayliss, residing at—'

'Maurice?' Roberta cut in.

'Yes?'

'As Dad would say, could you cut the waffle and get on with it?'

The lawyer let out a resigned sigh and shook his head. 'Oh dear, like father, like daughter.' There was a chuckle of amusement from the others. 'All right, then, if that's the way you want it, Bobby.' He laid down his paper and took off his spectacles and, linking his hands together, he rested them on the table. 'Mr Craig, Bobby's father, Simon Bayliss, was an entrepreneur of some note in Australia. He began as a young man in engineering, starting up his own company which he successfully adapted to producing munitions during the Japanese conflict. Thereafter, he began to diversify, investing mostly in small businesses that he felt had a chance of growing. I had the honour, Mr Craig, of being Mr Bayliss's lawyer for over fifty years, and I can quite truthfully say that I know of only two of those businesses that eventually failed. So, as you can imagine, he accumulated quite a fortune, in fact enough for him to retire at the age of fifty-two and concentrate on his one complete and utter passion – golf. It was one that was also shared by his youngest daughter, Roberta. They went everywhere together, all over the world, not only to play golf but to watch it as well.'

He coughed into his fist to clear his throat.

'When Simon Bayliss sadly passed away in March at the grand old age of ninety, he divided his estate among his three daughters, but – and it's a big but – the lion's share of his wealth was to go to his youngest daughter, with two major conditions attached. Firstly, that Bobby accompany his ashes over here to Scotland and to see to it personally that they were scattered on the furthest outreach of the Old Course at Saint Andrews. Secondly, that for the remainder of her mother's life, Bobby should stay to look after her in the family house. Both conditions were subsequently agreed to by Bobby.' He replaced his spectacles and shuffled through his papers, eventually extricating one from the middle of the pile. 'Now, this is where I have to rely on the written word, I'm afraid.' He held the paper up at an angle so that the light above the table played upon it. 'It is Bobby's intention to set up a fitting tribute to her father, one of which she feels he would not only totally approve, but also one of which he would be overwhelmingly proud. She has therefore asked me to draw up papers to inaugurate a trust, which will have as its sole purpose the investment of monies into the development of new golf courses around the world. Bobby has also intimated that she wants the course here at

Balmuir to be the first beneficiary, and I have here an agreement made up between the trust and Mr Davies's venture capital group which I very much hope we'll be able to sign this evening.' He took off his spectacles and sat back in his chair. 'So that's it really' – he shot Roberta a wry smile – 'without any legal speak whatsoever.'

The two men looked expectantly at Mr Craig, but he sat in silence, staring blankly at the lawyer, his elbow resting on the side of the table and his hand spread across his mouth, as if preventing himself from saying anything. Jonathan Davies shifted uneasily in his seat, realizing that the farmer's eyes were neither focused nor blinking. Both he and Maurice Roache turned simultaneously toward Roberta. She did not catch their look. She bit apprehensively at a finger-nail as she watched Craig, the glow of excitement that had been on her face now replaced by a frown of concern. Then she moved tentatively forward and placed her hand gently on his shoulder.

'Craig?' Roberta said almost in a whisper. 'What do you think?'

He started at the sound of her voice, as if being woken from a dream. He let out a deep breath, then, placing both hands on the table, he slowly pushed himself to his feet. 'Would you please all excuse me for a minute?' he said, his voice croaky. He squeezed his way between the armchair and the central work station, moving now like a very old man, and without casting a glance in Roberta's direction he shuffled his way over to the door that led into the hallway of the house. They followed him intently with their eyes as he left the room and then heard the door of

452

the front sitting-room opening and closing behind him.

No one spoke in the kitchen, the only sound being Maurice Roache putting together his papers and placing them back in the open brief-case. He closed the lid and softly clicked the fasteners shut.

'Maybe I should go and have a word with him,' Jonathan Davies volunteered quietly.

Roberta shook her head. 'No. I think it's up to me to do the explaining.'

'Should we make ourselves scarce?' he asked.

Roberta did not reply to his question, but simply held up her hand before she left the room.

She stood outside the door of the sitting room, her hand on the brass knob, ready to open it. She hesitated, then raised her hand and knocked quietly on the door. There was no response. 'Craig?' she called out quietly. Still no response. She turned the knob and opened the door and put her head around the side. There were no lights on in the room, but it wasn't entirely dark, only cold and unwelcoming. He sat in his armchair, his hands resting on its arms, staring straight ahead at the space where the one from the kitchen should have been. 'Craig? Can I come in?' He glanced at her for only a second, then looked away again. She walked around the side of the sofa and stood in front of him. 'Craig, are you all right?' She knelt down on the floor at his feet and placed a hand on top of his. 'I wish you'd say something to me.'

He looked at her, and she could plainly see the distress in his eyes.

'Craig, what is it?'

He slowly shook his head. 'Why have you done this?' he asked quietly.

'Why? Because . . . I wanted to, for my father.'

'But you knew the whole story, didn't you? I remembered. You were here when Jonathan Davies came round that time just before we left for the west coast. You knew that if he didn't find someone else to invest in this project, then it would never happen. So when did you speak to him?'

Roberta ran a fingertip up and down the back of his hand. 'When you were packing.'

The farmer nodded. 'Ah, yes. So it wasn't all about his naval times in Sydney, was it?'

'Well, we did talk about that . . . but not all of the time, I admit.'

'Then he would have told you about our insolvency problem, and how if this project didn't happen, then we would have nothing left.'

Roberta hesitated before replying. 'Yes, he did.'

He lifted his free hand and dislodged the tear that hovered on his bottom eyelid. 'Lass, I really can't allow you to do this. I can't let you save my family like this.'

Roberta pushed herself between his knees and grasped both his hands. 'Craig, listen, how else would I spend the money? I'm a spinster with an elderly mother. How else?' She paused. 'You know when I said back there in the car that I knew some pretty important people over here? Well, no one is as important to me as you are. You, quite simply, have single-handedly turned my life around. I thought that coming over here was going to be the end of everything . . . but it hasn't turned out that way. You have renewed me, Craig, my time with you has given me a new life, and I can't even begin to repay you for that.' She bent forward and laid her cheek on his knee. 'I can't bear to think that I'm going to have to leave you in a couple of days. I want to stay. But I can't. I have a duty to go back and look after my mother. Dad knew that I would anyway. He just wrote it up in his will so that he could leave me his money and to make it easier for my sisters to stomach the fact.' She looked up at him. 'But, don't you see, I can now use the money to my own advantage. If I invest in this golf course, I don't have to be away from you forever. I have a cast-iron excuse for coming back again and again.' She laid her head back on his knee. 'I can use it to buy some happiness.'

She felt the rough surface of his hand touch her neck. 'You're a great wee lass, you know.'

She looked up, resting her chin on his knee, and caught the look of fondness in his eyes.

'I really have grown so fond of you, Craig.'

He bent forward and took her face in both hands and planted a kiss on her forehead. 'Well, lass, I can tell you truly that it has come to work both ways.' He gave each of her cheeks a gentle pat. 'So maybe we should get ourselves back into that kitchen and sign those papers before your lawyer runs off home again.'

The tall blonde girl bounced her way across the brightly lit restaurant and placed the bill on the checkered table-cloth in front of Gregor and Alex. 'There you are, gentlemen.' She leaned over towards Alex. 'I've managed to wangle a staff discount for you.'

He shot a look at his father, then grinned up at Madeleine. 'Thanks for that.'

'It comes with my compliments.' She straightened up. 'So when will I see you again?'

Alex scratched at the back of his neck. 'I don't know. What are you doing tomorrow?'

'Nothing much. What are *you* doing?'

'Caddying probably in the morning, but if you want, we could meet up for lunch.'

'Okay, give me a call on my mobile.' She turned to see that a group of people had entered the restaurant. 'I'd better go. Duty calls.' She bent forward and gave Alex a kiss on his cheek, then turned to Gregor and held out her hand, a broad smile creating small dimples in her rosy cheeks. 'Really nice to meet you, Mr Dewhurst. That was great fun today.'

He took her hand and shook it. 'I enjoyed it too, Madeleine. And, as I said before, it's Gregor . . . please.'

'Oops, sorry,' she chuckled, putting her hand over her mouth. 'I promise I'll remember next time.' She gave Alex a quick wave and went over to welcome the newcomers.

Gregor reached across the table for the bill.

'I'll do that, Dad,' Alex said, shifting his bottom on the chair so that he could take his wallet from the back pocket of his trousers.

'No, you won't. It's my shout. It's the least I can do after butting in on your day off.'

456

'You didn't butt in at all. It was great fun. Madeleine thought that you were pretty chilled out.'

'Do I take that as a compliment?'

'Of course you do. It means that you're a pretty sound guy.'

Gregor gave his son an uncertain look. 'I'll take your word for it.' He picked up his glass of beer and drained it, and on hearing Madeleine let out her distinctive laugh, he looked over to where she was taking the order from the group of people. 'She's a nice girl.'

'Yes, she is. She's a good friend.'

'Is that all?'

Alex leaned towards him, his eyes widened emphatically. 'Yes, Dad, only that.'

'Right.'

'Anyway, I wouldn't tell you otherwise.'

Gregor laughed. 'I know you wouldn't.' He brought his hands down hard on the table. 'Right, shall we make a move?'

Alex pushed back his chair. 'Ready when you are.'

The cold night air immediately hit Gregor when he stepped outside. He fastened the zip of his jacket up to the neck and thrust his hands into the pockets and stood stamping his feet, waiting for Alex to come out. He turned and saw him through the fogged-up window saying a final good night to Madeleine. A young couple veered off the pavement to enter the restaurant and he stepped aside out of their way. As they opened the door, Alex came out.

'Hell, it's a bit cold, isn't it?' he said, rubbing at the sleeves of his jersey.

457

'Bloody freezing.' He gave his son a powerful thump that was designed to throw him off balance, then turned and began to sprint away up the street. 'Come on,' he called out, 'I'll race you back to the car.'

Alex laughed as he watched his father's compact figure race around the corner and out of sight, but he didn't bother following at his pace. Even with his extra height and longer legs, he knew that he still hadn't the speed to keep up with him. He decided therefore to take his time, and allow his father yet again the pleasure of being the victor, even though he knew that he would be teased unmercifully about his lack of stamina and pace all the way home.

But it was good to have been out with him again. He *was* a pretty chilled-out guy, even though he was his old man. And come on, he wasn't even that old. Hell, there were guys still playing professional football who were older than him. Even Madeleine said he was pretty fanciable.

He turned the corner into Market Street and saw his father in the distance, sitting on the bonnet of the Peugeot van with his arms crossed, his legs swinging nonchalantly over the side. He could imagine the smug grin that he would have on his face, so he decided not to give him the satisfaction of thinking that this was a famous victory. He slowed his pace, taking time to look into the windows of the shops and restaurants that he passed, stopping every now and then to make it seem as if he were genuinely interested in what they had on display. He was now in voice range, and he could hear the gibes that were being called out to him.

'Come on, you bloody tortoise!'

This he heard when he was only twenty yards away from the van, and he knew that if he looked towards him, his father would see the broad grin on his face. He turned away and studied intently the whirled-glass windows of a small Italian restaurant. He couldn't really see anything inside, the glass distorting any chance of clear vision, but it gave him time to bite at the sides of his mouth so that he could regain his composure and produce once more a perfect poker face. Then, as he walked slowly on, he suddenly found himself looking through a pane of clear glass that must have been put in as a temporary replacement. He could now see everything that was happening in the restaurant. It was one of those places that had booths, shaped rather like the old cattle stalls in the Winterton steading, where people could sit at their tables in privacy. He wiped at the pane with the sleeve of his jersey, as if trying to wipe away the reality of what he saw. But there was no doubting his initial appraisal of the situation. It was the hair he had recognized first, the short, bobbing blonde hair. At first he thought it could have been an innocent-enough liaison, but then it was the position of her hands that told him the whole story, clasped together with those of the man who sat opposite her. They leaned towards each other, their faces inches apart, then he watched as they both rose from their seats and kissed across the table before sitting down again, laughing at their actions.

'All right, come on, you've made your point.'

He turned to see his father walking towards him. He

gave a reactive glance towards the window, then made off quickly towards the car. 'Let's go, Dad.'

Even in the dim glow of the street-lights, Gregor noticed that his son's face had drained of colour as he walked past him. 'What's up with you?'

Alex turned and walked back to him and grabbed his arm. 'Nothing. Come on, Dad, we're going home.'

Gregor stood where he was. There were ten yards separating them. 'What did you see in there, Alex?'

'Nothing, Dad. Please just come home.'

Gregor watched him for a moment, then turned and walked back to where Alex had been standing.

'*Please*, Dad, just come away from there.'

Alex could make no further move. He had done all that he could to prevent his father from seeing. He watched as Gregor stood in front of the clear pane and peered into the restaurant, his hands thrust into the pockets of his jacket. He took a step nearer, then, looking for a moment longer, he lowered his head as if he didn't want to see any more of what was going on. He turned and began walking back along the street, and as he passed by his son, he glanced at him and Alex could see the deep hurt in his eyes. 'Thanks, Alex,' he said quietly, his voice quavering. 'Thanks for trying, lad.'

Alex stood watching him as he walked slowly back towards the van, his shoulders down, his head bowed, the body language of a broken man. He set off after him, and on reaching the car he unlocked the driver's door, then looked across at his father. 'Maybe it's just a good friend.'

Gregor blew out derisively. 'Aye, a *bloody* good friend.'

He shook his head slowly. 'She said that she wasn't going to be back until tomorrow.' He brought his fist down hard on the roof of the van. It resounded like a gong, and Alex stared at the large dent that the punch had made. 'What a *bitch!* What a conniving, good-for-nothing *bitch!*' He slumped forward, his forehead resting on his forearms. 'What a mess I've made of my life, Alex, what a sodding mess!'

Alex opened the door and reached across to unlock the other, then he walked around and put a hand on his father's shoulder and opened it for him. 'Come on, Dad, I'll take you home.'

They drove in silence out of St Andrews and climbed the hill, leaving behind them the ghostly amber glow of the floodlights that played upon the ruined walls of the town's ancient cathedral. Alex pushed the van fast, out of anger at the hurt that Mary McLean had caused his father and eagerness to get him back home as quickly as possible. He flashed through villages and swung the little van at pace through the bends, and for once, as he approached the stretch known as Smash Alley, he threw caution to the wind. There were, after all, hardly any cars on the road. He drove so fast over the first blind summit that the van lifted off the road and his head touched the plastic covering of the roof. He glanced to his left and could see the outside light of the farmhouse at Winterton shining out across the fields. He turned to his father. 'We're nearly home now, Dad.'

His father lifted his head, but he did not look towards Winterton. His eyes were suddenly wide open, transfixed on the road in front of him. 'Watch out, Alex!!'

Alex turned back to see the two sets of headlights, side by side, coming straight at them over the next summit of the road. There was no way that he could possibly avoid them. '*Shit!*' he yelled out at the top of his voice, and slammed on the brakes, pulling the steering wheel hard over to the left. The van hit the verge at pace, and as it rose in the air, there was a resounding bang as the bonnet caught the top of the drystone wall, and then there was a moment of terrifying limbo when he realized that he was probably in the last seconds of his life, and he gulped a breath as he watched the light of Winterton farmhouse floating away at the top edge of the windscreen. The van hit solid ground with a bone-jarring thud, but then it seemed to bounce off again, and the world spun around in the beam of the headlights before it thumped down for a second time. The lights went out, and there was the deafening noise of tearing metal and shattering glass as the panels crumpled around them and the windows disintegrated with the force of the impact.

In the sudden, unworldy silence that followed, Alex still held tight to the steering wheel, and it was only when he felt the cold night air on his face that he realized that he was still conscious. He tried to orientate himself, but his senses were then invaded by the excruciating pain in his neck. He attempted to move his head, but it was bent sideways, stuck hard against a solid object. He became aware of the seat-belt cutting into his shoulder, yet he didn't seem to be in contact with his seat. He tried moving his legs, but his right foot was numb and there seemed to be something heavy weighing it down.

'Dad!' He reached out and felt the sleeve of his father's jacket and gave it a shake. Something felt sticky on his hand, but he couldn't manoeuvre it around to see what it was. 'Dad! Are you all right?' He reached out again. 'Dad!'

He could now hear his father breathing heavily. 'Hang on, Alex,' he said weakly. 'Hang on, lad, we're upside down. I'll try and get my seat-belt off.'

'Dad, I'm stuck. I think I'm jammed against the roof and my foot won't move.'

'All right, lad, just hang on. I'll get you out.'

'Jesus, I think there's smoke, Dad. Something's burning.'

'Hang on, Alex,' his father shouted back.

He caught the desperation in his father's voice, and it was then that he knew that there was no way that they could help each other. He started to cry now, understanding the hopelessness of their situation.

He could hear his father thumping his shoulder against the caved-in door, then he let out a growl that crescendoed into an ear-splitting yell as he threw the whole force of his powerful body against it. There was a loud creak as it gave way a fraction, then he felt his father manoeuvring around and suddenly the back of his head came into sight below him.

'Just keep calm, Alex, we'll get out.' He kicked out backwards like a mule, kicking and kicking at the door, each one making its mangled hinges screech in protest. He could hear his father's breathing getting faster and faster with the effort.

'Right, Alex, I think I've got it.' He began to edge his way backwards.

'Don't leave me, Dad.'

'I won't leave you, son. Just hang on.'

He heard the sound of voices outside. A man's voice wailed, 'Jesus, I'm sorry, I'm so sorr—'

'*Fuck off!*' he heard his father yell. 'Just go and get an ambulance and the fire brigade.'

'*Dad! Quick! Look down at my feet!*' Alex coughed out, as a flicker of yellow flame appeared in the footwell, glowing through the acrid smoke in the car.

He felt his father crawling back in again, and this time he saw his face looking up at him. In his hand, he clutched a penknife, its open blade glinting yellow in the light of the flame. 'Just hang on, lad, I'll get you out.'

'My feet, Dad, look at my feet!'

Alex watched as his father reached up into the footwell and beat at the flickering flames with his bare hands. They seemed to die away, and then he felt his father's hand slide up the upper part of his leg.

'Right, I've got it now, Alex. I've got what's trapping you.' He felt his father's body shudder with exertion as he pulled at something in the footwell. 'Try moving, Alex.'

'*I can't.*'

'Right, I'll try again.'

'Dad, look above you! They've started again!'

He watched once more as his father hit out at the flames with his hands. Again, he managed to dampen them. 'Right,' his father breathed heavily, 'let's try again.'

This time, he let out a scream of effort as he pulled hard at the metal above Alex's leg. 'Okay!' he yelled out through gritted teeth. 'Try now, boy.'

Alex used his hands to give extra leverage to his legs and then suddenly the one that had been trapped came free. 'Yes, that's it, Dad. I'm out.'

He saw the knife blade come up and slide under his seat-belt. His father pulled hard on its handle, and the seat-belt gave way, pitching Alex forward on top of Gregor's body.

'Right, crawl, Alex; crawl for your bloody life!'

Mr Craig flicked on the switch at the back door of the house and light flooded into the courtyard. He opened the door and stood aside to allow Roberta and the two men to file out before him. They descended the steps and walked over to the car.

'We'll pick you up at ten o'clock on Tuesday then, Maurice,' Roberta said, as she opened the passenger door for the lawyer.

'I'll be ready, my dear.' He slowly clambered into the car. 'It'll be good to have some company on the way home.'

'That goes for me too.' She leaned inside and gave him a kiss on his cheek. 'And again, Maurice, thank you so much for coming over. I really do appreciate it.'

He smiled at her. 'I think you've got your father's business acumen, Bobby. I'm pretty sure that this one'll go as well as anything that *he* invested in.'

'You're right. I know it's going to be a winner.' She closed the door and gave him a wave as she came around the side of the car.

Jonathan Davies held out his hand to her. 'Thank you, Roberta, for everything. It's wonderful to know that we can just get on with things now.'

Roberta ignored the hand and reached up and gave him a kiss on either cheek. 'I have to thank you as well, Jonathan, for giving me the opportunity of a lifetime.' She turned and took hold of Craig's hand. 'You just keep me informed of everything that's going on.'

Jonathan patted the top pocket of his blazer. 'I have your fax number right here. I'll give you weekly bulletins, I promise you.' He put forward his hand to the farmer. 'I think Liz will be well pleased, Mr Craig.'

He shook his hand. 'Aye, I have no doubt that she will be, Mr Davies.'

Davies opened the driver's door. 'Have a good trip home, Roberta.' He hopped in and fired up the engine, then, reversing quickly, he took off around the corner at speed.

They stood for a moment until they heard the car accelerate up the farm road, then he gave Roberta's hand a gentle squeeze. 'Right, what say you to a wee glass of something to celebrate?'

She smiled up at him. 'I think that's probably the best idea you've had all day, Craig.'

They walked back over to the house and climbed the steps. Mr Craig turned off the courtyard light and was about to close the door behind them when he stopped, looking up into the night sky. He went back out and stood on the steps.

'Craig?' Roberta asked with concern as she came back out of the kitchen to join him. 'What are you looking at?'

He pointed above the roof of the steading where a red glow lit up the night sky, interspersed with the flicker of blue light. In the distance, coming from the direction of St Andrews, was the wail of a siren.

'What's happened?'

'Looks like there's been an almighty car smash up on the main road. There's one on fire at any rate.' He turned back into the house. 'I'm afraid that it won't be the last on that stretch, either.'

Roberta still stood out on the steps. 'Do you think we can do anything to help?'

'No, I don't think so. The emergency services are there. We'd just be a hindrance.' He held the door. 'Come on, lass, get yourself inside. I don't want you catching a cold before you go home.'

Annabelle crossed over the cobbled courtyard to the flower-bed that ran alongside one of the high enclosing walls, and began plucking off the deadheads of the rambling rose that grew abundantly across it. She had been meaning to do this for the past week, but she had never seemed to find the time. She heard the large oak door swing open and turned as Johnnie walked into the courtyard.

'So what have you got planned for this morning?' she

asked, throwing a handful of dead petals into a cardboard box that, conveniently, happened to be there.

Johnnie sat on the low stone wall that surrounded the small fountain in the centre of the courtyard. 'Nothing much. I thought that I might go into town and return that wine to Fidel.'

Annabelle smiled wistfully at him. 'Now, that's a very good idea.'

'Yes, maybe it is.' He let out a deep sigh. 'You know, my love, I don't often say this, but I think I'm going to miss our guests.'

Annabelle walked over and sat down beside him. 'I know. It's not often one gets on the same wavelength, is it?'

Johnnie shook his head.

She slapped him on the knee. 'Never mind, we've got a free night. No one to think about but ourselves.' She gave him a nudge with her arm. 'What fun we could have, eh?'

He laughed and put his arm around her and gave her a kiss on the cheek. 'You know, I just might hold you to that.'

The telephone sounded out through the open door of the kitchen. Annabelle smiled at her husband. 'That, though, could quite easily spell the end of our plans.' She got up. 'I'll answer it.'

She hurried into the kitchen and took the receiver off the hook on the wall. '*Digame*, Finca de Rodrigo . . . Yes? . . . Oh, hullo . . . No, I'm sorry, Mr Craig, you've just missed them. They left about five minutes ago . . . No,

I've no idea where they'll be staying. Will has a mobile phone, though . . . Oh, I'm afraid that I don't have it either. Is everything all right? . . . I see . . . Well, I'm sorry I couldn't have been more help . . . goodbye, Mr Craig.'

She hung up the receiver, but kept her hand upon it and stared pensively out of the kitchen window.

'Well, was it another booking?'

She turned to find Johnnie leaning against the door-post. 'No. It wasn't. It was Liz's father,' she answered quietly.

Johnnie noticed the look of concern on her face. 'Has something happened?'

Annabelle shook her head. 'I don't know. But there was definitely something about his voice.'

Johnnie approached her and put his arm around her shoulders. 'And there's something about my voice too,' he said in his most seductive tones.

She smiled at him, then pushed him away and walked over to the kitchen sink. 'I know there is, Johnnie. It's normally far too loud.'

CHAPTER 25

Mr Craig followed the lumbering figure of Maurice Roache across the crowded concourse at Edinburgh Airport, struggling with the unruly luggage trolley on which he pushed Roberta's two suitcases and golf clubs. There was nowhere near the same number of people waiting to check in as when he had seen Liz and the professor off to Seville, so they were able to zig-zag their way straight through the cordoned aisle to the desk. He positioned the trolley next to that of the old lawyer and turned to scan the area for Roberta. He caught sight of her through a blur of hurrying travellers, standing outside a newsagent's and leafing through a book. She looked up, and seeing that they were waiting at the desk, she hurried over, rummaging in her handbag for her tickets.

'Sorry!' she said, placing her tickets on the desk. 'I just wanted to get something to read before I left.'

Having booked them in, the cheery-faced girl handed back their tickets, informing them that their luggage would go all the way through to Sydney, so there was no

470

need to worry about it at Heathrow. They thanked her and wheeled their empty trolleys away to the stacking area.

'Right!' Maurice said, shifting his brief-case from one hand to the other. 'I've got a couple of telephone calls to make, so I'm going to head straight through security now.' He held out a hand to the farmer. 'It was a pleasure to make your acquaintance, Mr Craig. I'm only sorry that what should have been a happy occasion was overshadowed in such a way.'

'I know, Mr Roache, but nevertheless it was good to meet you too.' He shook his hand. 'I hope that our paths might cross again sometime.'

The lawyer let out a short laugh. 'I doubt very much that that'll happen, unless you come over to Australia. I think it would be wise for me to leave any foreign travel in the future to a younger colleague.'

'Aye, I can understand that. But I trust that you'll still be looking after Roberta's affairs.'

'Oh, I don't think I'll be wanting to pass up on those for a good bit yet.' He smiled down at her. 'I'll see you upstairs, Roberta.'

'All right, Maurice. I won't be long.'

'No hurry,' he said, making his way across to the escalator and lobbing a wave over his shoulder. 'You take as long as you like.'

Craig and Roberta stood watching until he was out of sight, then once more she delved into her handbag. 'Look what I've bought!' she said, an excited glint in her eye. She took out a small book with a tartan cover

471

and handed it to him. He held it out at arm's length and read the title. *An Idiot's Guide to Scottish Reels*. He smiled and flicked through the pages, then handed it back to her.

'It should have been the expert's guide that you got.'

'Oh, that's rubbish!' she exclaimed. 'I couldn't have done any of those dances without you. But you wait until the next time. I promise you that you won't have to give me a word of guidance.'

'I'll look forward to the pleasure of seeing that.' He gave her back the book, then immediately brought his hand up to his mouth in an attempt to stifle a long yawn. Roberta noticed it.

'Craig, there was really no need for you to bring us over. We could have just as easily got a taxi.'

'No, no, I'm absolutely fine. Just feeling a wee bit tired.'

'Not surprising. You've hardly had any sleep over the past two nights.'

'Neither have you.'

'I know, but I can catch up on the plane.'

The farmer reached out and took hold of her hand and gave it a pat. 'I've got to thank you for your support, Roberta. I don't think that I could have managed without you.'

She smiled at him. 'Oh, Craig, I was just so glad that I was around and that I could be of some use.'

'Well, you certainly were that, lass.'

'Are you sure you're going to be all right telling Liz about it?'

'I think so. I've just got to make sure that I get my

wording right so that she doesn't start jumping to the wrong conclusions.'

Roberta let out a sigh. 'It was just such a pity that you missed them in Spain.'

'Aye, it was. Mind you, I don't think she would have been able to get back here any quicker, so I suppose it's saved her a day's fretting over the whole thing.'

'When does their flight arrive?'

'In about three hours.'

'That'll be a bore for you having to wait around.'

'Not at all. I'll just pass the time in the Land Rover.' He smiled at her. 'I'll be needing to keep Leckie company now. He'll be missing that comfy knee to sit on.'

Roberta moved towards him and put her arms around his lean chest. 'I'm going to miss him and I'm going to miss you, Nathaniel Craig. I can't even begin to tell you how much I'm going to miss you.'

He placed an arm around her shoulders and drew her plump little body close to him. 'Aye, and I'm going to miss you too, Roberta Bayliss. You just come back whenever you can, and the three of us will head off again, and we'll golf by day and jig by night.'

Roberta looked up into his face, tears bubbling in her eyes. 'I'll hold you to that, my dear man. I really will.'

He gently pushed her away and cast a glance towards the escalator. 'You'd better be off, Roberta. You don't want to miss your plane.'

She wiped at her cheeks with the back of her hand. 'Will you come up with me?'

'No, lass, if you wouldn't mind, I think I'll just head

back to the Land Rover now. I'm not awful good at saying goodbye to my womenfolk.'

A broad grin stretched across Roberta's face. 'Am I one of your womenfolk, Craig?'

'Aye, you are. And a very special one at that.'

She reached up and pulled his head down towards her and gave him a kiss on either cheek. 'Goodbye, my dear. I shall write to you every week.'

'You do that.'

'And I shall expect you to write back.'

The farmer chuckled. 'Och, you'd have a hard time trying to read *my* writing.'

'I don't care.' She took hold of his hand. 'Now, don't you go caddying for any more strange ladies on the golf course, do you hear?'

The farmer shook his head. 'No, I won't do that. I'll tell everyone that I'm booked.'

She smiled. 'You do that, Craig. You tell them that you're well and truly booked.' She reached up and gave him a final kiss, then slowly letting go of his hand, she turned and hurried across the concourse floor and, without looking back, made her way up the escalator with the agility of a girl.

The Jack Russell caught sight of him as he approached his Land Rover, and began to tear back and forth across the front seats in excitement. He opened the door carefully, putting in a hand to prevent the dog from jumping out. He slid in behind the steering wheel, hardly being able to settle himself before Leckie bounced onto his lap.

'Well, my lad, it's just you and me again,' he said,

474

rubbing at the dog's head. He watched as a plane rose up above the terminal building, its engines roaring as it powered its way into the sky. He shook his head. 'Who would have thought that that would have happened to us, Leckie?' he murmured. 'Who would ever have thought it?'

The arrivals hall was already thronged with passengers from the flight by the time that they appeared. It was Arthur he saw first, being pushed in a wheelchair by a sandy-haired young man who wore a fawn corduroy jacket over his square-set frame. Arthur's son, he concluded. It was only then that he realized that the woman who bounced along beside them, chatting away to them both with such spirited animation, was his daughter. He could hardly believe the transformation. Her hair was much blonder than when she had left, and the features of her sun-tanned face were lit up with a happiness that he had not seen for many a month. She bent forward to hear something that Arthur was saying to her, then, throwing back her head with laughter, she cast a sweeping look around the hall. She caught sight of him and ran over to meet him.

'Hullo, Dad!' she exclaimed, reaching up and giving him a kiss on either cheek. 'How are you?'

The farmer smiled down at her. 'I'm well, lass, I'm well. My word, you look terrific.'

'I feel terrific, Dad. We've just had a truly wonderful time.' She took hold of his hand and began to drag him over to where Arthur and the young man now stood beside the luggage carousel.

'Dad, this is Will, Arthur's son.'

'Pleased to meet you, Will,' he said, extending his hand.

Will shook it. 'And good meeting you too, Mr Craig. Liz has told me a great deal about you.'

The farmer directed his attention to Arthur, placing a hand on his shoulder and giving it a squeeze. 'So what's my friend, the professor, been doing to himself?'

Arthur did not turn to look at him, but blew out a disgruntled puff. 'Why is it that because I'm in a wheelchair, everybody has to ask about my welfare through a third party?'

'I *was* actually speaking to you, you crabbit old devil!'

Arthur looked up and laughed. He nodded at Mr Craig. 'I can't tell you how good it is to be back. I've missed our time together.'

Craig glanced at the professor's leg. 'Aye, well, it looks as if we might be spending a good sight more of it over the cribbage board than we've done in the past.'

Liz touched her father's sleeve. 'Dad, I thought that you might have come over with Alex,' she said breezily. 'Is he working today?'

Mr Craig had not been prepared for this. He had been hoping to get her by herself before he told her. He took off his cap and scratched at the back of his head. 'No, he's not, lass.'

Liz's smile fell. She could tell instantly from the look on her father's face and by his actions that something was wrong. 'Dad, what's happened?' she asked, her mouth open.

'Well, before I go any further, I have to say that Alex is all right.'

'What's happened?'

'He's had a bit of an accident.'

'What kind of accident?' There was desperation in her voice.

'A car accident.' He noticed now that both Arthur and Will had turned to look to him, expressions of apprehension on their faces.

Liz clapped her hand over her mouth. 'Oh, my God! But he's all right, Dad?'

'Aye, he is. He's got a badly bruised leg and his neck's in a brace, but he'll mend.'

Her hand moved to her forehead. 'Oh, thank goodness! Thank goodness!' She let out a shuddering sigh of relief. 'So where did it happen?'

'Up on Smash Alley.'

'Oh, no – not there! Was it his fault?'

'No, it definitely wasn't. The young man who caused the crash has been charged with dangerous driving.'

'And there was no one else involved?'

Mr Craig swallowed hard. 'Aye, there was.'

'Who?'

He hesitated for a fraction of a second before answering. 'Gregor was in the car.'

'Gregor? Gregor was *with* him?' She paused, and the farmer noticed the colour drain from her lips as she pulled them tight against her teeth. 'Who was driving, Dad?'

'Alex.'

Her shoulders heaved and she crossed her arms, turning away from her father. 'Well, thank heavens for that. If it had been Gregor, I would never—'

'Gregor saved his life, lass.'

She slowly turned around to look at him once more. 'What?' she asked quietly.

'Well, I had been planning not to tell you the whole story, but I don't see how I'm going to avoid it now. It was a pretty horrific accident, Liz. Alex was trapped upside down in the car and it caught fire. Gregor crawled back in and managed to release him.'

Liz just stared at him, and he could see the look of hostility in her eyes drain away into one of deep concern. 'And . . . Gregor?' she asked, as if not wishing to know the answer.

'It's all right, lass. He managed to get out . . . just, but he got himself quite badly burned in the process. Alex told me later that he had actually used his bare hands to douse the flames.' He paused for a moment. 'It was an awful brave thing that he did, Liz.'

Liz nodded slowly. 'Yes, it must have been.' She gave her head a quick shudder as if to break herself away from the nightmare of the spectacle. 'Are they both in hospital?'

'No, back at Winterton. Alex was released yesterday morning, and then Gregor discharged himself last night. He said that he'd got things to do and that he'd rather be at home with his son.'

A questioning frown wrinkled her forehead. 'Yesterday morning? But when did this happen, Dad?'

'Sunday evening.'

'Sunday evening? But why on earth didn't you get in contact with us?'

'Because I wasn't informed about it until much later on that night, and I headed straight over to the hospital in Dundee. I never got home then until the next morning, and when I tried to phone you, the woman said that you'd just left.'

Liz turned to see Will pulling their suitcases off the carousel. He caught her eye and they stared at each other for a moment before she turned back to look at her father. 'I've got to go straight to Winterton, Dad.'

He nodded. 'Aye, I thought you might want to do that. That's why I'm going to suggest that the professor and Will take a taxi back to Brunthill. It'll be a more comfortable journey for the professor at any rate.'

They drove to the Forth Bridge without speaking, Mr Craig not wishing to disturb his daughter in her thoughts. He knew that as soon as he had told her about what Gregor had done, it would raise in her mind a turmoil of conflicting emotions. It was better that she had time to think about this and work out how she was going to react when she saw both him and Alex. He glanced across to where she sat, absently stroking the dog on her knee and staring out of the window at the ribbed surface of the cold grey water far below them.

'I've met someone, Dad,' she said quietly without turning to look at him.

He smiled to himself, but did not reply immediately. Then he pushed himself back in his seat, straightening his arms on the steering wheel. 'Aye, I thought you had.' He cast his eyes sideways without moving his head and saw that she was looking at him, a smile on her face. 'Is it Will?' he asked.

'Yes.'

'I'm glad.' He glanced in the rear-view mirror at the lorry that drove feet away from his back bumper and reacted by pressing his foot down further on the accelerator. 'I met someone too.'

'I know. Alex told me.'

'Ah, did he?'

'What's her name?'

'Roberta Bayliss.'

Liz waited for him to expand on the subject, but he said no more. 'And where is she now?'

'On her way back to Australia.'

'Right. And . . . how do you feel about that?'

He looked at her and gave her a wink. 'I feel very happy about everything. Very happy indeed.'

Liz smiled at him. 'You must tell me about her sometime.'

'I will, lassie. Don't you worry. I will.'

An hour later, Mr Craig pulled the Land Rover to a halt outside the Winterton farmhouse and switched off the engine. He turned to his daughter and saw that she was looking past him, staring apprehensively at the door into the house. 'Are you sure you'll be all right?'

Liz nodded. 'Yes.' She paused. 'It's just that this is the first time that I've been back.'

'Aye, I was thinking that. Listen, I can easily wait if you want.'

'No, I don't want you to do that. I'll just walk back across the fields.' She opened the door and got out. 'I'll see you later.'

The farmer watched as she made her way across the courtyard to the house. She stopped for a moment before entering, and he wondered to himself whether she wasn't considering knocking, but then she opened the door and went inside.

Liz was overcome by a disturbing melancholy from the moment that she walked into the house. She hadn't really expected that so little would have changed. The Wellington boots were still scattered about the floor of the back kitchen, despite the row of squint, but well-spaced shelves that she herself had erected specifically to house them. The long, windowless corridor still glowed with the orange paint that she had splashed on the walls one afternoon on realizing that Gregor's oily handprints were the first form of decoration one came across when entering the house. She let out a long sigh in anticipation of her feeling when she entered the kitchen.

She walked along the corridor and opened the door quietly, hearing immediately the sound of the television drifting over from the sitting area. She glanced around the kitchen, noticing once more that everything was much the same, then caught sight of the back of Alex's head over the top of the armchair in front of the television.

'Alex?' she called out softly.

She saw him straighten in his seat, but he didn't turn around. 'Is that you, Mum?' He pushed himself slowly to his feet and it was then that she noticed the white surgical collar around his neck. He reached onto the table for something, then turned slowly towards her and moved around the side of the armchair, supporting himself on a stick. He smiled at her. 'Hi, Mum. You look good. Did you have a good time?'

Hearing those words suddenly hit home. She might never have had a son to say those kind of words to her again. 'Oh, Alex, my darling boy.' She burst into tears and ran towards him and threw her arms around his neck.

She immediately felt his body go rigid against her. He let out a cry of pain. 'Ow, Mum! That's agony!'

'Oh, sorry!' She let go and stood away from him, gulping out a tearful laugh. She shook her head. 'I can't believe this happened, Alex.'

'I know,' he replied quietly. He shifted himself sideways to a kitchen chair and sat down again. 'I was bloody nearly dead, Mum.'

Liz's body shook as she fought to control her emotions. 'I know you were. Granddad told me.'

'If it hadn't been for Dad,' he paused, biting at his lip, 'I would have—'

'You don't have to say it. I know it all.'

There was a loud crash from somewhere within the main part of the house, followed by the sound of a heavy object falling down the stairs. Liz started. 'What was that?'

Alex looked towards the door. 'A suitcase, or should I say the third suitcase.'

Liz shot her son a quizzical look. 'What's he doing?'

'Well, he's not able to carry anything heavy because of

his hands, so he's just manoeuvring them to the top of the stairs and giving them a kick.'

'But where is he going?'

'He's going nowhere, Mum. It's Mary McLean who's leaving.'

Liz stared at her son. 'What's happened, Alex?'

'What do you think? She's been playing around, hasn't she.' He pushed out his long legs and folded his arms across his chest. 'I feel sorry for him, Mum, I really do, even though he's been caught out at his own game.'

They looked at each other in silence, then Liz pointed at the door. 'I think that I should go and see him.'

Alex nodded. 'Yes, I think you should.'

She moved towards the door.

'Mum?'

She turned back. 'Yes?'

'He saved my life.'

She nodded and walked out into the corridor.

The first of the suitcases that had descended the stairs had left a deep white scar where it had slid across the polished teak floor in the hall. She edged past the other two that had stacked up behind it and looked up the stairwell. She could hear him moving about in the bedroom.

'Gregor?'

The footsteps above her stopped, and then she heard him moving over towards the door. His head appeared over the banister, and she caught sight of his bandaged hands resting on them. He looked at her, upside down, but said nothing.

'Can I come up?' she asked.

He drew back out of sight. 'If you want,' he eventually replied.

She walked up the stairs and edged into the bedroom, not so much in trepidation of seeing Gregor, but of going into the room where they had once slept, where they had once made love. She glanced around, taking in the open wardrobe and the pulled-out drawers of the large pine chest. All the same furniture, just in different positions. Articles of clothing were strewn across the floor and over the lilac satin sheets of the unmade bed. It looked like a whore's boudoir. How fitting *that* was. At least he had had the decency to get another bed.

He was stuffing a pair of Mary McLean's pale pink trousers into a suitcase that she recognized as having been her own at one time, using his foot to compress its contents. He turned to look at her. 'Well, what do you think of this?'

Liz shook her head. 'I don't think anything of it. I'm . . . just sorry that it's happened.'

Gregor threw back his head in derision, then slammed shut the lid with his hands. He stood up, clutching them under his armpits and grimacing with pain, then brought his foot down so forcefully on its cardboard top that it ripped. 'Why the hell should *you* be sorry that this has happened?'

Liz bit at her lip. 'Gregor, I didn't come to talk about that, and I certainly didn't come to gloat. I had no idea that this had happened until Alex told me downstairs.'

Gregor looked at her, and a smile broke across his stern features. He shook his head slowly. 'You look good, Liz. In fact, you look terrific.'

Liz swallowed hard. She couldn't remember the last time he had said that to her. In fact, she couldn't remember if he'd *ever* said that to her. 'Gregor, I just came to say thank you for what you did for Alex.'

He snatched one of Mary's brassieres off the bed and began to ravel it up in his bandaged hands. He noticed that Liz was looking at it, and suddenly realizing what it was, he held it out at arm's length and let it drop back on the bed. 'He's my son as well as yours, you know, Liz. I would do anything for that boy.'

Liz nodded. 'I know you would.' She paused. 'You shouldn't be doing all this, you know. Your hands.'

He looked at his bandaged hands and gave a quick shrug of his shoulders. 'You're not going to offer to help, are you?'

She smiled and shook her head. 'No, I certainly am not.'

He let his hands drop to his side and let out a heaving sigh. 'Lizzie, Lizzie, what a bloody stupid idiot I am. None of this would have happened if I'd just used my damned sense.'

Liz didn't reply, but watched him as he walked over to the window. He stared out across the fields. 'I never actually fell in love with her, you know, Lizzie. Not like I did with you.' He turned to look at her. 'I just have to tell you this.' He turned away again. 'I just happened to get caught up in a situation that I was too bloody weak to handle. I'm afraid that my brain got firmly wedged between my legs. I never considered you, and I never considered Alex, and I'm truly sorry for that. I really am *sorry.*' He paused, bowing his head. 'I'm not just saying this because she's gone, or because I want you to feel pity for me. It's just . . . well . . . the truth.'

Liz stood immobile watching him, then she let out a long, calming breath. 'Fuck you, Gregor,' she said, almost incoherently.

He turned to look at her, his forehead creased into a frown. 'What was that you said?'

She shrugged her shoulders, almost to signify that she hadn't realized what she had said herself. 'I said, "Fuck you, Gregor."'

His face broke into a smile, then he let out a laugh. 'That's what I thought you said.' He shook his head disbelievingly. 'I've never heard you say that before in your life!'

'Well, there you go. You obviously don't know everything about me, do you?'

Gregor shook his head. 'No, obviously not.' He sat down heavily on the bed and looked around the room. 'I'm not going to start on about turning back the clock, Liz. That would just be selfish and futile. I know the damage that I have done and know that it's beyond repair. But what I would like more than anything else is to get the chance to win your friendship back. I have missed that so much. Over the past year, I have felt my soul being physically ripped from my body, hearing the hostility in your voice whenever we talk.' He paused and looked down at the bandaged hands resting on his knees. 'And I can't go on like that.' He slowly rose to his feet and walked back to the window. 'And even if you feel that you can't do it for my sake, please try to do it for Alex's.'

There was a silence, only broken by the distant sound of the television permeating through the house from the kitchen.

'Gregor,' Liz said quietly.

'Yes?'

'I've met someone.' Her eyes never left him as she said it. She wished that she could see his face. He stood motionless for a moment, then slowly nodded his head.

'In Spain?'

'Yes. He's over at Brunthill right at this minute.'

He turned to look at her, a smile on his face. 'Good. I'm glad for you. In fact, I'm really, really pleased for you, Liz, because you deserve every moment of happiness that you can get for yourself from now on.' She could hear his voice beginning to break with emotion. 'You just go right out there and nail him.' He clenched his fist to emphasize the point, forgetting about his bandaged hand. He quickly managed to turn the grimace of pain back to a smile. 'Because if he makes you look as beautiful as you do now, then he's the man for you.'

Liz's face crumpled and she felt the emotional convulsions well up from deep within her. 'Gregor, why are you such a bastard?' she blurted out. She turned and ran out of the bedroom. 'Why are you such a mean *bastard*?'

She ran down the stairs and along the corridor, narrowly avoiding running into Alex as he hobbled out of the kitchen to come see what was happening.

'Mum?'

She heard him call out but didn't slow her pace, and, opening the back door, she threw herself outside and slammed it shut behind her. Everything suddenly was quiet. She stood in the courtyard, gulping in the cold air with sobbing breaths, then she covered her face with her hands. 'Oh, God, what am I meant to do now?' She took off into the dark, following the track that was known so well to her that she had no need for a guiding light. If only, she thought to herself as she went, I could have made my way through life this easily.

CHAPTER 26

Nathaniel Craig placed the two logs on the sitting-room fire and stood over it until flames began to lick up around them. He walked back to his armchair and sat down with a thump. He picked up the glass of Jack Daniel's and raised it in the air.

'Well, here's to your speedy recovery, Arthur, and good health thereon.'

Arthur sat in the armchair opposite, his plastered foot resting on the low coffee-table in front of him. He raised his glass. 'And here's to you, Nathaniel.' He took a sip, then studied its contents. 'Mind you, I don't think we'll be able to drink each other's health for much longer if we carry on like this.'

'In what way?'

'Nathaniel, I haven't had a Jack Daniel's at eleven-thirty in the morning since the time in my life when I found myself in imminent danger of sliding towards alcoholism.'

The farmer laughed. 'Well, I was just thinking that a

wee celebration was in order, seeing that everybody is back home in one piece.' He eyed Arthur's leg. 'Or nearly.' He placed his glass on the table beside him. 'I didn't realize that breaking your leg was an integral part of your plan.'

'My plan! It wasn't just *my* plan. I seem to remember you having quite a hand in it, too.'

Nathaniel twisted up his mouth. 'Aye, you're right.' He let out a reprehensive sigh. 'I have to say, though, that after you'd gone, I had second thoughts about it all. I wondered if we weren't playing with fire.'

'I know,' Arthur replied quietly. 'I had the same notion.'

'Mind you, I never quite shared your confidence in thinking that Will would join you.'

'Well, if you want to know the honest truth, I wasn't that confident about it all, either. Okay, I had a hunch when he didn't return the itinerary with the tickets, but it was a long shot.' He leaned across to retrieve his glass and rested it on his lap. 'And then when he did turn up, I have to admit to you, Nathaniel, that I suffered a fairly prolonged moment of confusion during which I wished to hell that he *had* never appeared.'

Nathaniel noticed a heaviness come over Arthur's eyes. He nodded slowly, understanding the look. 'Do I take it that passion flickered in your own bosom for a time?'

'Yes. It did.' He blew out a long breath. 'And that was when I realized that I was just being a stupid old goat – old being the operative word.'

'Och, you shouldn't be so hard on yourself. You've got a good few years in you yet.'

'Yes, lonely years.'

Nathaniel laughed. 'That's a load of poppycock, Arthur! I can tell you that life has a funny way of throwing up the least expected things.'

'You sound pretty convinced of that,' Arthur replied morosely.

'I am, Arthur, I am totally convinced of that.' He picked up his glass and took a drink. 'So, you think that there's quite a spark between Liz and Will?'

Arthur laughed. 'A spark! I'm surprised that they didn't blow up the plane on the way over.'

'What do you think will happen now, then?'

'I can't be certain on that account. Depends on what Will's going to do.' He wedged his glass between his legs and delved into his inside pocket and took out his wallet. 'But, I tell you what. I am willing to bet you this crisp new Scottish ten-pound note that when they return to the house from their walk, they will have something to tell us.'

For a moment, Nathaniel eyed the note that he held up in his fingers. 'I'm not so sure.'

'Can I ask why?'

'Because she's back home, Arthur. She'll have a great deal more to consider here than she would have in Spain, especially in the light of that accident. You saw yourself how upset she was when she returned from Winterton last night.'

'But that's hardly surprising. She'd nearly lost her son.'

491

'And her husband.'

'Yeah, maybe so, but not much of a husband, regardless of his heroics.' He rustled the note between his fingers. 'So, what do you say?'

The farmer smiled at him and pushed himself out of the chair. 'You're a terrible influence on me, Arthur Kempler, trying to make me gamble for money under my own roof.'

'Are you on, then?'

Nathaniel took the bottle of Jack Daniel's from the mantelpiece and replenished Arthur's glass. 'I would be an ungracious host if I refused, now wouldn't I?'

Liz stood on the outcrop of rock, her hair blowing around her face in the stiff breeze, watching the sea-gulls out on the water dip and rise with the movement of the waves. A spatter of surf hit her cheek, and she put up a hand to brush it away, the action being sufficient to break her from her thoughts. She turned and looked twenty yards along the shoreline to where Will was using a long strand of seaweed to play a ferocious tug-of-war with Leckie. He looked in her direction and gave her a wave, and she set off across the rocks to join them.

'What do you think of it, then?' she asked as she approached him.

Will cast his eyes out to sea. 'It's great. Mind you, I've spent so much time on oil rigs that I've seen enough water to last me a lifetime.'

'Yes, but this is different.'

'Oh, really? Why?'

'Because it's mine.'

Will laughed. 'Oh, I'm sorry. I was under the impression that the oceans moved around, you know, with the gravity pull of the earth.'

Liz gave him a hard punch on the arm. 'Well, it's mine while it's here.'

'Sort of a surf-loan arrangement, is it?'

She made to hit him again, but he grabbed her in his arms. She didn't resist, but pressed her head against the now familiar feel of his corduroy jacket. He rocked her back and forth as they stood there in silence.

'It's different, isn't it?' he said.

She didn't move. 'What is?'

'Seeing someone on your own patch. You suddenly see them as alien.'

Liz smiled to herself. 'You're not alien, Will.'

'Maybe not, but you're the one that belongs here, not me.'

She looked up at him, a frown of concern on her face. 'What is that supposed to mean?'

He laughed and shook his head. 'No, sorry, that didn't come out right. All I meant was that I'm not enthusing about this place as much as you are.'

She laid her head back on his jacket. 'That's all right, then.' She felt the comforting warmth of his body against her. 'Will?'

'Yes.'

'What do you want to do?'

'I don't know. What do *you* want to do?'

'I asked you first.'

'Hmm, yes, you did, didn't you?' He paused. 'Well, I've got to go back to the Philippines.'

He felt her weight slump against him. 'I know you do.'

'And I would like you to come with me.'

She smiled up into his face. 'You could have said that in one sentence.'

'Yeah, I realize that. I just didn't want to push it.' He paused. 'What do you think?'

'I don't know. I just don't know.' She let out a sigh. 'It's a pity that things just couldn't have stayed the same as they were in Spain.'

'What's changed?'

She gently pushed herself away from him. 'Being back. That's what's changed. Having considerations other than myself.'

'I can understand that. But remember that I do come back here every two months, so you can always return with me then to see your father and Alex.'

'Yes, I know.'

'And anyway, I'll be wanting to see more of my own father.'

She smiled at him. 'Of course you will.' She turned and looked along the rocky coastline. 'I don't know if I can leave just now, though. So much has happened.'

She heard him sucking in his teeth in consideration of what she had just said. 'Do you want to flip a coin?'

She laughed. 'No, I do not.'

'Well, how do you want to decide the issue?'

'I'm not sure.' She was about to turn back to look at

him when her eyes came to rest on the thin jagged rock that protruded from the waves fifty yards out to sea. A smile slowly crept across her face. 'Yes, I do,' she said, almost to herself. She looked at Will. 'What are you like at throwing stones?'

'Throwing them at what?'

She pointed a finger. 'Can you hit that rock?'

Will narrowed his eyes against the glare as he scrutinized the target. 'I reckon I could. Why do you want me to do that?'

'Because that's my father's stone of destiny. He told me that his father wouldn't allow him to take over the farm until he could hit it. It took him years.'

Will laughed. 'And you're now willing to rest your own destiny on the throw of a pebble, is that it?'

Liz shrugged. 'It's no worse than tossing a coin.'

Will bent down and picked up a pebble. 'All right, then, you're on.' He eyed the rock. 'How many attempts are you going to allow me?'

'Three or four,' she smiled at him, 'or maybe seven or eight.'

'Okay. Here goes!'

He took off his jacket and handed it to her, then gave the ground on which he was standing a quick check to make sure that it was even enough. He weighed the pebble in his hand for a moment, then ran forward and launched it off. They stood watching as it arced through the air and landed, sending up a small plume of water six feet to the left of the rock.

Liz flicked back her head in scorn. 'You missed.'

'Not by much,' Will laughed, bending down for another pebble. 'That was just a range finder. You watch this one.' He moved ten feet farther back. 'Are you ready?'

Liz kept her eyes on the rock. 'Go on then.'

The pebble came over far quicker than she had anticipated. She watched again as it spun through the air and even at its highest trajectory she realized that this time he was right on target. As the pebble began to descend, she suddenly became aware of the metallic taste of panic rising in her mouth. Oh, no, she thought, why did I agree to this? This is not right. This shouldn't be decided like this. I'm not ready to leave Alex or my father, and I'm certainly not ready to leave here.

The pebble hit with such force that it splintered off a shard of rock. It tottered on its axis for a moment, as if it, too, were vacillating over whether to stay or leave, then it slowly keeled over into the sea.

Liz stood staring at the place where it had disappeared beneath the waves. 'Well done,' she said, her attempt at a light-hearted tone doing little to disguise the hollowness of her congratulations. 'You've done it.'

A pebble landed beside her right foot and she looked down at it, wondering where it had come from.

'That wasn't me,' Will said quietly.

Liz turned to look at him.

'What?'

He pointed a thumb over his shoulder, and Liz slowly followed its direction. On a rock twenty yards behind them stood Gregor, an unravelled bandage fluttering out of his trouser pocket in the breeze. He clutched at the

496

wrist of his throwing hand with the other, still bandaged, and just stared at her.

She glanced at Will, meeting in his eyes the same steely glare as Gregor's. She moved across to him and placed a hand on his arm. 'Just wait, Will. I'll be back in a moment.'

As she walked over to the rock on which Gregor stood she noticed that his eyes followed her every inch of the way. She stopped below him. 'What are you doing here, Gregor?'

He raised his face and looked out to sea. 'Just watching you throw stones at the Craig Rock.'

She was silent for a moment. 'How do you know that's called the Craig Rock? I didn't even know that myself.'

'It's what my father calls it.'

'But how would your father know?'

'Because he used to come down here most days after school with your father to practise hitting it. In the end, they were both equally good.' He looked down at her. 'It was my father who gave me a bit of coaching.'

'Why would you need coaching?'

'Because being able to hit it twice in a row was a condition laid down by your father before he allowed me to marry you.'

'Why would he do that?'

'Well, his actual words were that he was passing on to me something that was as precious to him as his own farm.'

Liz swallowed and lowered her head. 'He never told me all this.'

'No, he wouldn't. I think it's sort of a male thing.'

Still carrying Will's jacket over her arm, she picked at a small white thread that protruded from under its collar. 'And would it have made any difference if you had missed? I did have something in my belly at the time which I would have thought made the outcome of your little test somewhat immaterial.'

'But I didn't miss, did I? I hit with the second and the third pebble.' He stared at the rock once more. 'I've never hit it with the first pebble before now, but by God, this time I was willing for it to hit with every part of my being.'

She looked up at him. 'How did you know we were here, Gregor?'

'I saw you walking across the fields together.'

'But why did you follow us?'

'I'll tell you why, Liz Craig.' He squatted down on his haunches, still clutching at his hand. 'Because, before I never get the opportunity of saying this to you ever again, I just wanted you to know something that, for so many years, I realize now that I have just taken for granted.' He hesitated, and she knew only too well from the look on his face that he was scrambling for the right words in his mind. 'What I want to say is that I have always loved you, Liz, and I always will love you. I think you're beautiful, I think you're funny, and you have always been and always will be my best friend. And every day from this moment on, I am going to say those words, even if you're not with me. Because now, with Mary gone, I'm free to say them and, for about the first time in about two years, they have made me feel contented about myself.' He paused and took the bandage from his pocket and began to wrap it around his hand. 'I'm not trying to have my cake and eat it too, Liz. I know that I'm not in a position to fight for you any more. That's all passed. But I just had to tell you all that *once* to your face.'

Liz turned away from him and looked towards Will, using the moment to wipe away a tear that had come to trickle down her cheek. Will noticed the action and lowered his head.

'You screwed up, Gregor Dewhurst,' she said without looking back at him. 'I hope you realize just how much you screwed up.'

'I know I did, and I've got to live with the consequence of that for the rest of my life.'

'And so do I.'

'Yes, I know,' he replied quietly. She heard him rise to his feet behind her. 'But I did hit that rock, Lizzie, and I can keep on hitting it time and time again.'

Liz stood where she was for a moment, then slowly set off back across the rocks towards Will. As he watched her approach, the smile that he gave her slowly slid from his face.

'Uh-oh,' he said quietly. 'This doesn't look good.'

She ran her hand over the rough texture of his corduroy jacket before holding it out to him. 'Will . . .'

'Liz,' he cut in, taking the jacket from her. 'I can't even begin to negotiate on this one, even though I would love to try. It would be no use for me to influence you one way or the other. You have to be absolutely sure in what you choose to do. You're back in the groove now, everything should be right for you, and you will have to decide for yourself what is best for you.'

'I know, and I am so glad that you said that, otherwise it would have made this even more difficult for me.' She paused for a moment to collect her thoughts. 'Will, I belong here. I can't leave. My soul is part of this place, and I know now that I cannot physically take myself away from it. No matter how fond I am of you, I would be miserable in the Philippines, and I could never allow myself to burden you with that.'

Will glanced towards Gregor. 'Will you go back to him?'

'I can't tell you that at this minute, because you are far too prominent in my heart and in my mind. But he's not the only consideration, Will. I have to think of Alex, and if there's any way of giving him back his parents, then I'll push the boat out for it. If I were to go away now, it would be exactly the same as what Arthur did to you. You do understand that, don't you?'

Will nodded. 'You mustn't let him hurt you again, Liz.'

'He won't. I know now that he won't.' She moved towards him and took hold of his hand and looked up into his pale-blue eyes. 'What worries me more is the hurt that I'm doing to you.'

He threw his head to the side as if he had just received a heavy punch to the chin. 'Ouch!'

'I'm sorry, Will. I really am sorry. I didn't use you, I promise you.'

Will let out a silent laugh. 'I know you didn't, Liz.' He blew out a long breath and looked out towards the rock.

'Well, at least I lost in battle fair. It's just a pity that he arrived before I had a few more practice throws.'

Liz moved forward and reached up and gave him a kiss on the cheek. 'Thanks, Will.' She kissed his other cheek. 'Thank you so much for everything.'

He put his hand out and cupped it under her chin, tilting her face up towards him. 'And thank you, Liz. I think we both taught each other how to love again, didn't we?'

She took hold of the hand and kissed its rough palm. 'Yes, we did. We certainly did.'

The two men looked up from their game of cribbage as the door of the sitting-room opened, and both watched intently as Liz and Will walked in. Arthur caught the smile on his son's face and glanced quickly across to Nathaniel Craig, giving him an almost imperceptible wink.

The farmer, however, was less convinced of its meaning. It was not a smile of great joy and happiness, but more one of gentle kindliness and acceptance. And while Liz came to stand with her hands resting on the back of the sofa, Will remained distanced from her beside the door.

'Dad,' Liz began quietly. She stood up and stuck her hands into the pockets of her jeans. 'I have something to tell you.'

Arthur shot Nathaniel Craig a furtive smile over the fan of cards that he held in his hands.

'I've just had a long talk with Gregor.'

The fan of cards dropped like a stone onto Arthur's lap and he glanced from Will to Liz with an expression on his face that resembled that of a confused goldfish.

Will cleared his throat. 'I think while you're explaining it all, Liz, I might just go up and start packing.'

Nathaniel Craig saw both deep fondness and regret in his daughter's smile when she turned to acknowledge him. Once Will had left the room she took in a deep breath and proceeded to tell Arthur and her father of the decision that she had made, and how close she had come to choosing the alternative that had been offered.

'And now, if you will excuse me,' she said when her explanation was complete, 'I'm going to go upstairs to talk to Will while he's packing. So please feel free to continue your game.'

The two men sat in silence after the door had closed behind her. They even avoided looking at each other. Then Nathaniel Craig laid down his cards on the arm of his chair and rose slowly to his feet. He picked up the ten-pound note on the table and, taking a step towards Arthur, tucked it away into the breast pocket of the professor's tweed jacket. 'What did I tell you?' he chuckled quietly, giving his good friend a pat on the shoulder. 'Life does have a funny way of throwing up the least-expected things.'